STONE & SKY

**The international bestselling
Rivers of London novels
by Ben Aaronovitch**

RIVERS OF LONDON
MOON OVER SOHO
WHISPERS UNDER GROUND

Available from DAW Books:

BROKEN HOMES
FOXGLOVE SUMMER
THE HANGING TREE
LIES SLEEPING
FALSE VALUE
AMONGST OUR WEAPONS
STONE AND SKY

BEN AARONOVITCH

A RIVERS OF LONDON NOVEL

DAW BOOKS
New York

Copyright © 2025 by Ben Aaronovitch

All rights reserved. Copying or digitizing this book for storage, display, or distribution in any other medium is strictly prohibited. For information about permission to reproduce selections from this book, please contact permissions@astrapublishinghouse.com.

This is a work of fiction. Names, characters, places, and incidents are products of the author's imagination or are used fictitiously. Any resemblance to actual events, locales, or persons, living or dead, is entirely coincidental.

Jacket map illustration © Stephen Walter

Jacket design © Tomas Almeida/Orion Books

Jacket hand lettering © Patrick Knowles

DAW Book Collectors No. 1984

DAW Books
An imprint of Astra Publishing House
dawbooks.com
DAW Books and its logo are registered trademarks of Astra Publishing House

Printed in the United States of America

Library of Congress Cataloging-in-Publication Data is available upon request.

ISBN 9780756407230 (hardcover)
ISBN 9780756408251 (ebook)

First edition: July 2025
10 9 8 7 6 5 4 3 2 1

*This book is dedicated to Stuart MacBride and his creations
DI Roberta Steel and DS Logan McRae, who nobly stand as shining
exemplars to fictional detectives across the multiverse.*

Who does not dream of stone and sea
The depths below and the wild skies above?
—William Pageant (1920)

1

Monster House

IT ALL STARTED when Dr. Brian Robertson, retired GP, enthusiastic amateur ecologist and self-confessed cryptid aficionado, stumbled over a dead sheep a few kilometers west of the town of Mintlaw, Aberdeenshire. Normally, because they are famously geniuses at finding inventive ways of getting themselves killed, a dead sheep does not cause much concern beyond irritation in the farmer and speculation as to whether it can be disposed of off the books to avoid costs.

This, however, was a weird death even by sheep standards. It was difficult to tell the precise cause, what with the sheep's organs being spread over quite a wide area, but it looked to Brian as if something had taken a bite out of its belly. Something with a mouth the size and cutting power of a bear trap. So he took a series of photographs, bagged as much of the remains as he could stand, and sent an e-mail to an old friend of his who worked in London. When Brian had known him at Edinburgh Medical School he was plain old Ian Meikle, but then he'd got religion and a medical degree and taken to styling himself Dr. Abdul Haqq Walid, FRCP, AFSW.

Dr. Walid had thanked him for the pictures and said if Brian could stand to send him some samples, he'd be very grateful. Spring rolled around into summer, and while Brian had kept an eye out for any further attacks, he heard nothing more from his old friend and assumed that there had been nothing unusual about the dead sheep at all.

So he was a little surprised when, late one evening in July, he looked out of his window to find a vintage Jag, a bright orange Ford Focus ST and a heavily customized VW California camper van unsuccessfully attempting to cram into his driveway. He flung open his front door to find Abdul standing on the step. Beside him was a young colored girl wearing a fox stole.

"Good evening, Brian," said Abdul. "I'm sorry about dropping in so unexpectedly, but the decision to come up was made last minute."

"It's lovely to see you all the same," said Brian, and was about to ask the girl's name when he realized that the "stole" she was wearing was in fact a live fox—and a large one at that.

"This is Abigail," said Abdul.

"Delighted to meet you, Abigail," said Brian. "Would you like some tea?"

At that, the fox lifted its head and gave Brian an enthusiastic stare.

"Will there be cheese puffs?" it asked.

Before we continue, I'd like to point out that a) none of this was my fault and b) ultimately the impact on overall North Sea oil production was pretty minimal. I'm a dad now, so I don't go looking for trouble the way I used to. What *had* happened was that Abdul decided to spend his annual leave in Aberdeenshire to check out continuing reports of "big cat" attacks on livestock. My boss, Nightingale, who said he hadn't done any proper hunting since the 1930s, volunteered to join him, and could his youngest apprentice, Abigail, accompany them?

"It will be useful for her to see how magic operates outside an urban environment," he said.

And where Abigail goes these days, a fox is not far behind.

And it might have stayed bizarre but manageable if my better half and the love of my life hadn't decided that a Scottish holiday was just the thing for her, our twin two-year-old daughters, and me.

Which meant my mum demanded that she be included for babysitting purposes and, because my dad cannot be left unsupervised, he rode up in the back of the modified VW California, serenading the twins from custom sliding backseats with location-specific solos on his trumpet. Since he was coming up anyway, my mum figured that my dad might as well make a splash on Aberdeen's small but perfectly formed jazz scene.

So somewhere, probably just south of Perth, was an ancient Transit van containing his band, Lord Grant's Irregulars, and their brand-new manager Zachary Palmer, making its way inexorably toward us.

I was hoping for serious delays.

Dr. Brian Robertson was a tall, gangly white man with sharp features, small blue eyes and a thatch of hair that had obviously grown bored of being gray and was busily turning white. He lived west of Mintlaw in what was less of a barn conversion than an old agricultural building that was slowly evolving into a combination retirement bungalow and ecological laboratory. I noted at least three types of building materials, including what looked like granite blocks in the walls, but the roof appeared to have been replaced with modern slate, like so many of the local bungalows I'd seen driving up.

There was a caravan site across the road, which we offered to stop at, but Brian assured us that we were welcome to make camp in his garden. This proved to be the last vestiges of the farmland attached to the barn. Immediately behind the house was a terrace and formal garden, while the rest of the area formed a meadow that ran thirty meters to the woods that bounded the property. The grass had been mowed recently and a tarpaulin-shrouded roll of hay awaited pickup by the drive.

Brian said he had a farmer friend who mowed it for him in return for the hay. He offered the spare room to Mum and Dad, but they elected to stay in the camper van.

"It reminds me of when we were on the road," my mum said, and my dad had laughed.

"Not that our van then was half as nice as this," said my dad. "And we had to share with the drummer."

"You papa ein me not bein' say natin. We set we mot," said my mum, which I considered to be too much information.

Me, Bev and the twins glammed it up in a huge family tent complete with inflatable poles, double air mattress, folding table and a blow-up playpen. Despite not having any pesky poles, setting up was delayed as my beloved "surveyed" the back garden to locate the optimal location.

"We don't want to get waterlogged if it rains," she said.

Nightingale pitched his surprisingly modern pop-up tent between us and the house, while Abigail pitched hers at the bottom of the garden with the door facing the woods. Presumably so that Indigo the fox could sneak about to her heart's content. Once our tent was up, the twins ran around in circles for five minutes before dropping like sacks of sugar onto the air mattress and going to sleep.

After nearly twenty hours on the road, I was ready to join them, but Brian invited us in for supper, so we left Indigo to watch over the kids, with the promise we'd return with snacks, and went inside. Two things were immediately obvious: Brian mostly lived in his kitchen, and he'd used the grace period while we were setting up the tents to hurriedly tidy the place. He'd cleared enough of his scarred oak table for us to sit around it and eat, once we'd brought in some camp chairs.

I half expected an Aga, but Brian had installed an ecologically sound modern electric cooker which was wedged into a granite work surface that morphed abruptly at one end into what looked suspiciously to me like the wooden benches you find in school chemistry labs.

"It's probably best if you think of that side of the kitchen as being more akin to a laboratory," said Brian, who was still heaving piles of books and paper off the table and onto the work surfaces at that end when we came in. My mum was eyeing the clutter with a dangerously professional eye, but Dad, who never sleeps while traveling, was getting unsteady in his chair, so she concentrated on him. I wondered how long that would last.

Supper was toasted cheese sandwiches supplemented by rice and cassava my mum had packed, and the snacks left over from the journey up. I managed to stay awake right up to the point where Brian cracked open a bottle of whisky and poured us all a dram.

"Ah," said Abdul waving away the bottle, "the good stuff."

I'm not a whisky expert, but it went down fiery while simultaneously cleaning out my sinuses—but in a nice way. My dad declined, so I split his glass between me and Beverley, and as a result we both fell onto the mattress beside the twins and went out like a light. Until three in the morning, when the twins woke up and had to be changed into their pajama onesies and resettled.

Being a parent of two-year-olds means never having to set your alarm clock. Inspired by the ridiculously early sunrise you get up north, the twins woke their parents through the time-honored tradition of jumping up and down on us until sleep was impossible. Fortunately, having a river goddess for a partner meant she could do their early morning bath without getting out of bed. While the twins bobbed about in their individual floating globes of water, I went out to get the coffee in.

Nightingale and Brian were already up.

Brian pointed out that it was going to be a glorious day and that, this being northeast Scotland where glorious days were in short supply even in summer, I should definitely take advantage and hit the beach. Sounded like good advice, so Beverley and me threw the twins and a picnic in the back of the Asbo and headed for the sea.

Beverley had picked out a beach at a place called Rattray Head, and I faithfully followed the GPS for twenty minutes before turning off into a narrow lane. Around us, the land was flat and covered in wide fields of short yellowing grass. Silage or hay, according to Bev, who said they mowed early up here on account of the short summer. We continued on under a wide blue sky, past a ruined church and isolated farmhouse, at which point my poor Asbo started bumping along an unmetalled farm track.

I mentioned to Beverley that it seemed a bit excessively unspoilt, and she snorted.

"If we wanted crowds we could have gone to Southend," she said.

We topped a low rise and suddenly the horizon ahead was fringed with dark blue. Even the twins, who up until then had been engaged in competitive yodeling, shut up and made excited gurgling noises.

A couple more random bends and we arrived at a makeshift car park behind a two-story blockhouse of a building which had once serviced the offshore lighthouse, but was now, Beverley said, an eco-hostel. Somebody had parked a motorhome in the corner—probably as a cheap alternative to the eco-friendly accommodation.

We could hear the sea, but our view was blocked by three-meter dunes sprouting tufts of the unimaginatively named European beach grass.

"*Ammophila arenaria*," said Bev, who likes to remind me that I'm not the only one who can attach obscure Latin tags to things. Then she loaded me down with the half a ton of kit apparently required to take kids to the seaside, and we schlepped over the dunes. At least there was a cool breeze when we reached the crest and saw the sea, restless and turquoise, stretching out like the end of the world.

Beverley gave beach and sea a professional once-over.

"Tide is coming in," she said, and pointed to a third of the way to the water. "We should be OK there."

The Goddess of the River Thames, Beverley's mother, claims to have forgotten her birth name. She says that she abandoned it when she gave herself to the river back in the fifties. Despite a bit of surreptitious digging on my part, we know little of her life beyond what she has told us—that she was a trainee nurse from Nigeria. But you don't have to spend more than five minutes around her or her daughters to twig that she was raised a Yoruba.

And they have some particular conventions when it comes to twins.

The first out is always called Taiwo—the one who tasted the world first. The bold child. The second is always named Kehinde—the one who waited to see what was what. The cautious one. So it was a bit ironic that, of the pair, it was Kehinde who took one look at the sea and made a break for it. She had some legs on her, too, because she'd made it all the way to the surf before I caught her and hoisted her up, legs kicking, into my arms. I heard a rhythmic thumping behind me and disengaged my right arm so I could scoop up Taiwo, who was trying to sneak past while I was distracted. I hoisted a twin onto each hip and jiggled them to make them giggle. They were getting heavy—I wasn't going to be able to lift both of them for much longer.

"Bath," called Taiwo, arms wide, "bath, bath, bath, bath."

"Big bath," said Kehinde, who was the intellectual of the pair.

"Sea," I said. "That's the sea."

"Monster," said Taiwo, and pointed at the lighthouse that reared out of the waves.

"Lighthouse," I said. It was a classic cylindrical white tower, albeit a stumpy one, mounted on a cone-shaped stone base.

"Monster house," said Kehinde.

I carried them back toward their mother, both girls squirming to keep their eyes on the sea. Beverley had laid out a blanket, erected the wind and sunshades, and had the twins' wetsuits waiting. She was already sealed into her own blue and red suit with the hood up to cover her hair.

"You get them ready," she said. "I'm just going to check it's safe."

We watched as she ran into the sea, dived forward and vanished. Back home Beverley can submerge for hours, swim the length of minor rivers that you'd swear were only ten centimeters deep, and do other things that make me think she may not be entirely under the water. At least not in a mundane sense. But being a *genius loci*, the spirit of a locality, means her power fades the further she gets from her river's catchment area.

"And the sea," she says, "has a different set of rules."

So I worry a little bit more when she swims in the sea.

"Yeah," she says when I bring this up. "Remember that worry the next time you do something brave and noble in the line of duty."

She surfaced halfway to the lighthouse, and turned and waved before diving under again. I didn't see where she went after that because Kehinde made another break for the water, and I had to trap her with my leg as I finished dressing her sister. By the time I'd finished Beverley was doing her Bond girl impression, emerging from the surf with her hips swaying from side to side.

Although I noticed she was also breathing heavily. When she reached me, she slumped down on the blanket and fell on to her back, still panting.

"That was way more tiring than I was expecting it to be," she said. "Much harder than off Southend." She sat up again and pulled the water flask from its shady spot behind the cooler. "I was actually getting worried on the home stretch." She gulped down water and then looked back out toward the lighthouse—eyes narrowed.

"You should be more careful," I said.

"Yeah," she said. "Maybe I should."

"Anyone in the lighthouse?"

"Nah, it's automated," she said. Which was not really what I meant.

"Anyone else, though?"

She shrugged.

"If they wanted a chat, they would have made themselves known."

Which, to me, implied that Bev had half expected someone to do just that.

Once she'd recovered we took the twins out for a swim. Or rather, I supervised while Kehinde played tag with the wavelets and Bev kept a close eye on Taiwo, who seemed determined to drown herself in the breakers. When they got bored with that, we put them on our shoulders and did water jousting. Once we reckoned they were sufficiently worn out, we trooped back up to where our stuff was spread on the beach and broke open lunch. Beverley stuck her hand in the cooler and refroze the ice water in the bottom.

"That still works, then?" I asked.

"Sort of," she said. "But up here it's harder and slower." Then she flicked me and the twins with freezing water, so that the girls shrieked and ran around in circles until I enticed them back to the blanket with tuna sandwiches, cut into squares, and carrot sticks. The moment the food came out the gulls arrived, and were only kept at bay by flicking carrot sticks down the beach for them to squabble over.

After lunch it warmed up enough to strip off the wetsuits and sunbathe while the twins napped in the shade of the umbrella. We were slapping on the sunscreen when a scruffy yellow Labrador bounded over the dunes to sniff at Bev's BGF-Factor-30-covered hands before racing off down the beach. There it fell in with a pair of windsurfers—the first people we'd seen all day.

Unlike the twins, I found it difficult to settle. There was something desolate about the emptiness of the beach. The monotonous wash of the waves, unbroken by screaming kids and overheated parents, made me weirdly restless, so instead of lying down next to Bev I went for a stroll. From the top of the nearest dune I could see the car park, where the Asbo had been joined by half a dozen other vehicles. There were windsurfers out beyond the breakwaters and the rocks—red, blue and green triangles flitting across the waves. As I watched, one went arse over tit. I kept an eye on them until they righted their board and started up again. You could tell where other picnickers were by the way the gulls wheeled above them. Not counting the resting windsurfers, I spotted three couples and two families evenly spread along the beach.

The scruffy Labrador came bounding back across the sand, did a little dance around me, and skidded down the side of a dune to join its owners as they carried their sailboards back toward the car park.

I heard the distinctive happy cry of a pair of two-year-olds who have awoken to find themselves unsupervised, and picked my way down to grab them before disaster struck.

Beverley decided that it was warm enough to swim without the wetsuits. The water was still freezing, but at least the twins wore themselves out and fell asleep in the car. They stayed that way all the way back to Brian's house.

We arrived to find my mum had cleaned the kitchen while we were away.

"I told her not to bother herself," said Brian. "But we came back to find it like this." He had the look of a man who no longer knew, for sure, where his tea towel was—I knew the feeling. My mum has a platonic ideal of a tidy kitchen in her head and will impose it on any kitchen she cleans, regardless of the owner's preferences. This may explain why my mum mainly does commercial buildings these days.

At least she hadn't started cooking yet although, judging by the two-kilo sack of basmati rice sitting on the counter, it was only a matter of time.

We ate out on the terrace, where we could keep an eye on the twins as they explored the garden. Brian and Abdul had picked up a takeaway from the local bakery, the better to introduce us to traditional Scottish fast food. There was a selection of pies, including one that was filled with macaroni and cheese which, once I'd added sufficient chili sauce, worked really well. The twins had chicken pie and mashed potato—what Brian called "chappit tatties"—some of which even went in their mouths. Dad had the mince pie and Beverley, Brian and Abdul had steak, steak and macaroni.

"I was going to fetch some Irn-Bru," said Abdul. "But I can't stand the stuff personally."

Indigo snaffled up a mince pie, an egg and, at Abigail's insistence, some of the leftover carrot sticks.

"I admit I'm a little put out that you never told me about the foxes," said Brian as we finished off with coffee. This far north, sunset was late, but the color of the sky was deepening and the shadows lengthened among the trees at the end of the garden.

"To be honest," said Abdul, "I've got so used to them I stopped thinking of them as cryptids."

"Really?" said Brian. "Do you think they've spread up here as well?"

As one, Abdul, Brian, and I turned to look at Indigo, who was curled up on a warm patch on top of the patio wall.

"Indigo," asked Abdul, "do you have compatriots up here?"

"You know we never discuss operational deployments," said Indigo, which I reckoned meant yes.

After we put the twins to bed, I asked how the first day's big cat hunting had gone.

"When hunting," said Nightingale, "you always start with the known."

Which was why Brian had taken them to the location where he'd found the half-eaten sheep.

"I had a friend at Edinburgh Zoo estimate the mouth shape," said Brian, and showed us an image on his tablet. It looked like the sort of diagram the dentist shows you when they're thinking of drilling—although whoever owned this mouth would probably require something more than a local anesthetic. Assuming you wanted to keep your hands attached to your wrists.

"Robust canines," said Abdul. "Slicing teeth in the cheeks. Did your friend think it was a panther?"

"Yes," said Brian. "But she was sure it was a hoax."

Because while big cat sightings are common, big cat scat—that's hunter-speak for cat shit—is suspiciously thin on the ground.

"Although I believe the Chiltern deposit was verified," said Nightingale.

"But no scat today?" I asked.

"Not a sniff," said Indigo.

"And you should know," said Abigail, who was idly brushing the vixen's tail.

The kill site had been to the west, on the edge of Loudon Wood. Brian was certain the sheep had been dragged there by the owner of the big mouth. A cat Brian's zoologist had reluctantly estimated to weigh at least eighty kilos and be a meter and a half long—not counting the tail.

"There were no sheep pastured nearby," he said.

"We did a preliminary sweep," said Nightingale, and in the woods they had found the bones and other remains of squirrel, badger and deer. Possible signs of predation, but no cat poo.

"The sheep attack was six months ago," said Abdul. "The scat could have been subsumed by the environment."

"We'll widen the search tomorrow," said Nightingale.

I woke suddenly in the middle of the night, suffering that weird dislocation you get when you sleep in a strange place. I ran down the new parents' paranoia checklist—no choking, crying, or smell of baby scat, burning or Calor Gas. On the other hand, if I listened carefully I could just hear the pair of them breathing. Satisfied that I was able to stay tucked up with my nice warm river goddess, I refocused on the chatting I could hear outside.

"Were you always a fox?" I recognized Brian's voice.

"What else would I be?" That would be Indigo. I wondered if Abigail was also awake.

"You might have been born human and transformed into a fox."

"Is that possible?" There was an eager curiosity in Indigo's voice. These talking foxes think they're spies and live to gather intelligence—especially where it relates to themselves.

"There are stories," said Brian. "Of people that turn into foxes and vice versa. I believe they're common in Japan and China."

"Can you tell me the stories?" asked Indigo.

"Not off the top of my head, but I'm sure I can find you some books." He hesitated. "Can you read?"

"Of course," said Indigo. "Can't write, though—the keys are too small. You said vice versa? Can foxes turn into humans?"

"The Japanese think so," said Brian. "They believe that all

foxes, if they live long enough, gain the power to transform into humans."

"All foxes?"

"All."

"Wouldn't they be very small humans?"

"How do you . . . ? Oh, I see," said Brian. "Perhaps they grow bigger when they change."

Indigo made a skeptical noise deep in her throat.

"Do you have any brothers and sisters—" started Brian, but Indigo cut him off.

"How old do you think I would have to be?" she asked.

"To do what?"

"To turn into a human."

"I don't know," said Brian. "But if you do transform, you must promise to come visit me and tell me that story."

I think they talked about something else after that, but I must have gone back to sleep.

The next morning we found Indigo in the kitchen, sitting on a stool and staring at a tablet propped up against a pile of books. Amazingly, a plate of mini sausage rolls sat uneaten on the table beside her.

"Next page," she said, and I realized she was wearing a specially adapted microphone headset. I'd seen some of the foxes wearing these headsets before, but it had never occurred to me that they might use them to run electronic gear. This seemed to me to be a bad idea. I could just about cope with the foxes being all John Le Carré, but if they went full *Mission Impossible*, fuck knew where that was going to end. I asked what she was reading.

"*Low Intensity Operations: Subversion, Insurgency and Peacekeeping*," she said.

"Any good?"

"There's some wicked stuff about conducting counter-insurgency operations among a hostile population."

So me and Beverley left Indigo to her light holiday reading and whisked the twins back to the seaside, only this time to Cruden Bay. It was another beautiful beach, only with a golf course instead of sand dunes and, more importantly, shops that sold ice creams, flotation rings, buckets and spades. Not only were there a ton of other families on the beach, but also, when Beverley got bored of making friends, there was a nearby castle to explore. Between the swimming, the chatting and the castle, the twins were even more worn out than the previous day, so that evening me and Bev had an opportunity for some *very quiet* shagging.

2

Beach Boulevard

YOU DON'T *EVER* get a lie-in with two-year-olds, but you can have a leisurely morning if you prepare enough distractions. Thus, half an hour spent secreting "treasures" around the garden netted two hours of lounging around while Beverley drove the Asbo to Peterhead and the nearest Morrisons. Brian had been called into the Aberdeen Royal Infirmary to look at something "interesting" and had taken Abdul with him. So, what with Nightingale, Abigail and Indigo out big cat hunting, we had the garden to ourselves. This allowed Kehinde the opportunity to see if she could eat a worm—I stopped her just in time—and Taiwo to burrow into a bush with small pink flowers. This gave me an excuse to pump up the paddling pool we'd bought from London, and hose the twins clean. Unfortunately, when their mum came home I was dragooned into bringing in the shopping, and they took advantage of the distraction to escape naked into the grass and get covered in mud again. This got them hosed down for a second time, then moisturized, dressed and made presentable enough to make the inevitable lunchtime food fight satisfactorily messy. Satisfactory from the twins' point of view, obviously—not ours. Beverley cleaned their faces, but declared that they might as well get muckier before they got washed again.

That afternoon, it was my job to drive my mum and dad into Aberdeen for Dad's first gig. Both my parents were as excited as the twins had been at the seaside. My dad loves to play to an audience and Mum loves to be in that audience when he plays. As relationships go, it's about as dysfunctional as it sounds, and has given my shrink hours of entertainment. She keeps asking whether we couldn't do a family session, but I suspect she's only looking to get an academic paper out of it.

I've been out driving in the sticks enough times to know to never charge through the center of a strange town—however seductively straight the route looks. Instead, I followed the satnav to the west of the city center—across the river Don—where the city greeted me with a massive graveyard before spinning me through a roundabout and down a dual carriageway lined with bungalows.

There was a burst of corporate offices and characterless modern luxury housing blocks before what I was beginning to think of as the typical granite semi reasserted itself. The granite theme continued as we turned west down a narrower main road lined with ornate gray Victorian terraces and the accoutrements of an indisputably posh suburb.

Zachary Palmer, band manager, wide boy and possibly a goblin—although we don't use the G-word in the Metropolitan Police—had boasted that he'd ligged somewhere better than a five-star hotel. Given Zach's slippery relationship with the *actualité* I'd managed my expectations downward, right up until I turned into a driveway and was confronted with a genuine two-story mansion with an extension forming a half courtyard, hidden among its own grounds and screened by mature trees. The windows looked Georgian, but with Victorian embellishments around the roof and an overlay of Arts and Crafts around the doors and the wing extension.

Anyone can have a big house in the countryside. Something this big in a built-up area, even if it was a suburb, said serious money. I was instantly suspicious.

"This is a bit grand," said my dad.

It had to be the right place. My dad's drummer James Lochrane's grotty blue Transit was parked outside, and I pulled up next to it. I'd only just climbed out when Zach exploded out of the front door.

"At last," he said. "The talent is here."

Zach was a tall, skinny white man in his twenties, with a thin face, a big mouth and a mop of unruly brown hair that he'd recently taken to gelling into submission and sweeping back from his forehead. It made him look like a particularly streamlined ferret.

"You're going to love this place," he said.

And it was impressive. As he led us through the courtyard door, I saw that it wasn't made of brick but from granite blocks covered in white lime harling, which is Scotland's answer to pebble-dashing. There was probably a grander entrance somewhere, but like a working farmhouse, life here passed in and out of the back door.

"You had the key to this place, right?" I asked, because Zach could pretty much open any mechanical lock using a hairpin and what I suspected was a bit of innate magical larceny.

"Oh yeah," he said. "It's totally kosher. We're officially house-sitting."

We went through a vestibule lined with dark wood coat and boot racks and into the warm, red-tiled kitchen.

Disappointingly, this was your bog-standard expensive kitchen designed to be clean, airy and as characterless as a TV studio set. There were used plates scattered on the breakfast bar, and at least three jam and two peanut butter jars with their lids off by the Nespresso machine. Not even extreme wealth can resist the combined entropic effect of Zachary Palmer and traveling jazz musicians.

"Proper, innit?" said Zach, even as my mum eyed the mess and frowned. "It has two kitchens," he said, leading us through a series of small hallways with whitewashed plaster walls. "But best of all . . ."

We stepped into a long room with large bay windows. There, a black baby grand took pride of place, angled so the pianist could look out onto the lawn and tall boundary trees beyond. The floor was a fine but well-used herringbone parquet, black leather sofas were ranged against the walls, each with its own glass-topped coffee table. Amplifiers, speakers and an antique reel-to-reel recorder were neatly stacked on recessed white shelving in the dove-gray walls. Gleaming brass music stands sprouted like saplings in the empty center of the room.

"Belongs to a famous rock star whose name I am sworn not to

reveal," said Zach, and pointed to a row of pale rectangles ranged along the wall—missing picture frames.

I must have looked blank, because Zach sighed.

"That's where all the platinum records go," he said.

"Has he got a lot of platinum, then?" I said.

"Don't know," said Zach. "I don't like his stuff."

Behind me, I heard a click as my father unfastened his trumpet case.

"This will do nicely," he said.

"Does this rock legend know you're here?" I asked.

"Sure," said Zach far too quickly.

"He doesn't, does he?"

My dad walked into the pool of sunshine beside the piano and lifted his trumpet to his lips. My mum sat demurely on the nearest sofa and watched him as he ran up and down some preliminary scales. I dragged Zach out into the hallway.

"Does he?" I said.

"Relax," said Zach. "He pays a retainer to a servicing company. They come in once a week to restock and arrange any cleaning and repairs."

"Aren't *they* going to notice?"

"Ah, that's the genius bit, innit?" said Zach as my father launched into "My Funny Valentine." "They're paid to be discreet and not ask questions. Just as long as we give them a wide berth when they visit and don't burn the place down, they're just going to see it as show business as usual."

"Where's the band?" I asked.

The band, aka Lord Grant's Irregulars, were in town scoping out the venue and doing a sound check with the engineer/roadie that Zach had employed for the tour. No doubt under false pretenses.

"You need to be careful," I said. "This is Scotland—I don't have any juice up here. So if you get into trouble you're on your own."

And because the universe prizes irony above all other things, that's when I got the phone call from Abdul.

"There's something I want you to look at," he said.

"At the hospital?" I asked.

"At the mortuary," he said, and gave me directions.

It's one thing to know that Aberdeen is called the Granite City, it's another to get an eyeful of what that nickname actually means. I drove past kilometers of terraced Victorian and Edwardian houses, only what would have been built, on the southern floodplains of home, out of sensible brick was here constructed of blocks of granite. Big blocks of granite. You wouldn't want to carry them up a ladder on a hod; you certainly wouldn't want to risk standing underneath.

The occasional terraced house was coated with white harling or ugly brown pebble-dash but mostly it was a natural gray. Where the sunlight caught it, it sparkled. But in the shadows, it looked like footage from an old black-and-white documentary. By the time I turned onto Union Street I would have been willing to accept some modernist multicolored monstrosity in the Stacked Tupperware school of architecture just to break up the monotony. I had plenty of time to look around as the traffic slowed to a crawl.

Aberdeen was much less white than I'd imagined, although there was plenty of skimmed milk skin on display in the afternoon sunshine. There were young women in short shorts and halter tops pushing prams and sunning pink muffin tops, while dangerously sunburned young men who had stripped to the waist, the better to show off swirls of tattoos, strutted past.

I spotted a pair of definitely African young men waiting at a bus stop, and a smartly dressed middle-aged woman in a yellow and black headscarf striding purposefully toward the entrance to a shopping center. Seeing them, I felt a tiny bit of a tension, that I hadn't known I was holding, unwind.

There was a sign strung across the road that urged Aberdonians to rediscover the delights that existed on their doorstep. Past that was a series of monumental buildings so encrusted with Gothic towers, crenellations and pointed window arches that I nearly missed my turn-off.

Unlike London, Aberdeen's mortuary was directly attached to the city's police station. This was your typical graceless seven-story stack of dirty gray Lego bricks built to express the spirit of *joie de vivre* that permeated the mid-1970s. Mind you, unlike London, the shabby gray concrete façade, brutalist annexes and walkways fitted well with the granite sternness of old Aberdeen. If they'd only thought to add a few turrets, you wouldn't have been able to see the join.

Following Abdul's instructions, I avoided the visitors' car park, drove around the back of the mortuary proper, past a *No Unauthorized Access* sign, and tucked the Asbo into one of a trio of spots around the corner. Then, on the assumption that Aberdeen's traffic division had been as thoroughly gutted as the Met's, I went and found the pedestrian entrance. This turned out to be a steel fire door with a keypad intercom and matching CCTV camera for extra security. This is typical. Mortuary staff are paranoid about random members of the public sneaking in and interfering with their "clients"—apparently it's a lot more common than is comfortable to think about. Stealing corpses is only the start of it, but it only becomes my problem if the "clients" walk out under their own steam.

I rang, and a knackered-sounding Dalek with, weirdly, a London accent, asked me who I was. When I identified myself, the cockney Dalek laughed, said, "The more the merrier," and buzzed me in.

I could tell from the smell that the Aberdeen mortuary was probably overdue a refurbishment, a deep clean and good going-over with a flamethrower. As a result, the usual smell of decay hidden under layers of disinfectant had long since spread to the outer rooms. The attendant must have seen my reaction, because he informed me that they'd been waiting years to get new premises.

"The whole building is a bit of nightmare," he said.

As I was directed to the pathology lab proper, I caught a reek of coastal decay, the same seaweed, dead fish and salt water that I'd expected but didn't get from Rattray Head. I was getting it now even through my face mask as I swished my way through a pair of double doors and into the lab.

Seven figures, swathed like me in noddy suits, turned to look at me. I thought I detected a bit of frowning hostility, but what with the face masks, the eye protectors and the hoods drawn tight, it was hard to tell.

"Afternoon," I said cheerfully.

"Ah, Peter," said a familiar voice—Abdul. "You're here, excellent." He ushered me over and introduced me to the procurator fiscal, the deputy procurator fiscal, a DCI Mason from the Major Investigation Team, an anatomical pathology technician, the photographer, a second corroborating pathologist—as required by Scottish Law—and Brian. All totally anonymous in their Tyvek suits. I really hoped I wasn't going to be expected to put names to faces afterward.

And hidden behind them was today's "client," although I could smell him already.

"Is this entirely necessary?" said one of the figures—a man, possibly the Deputy Procurator Fiscal. "How many more of these 'experts' are we going to have to wait for?" You could hear the quote marks either side of "experts."

"Better to be certain we know what we're dealing with here," said the pathologist, who had one of those posh Scottish accents you hear reading the news on Radio 4.

"What is it you want me to look at?" I asked, before the man possibly known as the Deputy Procurator Fiscal could raise another objection.

The wall of Tyvek parted as the crowd shuffled around to give me access to the cutting table.

It was a man. His skin was very pale but the cast of his nose and mouth looked vaguely Eurasian, although the eyes lacked an epicanthic fold. He was plump and streamlined, his body hairless except for the short black fuzz on his head. The autopsy was obviously complete, the classic Y-shaped incision sewn up with thick black thread. His skin was mottled by bruising across his chest, arms, thighs, and groin. He'd lived with them long enough for them to have turned purple with yellow fringes—two to three days, at a guess.

As I approached, the smell of seaweed and salt water grew more intense until I realized that it was not actually a physical smell. It was a *vestigium*—the trace left behind by magic. I didn't really need to get any closer to know that the supernatural was involved.

There was a deep puncture wound in his stomach a few centimeters left of his belly button. The blade, if it had been a blade, must have been unusually thick, and the edges of the wound were ragged in a way I'd never seen before.

"There's another one there," said Abdul and pointed a gloved hand to another wound in the man's side—just below his armpit. Despite the width of the wound, it didn't look very deep.

"Is that the cause of death?" I asked.

There was a long uneasy silence as the masked anonymous figures looked at each other before the pathologist sighed and shook her head.

"That's unclear," she said. "He was admitted into Foresterhill at 02:03 last Saturday with severe bruising and puncture wounds to the chest and torso. He was unresponsive, but otherwise stabilized quickly. Just to be on the safe side, he was moved to HDU for monitoring. According to his notes, staff there expected him to recover, although they were worried when he failed to regain consciousness."

That worry was justified when the patient's condition continued to deteriorate over the next forty-eight hours. Then the lab reported anomalies in his bloodwork. His blood type was difficult to characterize and he had elevated levels of ferritin. When looked at under the microscope, his red blood cells were large and malformed.

"And he has gills," said Brian.

"And he also has anomalous structures in his throat and upper chest that seem to be associated with his respiratory tract," said the pathologist.

Brian pointed to where two vertical rows of slits ran down from under the man's chin, either side of his Adam's apple.

Brian reached out a blue-gloved hand.

"May I?" he asked the pathologist.

"If you must," she said, and Brian pulled back one of the slits to reveal a deep pink gash.

"They're far too small in relation to his body size to be functional," said the pathologist.

"And yet here they are," said Brian.

"Are you saying our mugging victim is Aquaman?" said DCI Mason.

"He could be Namor," I said.

DCI Mason snorted, but even from behind the eye protectors, the hood and the mask, I could practically feel the poisonous look the deputy procurator fiscal threw me. He turned to the slim figure I assumed was his boss—the procurator fiscal.

"We're wasting time here," he said.

"Detective Sergeant Grant," said the procurator fiscal. "In your opinion, is this a member of the supernatural community?"

Glasgow is one of the few Scottish accents I can tell apart, mainly because James Lochrane, Dad's drummer, is such a proud citizen of that fair city that he has chosen to live five hundred kilometers to the south.

This was obviously the middle-class version.

"Yes, ma'am," I said.

"You're certain of that?" she asked.

"Yes, ma'am," I said. "Apart from the victim's atypical physical characteristic, he exhibits a strong and persistent *vestigium* which—"

The deputy procurator fiscal interrupted me.

"What's a vestigial when it's at home?" he asked.

"*Vestigium*," I said. "Supernatural incidents leave a trace. Like other forensic techniques, you have to know what you're looking for."

"You had your eyes closed," said the deputy procurator fiscal, who was really beginning to get on my tits. My fault, really. I'd got so comfortable working with people familiar with magic, I'd forgotten how to finesse my way around the skeptics.

"It's something you sense rather than see," I said.

"Sounds like something you'd train a dog for," said the deputy procurator fiscal.

"We have a dog," I said. "But he didn't want to come."

"This is—" started the deputy procurator fiscal, but his boss had had enough.

"I think DS Grant should do an initial assessment," she said, and turned to DCI Mason. "David, can you facilitate that?"

"No problem," said DCI Mason.

"That way we'll have covered all the bases," said the procurator fiscal.

We all swished our way back to the locker rooms to get out of the bloody noddy suits, except for Abdul, Brian and the pathologist, who hadn't finished poking and sampling. They seemed particularly interested in the poor man's spleen, which appeared extremely enlarged.

"This has been commonly observed among successful free divers," Abdul had said. "Particularly among the Bajau people in the Philippines."

Out from behind his mask and goggles, DCI Mason was revealed to be a narrow-faced white man with fading red hair and an unfortunate nose. Once he'd donned a pair of sturdy black-framed glasses, he looked me up and down with a sour expression. I didn't take it personally.

The deputy procurator fiscal turned out to be a bit of a white hipster, in skinny black jeans, Converse and the traditional white and blue check shirt. He had a cultivated tan, squinty blue eyes and a sort of floppy mouth which was attempting a smile in my direction.

"It was my day off," he said, and held out his hand. "Chris MacEleny. Nothing personal," he said as we shook. "But Scotland Yard tends to forget where its jurisdiction ends."

I was tempted to put him right, but DCI Mason was clearly impatient to get going, so I followed as he banged through an exterior door and stamped down the stairs to the rear car park.

As we headed for the grumpy rectangular bulk of the main building, I decided it was time for a bit of preemptive placation.

"Look, sir," I said. "I'm supposed to be on holiday. The quicker I make an assessment, the quicker I get back to the beach."

Mason stopped so suddenly that I almost ran into him. He turned and gave me a dubious look.

"You came up to Aberdeen for the beaches?"

"And the castles and the scenery," I said. "And the culture."

"Not the cuisine, then?"

"I had a very nice macaroni pie."

"Oh aye?"

"You don't get those down in London."

Mason shook his head sadly before turning and leading me away.

"We'll see if we can't get you back to the sun-kissed shores of the Teuchter's Riviera by the end of the day."

A straggle of uniformed PCs had been loitering by the rear entrance, enjoying the sunshine and having a sly vape. Police Scotland had gone for an all-black uniform design, probably aiming for some of that Scandinavian chic, but had hit low-budget YA dystopia instead. The rest of the kit was familiar, though. Same Airwaves, body armor, ASPs, CS spray and speed-cuffs as down south. I made a mental note to look up the channel numbers for Police Scotland, just in case.

Like most seventies office blocks that were still in use, DHQ, as I learned it was called, had undergone numerous refurbishments, each one more desperate and uneven than before. The area at the back, being the preserve of lowly PCs, civilian staff and, worse, suspects, was all dingy magnolia with blue trim, the same economy thin-set terrazzo floors as the mortuary and the wet dog smell of police kit hung up to dry.

Mason eschewed the lifts and led me up several flights of concrete stairs and into a carpeted corridor with clean ceiling tiles and modern lighting. He opened one of the office doors and, asking me politely to wait outside, walked in and closed the door behind him.

I heard the low grumble of conversation and was tempted to stick my ear to the door. Somebody was being quickly briefed as to exactly how Mason wanted me handled. That somebody emerged from the office behind Mason three minutes later.

He was a short white man in his early thirties, brown hair, curls on top and short at the sides that didn't really suit a square face with a prominent nose and thin lips. At least his head matched the rest of him—broad shoulders, short legs, but a much better suit than I would have risked wearing to work. Dark brown wool, bought off the shelf, I reckoned, but then tailored. Despite the weather, he wore a lambswool pullover over his shirt.

Mason introduced him as DS Martin Blinschell. His hands were as rough as a bricklayer's and his grip firm but, mercifully, he didn't go for the posturing hand crush beloved of men who have something to prove.

"Pleased to meet you," he said in what I was beginning to recognize as an Aberdonian accent. "Do you want to see the crime scene first?"

"Yes, please," I said.

Mason left us to get on with it and I followed Blinschell back down the stairs. Unless they have to, nobody enjoys using a pool car on a hot day, when the three months' worth of discarded food wrappers in the rear footwell have started to ferment. So we decided to take the Asbo instead.

Blinschell patted the orange roof.

"Is this what passes for inconspicuous in London?" he asked.

"It's reverse psychology," I said. "Nobody believes that a Fed mobile is going to be this obvious."

I plipped the locks and he climbed stiffly into the passenger seat.

There was something awkward about the way he moved, which bugged me until I realized that he was wearing a stab vest in an "undercover" sleeve. Since one of the joys of going plain-clothes is shedding your MetVest and the five kilos of associated kit that goes with it, I wondered what he knew that I didn't.

Since I'm allergic to sudden upsets, I asked him why he was wearing it.

"Is there something I should know?" I asked as we pulled out.

"These thievin' tinks keep trying to stab me," he said. "After the third attempt I started wearing the vest."

He directed me back up Queen Street and then left, into the heavy traffic on Union Street.

"Mind you, seven years in uniform and nobody so much as had a go with a knife," he said. "Sticks, bricks, and one time a JCB. But nothing with a blade."

"Is this stab thing contagious?" I asked, thinking of my own MetVest currently six hundred kilometers to the south.

"Dinna tell me you're feart of a little stabbing?" said Blinschell. "I thought you were a' supposed to be hard men in the Met."

"There's hard," I said. "And then there's stupid."

This got a grim chuckle.

"Follow my lead," he said. "And you'll be all right."

The crime scene was a forlorn stretch of grass beside a wide treeless four-lane road with a gravel divider that was named, presumably ironically, Beach Boulevard. Although Blinschell assured me there was actually a beach less than half a kilometer further on. What Blinschell called the Scene Examination Team had staked out a square with blue and white police tape, back from the pavement in a gap between several mature trees of the possibly oaks variety. One poor sod had obviously been detailed to empty the dog poo bin and was reluctantly approaching it, clutching a sheaf of evidence bags. Even in the full noddy suit they radiated reluctance.

The rest of the scene examiners had their hoods down and their masks off. Obviously they weren't expecting much in the way of trace evidence at this site.

"Three days," said Blinschell, by way of explanation. "And it rained the night before last."

"House to house?" I asked.

Blinschell shook his head.

The grass strip on our side of the boulevard was bounded by the blank windowless rear walls of a row of light industrial units.

"We've checked the rear loading doors of them," said Blinschell, and turned to indicate the bland block of modern "luxury" flats made of tan brick across the boulevard. "Nobody saw or heard anything."

"Who called it in?"

"Passing driver," said Blinschell. "Oor laddie practically fell into the road in front of them. They called an ambulance and didna' see onibody else. They thought he was blootered—drunk. It's not unusual down here."

He gestured at the boulevard that managed to be bleak and depressing despite the bright afternoon sunshine. I doubted it got any lovelier at night. The scene examiner fishing in the dog shit bin took a sudden step back and turned away—panting.

"Something?" asked Blinschell.

The man pulled off his mask, took three quick steps out of the locus and vomited into the gutter. One of his colleagues brought over a bottle of water but, of course, wasn't required to hold his hair back while he threw up again.

"Did you find something?" called Blinschell from a safe distance.

The man shook his head.

Blinschell turned back to me.

"I'd say it was time for you to do whatever it is you do," he said.

And I did, although we checked with the Crime Scene Manager before I did it.

I was very conscious of Blinschell's gaze as I walked slowly up and down inside the taped area. Grass, like most growing things, is crap at retaining *vestigia*. Abdul and Abigail have hypothesized that plants somehow metabolize ambient magic, sucking away the trace the same way they soak up water. After three days the sad grass verge was metaphorically dry and the CE team hadn't found so much as a pebble, let alone a knife blade or some other metal object that might have kept its trace.

No *vestigia*, no blood or footprints. It looked like Locard's exchange principle was getting a beating today. Whatever Aquaman's assailants had brought to the party had either left with them or been washed away by the rain.

I looked up to find Blinschell giving me a studiedly bland look.

"Anything?" he asked.

"Fuck all," I said. "Do we even know how he got here?"

"We know he walked up from the Esplanade," said Blinschell. "Because he mugged some poor bastard for his clothes."

"Where was this?" I asked.

3

The Lemon Tree

THE ABERDEEN ESPLANADE appeared to be suffering from a bit of an identity crisis, being unable to decide whether it wanted to be a shopping center or a pleasure beach. There was a steep slope down to the beach on one side, and a sort of strip mall/entertainment complex that appeared to be trying to hide from the sea. Perhaps it was a weather thing. Perhaps giant waves driven by howling storms lashed the shop frontage in the winter. When I asked Blinschell about it, he said that was pretty much the case.

"Also in the springtime," he said. Then, after a pause, "And the autumn, of course." Another pause. "Once or twice during the summer."

The top of the Esplanade looked to be a good ten meters above the level of the beach, so I hoped he was joking about the waves.

I guessed the tide must be out, because the beach was exposed almost to the mounds of rocks that anchored the groins that reached out into the breakers along its entire length. And the beach was a long one, extending out of sight to the north and all the way to the harbor mole, at least a kilometer to the south. Gulls wheeled and dived—looking for chips, or possibly a macaroni pie.

Every ten minutes a big helicopter would clatter off across the sea.

Down south, on a sunny day, the beach would have been

rammed. But while there were plenty of families, dogs, kids, and strategically placed windbreaks and parasols, you could have staked out an Olympic specification volleyball court in the gaps.

Most of the kids, I suspected, were either in the indoor or outdoor amusement park, which promised all-weather fun and more sugared carbohydrate than was good for you, plus a big wheel and a go-kart track. Growing up, I'd have killed for entertainment like that—assuming I could have wheedled the pounds out of Mum.

I also noticed an inflatable play space that might provide some suitable low-energy twin-wrangling possibilities. Mine and Bev's low energy, that is—not the twins'. I made a note to look up the details once I was done here.

But not in front of Blinschell, who was giving me the eye from the bus shelter.

The shelter was transparent and open at the front that faced away from the sea.

"That's where he alleged the attack took place," said Blinschell.

"He" being Bernard Fontaine, who'd claimed to have been assaulted and stripped in a bus shelter around 1 a.m. the same night as our victim had been taken to hospital. As soon as that became a major incident, three days later, Aberdeen MIT had checked all the reported incidents for that night. They were looking for commonalities, because nothing is more embarrassing than finding you've already arrested the suspect for something else, but have since processed them and released them back into the wild.

It's the sort of thing that provokes comments—often on the front pages of the tabloids.

Bernard Fontaine had been discovered naked, drunk and confused near the Esplanade bus shelter. He told the response officers that he'd woken up to find some guy stripping off his clothes. The description he gave was IC1 male, fat and in his thirties.

"Could be our victim," I said.

"Aye, could be," said Blinschell. "Could be the ten percent of the city that gets pissed every night."

"As low a percentage as that?"

"I was only counting the IC1 males below forty," said Blinschell. "As a nation we just don't drink like we used to." He waved a hand at the shelter. "Are you going to do your voodoo thing?"

Although it had been over three days since either attack, I was hopeful about the shelter, which was a bog-standard Trueform with metal structural supports. It would definitely retain any *vestigia* much better than the sad grass verge of Beach Boulevard. It also had one of those narrow benches designed to discourage rough sleepers from dossing down.

"I doubt he was sleeping on that," I said.

"He must have passed out on the floor," said Blinschell.

I started with the support closest to the bench. These days I can do an Initial *Vestigia* Assessment on the fly and with my eyes open, but it's still worth trying to look for a bit of inner stillness.

It was faint but persistent... like someone watching TV in the flat below your own. The same sense of seaweed and salt water as I'd felt clinging to Aquaman in the mortuary, although with less dead fish and more...

The cry of a gull, bird shit smell—something greasy, like an old packet of chips.

A separate *vestigium*, I realized. And opened my eyes to look around. There were a ton of gulls hovering like kites above the beach. Occasionally one would peel off and slide sideways—hunting for a fish, or more likely an unattended sandwich.

Animals hardly ever leave a *vestigium*—not even the talking foxes, who were definitely magical themselves—so where had that gull trace come from?

To be thorough, I checked the other supports, the bench and even the ground in front of it. Blinschell paced up and down like a man who had just quit smoking. The *vestigia* mix remained the same, but was definitely centered on the area in front of the bench.

Aberdeen MIT had managed to recover Aquaman's effects from the hospital. The contents of his trouser pockets had consisted of a wallet belonging to the mugging victim, Bernard Fontaine, a single condom still in its foil, and a tourist map of Aberdeen with a circle drawn around a location in the west of the city. I wondered if the last two items had belonged to Fontaine or his assailant. Perhaps Aquaman had been hoping for a romantic night out.

It had been a busy Friday night when they picked up Bernard Fontaine. The statement he'd given had been just the facts. *A big man stripped me naked and ran off with my clothes.* Maybe we needed a bit more.

I told Blinschell that I wanted to re-interview Fontaine.

"He's going to be on the action list as a TIE anyway," I said. In a homicide, just about everybody who had any connection to the victim got Traced, Interviewed and Eliminated from the inquiry. Or, if you were really lucky, they spontaneously coughed to the crime when you turned up on their doorstep, but I've got to admit that's never happened to me.

Blinschell agreed, and we called in to the incident room to get his work address.

"Unfortunately, I appear to have picked up some bad habits from the locals," said Bernard Fontaine. One of which was getting unreasonably hammered on a Friday night. To the point where he didn't even know how he had managed to rock up at the Esplanade bus stop.

"That's all a bit of a blur," he said.

We'd caught up with Bernard at his place of work. It was the sort of office that has been created by hollowing out a line of terraced houses in the hope of pushing the hoi polloi out to the suburbs, where they belong. With its spider-legged beechwood desks, flat-screen workstations and the prevalence of noise-canceling headphones, it could have been working on anything from computer games to accountancy, but was, in fact, developing plans for offshore wind turbines.

Bernard himself was French. But, having worked in Aberdeen for ten years, his English—or more precisely, his Scottish—was fluent, although he'd kept his accent. "On purpose," he admitted. "Because it goes down well with both the ladies and the gentlemen." Round-faced, sad-eyed, floppy-haired, with a gym-fresh physique, I suspected he was hoovering them up on both sides of the aisle. He obviously hadn't scored on the night in question—or, if he had, he must have been too "blootered" to follow through.

Although he admitted to a certain amount of confusion when he woke up to find someone stripping off his underwear.

"I thought I was dreaming," he said. "Only I realized I was lying in a bus shelter. I have my standards."

His description of his assailant remained the same as his

initial statement—white, male, plump but hefty. We showed him a touched-up image of Aquaman's dead face and he made a positive identification.

"He looked better, though," said Bernard.

I asked Bernard what his immediate reaction had been—once he realized what was going on.

"I hit him, of course," said Bernard. "As hard as I could. Not that it made any difference. It was like punching a granite block wrapped in leather."

"Did you hurt him?" asked Blinschell.

Drinking was not the only local habit Bernard had acquired, because he was immediately suspicious.

"Why?" he asked. "Has he made a complaint?"

"What happened after you hit him?" asked Blinschell.

"He grabbed me by the throat, one-handed," said Bernard. "Lifted me off my feet and whipped off my knickers. Then he dropped me, and by the time I'd recovered he was gone."

This tallied with the bruises on his neck documented at the hospital on Saturday morning.

"I don't think he was trying to kill me," he said—touching his neck. "Or I would be dead. You understand?"

I thought of Aquaman's anomalous structures in his throat and upper chest, and asked Bernard whether his assailant had been wet or smelled of the sea. This got me a blank look. Then he shot a questioning glance at Blinschell and then looked back to me.

"Wet? Perhaps. Maybe. I didn't notice any smell." Bernard paused and thought about it. "The smell of the sea?"

"Seaweed, fish," I said. "That sort of thing."

"Well, yes," said Bernard. "Given where we were, it didn't seem unusual."

"Did you notice anything else that was unusual?"

Bernard puffed out a breath.

"He was attacked by a bird," he said. "When he was bundling up my clothes and leaving, this huge bird swooped down and tried to peck him."

Bernard didn't know what kind of bird it was beyond big and white, so presumably a gull of some kind.

I took Bernard around the questions again, but varying the

emphasis to see if I could wheedle anything extra out of him. We showed him images of the condom and the tourist map we'd found in "his" trousers, and while he copped to the condom he said the map wasn't his. After ten years he knew his way around.

When we circled around to the bird section, Bernard volunteered that he thought he'd imagined the bird because he was sure it had vanished mid-attack.

"One moment it was there and the next, gone," he said. "I was disappointed because I was supporting the bird at this point. Then it came back in the same place, but it must have been a trick of the light."

After we'd finished the interview, we finished writing up Bernard's statement in front of him. He obviously wanted us gone, but you don't want your police writing *après* interview out of your sight. Trust me on this. Then we got him to read it and sign it.

"What was so interesting about the gull?" asked Blinschell once we were back outside.

The bonnet of the Asbo was hot, so I opened the doors to let the air circulate.

I said I didn't know, but I was suspicious about the way it attacked in the middle of the night. "Is that usual?" I asked.

"Wherever there's spare food you're going to get a gull," he said. "Day or night."

I asked Blinschell when he was getting off shift, and he said whenever I was safely gone from the city.

"I have to pick up my parents," I said. "But can you meet down at the bus stop later?"

"How much later?" he asked.

I checked my watch and added an hour's faffing time and an extra half hour for waiting for Mum time.

"About eight o'clock," I said.

"What precisely will we be doing?"

"We're going to catch ourselves a seagull," I said.

I dropped Blinschell off at Divisional HQ and, following his advice, avoided Union Street for the return trip to chez rock star. There, unsurprisingly, Mum had cleaned the kitchen and Dad had gone to sleep on one of the sofas in the music room.

An hour and a half later I drove them both to the Lemon Tree, which was, ironically, one street away from DHQ. I took advantage of my new semi-official status to park in the official car park at the back, and followed Google Maps down an alleyway to yet another bleak, treeless boulevard. The club proper was a big plain granite box with a gray institutional interior that kind of matched the inside of DHQ.

"It was a community center built by the Young Women's Christian Association," said Zach. "So they could have alcohol- and fun-free dances."

Which explained why the green room on the first floor had a simple stained-glass bay window, wood-paneled walls and a brass bell mounted halfway up one of the walls. There was also a plaque honoring those from the community center who had given their lives in World War II. Either this solemn reminder or—more likely—the teetotal history of the club had obviously infected the band, who were unusually quiet. Not that they were particularly rowdy at the best of times, coming as they did from the respectable middle-class school of weekend jazz. They were all good musicians but the legendary "Lord" Grant, now on his fourth comeback, was who would be pulling in the punters.

All three were white and in their early forties; all of them had proper jobs. Daniel Hossack was thin, blond, bespectacled, and unassuming. Derek "call me Max" Harwood was so average-looking as to be almost invisible, although at least the band's elevation to almost-stardom had persuaded him out of the diamond-patterned M&S jumpers.

James Lochrane, the drummer, was as close to a hellraiser as they were going to get, and that was only because he was from Glasgow and didn't want to let the side down.

"It's not that we're particularly violent," he once told me. "It's just that the bastards keep trying it on."

The bastards, as far as I could tell, included everyone born more than ten kilometers from George Square. Including, I assumed, the entire faculty of the Humanities and Social Sciences at Queen Mary's, where he taught seventeenth-century French history. I'd actually looked him up on the Police National Computer, but if he'd nutted anyone in real life it hadn't made it to the attention of the police. None of them had, which my dad thinks says something about the modern jazz scene.

"Not one would have lasted five seconds around Tubby Hayes," he says, but my mum never cared for the lifestyle—only the music. So Lord Grant's Irregulars suited us both.

With my parents safely installed in the green room, I popped downstairs and called Bev. Once I'd established that the twins' environmental damage was at an acceptable level, I asked her about people with gills.

"I've heard rumors of them," said Bev. "Never met one, though. Did they give a name?"

"This one was dead," I said, and told her about the body in the morgue, his *vestigium*, gills and enlarged spleen.

"Could be a selkie," she said.

"I thought they were seals?"

"Don't know—they never come up the estuary," said Beverley. "Sorry. But if you meet a live one, don't forget to give them my card. Then maybe we can ask them who they think they are."

"Perhaps if you come down here tomorrow they'll talk to you," I said.

"Don't count on it," she said. "Speaking of which, they met their panther today. At least, Abigail did."

I asked whether it was really a panther, and Bev said that Abigail's description matched the Wikipedia entry.

"Is she all right?" I asked.

"Abigail? 'Course," said Bev. "She says it was more scared of her than she was of it. Although Indigo says she wants hazard pay in future. The thing is, Thomas couldn't find any trace of it. He thinks it might not always be present in the here and now. Remember the unicorns?"

Carthorses with spikes on their heads, translucent in the moonlight, horrifyingly really there when they'd absorbed enough magic. Creatures of fairyland that crossed over into the real world at seemingly random intervals—the better to mess up my paperwork.

Also carnivorous.

"I remember," I said, and Beverley laughed.

I don't like using the word "dimension" for this stuff. Apart from anything else, the cosmologists get all snooty when talking about alternative dimensions and parallel worlds. To them, dimensions are mathematical abstractions that they plug into their equations to explain stuff like quantum mechanics and gravity—not a place where unicorns come from. At least, not unless they've imbibed something seriously mind-altering.

The posh wizards of old called them *allokosmoi*, and until some clever bugger comes up with an explanation I can understand, that's what I'm going to call them. Fairyland, where the unicorns and the High Fae originate, is one. There are others that I have glimpsed in passing. And a glimpse was all I wanted.

I like to stick to just the one world when I can. Real life is complicated enough.

We chatted for a bit more until I noticed that one of the Lemon Tree staff was trying to attract my attention. I told Beverley I loved her and would see her that evening, and hung up.

"There's a couple of guys outside who'd like a word." He sounded weirdly like he'd came from Belfast via Dallas, or at least hung out with way too many American oil workers.

"Did they say who they were?"

The guy gave me a slightly bewildered look, as if it had never even occurred to him to speculate as to their identities. Let alone actually ask. I recognized that look, so I knew better than to ask any more questions.

Parked outside in the bus stop on a double yellow line was a brand-new bright red VW Polo. Two young white people were leaning casually against it and watching me walk down the steps. The young woman was fashion-model tall and skinny, wearing cream-colored wide-leg trousers, heeled boots and a black and gold collarless blouse. She had red hair, and the sun had smeared freckles across the pale skin of her face. A pair of blue metal-framed sunglasses were pushed up on her forehead to reveal green eyes.

Her companion was almost as tall, dressed in Neil Gaiman black, with a matching pair of round smoked-glass sunglasses.

"Hi," I said. "What can I do you for?"

"Haud yer wheesht!" said the man, and in his voice I heard the clank of steel pipes and smell of diesel. The bellow of huge engines and the thump-thump of big industry. *I am huge*, his voice said, a mad ferment of activity and power . . . *Who are you to disobey me?*

I couldn't think of anything clever to say, so I gave him what I hoped was an enigmatic smile. For some reason, every single bloody entity I meet tries the glamour on me—at least once. To be fair, half the time they don't even know they're doing it. The really powerful ones probably can't even stop themselves, and these two were definitely in the serious river god class. At a guess they were the Dee and the Don—the two rivers that mark the north and south of Aberdeen.

"I take it you two are the rivers," I said.

"You can call me Bridget," said the woman. "You can call him Elric, because he's an eejit."

Elric rolled his eyes and I caught a glimpse of pink behind the smoked lenses.

"Is your missus about?" asked Bridget. "Only we're supposed to stay clear of your missus."

"To be honest, we're not even supposed to be talking to you," said Elric.

"The aul mannies divven like us fraternizing with the Issacs," said Bridget.

"So why are you talking to me?" I asked.

"Well . . ." said Bridget—stretching the word until it sounded like *wheel*. "We were curious what you were doing up here."

"I was supposed to be on holiday," I said. "Speaking of which, is it all right if Beverley comes down to the beach tomorrow?"

As I hoped, this caught them nicely off guard, and there was a period of fidgeting until Elric said, "Sure, why not?"

"Just the beach, right?" said Bridget.

"Come on," I said. "Some lunch, a bit of shopping, a bit of sightseeing."

Elric snorted a laugh and Bridget slapped his shoulder with the back of her hand.

"They said this would happen," said Elric.

"Said what?"

"That it was dangerous getting into a conversation with you," said Bridget. "You start by saying hello and the next thing you know it's tea, biscuits and obligations."

"Really? Who says that?"

"See what I mean?" said Elric.

"Fine," said Bridget. "Beach, shopping, sightseeing . . . whatever you like. Just so long as you don't get involved."

"Involved in what?" I asked, and this time it was Elric's turn to thump Bridget.

"Look, are you going to promise or not?" she asked.

"I promise Bev will keep her nose out of whatever it is you don't want us to know about," I said. "But you'd better tell me what it is you don't want us to know about."

"Are you trying to be funny?" said Bridget.

They gave me identical narrow-eyed looks, which was impressive since Elric's eyes were hidden behind his sunglasses.

"If you want us to steer clear," I said, "you're going to have to tell us what to steer clear of."

Bridget folded her arms.

"You don't know, do you?" I said.

"Busted," said Elric quietly.

Bridget sighed.

"Onything that's nae right, just tell us," she said.

That seemed fair, so I told them about Aquaman—which seemed to upset them.

"Was he a selkie?" I asked.

"Can't say without meeting him," said Elric.

"You could come and have a look at him in the mortuary," I said, thinking I could probably justify it as an attempt to identify our victim.

"Dead is no good," said Elric.

"We'd need to meet him when he's alive," said Bridget.

"Why's that?"

"He doesn't stop, does he?" said Bridget.

"No, he doesn't," said Elric, and then to me, "Just don't call anyone a selkie until you're sure."

"Even better," said Bridget, "don't get involved."

"There's other things that swim out there in the sea, and tifts that go back a long way," said Elric.

Bridget handed me a card.

"Better that you call us," she said.

I said that I would strive to keep them apprised of developments, and they gave me the same look Bev does when I promise not to tidy up her wardrobe.

"Remember," said Elric as they climbed back into the red VW.

"This isn't London. The rules are different up here, and so are the allegiances."

Despite staying to watch Dad's opening number, I managed to meet Blinschell on time. Aberdeen has two-thirds of the population of my home borough, although its compact nature and sheer busyness makes it feel bigger. Being smaller than it looks, it took less than ten minutes to drive back down to the Esplanade bus stop.

The sun was dropping toward the hills, and the Ferris wheel and the tower of the Pizza Hut were casting long shadows across the road. The beach was in shadow, but sunlight glinted off a huge orange ship and off the tips of windmills near the horizon. The crowd had changed, too; it was older teens and young people congregating around the cafés and the entrance to the funfair.

I found Blinschell propping up the railing and keeping a wary eye out for potential customers among the passersby. By his feet was a large Save the Planet shopping bag, hopefully containing a nylon fishing net. As I approached he lifted the bag and waved it at me.

"What are we doing with this?" he asked.

"We're going to catch that gull," I said.

There was a second path on a terrace a couple of meters lower than the Esplanade. There were fewer members of the public down there, and it had a metal railing that would do nicely for this evening's entertainment.

We walked down the steps and went left along the path until we got to an empty section.

"Do you know how to use one of these?" asked Blinschell, holding up the net. It was a round coarse mesh with weights around its circumference and a line attached to the center. I'd watched a couple of YouTube videos while waiting for my parents to stop faffing, and it seemed simple enough. Especially since I had no intention of casting it any distance at all.

"How hard can it be?" I said, and took the net from him. I tried a couple of experimental casts, which mostly caused it to tangle up around my arms. I had a feeling I was making this far too complicated.

"Look," I said. "You take that side, I'll take this side, and when the bird lands there . . ." I pointed to the nearest upright post on the railing. "We throw it on the count of three."

We practiced it a couple of times until we could cast the net reliably. Blinschell looked up at where the gulls were wheeling above, lit up by the last of the sun.

"How're you going to lure it down?" he asked. "Birdseed, chips, a nice fresh herring?"

"Since we're looking for a magic bird," I said, "I'm going to lure it down with magic."

Blinschell stared at me for a whole minute. As police, you learn to be almost as good a liar as any random grifter or multinational CEO, so it said something that I read every expression as it passed across his face. Suspicion . . . *Is he taking the piss? Are the rumors true? No, I'm fairly certain he's taking the piss. But what if he isn't? You hear stories. Yeah, stories, right. Rumors, more like, because that's reliable . . .*

I felt this could go on for some time, so I held up my palm and conjured a werelight. Six years of practice with that particular spell meant I could make a low-powered one that wasn't going to burn out any phones, but was nice and flashy—like a miniature photon torpedo, a sexy red Klingon one, complete with lens flare.

"Fuck," said Blinschell.

"Yeah," I said. "That's what I said the first time."

"So that's going to attract a bird," said Blinschell. "Because it's a magic bird."

Right on cue there was a long, drawn-out screech somewhere far overhead.

I shut down the werelight.

"Let's catch it first and then I'll explain," I said.

We practiced the capture movement a couple more times. An old couple wrapped up against the evening chill stopped to ask us what we were doing.

"It's a science experiment," I told them.

"We're looking to net a gull," said Blinschell.

"You'll need to watch out," said the old man. "Because thon can be ill-trickit vratches."

The old woman shook her head in sad agreement.

We assured them we would, and they said goodnight and headed off.

Since we were the most interesting thing on the Esplanade at that moment, I started our "experiment" before any more members of the public took an interest.

I've attracted supernatural thaumavores—organisms that consume magic—before. Mostly ghosts, but also the occasional unicorn. Through a bit of trial and error I've developed a werelight variant that omits visible light, UV and infrared, making it pretty inconspicuous, although a friendly astronomer has asked me not to use it in the vicinity of working radio telescopes. It does put out a fair bit of magic, so I told Blinschell to leave his watch, phone and Airwave a couple of meters away—just in case.

He must have been getting used to me because he didn't even ask why.

I switched mine off and then I cast my spell, focusing it on the post cap where the handrail met the upright.

"Is that it?" asked Blinschell. "No chanting or wands? Shouldn't you have a wand?"

"I've got several," I said, and left out that they were mostly experimental. "All back in London with the rest of my kit."

"I can't get used to this," he said.

"What?"

"The way you talk about magic," he said. "As if it's real."

"I showed you."

"I know, I know. But I don't think my brain believes my eyes."

Nothing happened for at least two minutes, so I juiced the spell a bit.

"You know they're a protected species?" said Blinschell.

"What are?"

"Gulls," he said. "Under the Wildlife and Countryside Act (1981) and the Nature Conservation (Scotland) Act (2004)."

"I do, as it happens." I'd used the office back at the rock star mansion to look up the details while Mum and Dad were finishing their preliminary faffing. The acts made it illegal to recklessly or intentionally kill, injure or seriously inconvenience any gull. You're also not allowed to take, damage, destroy a gull's nest or obstruct a gull from using the same.

So far, so clear—don't mess with gulls if you don't want your collar felt.

You can apply for a license from the appropriate authorities to kill or capture gulls. The appropriate authority in this case being the Scottish Executive, who might or might not regard the fact that I suspected the bird in question might originate in an alternative dimension as suitable grounds for a permit. I don't think even Peter Capaldi would get away with that argument, and in any case it might lead to awkward questions about jurisdiction that have yet to be tested in court.

"We're just going to have a good look," I said. "And then we let it go."

I reckon its ears must have been burning, because that was when the gull, if that's what it really was, chose to make an appearance. It swept in with its wings sculling to land neatly on the top post. And it was big, too, with a wingspan wider than I was tall and a long solid body, white head, black back, yellow beak. As it settled on the magical hotspot the colors became brighter, the white tinged with silver, the blacks veined with dark greens and blues.

It perched primly on the top post and furled its wings, turning its head to watch me with one eye after another and back again. The eyes were black, but I thought I saw a glint of red fire at their centers.

Blinschell made an incoherent sound. I think he wanted to swear, but was having trouble coming up with something dramatically appropriate. Faced with the huge bird, "fuck" didn't really cover it.

"Are we doing this or not?" he hissed.

"On three," I said, and on three we cast the net over the bird.

Given it was our first attempt, it was a good cast. The net flew cleanly and landed dead center, the weighted ends dropping down to entangle its wings. The reaction was instantaneous. The gull seemed to explode, rearing up on its legs, neck stretched, wings spreading as far as they could, the beak opening wide to show a long pink tongue and double rows of white serrated teeth.

"Get it," I shouted, and lunged forward to grab one side of the net. Blinschell grabbed the other and we both pulled—trying to sweep the bird off its feet so we could bundle it up.

This did not go down well with the bird, which snapped at the mesh, biting through the nylon with terrifying ease. Close up, I got the strangest sensation of wet heat and the smell of dirty water. We bunched up the net in our hands, the coarse strands cutting into my palms, and the gull started to thrash harder. It got its head and neck out of the hole it had made in the mesh, and lunged for my arm. The toothed beak ripped through the cuff of my jacket and the shirt sleeve below. I flinched backward and lost my grip on the net.

"Let it go," I yelled, but too late.

The gull swung its head around and, quick as a snake, struck at Blinschell's chest. Closed, the beak was as pointed and as lethal as the tip of a spear. But it hit with a strange *boing* sound and Blinschell fell back with a shout—letting go of the net. Bird and net tumbled backward off the railing and out of sight.

I rushed over to Blinschell, who was standing bemused, looking down at his chest.

The beak had ripped through his M&S lambswool pullover and the beige cover on his stab vest, but bounced off the vest itself.

"Shit," I said. "That was lucky."

"Fuck luck," said Blinschell. "Proper preparedness."

I checked my own sleeve and found a long scratch along the inside of my forearm. As soon as I saw it, it started to sting. Any deeper and it would have opened a vein.

Cautiously we looked over the railing. Below on the beach were scraps and tangles of orange nylon—all that was left of the casting net.

"Next time we're using a tranquilizer dart," I said.

"Never mind that," said Blinschell. "What the hell am I supposed to put in my notebook, and how can I claim for the jumper?"

4

What Abigail Got Up To in the Woods

I'M LYING IN a ditch in Scotland because Paul is dead and there is a hole inside me and I'm scared I'm going to fall into it and disappear. I reckon it must be written all over my face because the olds have been tiptoeing around me as if I'm going to explode, and maybe I will. I don't know—maybe I will.

So Nightingale decided to drag me out of my ends, away from my memories and my relatives who say *passed* when they should be saying *dead*. As if Paul has done really well on an exam or qualified for a new body or something. Away from Mum and Dad, who have shit to work out for themselves because most of their life together orbited around Paul, and now that fixed point has gone and we're all whirling off in space like rogue planets looking for another sun.

Although you know I would have settled for Crouch End, not the middle of nowhere. Although I guess the idea is that if I do explode, I'm only going to be a risk to sheep.

So I'm lying in a ditch in Aberdeenshire and trying not to cry again. Which keeps happening at random intervals, which is bare vexing because people stare and it upsets Indigo and the rest of the foxes.

So I am lying in the ditch, which at least is dry, in a temporary hide like what Nightingale showed me how to make once when we were surveying the woods behind Ambrose House. The world has completely turned to face the sun, and it's getting stuffy because Nightingale insists that I wear cargo trousers tucked into boots and a long-sleeved shirt. Nightingale says you've got to buss sleeves and ting when you're finessing the bush—only he don't say it like that.

Given the most amount of stinging nettles, I think he might be right.

Indigo is curled up asleep against my side. Even though it's hot I like the little bit of warmth because it reminds me that I'm not alone. Which is bare stupid, given all the people who worry about me and get up in my business whether I want them to or not.

Peter wants me to do grief counseling, which is rare coming from him, but I said it's my grief, innit? And I ain't finished with it yet.

Still there's a hole in me, and sometimes I think I'm going to implode like a moon with a singularity at its core. Just shrivel down and become so small and massive that nothing can escape—not even sadness.

Indigo wakes up, yawns, stops, her ears swivel.

"What is it?" I ask quietly.

"Something's coming," she says.

I ask her what, but she can't be sure.

"Very stealthy," she says. "But big." The ears twitch again. "Something else as well. A human."

"Nightingale?"

"Don't know."

I am shifting position to get a better view. The ditch I'm in runs along the edge of a forest of tall evergreen trees. Right in front of me is a section of ground that has been recently felled, the stumps torn up and laid on their sides to promote insects. Ten meters away, hanging on an upthrust root, is a string bag with a piece of a sheep in it. Nightingale reckoned that the big cat obviously likes themselves a bit of mutton.

"Closer," says Indigo.

I raise the Leica and check that it's wound on. The thing is manual and you've got to remember which bit to look through for framing and which is the rangefinder. But nothing magical, not even Nightingale going full Darth Vader, is going to mess up this camera.

Somebody, a long time ago, scratched their name, P. Möller, on the case. Nightingale says he picked it up in the war, and I'm too shook to ask whether P. Möller survived the encounter or not. I can't help but think of that war as a million Pauls—all dying for no reason.

"Movement, three o'clock," whispers Indigo, and I shift the camera over to concentrate on the treeline to my right. Because I'm low, the stumps and ridges are getting in the way. Whatever it is, it's going to have to come a way into the clearing for me to see it.

And it has, almost before I can register it. A low-slung shape longer than I am, black as the inside of a coffin and definitely not in a zoo, not safe. I take a photograph but I think my hand was shaking. I thumb the manual winder as quietly and as gently as I can. Indigo is trembling against my side. I take a deep breath and let it out slowly and evenly—the way Varvara Tamonina, who teaches me Russian, combat spells and applied irony, has taught me.

I don't bother with the framing viewfinder. I ain't looking for a composition, just a clear shot in focus. The cat fills the rangefinder from end to end. I take the picture. Another slow breath as I wind on. Another picture.

The head turns toward me.

It's a leopard—a melanistic leopard, a black panther. It's got the short limbs and the cute anime ears. The eyes are golden, slotted, and even as I take another picture, I realized they're fixed on me.

There's like a shiver running down my body and out through my toes. I'm so totally scared that I keep taking pictures because the decision-making part of my brain is too paralyzed to even tell my hands to stop.

The panther oozes toward me, head low, shoulders bunching and relaxing, the rest of its body vanishing from view as it lines up, although I can still see the tip of its tail swishing back and forth behind it.

I've never had to do magic under this much stress before, and when I go looking for the *formae* for a shield or a fireball or even a snapdragon, my brain is just going, *Oh pussycat, what big teeth you have.*

And I'm embarrassed because it's my first real test as an apprentice and I'm going to fail it. Plus I'm about to get totally fucked up by a black panther, and if that ain't ironic then I don't know what is.

The panther stops, the head drops lower, a large pink tongue licks the points of sharp white teeth. I take another photograph because I can't make myself do anything else.

"Run," I hiss at Indigo.

"You first," she hisses back.

I tense, ready to roll over and jump. Big cats don't like sudden movements, and they don't like eating scavenging monkeys like us if they can find something else easier and tastier.

Unless they've got a taste for it, like the lions at Tsavo.

I've finally got the *formae* for a snapdragon ready in my head and I'm about to roll when the panther stops. Its ears twitch, and it slowly turns its head and then its shoulders to look behind it.

I'm never going to get a better chance.

I roll away from Indigo, bits of grass and netting dragging at my hair. I'm lining up the *formae* for a snapdragon, just two of them and a couple of modifiers. It's a simple spell that makes a loud bang and a flash. Developed, so I'm told, to scare off wild animals. But even as I start, I see a girl running in from the treeline.

I'm registering short shorts, pale legs, midriff and arms, white face, black hair, and not much else 'cause she's brandishing a spear. Charging in like she's going to skewer the panther.

I'm releasing the spell, but the cat is rearing up and twisting. And I knew I'd got it wrong the moment I cast it because there was no flash, but there is a bang and a sharp sting on my cheek.

The panther is yowling just like a cat and the girl is doing a knee slide, skidding to a halt, one hand behind her as she falls over backward. There's a plume of smoke rising from the ground in front of her, and I realize I've done a Peter and blown up a tree stump.

Then jagged bits of wood are falling from the sky.

The yowling cuts off suddenly and I can't see the panther any more. I jump back and spin around, looking for where it went, but it's gone.

"Indigo," I shout. "Can you hear it?"

"It's gone," says Indigo from somewhere behind me.

There's a deep sigh and the girl rises from a crouch, reversing her spear to rest on her shoulder. I'm getting a better look now and she definitely isn't from the Nightingale school of forest wear. The shorts and her crop top are bright green Lycra gym-wear, all the better to show off her muscle definition and pale creamy skin. Around her waist is a shimmering silver wrap with a sheen like petrol on water. There are scratches on her calves and her feet are bare.

She's got wicked sharp cheekbones and blue eyes that seem too widely set on her face. Her lips are unnaturally red and I swear it's not lipstick. While I'm looking at her she's looking at me. She slowly looks me up and down and those red lips curve up in a lazy smile. I'm thinking that maybe she likes the look of me, and for the first time since Paul died I'm really wondering what it would be like to kiss someone again.

"Hello," I say. "My name's Abigail."

There's a scratch on her cheek and blood is trickling down toward her jaw.

"Sorry about that," I say. "Got a bit carried away."

Her eyes dart to the right, back toward the trees, then she lifts her spear in a salute, turns and legs it in the opposite direction.

"Nightingale's coming," says Indigo from her hiding place behind me.

"So who was she?"

I am sitting in a deckchair in Brian's back garden, drinking a beer and watching while Abdul burns halal sausages on the barbecue. Beverley is lounging beside me on an inflatable mattress she dragged out of their bungalow-sized tent. The twins are sleeping in a heap beside her. Indigo has sloped off somewhere "classified" and Peter is settling his parents for the night. Which is bare strange, but then it makes me think of doing the same with Paul and the beer suddenly tastes like metal on my tongue.

There's things they don't tell you about grief—like it can alter your sense of taste and drain all the color out of the world.

Nightingale and Brian have unpacked Brian's telescope and are setting it up away from the lights.

"Abigail," says Bev. "Do you know who she is?"

"She didn't say," I say.

"Yeah, but . . ." says Bev, stretching out the "but." "Apart from her name—who was she?"

I'm thinking of the bare feet and the spear and the way she moved. And the silver wrap that glistened like fish scales or petrol—exactly the way real photons don't reflect off anything.

I don't like the word "demimonde" and not just 'cause it's an old French term the boujees stuck on any women if they had sauce, and I've never liked the idea of us and them, but, that said, there's definitely "us that's not quite the same as us."

"Was she something?" asks Bev.

"Oh yeah, she was something all right," I say, and feel a flash of heat in my stomach that has nothing to do with the can of Tennent's in my hand. "But I don't know what. Really I don't."

I've already debriefed, as Indigo loves to call it, the others about the black panther plus strange woman with bare feet and spear. Brian and Abdul got all excited about the big cat, of course, but I know Peter—he had that crease between his eyebrows that he hasn't twigged gives him away.

Two things we all agreed on, though. One: either Aberdeenshire is overrun with supernatural creatures, or the panther and the seagull were probably linked. And two: we were going to have to investigate.

"Could your friend be related to our dead guy?" Peter had asked.

I remembered the perfect smoothness of neck and chest.

"I didn't see any gills," I said.

Peter thinks the magic gull is related to the physical attack on what I'm calling Gillman but only in my head. He's planning to head back to Aberdeen in the morning and see what he can dig up. He's already emailed the Folly and told them to action an analyst to trawl Police Scotland's databases and see if they can't find some connections.

Action an analyst—say that five times quickly.

Beverley reaches up and puts her hand on my arm, and I flinch.

"Are you all right up here?" she asks.

"I'm worried about Mum and Dad," I say.

Beverley squeezes my arm.

"Do you want to go back to London?" she asks.

I want to tell her about the hole in my chest, but it's hard to say things like that, innit? Excuse me, but I feel like I'm going to implode and warp space-time all around me. And then you, my mum or anyone else who tries to get too close will get themselves spaghettified on the event horizon.

I don't say these things—it's not part of my style.

"No," I say. "I want to find out what's going on."

Beverley sighs and shakes her head.

I'm crying in my tent, keeping it quiet so nobody will know, not even Indigo, who I think is out jamming in the woods. I never used to cry like this, not even when Barry Steelhaven sat on me in primary school and tried to tickle me until I weed myself.

I looked him up on Facebook the other day and found his memorial page. He died of leukemia when he was thirteen. He was probably at Great Ormond Street, too—I might have walked right past him when I was visiting Paul.

The tent thrums as Indigo wriggles through the gap I've left in the door flap. A sudden weight on my side and fox breath in my ear.

"I've activated some local contacts," she says. "They want to meet."

"Now?"

"The moon is up, the mice are prancing and the owls are nervous," she says. "Now is the time for covert operations."

I drag myself out of my sleeping bag and get dressed. Once I'm back in my sensible water-resistant cargo trousers I pull out my phone and text *walking-man, evergreen, evergreen* to Nightingale.

A couple of seconds later he texts back, *fox-face?*

I text *thumbs-up.*

I'm pulling on my boots when Nightingale texts a clock symbol I don't recognize. I stop lacing and scroll through the emoji list on my phone. It's a *timer-clock*—he doesn't want me to be too long.

Nightingale took to emojis suspiciously fast. I think he uses them as shorthand with Molly and Foxglove.

I give him another *thumbs-up* and turn my phone off. I don't think he's got me lo-jacked, but I wouldn't put it past Peter—or my mum, for that matter.

Once I'm in the trees I cast *ómma alópekos*, or Fox-Eye for easies, which is my very first original spell. Actually it's a modification of *telescopium* which alters the air in front of your face to create a pair of lenses like a telescope. My version creates a pseudo-lens that shifts some of the ambient infrared into visible light and creates an image that hangs in front of my eyes and stops me walking into trees. I think it converts photons into electrons and then back into more photons, but I can't be sure. That's the real problem with magic, you can think of the *formae* as a series of black boxes. You can find out what they do, if anything, and how they can be modified. But not how they're doing it. It's a vexation, is what it is.

And the intensification effect is not that good and your eyes start to water after a while—and if someone flashes a torch in your face you're gronked for at least ten minutes.

Swear down—I was trying to create a more efficient ghost detector but things went wrong. One day I plan to enchant it into a pair of shades, which you've got to admit will be bare sick and get me points with the Sons of Wayland.

We walk on until we reach a small clearing where a pair of foxes are waiting for us. I shut down Fox-Eye and conjure a daylight-quality werelight.

"Ooh," say the foxes.

"This is Sax William and Reid King," says Indigo. "From the Grampian Operations Group."

"Hello," says Sax William, who is one of the most beautiful foxes I've ever seen. He has a long beige coat shot through with orange, red and flecks of yellow.

"Aye aye, min, fit like?" says Reid King, hanging back at Sax William's shoulder. Her coat is a dark rusty brown and has black flashes at her ears and legs. I've noticed that the talking foxes have a greater degree of color variation than ordinary foxes. In London this is seen as an operational hindrance, where looking like you're an average bin-bandit is considered the peak of tradecraft.

I squat down and hold out my hands so the foxes can sniff them. In some ways this is more important than giving your name. Indigo says they have a whole vocabulary to describe smells, but it's in Vulpenese or whatever you want to call it, so impossible to explain to humans.

Actually I think she could if she wanted to, but the foxes like to keep secrets—even from me.

"They've got some useful intel on our ALF," says Indigo. ALF being Anomalous Large Feline, or Alfa for short.

"We've been tracking it since spring," says Sax William. "But if it has a den it must be on the other side of a soft spot."

Soft spot is fox-speak for an *allokosmos*. Me, Peter and Abdul argue this a lot, because Peter thinks they have to be whole separate universes with their own galaxies and quasars and reh-teh-teh, but I think they can be pocket-sized and stacked up like a block of flats. Only the stairs go sideways into a soft spot, not up and down.

But whatever, the pattern matched Nightingale's missing poo suspicions and Peter's vanishing seagull, which was confirmation. But it could still be a coincidence 'cause that shit happens all the time, whatever our monkey brains think.

"Tell her aboot the fishy quine," says Reid King.

"Hud on. Ah wis jist getting there," says Sax William, and then to me, "There was a lang-shankit female also tracking the target."

"Was she barefoot and carrying a spear?" I ask.

"Roger," says Sax William.

"She was affa canny and sleekit," says Reid King.

I ask what *sleekit* means and Sax William tells me "sly," which from a fox is a major compliment. This sly girl started turning up at least a month ago, but today was the closest she got so far.

"If it goes in and out a soft spot," I say. "How is Little Miss Sleekit following it? Does she go through the soft spot, too?"

"No," says Sax William. "She comes on the bus from somewhere in the north." On the bus, she proves too fast for the foxes to track. One of the reasons they've broken protocol and made direct contact.

"Then how is she picking up the trail?"

Because the panther had a large but finite number of routes it liked to follow when moving about the woods.

"Tell me you've plotted them out," I say, and all three foxes give me the same offended look.

"Of course," says Sax William.

"And made a frequency analysis?"

Also, of course, which is why the next morning I am up a straggly oak tree on one of the established panther trails plotted by the foxes. Or, more precisely, the center of a fuzzy line of increasing probability, since Mr. Anomalous Large Feline doesn't follow precisely the same path each time and the foxes are well literal when it comes to tracking. The tree I'm in is at one of two pinch-points where the fuzzy line narrows to its thinnest.

"It's almost like a patrol route," Nightingale said when I showed him the maps.

"Patrolling for what?" I asked.

"Perhaps your friend with the spear knows," he said, and winked at me. Real ting—totally winked at me, and I got all hot and bothered and worried that he knew, even though I was fucked if I knew what it was supposed to be that he knew.

The other pinch-point was a thousand meters further down the fuzzy line toward Old Deer, where there was a Scottish heritage country house ting. We were using shielded disposable walkie-talkies to communicate, and if they didn't work Sax William and Reid King were going to act as runners.

"Fox news," Peter said when we outlined the plan.

"Wash your mouth out," said Beverley.

Meanwhile, Nightingale is casting a magical point source—like the one Peter says he used to attract the unicorns in Herefordshire.

"And then what?" I asked.

"We see if we can follow it," said Nightingale, which is why I am a thousand meters away, up a tree with a fox with radar hearing. If it follows its normal trail the cat should pass by me, letting Nightingale hang back and stalk it from a distance.

"This is just an initial recce," Nightingale said, using his serious elder voice. "Try to avoid direct contact."

"Roger that," I said. Which got me the side-eye, but Nightingale's too English to do a proper bad look.

I could feel him doing the magic a thousand meters away—a whisper of silver clockwork far away through the trees to the northwest. If I am sensing that here, what must it be like close to?

"How long are we up here?" says Indigo, who is vexed about being up a tree. Indigo is a town fox, she likes roofs and lintels, trees are bare random. And, she likes to point out, leopards are famously good at climbing trees. She knows because she read the Wikipedia article on her Kindle.

Nightingale reassured her that the high ground is always better. "After all, it has to come up the trunk face first," he said. "Should be easy enough to give it a good kick."

Real talk—my dad says that there's a ton of folklore and legends about leopards in Sierra Leone, and not one of them mentions giving one a kicking while up a tree. So in that eventuality I'm going to drop a snapdragon on its face, and if that don't work I'll merk it off the tree with an ice bomb.

I am just considering getting the snacks out to keep Indigo from moaning when she shuts up suddenly—ears twitching. I ready the Leica again. Peter has taken the first roll into Aberdeen to get it developed, but this time I'm hoping to get some lengthwise shots as it passes by. Then we can run it by one of Abdul's tame zoologists to see if we can get it properly identified.

"Where?" I ask, not even in a whisper, practically subvocalizing, because fox hearing is that good.

"One o'clock," says Indigo softly, and I shift my camera to the right.

I pick it up twenty meters away, casually slinking through the trees. The trees look wrong, too straight, the rows too regular. Western hemlock, according to my plant identification app, not native to Scotland and not native to the panther either.

This is a cat that belongs in hotter sunlight, deeper shadows, brighter colors.

I get some good shots and this time it ain't looking in my direction. I'm thinking that it's too big, like Peter's gull, and it's definitely not from here. Does it know where it is? Is it confused? Is it flicking in and out of its home and getting vexed because the landscape keeps changing? That would explain its bad temper.

It's heading in the right direction—toward where Nightingale is casting his lure—but it's going to pass real close to the tree.

We may get to find out whether the high ground is worth anything at all.

5

What Abigail Did About the Panther This Time

IT'S ALL GONE Pete Tong.
    I was supposed to be eyeballing the panther as it slunk past heading for Nightingale's lure, getting some sick pics, and then ninjaing back to where we'd left the Jag.

But the Panther—and this close up it def gets a capital—has other ideas. I don't know if it can smell me and Indigo, but it obviously knows something is sus because it's slowing as it approaches.

Then it pauses just two meters from my tree. Its head sways slowly from side to side—I'm sure it smells me but it hasn't looked up yet. I think that's about to change. But suddenly there is a noise.

Or maybe a song.

Definitely a something, because Indigo's ears are flat against her skull.

The Panther's ears flatten as well, and it crouches down with its belly flat against the ground.

Definitely a song because I can hear notes, and maybe a tune and a promise.

And suddenly I'm thinking I can almost see what the *formae* in Fox-Eye are doing to photons, and how *allokosmoi* stack up in a jumble like bits of a hamster habitat, and how this is all lies because I know a grift when I hear one. Even when it's backed up by a thousand watts of glamour.

The Panther doesn't have my mad skills, though, and lies down on the ground and starts to curl up like a kitten in the sun. Once she's over on her side I can see it's a female, even as I'm fighting this mad urge to climb down and stroke her belly.

Indigo tenses and her ears come back up.

She doesn't have to tell me what to look for. Ms. Panther is at maximum vulnerability, and so I'm not surprised that the song stops and the barefoot assassin is running in with her spear. I get the camera up and refocus on her.

She's traded up to a camouflage sports top and matching cycling shorts, still barefoot, spear raised above her head, hair streaming out behind her.

She's timed it well but cats have sick reactions—twenty times faster than yours or mine. This is why a cat can twist itself right way up in less than half a meter of falling, and Ms. Panther went from rub-my-belly to halfway up our tree before my brain could process the fact that she was moving.

There's about eighty kilos of melanistic leopard up in my face, and I'm so prang that I monkey-jump straight backward and suddenly run out of tree. Gravity gets a grip but I grab a branch before I fall.

Indigo jams her claws into my rucksack and hangs on—once again proving the utility of cross-species social cohesion in improving individual survival probabilities. As does the fact that I get both hands on the branch, improving mine.

So I'm hanging from the tree with a good view of the Panther as it parkours off the trunk and throws herself at the woman with the spear. But, dangling as I am with a terrified fox on my back, I'm not getting the best view of the action.

Twisting, the woman with the spear flings herself out of the way but the Panther gets a swipe in at her back. The woman goes flat on her face and the Panther turns to finish the job.

"Get back," I yell in my best imitation of Stephanopoulos's command voice, and the Panther shifts her attention to me. Two-meter drop or not, it's time to let go of the branch, and I fall and try to roll the way Nightingale has taught me.

I come up and the Panther is less than three meters away. It's hard to tell with a cat, but I think she's a bit puzzled and curious about me. And if you know anything about cats, and swear down Indigo can bore you to death talking about them, you'll know that what they're probably being curious about is whether you'd be fun to play with.

I'm thinking this is where we get to find out whether I can cast magic under pressure when the woman with the spear leaps up and drives it into the Panther's side. The Panther snarls, turns and rears up, batting with both paws.

But the woman jumps back and keeps her spear up, rotating the point to keep the Panther confused.

The woman jabs for the Panther's face—driving it back.

I reckon if I'm going to clap the cat, it's got to be now, and I have the spell ready and everything, but watching it back away from the woman who's trying to chef it with her spear, I'm wondering if I wouldn't be picking the wrong beef.

Then it's gone.

Just like that.

"Soft spot," says Indigo smugly from somewhere safe behind me.

No implosion, no sudden vacuum as it vanished. So Ms. Panther wasn't getting displaced stroke teleported stroke whatever.

Question: if a large melanistic leopard leaves no scat and vanishes without a trace in the forest—does it really exist?

The woman with the spear is suspicious. Ignoring me, she turns to look around, spear extended. As she does, I see her back is covered in blood from her left shoulder to her waist.

Obviously the Panther existed enough to do that.

"Hold up, gal," I say. "You're cut."

The woman looks at me.

"On your back," I say.

She cranes, trying to see—awkwardly feels her back with her free hand and looks shocked when it comes back red.

"Ah shite!" she says and drops her spear.

"Stay still and let me have a look," I say.

"Who are you?" she asks.

I fish the first aid kit out of my rucksack and show it to her.

"I'm the girl with the first aid kit," I say.

She nods and turns her back as I approach.

As I lean forward to check the cut, my other hand brushes against the sash around her waist. There is a rush of sensation, like bubbles racing over the skin of a dolphin. Which is well sus, because how would I know how that felt?

"What are you doing back there?" she asks, but she pulls her hair out of the way.

"Sorry," I say, and lean in to get a closer look.

The fabric of her top has been ripped open and blood is cascading down her back. I open the brand-new kit and rummage around for the wipes. With those, I clear enough of the blood to reveal three long scratches horizontally across her shoulder blade. The top one is deep—scarily deep—and blood is oozing out as fast as I can wipe it away.

I've done a bit of first aid and you don't spend half your life around a children's hospital without picking up stuff. Bruises, scrapes and grazes, yes. Claw damage, not so much. But even I can see this needs professional help.

It's only a little travel kit and its non-adhesive dressings are too small for the gash, so I grab my emergency packet of sanitary pads from my rucksack.

"This needs stitching," I mumble—ripping open the packet with my teeth.

She flinches away.

"No," she says. "No doctors."

"Stay still," I say, and amazingly she does. I slap down a pad on the deep cut and tell her to put her arm out. I hold it in place with my cheek as I fiddle the bandages out of their packet and wrap them around under her armpit and over her other shoulder. I keep going until I run out of bandage. I ask her to hold it while I get a safety pin. Her hand brushes mine and my heart thumps like it's turning over or something, which is a distraction I don't want because I'm trying not to stick her with the pin.

I finish and she tries to pull away, but I keep my hand on her shoulder.

"I need to clean the rest," I say.

"You've got kind hands," she says, which I guarantee nobody has ever said to me like ever. Then she puts her hand over mine and gives it a gentle squeeze. Then she notices the foxes, who have crept up to watch us from a safe distance, and lets go.

"Who are you?" she asks me, but it's Indigo who answers.

"We're foxes," she says. "Who are you?"

"Awa an' bile yer heid, ye wee rodent," says the woman, and I catch the edge of that same compulsion she used to make the Panther play sleepy kitten. She's wasting her time. Me and Peter once lined up the foxes at home and had Beverley put the glamour on them. We repeated the experiment at different distances and with variable numbers of foxes, but they were never affected.

"Of course not," said Indigo when we asked her if she knew why. "We have man's wisdom, remember?"

"Fa' are ye callin' a rodent, fish face?" says Reid King.

The woman gives a surprised little start, twists to catch my eye and raises her eyebrow.

"Indigo, Sax William and Reid King," I say, and gently push her shoulder back so I can keep working on it. "My name is Abigail," I say. "And you need stitches."

"You're English," she says as I use the last of the wipes to clean the bits of the other scratches that poke out from beneath the pad.

"No shit," I say. "I'm from London. What about you?"

"I'm from the Broch," she says. "That's Fraserburgh."

I've done all I can with what I've got, but the pad is already turning red.

"What's your name?"

"Ione," she says.

"What, like the sea nymph?"

Ione twists away again and turns to face me.

"What do you know about it?" she asks.

"It's just an old name," I say, because people can get bare strange if I tell them I read ancient Greek for fun. Well, maybe not for fun, but I like it more than Latin because of the shape the words make in my mouth.

Her lips are red and she's way taller than me. I want to put my arms around her neck and pull her down so I can kiss her on those red lips. It's all those hormones making me wavy because I'm thinking maybe she wants me, too, but you can't just go around kissing strange women until you know for certain.

Also, Indigo might get jealous.

I make myself get all practical and undistracted.

"You def need stitches," I say again. "Or you're going to bleed to death."

"I can't go to the hospital or the clinic," she says. "My uncle will find out."

"And that's worse than dying?"

"He'll kill me," she says, and I must have looked skeptical because she says, "You think I'm joking. I'm only his brother's daughter—he wouldn't think twice."

"Someone's got to stitch you up," I say.

Then Indigo turns to Sax William and Reid King.

"Have you got any medical assets near here?" she asks.

"Oh, aye," says Sax William, sounding smug as only a fox can.

Her name is Kirsty MacIntyre, BVMS, RCVS, top local vet and, according to Indigo, Grampian Operational Group's auxiliary medical officer. Following Sax William's instructions I'd called her number, and ten minutes later she'd picked us up at a designated "exfiltration interface"—that is, a nearby road—in a battered ten-year-old Range Rover.

She had a practice in the nearby village of Strichen, with a gray granite face on the high street and a big enclosed yard at the back. It smelled, like all vets, faintly of worried animal.

"Do you have contacts like this in London?" I ask Indigo while Ione is in the treatment room with Kirsty getting her stitches done.

"Of course," says Indigo. "Vets, charities, tech support—whatever needs an opposable thumb."

The vet is obviously used to working only on animals because she's left the door open, and I can see Ione stretched out on the treatment table with her top off. I watch her flinch, but stay silent as Kirsty stitches up her back. I've got this fantasy of kissing the small of her back and letting my tongue run up her spine.

I'm well smitten, which is, as the foxes say, detrimental to operational efficiency.

The foxes snigger.

"She's a right wee stoater," says Sax William. "Nae muckle wunner she funcies her."

"She's slabberin' and acting fiel," says Reid King, and they both snigger again. Indigo gives me an innocent look that isn't fooling anyone.

I shift seats so I can't see into the treatment room and text Nightingale so he doesn't get vexed.

He texts back a thumbs-up emoji and *maintain contact*.

After she's finished, Kirsty ushers the foxes into the treatment room while Ione goes into the bathroom to clean up. She holds the remains of her top in front of her chest but it's not like I'm looking . . . honest. I move back to the seat where I can keep an eye on the door and the treatment room. I don't want Ione slipping away without me.

I checked the bathroom earlier to make sure there wasn't a back way out.

I can hear Kirsty talking to the foxes in the treatment room.

"Up on the table, people," she says. "Let's be having you—you, too, Indigo."

I go and stand in the doorway and watch as the foxes leap obediently onto the treatment table and sit upright on their haunches like a row of china dogs. Kirsty runs her hands over the fur on Sax William's head, back and flanks.

"Any itches, mange, snuffles, ticks, bites or abscesses?" she asks as she checks Reid King.

"No, ma'am," chorus the foxes.

"Any strange things in your jobbies?"

"No, ma'am," say the two local foxes.

"Jobbies?" asks Indigo.

"Scat," says Kirsty. "Droppings, poo."

"Definitely not," says Indigo. "I watch what I eat."

"Glad to hear it," says Kirsty. "I wish this lot would. Everyone show me your teeth."

One by one the foxes open their mouths while Kirsty uses a tongue depressor to check their teeth. It's dope how wide the foxes can open their mouths, all those sharp white teeth on display. Healthy white teeth according to Kirsty, who clucks her approval before moving on to their ears. She asks whether the foxes have been using the medicated shampoo she's given them.

The local foxes all promise that they have, and using clean water as well—yes, ma'am, you won't catch us washing in ditch water, we're good little foxes.

"Not so little," says Kirsty.

She finds something in Reid King's ear that she doesn't like the look of. She cleans it out with gauze pad and an antiseptic. Reid King flinches as she cleans the tender spot.

"You haven't been checking your ears?" she says, and the local foxes fidget while Indigo looks smug. I check her ears every other day, and I also nick the twins' baby shampoo for her bath.

Ione emerges from the bathroom in a white sweatshirt with *Non inferiora secutus* printed on the front.

"Having not pursued the inferior," I say, because I've got this mad need to impress her.

"What?" she says.

"The Latin," I say.

She looks confused, but then susses it and looks down at her chest.

"It's the motto of the Buchan clan," she says.

"Is that your clan, then?"

"Awa' an' shite!" she says. "Look, I can't be staying here. I've got to get hame." She's heading for the door, and I follow because I'm not ready to let her out of my sight.

"Wait up," I say as we go out the front door. "How are you getting home?"

She points down a street lined with squat gray terraced houses, with narrow pavements and no trees.

"I'll get the bus," she says, and then asks me if I can lend her the fare. "I lost my bag in the woods."

Along with her spear, I remember, but she doesn't mention that.

I lend her the paper and we stand awkwardly looking at each other until she decides I'm total resistible and heads down the high street. I stay with her, because apart from anything else we've got unfinished business. I'm walking behind because the pavements are that narrow.

"We haven't talked about the cat," I say.

"Stay away from the cat," she says. "It's no business of yours."

"Why are you trying to kill it?" I ask.

"Because it shouldn't be here," she says.

"Where should it be?"

"How should I know?" she says. "Just not here."

We stop at a minimalist bus stop by a big flat field that I think must be a park, although why you need one when I can literally see open country just the other side of it is beyond me.

"Do you know what it's doing here?" I ask.

"Why do you want to know?"

"Because it is my business, innit?" I say, and she takes a step back and frowns down at me.

"Who are you working for?" she asks. "Is it FPXPLORE? Is that it?"

"I'm working for the Folly," I say, which is sort of true, me being a sworn apprentice and all that. Although I prefer "working with" since I don't have any plans to be a Fed.

"Fa' the fuck are they?" she asks.

"Things like the cat," I say. "That's our business."

"Not in this place," she says. "Not now, not then, not ever."

But I can hear some doubt creeping in and I think I can maybe work a bit on that, but that's when the bus turns up and I blurt out the first thing that comes into my head.

"Can we meet?" I say.

She hesitates, looking surprised, then suspicious, then sort of shy—and my insides do that flaky flip and tightening thing and my face is hot. She's blushing, too, and my insides flip the other way.

The bus hisses to a stop beside us and we're out of time.

"Where are you staying?" she asks quickly as the doors open.

I give her Brian's address.

"Stay away from the cat," she says, climbing on board. "Ye dinna ken fir ye're messing with."

The door closes, the bus moves off. I watch it until it's out of sight and then I call Nightingale.

"Where are you?" I ask when he answers.

"I'm having tea with the vet," he says.

"Has Indigo briefed you?" I ask, and start walking back up the high street.

"In precis only," he says. "What's our next move?"

"We buck up to the woods again," I say.

The thing about the foxes is that they can smell where they've been—especially when they've "marked" a couple of spots. I'm climbing the tree to recover my camera, whose strap, luckily, caught on a branch when I dropped it. Meanwhile Indigo and Reid King race each other around the bottom, chasing each other's tails while pretending to be huge scary cats. Sax William is playing sensible older brother and hunting for Ione's bag.

Nightingale is lying face down with his ear to the ground, "listening" to the forest. Or so he says.

I climb carefully out of the tree. It's shameful, right, but I realize that the big scary drop this morning was like seventy centimeters from the soles of my creps to the ground. It seemed further at the time.

I walk over to where I saw Ione drop her spear, and there it is. I pick it up and have a good look without touching the point. Forensically aware—that's me. At first I think it's got a stone tip, but I'm quickly deeping that it's a shell. One of them fan-shaped ones like you always get in kids' comics, but snapped in half. It doesn't have a point. The fan end is at the top, but when I look closer it's wickedly sharp.

I think there's blood staining the edge.

Or it could be moss—either way, I pop a paper bag from the sample kit in my rucksack over the top and secure it with Sellotape. Beverley says you should always take your sample kit with you when you go for a walk. You never know what you're going to find.

In Bev's case, it's mostly creepy crawlies and rare bits of plant. In mine, it's a potentially offensive weapon.

"Found it," calls Sax William from a place where the undergrowth has choked a spot. One of the conifers has fallen against another and created a tent-shaped hollow beneath a screen of ivy. Inside it is hot and booky and filled with dry grass.

Sax William is looking pleased with himself, with one paw on top of a bright blue cylindrical bag. It's a drybag made from PVC with radio-welded seals so that it stays dry underwater. They're designed for kayakers and windsurfers and other cracked people. Beverley and her sisters use them all the time, especially when they're going clubbing and want to keep their party gear dry.

There was a sealed external pocket for a phone, but no phone.

Sax William snuffles around the dry grass for a while and looks up.

"She was here for a long time," he says.

I lie down on the grass and can just make out the oak I was hiding in. The trunks of other conifers make it hard to see clearly, but I reckon she must have watched me climbing into it.

"And using me as bait," I say, because that's how it must have been.

Indigo and Reid King buck up and I make them hang back while I check the hollow for clues. When I find nothing I let them snuffle around in the grass. They say they're sniffing out trace evidence, but I ain't fooled. Especially when they start playing run away and bite me. When even Sax William joined in, I climbed out of the hollow, pulled on my nitrile gloves and went through the drybag.

There's a pair of creps plus socks. I give them a cautious sniff. They smell about what you'd expect, but I get a funny feeling in my stomach which vexes me. I don't like it when my endocrine system tries to one up my brain. Life's complicated enough. Then I'm thinking about Paul again, and Mum, and Dad, and I can feel my face scrunching up like I'm one of the twins when she doesn't get what she wants.

This won't run, I won't let it run. If I'd wanted to be this sad and emo, I'd be wearing vintage black and listening to Somali Yacht Club.

Besides the creps, there's a rain poncho still in its drawbag and a white plastic card wallet with a blue and yellow card with a goofy picture of Ione's face. It's marked Young Scot and looks like a travel concession card, like what I used to have in London. There's a pair of funny-colored Scottish tenners stuffed in the back of the card. No wonder Ione had to borrow money for the bus. Best of all, the card lists her full name as Ione Seaton.

I know her name and I know her ends. Finding her should be easy now, and I won't even have to beg Peter to use his Fed access to do it. I stuff everything back in the bag and head back to where Nightingale is still listening to the ground. I sit down where he can see me.

"Anything interesting?" I ask.

"Peter claims that he once read the whole history of a crossroads in Herefordshire," he says in a dreamy voice. "But I'm not sensing anything here."

"Crossroads is people," I say, because I've been deeping this ever since I learned what *vestigia* are. "Because it's people, we understand it. If it's just nature, then we might not even recognize it for what it is."

"Quite so," says Nightingale. "Now, I don't want to alarm you and I don't want you to do anything sudden, but I believe we're under observation by someone behind you."

I don't spin round or anything lame like that. Instead, acting natural, I get to my feet and turn to look.

A man is standing ten meters away. He's dressed in a sleeveless jerkin over a green shirt with the sleeves rolled up, and those old-fashioned trousers that get tucked into green socks poking out of the top of his boots. He's white, but I can't tell how old he is. Not young or old, but his face has crinkles—what they call weathered in books. His hair is thin and red. There's also a double-barreled shotgun held casually in the crook of his arm.

"Afternoon," he says, and I hear him clearly despite the distance and the softness of his voice.

"Wagwan," I say, before I can stop myself.

"You up from England," he says, not a question.

"Yes," I say.

The man nods but there's something odd about his face, like my brain can't get a grip on what he really looks like. The foxes, I notice, are nowhere to be seen.

"He's got a shotgun," I say as quietly as I can.

The man smiles.

"There's no need to be afeart," he says. "This is for pests. This is not for you. Unless you're a pest—are you?"

I know a threat when somebody makes one. And so does Nightingale, who rises from the ground behind me like the overprotective brother Paul would have been if he could.

"I assure you," he says, "we are here as authorities, not pests."

"Authorities?" says the man. "Is that so?"

"My name is Thomas Nightingale and this is my apprentice, Abigail."

"Ah," says the man and nods.

"And may I ask your name?" asks Nightingale.

"I think that comes later, don't you?" says the man, and starts to turn away. "We'll meet again soon enough."

And then he walks away into the shade of the trees and is gone.

"Who was that?" I ask.

"I honestly have no idea," says Nightingale. "But I'm sure we'll find out presently."

6

The Cream of the Well

THE NEXT MORNING we drove back down to Aberdeen while the twins engaged in a merry screaming duet from their child seats in the back. Early on, I asked Bev whether she couldn't use her mystical riverine glamour powers to keep them quiet, but she said that it doesn't seem to work on them. Then she punched me on the arm for using the term "mystical riverine glamour," and once more for making such an unethical suggestion. Being sensible, I didn't point out that the fact that she knew it wouldn't work implied she'd tried it at least once.

I parked on the Esplanade and helped wrangle the twins into the entrance of Innoflate, kissed all three, and went back to work. A quick google had located a Jessops willing to develop old-fashioned 35mm just off Union Street so I stopped off there on my way to Police Scotland's Divisional HQ.

There, a thin white guy called Donnie, in a black T-shirt with a name tag on a lanyard, turned out to be a film enthusiast, and became especially keen when I explained that the shots had been taken with an antique Leica. I promised to have its owner come in and talk comparative cameras with him if he could get it processed overnight. He said he could.

That done, I drove up to DHQ and presented myself to the reception officer. Blinschell was summoned and he walked me in and led me to the main stairwell. On the first landing, he stopped abruptly and put his fingers to his lips.

From above came a woman's voice shouting, "Oh, for God's sake, stop being such a motherfunking baby."

Then the sound of a door closing.

Blinschell visibly relaxed and resumed climbing the stairs.

"What was that?" I asked.

"You don't want to know," he said.

We ended up in a narrow rectangular office, with a bench desk along one wall and just enough room to stick a pair of operator chairs on the other side. It had been recently repainted and the light fittings were brand-new LEDs. I recognized it at once as the spare space "where we stick the Folly to stop them getting in the way of real police work." I've been working out of offices like that ever since I took my oath as an apprentice.

It did have a whiteboard, a HOLMES-enabled terminal, and since I'd wangled access to the Police Scotland intranet, it would do for our purposes.

Me and Blinschell sat down and planned out our morning. I'd work my way through incident logs, while he went and rounded up the CCTV footage from around the time Aquaman was relieving Bernard Fontaine of his trousers. As he was leaving, another thought struck me.

"Collect the footage from when we were trying to net the bird yesterday," I said. "Two hours . . . no—better make that three hours after, as well."

"What are we looking for?" he asked.

"People taking an interest," I said.

Once he was off, I sat down and composed a long e-mail for the Intelligence Section back at the Folly. I say Intelligence Section, but the truth is that unless we have a major operation going, it's one guy called Nathan Fairbright, who spends most of each day trawling for weird bollocks on the C.A.D, CRIS, CRIMINT databases, the vast sea of misinformation otherwise known as "open source material," and at least two hours a day playing on the Discworld MUD.

That done, I started wading through six months' worth of theft, shoplifting, drunk and disorderly, and the kind of scuffles I'd expect from an entertainment district. The real action was in and around Union Street on a Friday night, where the young men strutted their stuff in front of the young women, got "blootered" and occasionally stabbed each other. It reminded me of my days as a probationer in the West End.

A MISPER caught my eye almost immediately.

Alice MacDuffie, PhD student Geologist at Aberdeen University. Her car was found parked on the Esplanade after she was reported missing by her supervisor, Kristian Jørgensen. She'd missed some faculty meetings and hadn't answered her mobile or her landline. Somebody from the university had visited her house in Westhill, but there was no sign she was home. What bumped her up to high risk was the revelation that she was supposed to be on holiday for a month prior to her being missed, and nothing—not her phone, her bank cards or Twitter account—had been active for that period either.

Despite the new risk assessment, the officers assigned quickly ran out of leads. Obvious suspects such as male members of the university faculty all had alibis and no motive. It took the Aberdeen MIT only seven days to run every lead into the ground. The favored theory was that, for reason or reasons unknown, Alice MacDuffie had gone for a terminal swim of her own accord.

Nobody believed that. But until additional lines of inquiry or a body appeared, the case was left open but dormant. A routine review was scheduled for twenty-eight days after the date she was reported missing.

What caught my eye were reports of a particularly aggressive and large gull which had menaced the officers who'd located her car. The location and the gull seemed a tenuous link, but I flagged her file and noted some of the particulars in my notebook anyway—on the off chance.

I asked Blinschell about the case when he returned with the CCTV footage. One advantage of a compact city like Aberdeen is that it has good centralized CCTV, so grabbing footage is less of a faff than London.

There was nothing from the crime scene on Beach Boulevard, but Aberdeen MIT had already pulled footage from any cameras covering nearby access points. They'd also flagged up potential suspicious behavior, so that's where we started.

"There he goes," said Blinschell.

On the screen, the man identified by the MIT as our victim clipped the view of the traffic cam monitoring the boulevard's intersection with Links Road. Distance meant the image was small, but something about the set of his shoulders as he hurried across the intersection made me think he was determined but terrified. Aquaman definitely looked like he was in a hurry.

Less than a minute later came the group of five identified as his possible attackers.

Again the figures were too small for details, even zoomed in, but there was something wolf-like in the way they trotted after our victim. One figure in the lead, the rest of the pack clustered behind him in a loose string. They were dressed for urban invisibility, in hoodies and jeans.

The lead figure definitely had something long and thin in his right hand.

I thought of the spear that Abigail had recovered from her "friend."

"Any more information back on the wounds?" I asked.

Blinschell got on HOLMES and had a look.

"Not much, but they found traces of calcite in the wound track," he said, and then switched to Google for a further search. "The clear stuff was used in gunsights during the war, agricultural uses for soil stabilization—whatever that is—repairing concrete and in mass spectrometry."

Building sites, farms and material depots didn't really narrow things down, although the mass spectrometry did make me think back to our missing geologist.

"And the ancient Egyptians carved cats out of it," said Blinschell. "Also shells."

"Artillery?"

"Sea shells," he said, and I remembered my building materials.

"Limestone," I said.

The same group of figures had been caught by the same camera, running back the way they'd come less than ten minutes later. So far they hadn't appeared on any other CCTV, or at least none that had been accessed yet.

We switched to the footage from the Esplanade from ten to fifteen minutes. There was a relatively good view of the bus shelter. Enough to know that Aquaman, living up to his nickname, had arrived, stark bollock naked, up the stairs from the beach.

Low light levels blurred the details, but the shadowy figures struggling and the arrival of an outsized gull confirmed Bernard Fontaine's account.

Aquaman departed frame left with a weird hopping gait, which puzzled us until we rocked the footage back and forth and realized he was pulling on Fontaine's trainers as he went.

"Is it true he had gills?" asked Blinschell.

I thought of the pathologist's *anomalous structures in his throat and upper chest that seem to be associated with his respiratory tract*, and allowed that he might have.

"Do you think he swam in from the sea?" he asked.

On the screen, a nude Bernard Fontaine staggered out of the shelter and went looking for help.

"I don't know," I said. "Are you volunteering to go through all the CCTV?"

"No," he said. "But we could raise it as a potential action on HOLMES."

So that some poor sod on the MIT would have to do it for us.

"I think it's only sensible to pursue all viable leads," I said.

"But you think he came from the sea?"

"Yes, I do," I said. "But I can't see how to prove it."

We wound forward through the footage. Eleven minutes after Bernard Fontaine went looking for help, a group of individuals—we counted five—arrived at the bus shelter. They ran in from the south and, despite the blurriness, I got the distinct impression that at least three of them had to stop to catch their breath.

One of them was carrying a long stick tipped with something. It didn't look like a spear point to me, but it was hard to tell. Maybe it was a staff of office, because he was definitely in charge. As soon as it was clear that the shelter was empty, he pointed north and the others dutifully trotted after him. One of them made the mistake of glancing up as he went past the camera and we got a half decent look at his face.

Blinschell went back and forth on the footage to get as clear a still as he could.

"Anyone you know?"

"Could be anyone," he said, and requested that the image be attached to a nominal in HOLMES.

The face was pale, grim, youthful and sharp-featured. He looked worried. I thought I might recognize him if I met him, but I wouldn't want to bet a court case on that identification.

"Definitely the same group as on the Beach Boulevard camera," I said.

"Oh, aye," said Blinschell. "That's for certain."

We ran the footage forward until the officers who had responded to the attack on Bernard Fontaine appeared at the bus shelter. Then we spent a fun couple of hours checking footage from other nearby cameras, but found nothing but some unrelated drunks, a girls' night out that seemed to be going spectacularly well, and an urban fox. I think the fox was just an ordinary fox, but one of the adverse symptoms of policing is you get suspicious of everything.

I checked the time and saw that the twins' session at the soft play area was almost over.

"Right, I think it's time for lunch," I said. "Come on, you can meet the missus."

"Do you want me to go have a look?" asked Beverley as we settled into the ice cream sundae portion of lunch.

Blinschell had recommended a café less than a hundred meters from the Esplanade bus stop, which served bacon butties and burger and chips and had a children's menu, which at least kept the level of food waste down. Upon meeting Beverley, Blinschell gave me that *you jammy bastard* look that does so much for my self-esteem. He then sensibly sat as far from the twins as he could get. The twins ate their chips and the inside of their burgers, and would have used the buns as impromptu frisbees if I hadn't moved to confiscate them.

A couple of gulls came in for a cheeky snatch, but kited away when Beverley gave them the death glare.

Between wrangling the twins, I'd filled her in on our suspicion that Aquaman had walked up from the sea. Hence her offer to have a quick dip and have a look. I considered it while striving to make sure that most of the chocolate sauce sundae went inside the twins and not on their outsides.

"Only if you're careful," I said.

After coffee and hilarious burping, we trooped down to the

beach. Blinschell helped with the bags while I kept a firm hold on the twins to stop them racing into the sea after their mother. She'd been wearing an eye-wateringly tropical one-piece under her outer clothes, which she discarded with the cheerful indifference of someone who has never, ever, had to clean up after herself.

She was out beyond the groins before I'd dusted her top off and stuffed it in the travel bag.

It was cooler than the previous day—not what I would call beach weather, but bright enough to put a sparkle on the waves and light up the big orange ships that patrolled in and out of the harbor. The twins peaked in their sugar rush, crashed and went to sleep on the rug. Me and Blinschell eyed them warily until we decided it was safe to sit down on the folding camp stools and chat.

"I've got a mate in the Met," said Blinschell, and I thought, of course you do. A good copper makes a point of having mates everywhere. "She said that you deal with a lot of weird bollocks—exact words—*weird bollocks*."

"Did she give you any good advice?"

"Stay calm and get ready to bolt."

"Isn't that good advice for doing the job generally?" I said.

"That's what I said. And she said, 'Like normal policing—only more so.'"

I couldn't argue with that, so I changed the subject.

"What's south of here?"

"The harbor," said Blinschell. "Lots of warehouses, storage, chandlers . . . You know, ship stuff."

I was thinking of the group that had run in from the south, the ones we suspected went on to waylay Aquaman on the Beach Boulevard.

"What about housing?" I asked.

"There's Fittie," he said. "That's an old fishing village right up against the harbor."

"Who lives there?"

"Lawyers, artists, oil industry types . . . The usual. It's pricey now and most of the old families have gone. It's all a bit touristy these days—or would be if the tourists ever went there."

"Any pubs?"

"Just the Cream of the Well on Pocra Quay."

"Reputation?"

"There's never been a complaint."

"What, never?"

"Never."

There's not a pub in the country that hasn't come to the attention of the police at least once—even if it's just a noise complaint.

"That's a bit suspicious," I said. "You ever gone in?"

"Aye," said Blinschell. "It was very quiet, just some old mannies having a brew."

"Was it strange?"

"Strange?"

"Did it feel odd?"

"What are you asking?" said Blinschell. But his expression gave me my answer. It had been odd in a strange indefinable way that he was barely conscious of. Six years investigating weird bollocks and you learn to spot this sort of thing.

"It was just a thought," I said.

The twins woke up, going from unconsciousness to making a mad dash for the sea with the same abruptness with which they'd gone to sleep. I grabbed Kehinde and Blinschell went beyond constabulary duty by grabbing Taiwo.

I considered bribing them with snacks but Bev is dead set against that sort of thing, so I handed them toy spades and encouraged them to dig a hole. Surprisingly, that lasted five minutes before degenerating into a sand-flicking contest and finally a duel with pink plastic spades.

Taiwo won, three touches to two.

We were saved from Kehinde's no doubt devastating and fiendish revenge by the return of her mother. Who walked out of the surf wet and wonderful, and sparkling with water droplets.

"Anything," I asked as Kehinde lurched into motion in her direction.

"I was being watched," she said as the water evaporated off her skin.

"Who by?" I asked.

"Couldn't tell," she said, and picked up Kehinde and turned her upside down. "It wasn't my place, but it was theirs."

"Meaning?"

"Say you're from here." She dangled Kehinde by one leg so she could gesture at the sea with her free hand. Kehinde giggled, and Taiwo squirmed in my lap in an attempt to join the fun. "And if you came to London for a visit and went for a dip by Tower Bridge, I could be swimming right behind you and you would never notice."

"But you noticed something," I said.

Bev swung Kehinde the right way up and settled her on her hip.

"Whoever they are," she said, "they wanted me to know they were watching."

"A warning?" I said. "Hostility?"

"More like a sign," she said and jiggled Kehinde. Taiwo squirmed more and made jealous noises until I jiggled her up and down, too. "Like *keep off the grass* or *no fishing.*"

"So who put up the sign?"

"Couldn't tell," said Beverley.

"Wait . . . Are you saying . . . ?" said Blinschell, and then stopped. "All right, if there are people living in the sea, do you think our victim came from there?"

"He could of," she said. "That's the best I can do."

"I think we should check out your pub," I said, and then looked at Beverley.

"You two can go off and do some policing," she said. "Abdul's picking me up and taking us back to Mintlaw."

"What's in Mintlaw?"

"Your mum is going to babysit while Abdul and I do some sampling around the River Ugie."

"You remember what Tweedledee and Tweedledon said?"

"They never said anything about the Ugie. And I might as well get some work done while I'm up here."

"Is that environmental survey work, or your mum's òrìṣà outreach program?"

Beverley kissed me.

"You say that as if there's a difference," she said. "Now help me get them into their wetsuits so I can wear them out a bit more."

Pocra Quay—where the whaling ships used to unload their harvest of oil, blubber and baleen. And, according to Blinschell, create such a stink that you could smell it all the way up the hill at Castlegate.

The Cream of the Well pub was sandwiched between a row of blue and white Nissen huts and a gas storage tank, and built from the same granite as everything else in old Aberdeen. It was squat, ugly, and any sea view it might have had once had since been blocked by a row of five-meter storage hoppers painted bright blue.

I asked Blinschell what was in the silos as we parked up.

"I've no idea," he said. "Why do you want to know?"

"Just curious," I said, and eyed what definitely looked to me like gas storage tanks just spitting distance from the pub and thought, No sudden fireballs—check.

Policing, at least in London, is not the same marinated culture it used to be, but even so, as police you spend a lot of time in or just outside licensed premises. Especially if you do your probation in the West End. The interior of the Cream of the Well was like something frozen in the 1950s—and not in a good way. It was gloomy, dark, and filled with cracked leather furniture and stained wooden tables. The only thing it lacked was a linoleum floor, but I got the distinct impression that was because lino hadn't been invented the last time it had been redecorated.

Rushes would have fitted the ambience better.

They might have masked the old cigarette and beer smell.

The background *vestigia* were pub standard—vague sensations of sadness, laughter, flashes of anger and violence. The smell of the sea was stronger than you'd get in London, but that was to be expected.

There was a scattering of what Blinschell would have called "old mannies" hunched around the tables. One pair playing dominoes in a decorously white manner. Four white hoodies lurked in the one and only booth, hoods still up and faces hidden in the shadows. I made a point of keeping an eye on them.

As agreed, Blinschell took the lead, strolling casually up to the old-fashioned wooden bar with the remnants of its traditional brass trimmings. Behind the bar was a short, red-haired white woman who scowled at us as we approached.

"You police," she said—a statement not a question.

"Aye," said Blinschell, but didn't show his warrant card.

The bar woman turned her gaze on me.

"Him as well?"

"Do you have something against the police?" asked Blinschell.

"Not if I can help it," said the bar woman. "But I haven't seen you in here before."

"Never had cause," said Blinschell.

As per standard procedure, Blinschell was talking to give me time to scope out the people in the pub. There was a curious sameness about the patrons. All the elders were small, stocky, with long thin fingers. Their faces were pale and there was a cast to their features that made me think they were related—at least distantly.

The young hoodies shared a similar body type, and although I was only getting glimpses of their faces I noted pale skin, broad features and pink lips. This could be normal for Footdee, for all I knew. As Abdul says, it's dangerous to make assumptions based on phenotype. But still, I was getting a definite "vibe."

Also, one of them was making damn sure that he kept his face hidden. That's what we call in the trade a positive indicator. So while Blinschell kept the bar woman talking, I snagged a stool and sat down at the open end of the booth. Three of the hoodies gave me the stare, but the fourth turned away.

"Hello, lads," I said. "Seen anything odd recently?"

One of the hoodies, who I christened Stud because he had an infected one in his nose, opened his mouth to say something insulting. You can always tell, because they have to nerve themselves up a bit first. He got as far as the first consonant of "fuck" before his cleverer friend cut in over him.

"What kind of odd?" he asked.

"Animals behaving aggressively, unusual weather phenomena," I said.

"This is Fitty," said the Brains. "The gulls will have your eye out, and we've never had what you'd call usual weather. Where you from?"

"London," I said.

Stud snorted, but got shut down by a look from Brains. I looked at the guy who was keeping his face hidden and wondered how long he could keep it up. I mean, he was practically facing the wall. But his hoodie friends were studiously ignoring him, which meant they either knew he'd been up to no good or they were all in it together.

This could have been the whole gang of five, minus the leader with the stick/spear.

"What are you doing up here?" asked the third hoodie, who sported a goatee. A neatly trimmed one that kind of suited his face, which made it a rare goatee indeed.

"My job," I said.

"Which is?" asked Brains.

"I deal with the odd, the unexplained, anything on earth . . ." I said.

"I don't believe you're police," said Brains.

"He's definitely from Scotland Yard," said Blinschell, who'd come to stand behind me.

"Then he's no' police up here, is he?" said Stud, which caused Brains to shake his head.

"We have been mercifully free of the upside down," said Goatee.

Blinschell, who was obviously from the school of not-fucking-about policing, nodded toward the guy with his face hidden.

"What about you?" he said. "Yeah, you at the back. Let me see your face."

The mood immediately changed; the hoodies shifted position and I went into dynamic risk assessment mode. You don't want be sitting down when things kick off, but you don't want to make any sudden moves either. There were four pint glasses on the table, two phones, no cutlery—thank God. The table was fixed in place so it couldn't be flipped, and I was sitting on a stool, which meant no backboard to trip me up. The hoodies might have who-knew-what hidden in their pockets, but they'd have to reach for them first.

"Fit ye saying?" said Stud. "He disna hae tae dee anything."

"I just want to see his face," said Blinschell, and I shifted back a tad so I could clear the table when I stood. "He can't be that ugly."

"Are you sure about that?" said Brains—obviously trying to defuse the situation. I assigned him as being the lowest threat. Goatee was subconsciously shifting back—away from us: second lowest threat. Stud put his hand on his pint glass and went to the top of list. Blinschell must have noticed, too, because he told him not to be an idiot.

My current theory was that, of the hoodies, three didn't even know about the murder or they'd be tenser. The Shy Hoodie could be our suspect, or a suspect for something else entirely. Only one way to find out.

"Show us your face and we'll go," I said. "We're not interested in anything else."

"Or," said Blinschell, "I'm going to arrest the lot of you for wasting my bloody time."

"Or," said Stud, "you could just—"

"We don't want any trouble," said Brains, but it was too late.

Shy Hoodie came out of his corner like a rat from a biscuit barrel. The speed took me and Blinschell by surprise. I tried to stand up, but he was so fast he literally ran over me, leaving dirty trainer tracks on my thigh and shoulder.

I fell on my back, tucking in my chin so I wouldn't crack my head. The less than bright Stud went to stand up, but I kicked out with both legs and knocked his leg out from under him. He slumped over the table to catch himself and I saw Brains, living up to his nickname, reach out to restrain him.

"Fucking leave it," he shouted.

I rolled to my feet to find Blinschell and Shy Hoodie nowhere to be seen, but the front door was still swinging so the direction was obvious. I followed them out into the surprising sunshine and looked left, to see Blinschell running after our suspect. I hoped he'd called it in because I'd left my Airwave in the car. Even assuming I could remember the right channels for Police Scotland.

The fresh bruise on my thigh complained as soon as I started to run, but I was obviously fitter than Blinschell because I caught up in less than ten meters. You're supposed to wear respectable shoes or boots when working, but I was technically on holiday so I was wearing birthday present trainers and adding length to my vector.

"Where the fuck's he going?" I asked as I passed Blinschell.

We were running down Pocra Quay. To our right were the blue silos of indeterminate contents, ahead was a car barrier and the open expanse of the harbor. To the left was housing, complete with alleyways and nooks and crannies. Or even possibly his mum's house. If I had to guess, I'd say it had to be his mum's house.

I expected him to go left but he bore right, jumped the car barrier and headed for the harbor.

Police hate chases. Foot chases, car chases, any kind of chase. The longer they go on, the more likely something operationally challenging will happen. Sprained ankles, sudden falls, car collisions—an unforeseen encounter with a sharp instrument or a shotgun. When you're in uniform you're weighed down by a metric ton of gear, and in plain clothes you always get shit all over your suit or ruin your shoes.

This is why I have taught myself to do one spell in particular while I'm running.

I threw a tanglefoot, which is an *impello* with half a dozen modifiers, including two controlling range, at his legs, and followed up with a second because judging distance is hard on the run.

One of them must of hit, because Shy Hoodie suddenly found his feet inexplicably stuck together. Down he went on his face, two meters shy of the harbor railings. He was still dragging himself toward the edge when I hopped the vehicle barrier myself and caught up with him.

I put my hand firmly on his back to encourage compliance and told him, between deep breaths, to stay down.

"It wisna me," he said. "Ah did nuhin!"

"Then you shouldn't have rabbited, then, bruv," I said. "Should you?"

7

Cheerz

IF I'D HAD my speedcuffs and a clear idea of my jurisdiction I would have cuffed Shy Hoodie there and then. Instead I did the next best thing, applying gentle but firm pressure on his back and asking him a stream of unanswerable questions to keep him disorientated until Blinschell arrived.

"That was a bit of a jump, weren't it? Do you do athletics at school? I mean, you're fast—what do you do a hundred meters in? I bet you're middle distance, aren't you? Four hundred meter? School champion? Regional? National? You running for Scotland?"

I was about to move on to recent films when Blinschell arrived.

"Fuck," he said, and panted for a bit.

"Swimming," said Shy Hoodie, his voice muffled by the tarmac. "Fifteen hundred meters freestyle. Only *they* won't let me."

I was going to ask who *they* were, but Blinschell had got enough of his puff back to do some practical policing. He squatted down by the boy and patted him on the shoulder.

"Now I'm going to give you a choice," he said. "We can cuff you and drag you back to the station, or you can stand up and take your consequences calmly—like a proper man. Which one do you want?"

Shy Hoodie chose manly fortitude and, taking an arm each, we helped him to his feet. I caught Blinschell's eye and nodded at the nearby railing and the open water beyond. He nodded, and we guided the lad back to where the car barrier separated the harbor access from the road.

Blinschell was probably thinking suicide, but I was thinking possible escape attempt—and not just because of the fifteen hundred meters freestyle. I was thinking gills and an affinity for the sea.

To avoid future jurisdictional debate, Blinschell did the search while I kept a grip on Shy Hoodie's arm to avoid him getting any funny ideas. He came up with keys, wallet, a Young Scot card tucked away in a back pocket—conveniently providing us with his full name, Robert Tarry Smith—and lastly, an antique clasp knife. Blinschell pried the blade open and tested the ring lock to see if it engaged. He showed it to me.

"I'd say that was over three inches," he said.

"More like six," I said. The handle was well made, of what looked like it might be bone, with steel fixings.

"Oh, dear," said Blinschell and, folding the knife, pocketed it. "That's not looking good, Robbie."

"That was ma dad's," wailed Shy Hoodie. "I use it for work."

"What kind of work?" said Blinschell.

"Gutting fish, cutting ropes, that sort of thing."

"Show me your hands," said Blinschell.

I relaxed my grip a little so Robbie could show his hands to Blinschell, who held them and turned them this way and that.

"You're no fisherman, Robbie lad," said Blinschell. "The only callouses you've got are from playing with your joystick."

We arrested him on suspicion of murder, because it's always better to start with the more serious offense. This makes getting warrants and detention extensions easier, it scares the wits out of the suspect, and it stops defense lawyers from claiming you racked up a more serious charge to avoid going out and looking for another suspect.

"Robert Tarry Smith, I am arresting you under Section One of the Criminal Justice (Scotland) Act 2016 for murder," said Blinschell.

Robbie went even paler—if that was possible.

"Murder?" he croaked. "It was nae me."

He didn't deny that there had been a murder, or ask who'd

been killed, which was a dead giveaway. I was tempted to push for details, but for legal reasons it's important not to fuck up your arrest, especially for something serious. Blinschell ignored him and plowed on with the caution, which, being the Scottish version, went on for some time.

"The reason for your arrest is that I suspect that you have committed an offense and I believe that keeping you in custody is necessary and proportionate for the purposes of bringing you before a court or otherwise dealing with you in accordance with the law," he said. "Do you understand?"

Robbie mumbled that he did, and Blinschell launched into the old-fashioned bit of the caution, about evidence being used against you, and then asking whether Robert Smith understood—which again, mumbling, he said he did.

I thought that was going to be it but, no, Blinschell demanded his name, date of birth, place of birth—presumably in case he was secretly English or something—his nationality and his current address.

Robbie gave a name that matched his Young Scot card, his DOB, which made him 23, and looked a bit confused about the place of birth.

"I'm fae the Don," he said. "Far the fuck d'ye think I'm from?"

Nationality was of course "Scottish!" but the address, somewhere called North Square, meant nothing to me.

Again, I thought we'd finished, but Blinschell went on to explain that Robbie had the right to have access to a solicitor and that further explanations would be given at the police station.

Both mine and Shy Robbie's eyes had glazed over by the time he'd finished, and I was willing to bet pounds sterling, Scottish or otherwise, that the whole procedure got drastically abbreviated on late Saturday night shifts.

At least it did mean that by the time the caution was over, the van arrived.

I wanted to go search Robbie's gaff, but apparently in Scotland it takes a bit more than some creative suspicion and an inspector's say-so to enter a premises without permission. So we followed the van back with Blinschell calling his boss, who promised to take it up with the procurator fiscal.

"There could be forensics lying about," I said. "He had accomplices, any one of which could pop round any minute for a bit of spring cleaning."

"We're not daft, Peter," said Blinschell. "We've put a couple of uniforms outside just in case."

One advantage of being currently a cop of dubious jurisdiction was that I was spared the mad excitement of supervising Robert Tarry Smith's introduction to DHQ's custody suite. While Blinschell organized that, and the request for a search warrant, I headed up to our assigned office. There I logged into the secure internet to see if Nathan Fairbright, of the mighty Folly Intelligence Section, had dug up any dirt for me.

The answer was tons and tons of dirt, most of it rated as interesting but not very useful, and relegated to the appendices of the briefing document he'd sent as an attachment. Fortunately Nathan was good, which is why we kept him full-time, and he had cross-referenced with the Folly's own records. These had yet to be computerized, but they had been seventy percent index-carded. Thus the Folly had been dragged kicking and screaming into the 1960s, and was taking a much-needed breather before tackling the information revolution.

I planned to leave that bit to Abigail.

There was a lot of stuff about witchcraft, of which there was a ton in the sixteenth and seventeenth centuries. In fact, Scotland was top of the European league when it came to judicially executing suspiciously clever women—in contrast, England barely made the top ten. Most of it happened in the Lowlands, but there was plenty enough in Aberdeen, and Footdee played a prominent role in providing the leading ladies. The victims were tried in secular courts under the 1563 Act signed into law by none other than Mary Queen of Scots, and the Aberdeen courts kept particularly meticulous records.

When Newtonian magic had its first great flowering along with the Scottish Enlightenment, the newly respectable practitioners sifted through the records in a quest to see whether anyone actually magical had been strangled and then burned at the stake. Nathan had paired down several volumes of speculation to four cases in Aberdeen, of which two occurred in Footdee. I noted down those two—Janet Wishart, executed 1597, and Lorna Smith, tried but acquitted in 1598. Ms. Wishart was a witches' witch, accused of everything from souring milk to shagging the Devil. The last she did down Pocra Quay, the site of the Cream of the Well. That was her only connection to Footdee.

Ms. Smith was a Footdee local, from a Footdee family, and had been accused of swimming naked in the harbor and consorting with fairies. There was a report on the case by William Farquharson, accredited wizard, student of the famous Joseph Black and member of the Poker Club—*the parsimonious heart of the Scottish intelligentsia*, according to Farquharson. He wrote, *It was not unusual for the denizens of the village [Footdee] to swim in the harbor, the river or indeed the sea. There were many fantastical reports of mermaids taking Footdee men as husbands and that on certain nights many of their daughters would take to the water in the manner of their mothers and grandmothers.*

Farquharson would have discounted these reports, had he not ventured out in a boat and seen *these creatures with my own eyes. I sought to communicate but they replied only with scornful laughter.*

Nathan had added in a note that he wondered if H. P. Lovecraft had heard the story.

I had one of those moments of irrational worry that you know is irrational, but you have it anyway. My knowledge of Lovecraft was mainly filtered through playing the role-playing game and in that, the Deep Ones, whose fishy genetics had tainted the inhabitants of Innsmouth, had been servants of greater entities. Including great Cthulhu himself, who lay undying beneath the waves.

Bev had once told me that the whales thought there was something living in the North Sea that might be a giant squid.

I used to be able to make such a clear distinction between fiction and real life . . .

Which made an immediate appearance in the form of a call from my mum.

"Peter," she said in a tone that had not changed since I was little and being ordered to tidy my room. "Make sure you keep an eye on the boys tonight. I don't want them getting frisky."

My dad had a heart attack a couple of years ago. Not serious, but dangerous enough. Since then, he's strictly forbidden from doing gigs on consecutive nights. This left the Irregulars and manager Zach at a loose end in a strange city. Even with tame jazzmen, like my dad's band, this is a dangerous proposition, especially given their manager's ability to get into trouble while standing in the middle of a deserted football pitch at three in the morning.

I assured her I hadn't forgotten, and I asked what her plans were that evening.

"I'm going to cook," she says. "These pies are all very well *'Nas for go buy res if you want me ein the girl pekin dem for live.'*" I told her to save some for me and got back to my intelligence report. I just had enough time to read up on the verified fairly reliable history of Footdee before Blinschell leaned in through the door to report that they had the search warrant for Robert Tarry Smith's home.

Footdee was settled in the late twelfth century by fisherfolk desperate to escape the crushing urban lifestyle of medieval Aberdeen. Some claim that Fittie was its original name, after the Celtic *feihe* or "morass," but most reputable local historians regard this as "a pile of shite."

The locals were famously taciturn, superstitious and clannish, even by Grampian standards, and Nathan had dug up plenty of folk tales featuring witches, warlocks, drowned men appearing on shore and dreadful premonitions.

Aberdeen itself, apart from being occasionally burned down by the English or sacked by neighboring Scots, expanded until Fittie was swallowed up. In a burst of Victorian paternalism, the town council built two squares lined with cottages made out of the same indestructible granite as the rest of the city. The original one-story cottages were expanded upward to increase capacity, and then informally expanded further in the interest of renting out attic rooms to itinerant workers and the like. It was in one of these attic bedsits that Robert Tarry Smith lived.

"Not in his mum's house, you notice," said Blinschell smugly. Since I'd bet him the other way, I now owed him a fish supper.

Searching the bedsit didn't take long. There's such a thing as being too paranoid about forensics, so thankfully we decided against noddy suits and went in wearing gloves and booties. It was a minimalist attic conversion reached via a narrow staircase from a side door. There were two dormer windows, one facing out across the sea and the other across the square. A double futon on a tatami mat filled half the space. The bedding had been recently changed and the duvet was rolled up neatly at one end. The only other furniture was an old kitchen chair that sat in the opening of the dormer that faced the sea. A haphazard stack of paperbacks was piled next to it.

I squatted down and had a look.

It was ninety percent manga—*My Hero Academia*, *One Piece* and something called *Ancient Magus Bride* which I'd never heard of.

There were three four-liter clear plastic storage boxes stacked at one end of the room. The top two boxes held clothes—T-shirts, jeans, boxers, socks, spare Adidas hoodie, all laundered and neatly folded. It was all indicative, as my shrink would say, of institutionalization. Blinschell agreed.

"What do you think?" he said as he searched through the clothes. "Prison, the army?"

"He'd be in the system," I said. "Maybe a tyrannical parent? Or OCD?"

The bottom box was full of mostly manga again, although there was a hefty textbook titled *Essential Math for Geoscientists: An Introduction* and stamped University of Aberdeen inside the cover—I put it in an evidence bag for later. There was a phone charging cable, but no phone. He hadn't been carrying one when he was arrested, either. If he dropped it during his escape from the pub, no doubt one of his friends had pocketed it.

We didn't know who Stud, Brains and Goatee were, either, and the bar woman had adopted the "never seen them before" approach of dodgy pub landlords who know they've got to keep on serving drinks in that particular community.

We were going to check the mug sheets when we got back to DHQ, but Blinschell was sure that if they'd had form he'd have run into them before now.

Footdee—a closed and clannish community?

Out in that community, most of the doors were brightly painted and the doorsteps flanked by potted plants and park benches. The sheds in the squares, where once nets and rigging were hung, had become art shops and psychedelic happening venues. Half the parked cars were BMWs, Audis and Mercedes. But I knew from London that gentrification often only masked the history of a place.

In Robert Tarry Smith's bedsit, the tiny bathroom, just big enough for a loo and a power shower, was as scrupulously neat as the rest of the place. The cupboard above the sink was predictably masculine—disposable razors, shaving gel and, interestingly, a wholesale tub of hypoallergenic moisturizing cream. I knew white boys were beginning to wise up to proper skin care, but Robert hadn't seemed the type.

Extra relief for dry itchy Deep One skin?

There was a separate section for household cleaning products, including an old toothbrush obviously kept for scrubbing the grouting clean—my mum would have approved.

I couldn't get a handle on Robert the OCD weeaboo hoodie at all, and it was beginning to seriously vex me. Where did he keep his illegal substances, his contraband? Where were his snacks, for God's sake?

I went back to the chair in the dormer window and sat down. Lots of daylight for reading, nice view of the sea. Scuff marks on the roof tiles.

The window was a modern casement with thick layered glass, that swung smoothly outward after I unlocked it. There were definite scuff marks. And at least two obvious footprints, made by a trainer, on the gray slate tiles. When I looked down, I saw that there was a footpath built on top of a sea wall that was less than a meter below the roof line. The dormer I was looking out of, and the slanted attic windows running either side, were the only openings on the seaward side.

I asked Blinschell if the waves really came up that far.

"I've heard they've gone right over the roofs," he said.

Using the chair—very conveniently placed, I realized—I cautiously stepped out of the window. The roof was steep, but if I hung on to the windowsill there was barely a drop to the walkway. I looked around. To the north was the curve of the beach, with the bus stop clearly visible less than a thousand meters away. To the south, the walkway joined a footpath across a small park with a children's playground and the port authority control tower, which looked like it had been designed by Gerry Anderson.

Blinschell stuck his head out of the window and looked around. "Convenient," he said.

"I bet he never ever went out his front door," I said.

"Doesn't help us, though," he said. "Does it?"

Joyless functionalism, one of the hallmarks of the modernist style, might be terrible for the built environment, but it's just what you want in an interview room. Interview Room Four was every bit as manky and old-school as an interviewing copper might want. Right down to the cigarette burns on the sturdy laminated table. Which was weird, given that Police Scotland had had a no smoking anywhere policy since before it was Police Scotland. There was a faint whiff of sick underneath a layer of disinfectant and a vague patina of anxiety, fear and anger imprinted into the walls.

Blinschell turned on the recorder and did the introductions. DCI Mason had been against me taking part, on account of the jurisdictional problems, but I pointed out that I was going to spot stuff that they wouldn't. Once Blinschell backed me up, he relented.

Robert Tarry Smith's brief raised an eyebrow when I sat down. He was a thin old white man with thick white hair worn swept back from a wide forehead. The eyebrows were gray, his eyes were pale blue, and his lips and nose were thin. His three-piece suit was of an expensive conservative cut in lightweight charcoal wool. His name was Gerald Tully, of Tully, Stonehouse and Park, and his appearance as Robert's solicitor had surprised both DCI Mason and Blinschell.

"What the fuck is he doing here?" Blinschell had asked— apparently Gerald Tully was the most senior partner in his firm and had never directly represented a client in living memory.

"Obviously our Robbie has influential friends," said Mason.

Not his parents because they were missing, presumed dead or indifferent. So far we'd turned up minimal records for Robert. There was no birth record or criminal record, and the only official reference we could find was his attendance at the Torry Academy—which didn't impress Blinschell at all.

"It's on the other side of the harbor in Torry," he said, and explained that this was an area of high crime and deprivation. Although he didn't use those terms exactly. A pair of luckless PCs had been sent off to see if anybody at the school remembered him. The school had actually closed at the end of the last term, so tracking down individual teachers was going to be the kind of fun job I don't have to do any more.

Well—not often, anyway.

"He left in 2016," said Blinschell. "After that, *nada*."

And there was something "*nada*" about Robert's expression as he sat across from us. His eyes were fixed on a point somewhere above my right shoulder, his posture was listless and, unusually, there was no fidgeting. People nearly always fidget during an interview, innocent people often more than the guilty ones. Robert's stillness was unnatural, and when I say unnatural I know what I'm talking about.

"My client wishes to make a statement," said Tully as soon as we'd finished advising his client that he was under caution and all that entailed.

"OK," said Blinschell. "Let's hear it."

"I beat that man," said Robert in a dull monotone. "He came on to me when I was taking a pish and I freaked out and started beating him. When he stopped moving I panicked and ran away."

Me and Blinschell didn't do anything so unprofessional as stare at each other in stunned surprise, but we really wanted to.

"OK," said Blinschell. "Why don't we start from the beginning?"

He'd been out drinking with some people.

"What people?"

"I don't remember."

"Where were you drinking?"

"I don't remember."

What he did remember was getting separated from the people he didn't remember and peeling off for a "pish" in the trees along Beach Boulevard. While he was standing there with his willy out, a man had approached him and asked whether he needed a hand.

"A hand in what way?" asked Blinschell.

"I don't know, but he was standing right by me."

"What did *you* say?"

"I don't remember."

"Did you say anything at all?"

"I don't... think so," said Robert, and glanced at Tully before returning to gaze at whatever was so fascinating on the wall behind me.

"And then what happened?" asked Blinschell.

In the same listless monotone, Robert described how the man had put his arm around Robert's shoulders and grasped his penis with his other hand. I made a note to ask whether the man had led with his left or his right.

Robert had tried to pull away, but the man's grip had tightened. He struggled, panicked, used his elbows and broke away. The man lunged again and Robert hit him in self-defense, but then "totally lost it."

The man fell down, and Robert kicked him a bit more and then ran for it.

Now, I like a spontaneous confession as much as the next copper, but this smelled worse than an overflowing backed-up toilet in a public loo during a food poisoning epidemic. And I'm speaking from experience here. Not to mention that Tully was obviously angling for the gay panic defense, which was just insulting our intelligence.

Still, proper interview procedure in these circumstances is the same whether you believe the lying little scrote or not. You go back over their story and see if you can pull it to pieces.

Does he have any clue where he went drinking?

No, he doesn't remember.

How far up Beach Boulevard did he stop to relieve himself? Where did his drinking companions go?

Doesn't know, doesn't know—was drunk.

Which hand did the victim use to grab his penis?

That got his attention.

"What the fuck," he said. "Does that have to do with anything?"

"Which hand?" I asked.

He gave the solicitor a desperate look.

"Just tell them what you remember," said the solicitor.

"I don't remember," he said, and abandoned the spot behind my shoulder and instead concentrated on the table in front of him.

"So you went totally radge and battered him," said Blinschell. "How many times did you hit him?"

"I don't remember."

"Oh, come on, Robbie," said Blinschell with feigned impatience. "I'm not asking for an exact figure. You hit him, what . . . ? Once, twice . . . lots?"

"Lots," said Robert. "I hit him a lot of times."

"Until he fell down?"

"Yes, I couldn't stop myself—I just kept hitting him."

"Hard," said Blinschell. "You must have hit him really hard."

"Yes, I hit him hard."

"Really hard?"

"Yes."

"As hard as you could?"

"Yes!"

"Only the thing is, Robbie . . ." said Blinschell. "The thing that's puzzling me is that your knuckles show no signs of bruising whatsoever."

The solicitor coughed and creaked into life.

"The alleged incident took place five days ago," he said. "That's plenty of time for any superficial injuries to heal."

"Alleged incident?" said Blinschell.

"Apologies," said the solicitor quickly. "Force of habit—the incident in question."

"Can I remind you that you are here to advise your client?" said Blinschell. "Not answer questions for him."

That got us a poisonous look from the solicitor—he obviously wasn't used to getting pushback.

We asked Robbie about where he'd gone after the attack, but he said he didn't remember but had woken up in his bedsit late the next morning.

What clothes was he wearing and did he change his bed sheets? He couldn't remember.

What did he do after waking up?

Tried to pretend it hadn't happened.

Didn't he feel guilty?

He didn't feel anything.

If there'd really been such a thing as a reliable lie detector, the needles would have pinged off the walls.

Since he didn't have a job, he'd stayed in his bedsit. His mates had staged an intervention and dragged him to the pub, and that was where we'd come in.

"Who are your mates?" Blinschell asked.

"No comment," said Robert, which at least made a nice change from "I can't remember."

We went back over the events in reverse order and then started randomly shifting up and down the timeline, but Robert remained stubbornly consistent in his lack of memory. So we changed things up a bit.

"You ever go up the university?" I asked.

"What?" asked Robert.

He was surprised, but his solicitor was annoyed, not worried, by the change of tack.

"Got an interest in geology?" I asked, and put the *Essential Math for Geoscientists: An Introduction*, in a clear plastic evidence bag, on the table in front of him. Blinschell duly described it for the recording. I kept my eye on the solicitor while I did it, and there was definitely a spark of recognition before he clamped down on it.

"We found this in your room," said Blinschell. "Where did it come from?"

Robert looked confused, surprised, uncertain. He opened his mouth to speak, but Tully stepped in.

"He's confessed to the offense," he said. "What more do you want?"

"Robert," I said in my patented gentle we-just-want-to-help-you voice. "All we want is the truth."

"I've telt ye the fuckin' truth," he shouted. "He come on tae me an' I kicked his fuckin' heid in. Fit mare d'ye want? I fuckin' killed him. Now away and leave me."

"My client is obviously distraught," said Tully. "Perhaps we may take a break."

We paused the interview for tea and discussion.

"That was bollocks, right?" I said.

"Oh, yeah," said Blinschell. "The only question is who's he covering for?"

DCI Mason jerked his head toward the interview room door.

"Tully's feeding him the answers right now," he said.

"Conspiracy?" I asked.

"With who?" asked Mason. "And why? What possible reason would an old firm like Tully's get involved with a ned like Robbie for?" He gave me a sharp look. "Is this something to do with your lot? Is there something you're not telling us?"

"I came up here for a holiday, remember? Sun, sea and macaroni pie," I said, but left out the giant cat because I felt my goodwill at Aberdeen DHQ was hanging by a thread as it was. "As soon as I know anything, you'll know it."

Both Blinschell and Mason gave me the hard stare, but I've been stared at by true masters of the bad look—not least my mum—so I merely shrugged and shook my head.

"Right," said Mason, checking his watch. "Get back in there and see if you can get him to pop. I'll see if I can contact the PF before she pisses off to the next soirée. She can decide whether we have enough evidence to charge him or not."

Back we went to try and "pop" Robert Smith, which was weird, because according to Blinschell, you usually pop a suspect by getting them to make a confession, not to retract one. After two hours raking over the events of the night in question, we decided we'd got all that we were going to get and then we called it a day.

"Want to come down the pub?" asked Blinschell.

"Can't," I said. "I have to babysit some jazzmen."

In an attempt to keep my mum happy and forestall any potential friskiness, I had agreed to meet up with the band at Cheerz, which turned out to be Aberdeen's self-proclaimed premier gay bar.

"We played rock paper scissors," explained James. "And Danny won. Anyway, unless you're looking for a heteronormative hook-up, gay bars are always more fun."

And Cheerz was definitely more fun than the Cream of the Well, at least. Even on a Thursday night it had a drag act and Zach doing an impossibly cheerful version of James Bay's "Pink Lemonade" on the karaoke stage. The place boasted a truly ridiculous number and variety of bottles behind the bar, but unfortunately, as that night's designated grown-up, I was off the booze. On the upside, this meant I was sober enough to spot one of Robert Smith's friends across the dance floor. It was Stud—who had scrubbed up nicely in tight jeans and a blindingly white

T-shirt, marred only by the plaster he'd stuck on the infected bit of his nose. I suspected he'd left the stud at home. I was going to have to rename him.

I made a quick scan to see if Brains or Goatee were out with him, but there was no sign. Coast clear, I deliberately sidled around the dance floor so he wouldn't spot me coming.

"Hi," I said, when I'd got close enough to be sure he couldn't escape.

He literally went bug-eyed when he recognized me. After he calmed down, we ended up having one of those nightclub conversations where you have to stand close and make short declarative statements.

"You," he said.

"Me," I said.

"Are you off duty?"

"I'm babysitting," I said, and pointed at the Irregulars who, since they'd been watching me the whole time, waved back.

"So this isn't . . . ?"

"In a relationship," I said.

He looked relieved.

"I need to talk to you about your friend."

"What?"

"Your friend Robert," I shouted. "We need to talk."

"I'm not cliping," he said, rhyming cliping with swiping. I assumed he meant grassing, and shouted that I wasn't asking him to.

"But I need you to help me help your friend," I said—which wasn't easy at volume.

"Fuck off."

"He's pleading guilty to murder," I said.

There was what might have been, without the loud bass, the shouting and the laughter, a long silence.

"No," said Stud.

"Yes," said I.

We went outside and stood a little way away from the vapers and their individual puffs of candy-flavored steam.

"He didn't fucking murder anyone," said Stud.

"He signed a confession," I said, and gave him the edited version.

"No no no," said Stud.

"Off the record," I said, which was bollocks, of course. Anything you do say, etc, etc. "You were out with him that night."

He wanted to say yes, to alibi his friend, but he was scared that it might implicate him—which it would. Not to mention attempting to pervert the course of justice.

"He claims that the guy came on to him and he lost his rag," I said.

This had the desired effect of shocking Stud out of vacillation.

"Robbie wouldn't . . ." he said. "Would never . . . Fuuuuuck." The last came as a groan.

"That's what we're taking into court," I said.

"I'm going to tell you something," said Stud once he'd got a grip. "But you didn't hear it from me—right?"

I said right.

"We're from Torry, the other side of the harbor, we're the shithole of Aberdeen," he said. "If you go on the worst places in Scotland list, we're ahead of Paisley and the Gorbals. Where me and Robbie went to school, the drug dealers used to turn up for careers day. We fucking hate the police, ourselves and everybody else in the entire world."

He stopped, having obviously lost control of his rant.

"Nah," he said. "Forget all that. My point is, if you're from Torry you dinnae clipe, you dinnae talk to outsiders and you dinnae trust anybody for shit. Then there's those that think we're much too open and forgiving. I'm telling this wrong." He visibly pulled himself together. "There's families from Fittie that do their own thing, they have their own rules and their own connection with the sea."

"What kind of connection?"

"I've nae idea. But nithin normal, ken?"

"But not fishing?" I said.

"Definitely not fishing," he said.

I smelled supernatural in that statement—or smuggling, maybe.

"Then there's people like me," said Stud, "who are from the next family along. Like we're related but not *in* the families. I'm on the outside, but if I wanted to, if I really wanted to, I could join up—it's like the Mafia. I could be a made man."

"Why didn't you?"

Stud glanced back at the cheerful loudness of the club.

"They can be a bit old-school about certain things," he said.

"But Robert joined up?" I said. "Yes?"

"Yes."

"I need names," I said. "I can't do nothing without names."

"I'm nae giving you any names," said Stud. "I'd die or go live in Manchester before I did that."

"OK, but these families are based in Footdee?"

"Started in Footdee, now they're all over."

"You're just going to let your friend do time?"

"Where I'm from, everybody goes inside sooner or later," said Stud. "If he does what they want, Robbie has it easy, he'll be looked after inside and out."

And that was pretty much all I got. I didn't even get Stud's name, but short of arresting him right there and then I couldn't make him tell me more. I did scribble my personal mobile on one of my plain-clothes business cards, the ones that don't have the Metropolitan Police crest on it, and hand it over. He didn't ostentatiously tear it up or drop it in front of me, which I took as a good sign.

When he went back inside, I saw that Zach was loitering by the door.

"What?" I asked.

"I was told to keep you out of trouble," he said.

"By who?"

"Your mum—among others."

"You're having a laugh."

"That's what I said."

It had been a long day and I wanted back to my kids and my nice warm river goddess, so I didn't dignify that with an answer. We went into the club, where Daniel was doing Gloria Gaynor's "I Will Survive" in a doomed attempt to impress somebody in the audience. It obviously didn't work, because at the end of the evening he piled into my illegally stuffed Asbo with the others when I drove them back to their rock star squat. It wasn't even eleven at night, which tells you everything you need to know about my dad's band.

Having dropped them off, I headed homeward.

I swished through the quiet streets of outer Aberdeen, out onto the even quieter open road. I was aware of a sudden stillness in my head. As if a noise I'd got used to had suddenly stopped. I wondered if it was a magical phenomenon or just my brain unwinding.

I arrived back at Mintlaw to find Beverley sitting outside the tent with a grumpy Indigo.

"Where's everyone?"

"The twins are asleep, Abdul and Brian are off visiting childhood friends, and your parents have just finished rocking the van," she said with a sly smile. "So they've probably gone to sleep, too."

"What about Abigail?" I asked, and Indigo made a huffy "ha" sound.

"Abigail and Thomas rode away on a magic horse," said Bev.

8

What Abigail Did at the Horse Fair

I WAKE UP just as it's getting dark. The sun is pretending to be just above the horizon, but if you know the truth you know it's already gone. I'm just seeing the memory of where it was eight and a bit minutes ago.

I didn't mean to go to sleep. I just went to my tent to use my laptop to find Ione. It was easy, 'cause she has a twelve-year-old sister with a Snapchat account. Same surname, school in Fraserburgh, and she even looks a bit like Ione, only with a rounder face and spiky hair. There's a picture of her and Ione on a beach somewhere foreign, with white sand and palm trees. Ione is in a bikini, showing off her shoulders and her smooth round stomach. There's pictures of her mum and mum's Greek boyfriend, but no dad. More pictures with Ione in them—in a taverna, at the airport—but the bikini shot is the best. I'd zipped up the door for a bit of privacy and it was warm in the tent. I got out of my stinging-nettle-resistant trousers and lay down on top of my sleeping bag. I imagined Ione lying next to me, so large and smooth, strong and soft, my head on her arm, our legs touching.

I wanted to kiss her so badly that I puckered my lips, and then felt stupid. She wasn't there—nobody was. I curled up around the hole in my chest. And I must have gone to sleep.

Indigo is scratching at the tent flap and calling my name.

"Something's coming," she says. "Something big."

I am out of the tent in under a minute, with my belt and creps undone.

The memory of the sun has filled the garden with golden light, which glints off Uncle Richard's trumpet as he plays a sad tune on the patio. His only audience is Aunty Rose, who sits in a deckchair, crying with her eyes closed.

I thought my parents were weird, but those two are cracked.

Indigo scampers on top of the table outside Peter's tent and sits upright—ears twitching.

"Where's it coming from?" I ask.

"The woods."

"Go find Nightingale," I say, and Indigo runs off.

Beverley is suddenly beside me—I didn't hear her arrive.

"You expecting anyone?"

"No."

"Get behind me," she says. "If things kick off, you and Indigo are responsible for the twins."

I do as I'm told—yeah, it happens from time to time. Beverley bounces a couple of times on the balls of her feet like an athlete warming up. Takes a stance.

"How did you know it was coming?" I ask.

"It's not hiding itself," she says.

Uncle Richard is still playing his solo, and I have a mad idea that it might be what's attracting whatever it is coming toward us.

Nightingale trots up and takes a position, a careful three meters to the left of Bev.

He asks Bev if she knows what it is, but she says no.

I almost scream when Indigo runs up my back and peers over my shoulder.

"Ten yards," she says.

"Proper units," I say.

Indigo sighs.

"Eight meters," she says.

We can hear it ourselves now. A heavy thudding sound coming from the shadows between the trees.

"Indigo," says Nightingale sharply. "Flanks."

"Nothing," says Indigo. "Three meters."

"It's a horse," says Nightingale.

It's a bare massive horse, gray and black in the twilight as it walks out from beneath the trees. It ambles toward us, slow, unstoppable, white legs ending in huge hooves clumping down on the grass—making the ground shake.

I've met horses before, all right. That time in Wales, when I did the thing with the lake and the power station. But this horse is looming over me. If I stood on tiptoes I might just be able to reach the flowers plaited into its mane. It's wearing a bridle but no bit or rein. No saddle, but a patchwork blanket and a girth to hold it on.

It snorts and lowers its head and blows out through nostrils the size of shotgun muzzles. It bobs its long head a couple of times and its feet shuffle back and forth.

"I think he wants to be friends," says Bev and, reaching over, plucks Indigo off my shoulder. Indigo squeaks, but knows better than to vex Bev. Once she's off my back, the horse shuffles forward and looms in front of me, smelling of sweat and flowers.

It lowers the long blaze of its face until it's level with mine, and the big soft lips nibble at my shoulder.

Nightingale leans in and whispers something in the horse's ear and, swear down, it starts sniggering. Then it nibbles my shoulder again.

"He wants to say hello," says Nightingale.

I'm shook, I ain't lying, but the horse's eyes are so dark and calm that I reach out and touch his mane. The hair is wiry under my hand, the skin of his neck warm and alive. The horse makes a dribbly snort of contentment and leans in a little. I stroke his neck some more—another contented dribble.

"Why are you here?" I ask as the horse butts me gently with his face.

He pulls back and, stamping his hooves, turns sideways. What he wants is obvious. What isn't obvious is how I'm going to get up there. I can't even see over his back and there ain't any stirrups.

I look at Nightingale, who bends down and cups his hands so he can boost me onto the horse's back. I've never ridden a pony, let alone a horse, and I don't have a saddle to hold on to. The horse's back is wide and his skin radiates heat through the blanket and into my thighs.

Nightingale puts his hand on the horse's back behind me and hesitates.

"It's been a while since I've performed this particular maneuver," he says, and laughs. Then he sort of does a hop, skip and jump, and suddenly he's sitting behind me. "That," he says, "was remarkably satisfying."

As soon as he's settled, the horse turns and starts to amble back toward the woods. I hold on to the mane and twist to look behind us.

Beverley has a firm grip on Indigo—who doesn't look happy.

The horse shifts his gait, and I face forward and concentrate on not falling off. It's not like riding a motorbike, or even that time Varvara took me gliding. With machines, I'm in control—it's all engineering and physics. With a horse, your method of transportation has its own opinions. It's about trust, and I've never been good at that.

It's dark in the woods, and my kit is all back in the tent with Indigo the—probably unhappy—fox. But when I go to cast a werelight, Nightingale puts his hand on my shoulder.

"Best not," he says.

There are branches swishing around us, but either we're lucky or the horse knows what he's doing as he clumps and sways down a slope and out onto a track.

I know a repurposed railway trackbed even when I'm perched on a horse and riding in the dark. Not even the Romans used to drive a line so straight and level.

"This is the Buchan Way," says Nightingale when I point this out. "I remember watching steam trains from the bridge ahead."

"When was that?" I ask.

"The last time would have been 1912—perhaps," he says. "My uncle used to bring me up here during school hols. We would do a tour of the horse fairs. He was one for the demimonde and the fae, was my uncle."

In London we have the Goblin Markets, where the demimonde goes to shop for the sort of thing that don't get sold in Aldi, or even on Etsy. They also have what Miss Redmayne, my old humanities teacher, called a wider community function. One of which, Peter says, is probably selling stolen goods. The foxes won't go in because they think Uncle Oboe keeps a presence at the fairs, so I have to do their shopping for them. According to Nightingale, some of the older country fairs served the same function—only with extra livestock and traction engines.

"My uncle had this enormous Vauxhall B-type, and we would throw our camping gear in the back and off we'd go," says Nightingale. "He was well known up here. I suspect that's why we've been sent this invitation."

"That explains you," I say. "What about me?"

"That's a good question," he says, which is not helpful.

I've heard rumors about myself—which is seriously weird, if you think about it. And I was once told by the ghost of Christmas present, or somebody a bit like him, that people are all up in my business and chatting behind my back all over the country. This is worrying because I'm not looking to be a celebrity influencer—at least not yet.

I wonder if they know about Paul, and suddenly I feel sick.

We cross a river on what was obviously a Victorian railway bridge.

"The South Ugie," says Nightingale, and says he thinks he remembers fishing in it when he was nine. "It was a long time ago," he says. "I think some of my older memories are fading. I dreamed I once had a fight on the Orient Express, which might have been a memory, although you'd think that would be more memorable."

He didn't used to talk to me like this. He used to be crisp and efficient, like he was trying to be an old-fashioned teacher. All this dim and distant memory stuff only started when Paul went into what his doctors referred to as his final decline. Suddenly it's all how he might have met a Yeti or worn a dress to a ball in New York. It was ages until I figured out that it was his way of trying to distract me.

Peter teaches me spells because that's what distracts him. Indigo demands scratchies and grooming and cheese puffs. Nightingale tells me stories that might be true. Well, the Yeti one, maybe. I'm not sure about the dress.

The horse turns off the path, up a slope and onto a modern road. His hooves echo off the tarmac as we amble along in the middle of it. I was expecting cars to be piling up behind us, but obviously nobody was out for a moonlit drive that night.

A dog barks as we pass a farmhouse. Gray fields run up a hill to our left and down a slope to our right. The air is still and cool, and it is so quiet I swear I can hear the fox-food scurrying around in the hedges.

The horse turns off the road and onto a track, his hooves muffled by a softer surface. The track is a pale line heading straight up a gentle slope. Darker patches on the horizon could be woods, or clumps of encroaching alien fungus.

"I think I know where we're going," says Nightingale.

"Where's that?"

"The fair at Aikey Brae," he says.

"They have fairs in the middle of the night?"

"Actually," he says, "I believe the official horse fair ceased to meet in the 1940s."

"Could be a rave," I say, but I'm thinking of the Goblin Markets and the way they are held in quiet, hidden places, away from where the tourists and the wastemen can find them.

And soon we can hear it, and it does sound a bit like a fair ... only with something missing. The horse takes us through a bunch of tall pines, and as the noise of the fair gets louder I realize what's missing—the sound of generators and proper beats. What I can hear now is a big outdoor pub hosting a folk music festival.

Unless you're a fox or a cat or somebody else that has a reflecting coat at the back of your eye, bouncing photons back at your retina, moonlight is fake news. You get a max of 0.3 lux from a full moon on a clear night, which is like less than one percent of what you get on a badly lit street. The only reason you can see anything is because your brain can take the most basic cues and interpret them into trees, figures, horses. The moonlight you get in films is an illusion created by lighting or special effects.

So when we ride out of the woods to find a fair laid out in moonlight so bright I can make out faces a hundred meters away, we know there is some serious magic underway.

The unicorn is a bit of giveaway as well.

It's tied up beside one of them old-fashioned Roma wagons with a horseshoe cross-section. Peter and Bev have always said that unicorns are a metric ton of psychotic killing machine, but this one is the size of a pony and seems more interested in its nosebag.

"Interesting," says Nightingale. "Peter said they were carnivorous."

"Different species, maybe," I say.

Just beyond the trees is a ragged stone circle fifteen meters across. To the left are the handful of Roma caravans, including Our Little Unicorn and, extending in a semicircle around the stones, a collection of tents and booths. It isn't rammed, but I can see enough mandem jamming outside the booths and gyaldem strutting past and pretending not to catch each other's eye. There's no other horses but the few tied up by the caravans, so whatever is being traded at the fair, it probably isn't ponies.

Our ride stops short of the stone circle and I slide off his back myself, 'cause you've got to assert yourself sometimes. I finesse the landing and sort of bounce, and it feels right—like it was natural, like it was something I already know.

I stroke the horse's neck and say nice things like they do on YouTube, and that seems to work. The big head butts my shoulder and I put my face against his smooth warm skin.

I always made fun of the posh girls and their ponies, but I think I'm beginning to get it. Not so much that I'm going to get myself a pair of wellies and a spade, though.

Nightingale dismounts and stands beside me, checking out the crowds.

"There," he says—pointing.

I look and see a figure standing near the center of the stones. It's the gamekeeper geezer from the woods, only he's left his shotgun at home. He's looking right at us and when he sees he has our attention, he nods.

The horse gives me one more bump with his head and then turns away. I feel the thump of his hooves through the ground beneath my feet.

"I believe my business is with this gentleman," says Nightingale. "But if I'm not mistaken, yours is over there."

I can see Ione across the stones. Glowing in the fake moonlight, in loose, light-colored trousers, boots and a sleeveless waistcoat thing with pockets. Her hair is a braided ribbon of darkness down her back. I can see flecks of bling glinting in the plait. She's still wearing the mesh scarf, shawl or whatever around her waist, but it's definitely glowing an unnatural silver.

Half the stones have fallen over, but I'm small enough to hide behind the nearest upright so I can deep the situation before I do anything stupid. I lean against the stone and act casual. Nightingale has joined the groundsman and I glance back at Ione.

She catches my eye as if she's been waiting for me to look at her and does a little shake of her head before looking away.

I'm feeling rejected, but I check the mandem she's with. They're all pale, like her, and dressed like a Two-Tone revival in dark-colored suits and light-colored collarless shirts. There's a couple of young ones in their twenties with some style in their suits, but the elders are rocking pork-pie hats.

And then I notice they're all wearing the same silver mesh shawls, some round their waists, some around their necks, like oversized cravats. One elder, with a face like a punchbag and a fedora clamped down on a tangle of white-blond hair, has his over both shoulders like a prayer shawl or a priest's stole.

I can feel his density from across the circle of stones—as if he's more solid than the people around him. He's talking to some of Ione's mandem, jabbing his finger to make his points.

This is the uncle, I think. The relative Ione's scared of.

He hasn't clocked me yet, and don't think it's a good idea if he does. So I do a quick fade around the back of my standing stone. I lean my back against it and catch my breath.

Then Ione is beside me.

She puts her fingers to her lips and lowers her head so she can talk softly. I'm weirdly reminded of the horse as her breath tickles my ear.

"What are you doing here?" she asks.

"We were invited by a horse," I say. And, to avoid long explanations, I ask whether the so solid geezer she was with was her uncle.

"Yes," she says. "That's why you can't be seen with me. I don't suppose you brought my bag?"

"I didn't know you were going to be here," I say.

Her face is so close that I can feel her breath on my cheek. She has her hand on my arm, but cautious, like she's worried she'll vex me. I put my hand on hers to show that I want her touch, and her eyes lock on mine. There's actual fear in them, which don't suit her none. Her lips part, but she stops as if she can't think of anything clever to say. The stillness and hesitation is killing me. Killing us both.

But one thing about growing up as the child that "can take care of herself" is that you learn to take what you need when you can get it. I check no one can see us and, before she can chicken out, I put my arm around her neck and kiss her on the lips.

She puts her arms around me and I'm melting.

Swear down—I've lipsed up and down the spectrum and most of them were nice, except for that one wasteman in Cricklewood. But none of them made me feel like I'd just stuck my tongue in the mains. I'm lit from lips to lips. I don't ever want to get out of the circle of her arms. I'm pushing my hand down the back of her pants, desperate for the feel of her bare skin.

"Slow down, girl," she whispers, and I stop pushing, but it's hard.

I want to tell her I love her, but that's stupid, and I'm not going to do that because I don't want her thinking I'm one of these sad emo kids from English Literature. I'm so desperate to stay in her arms that I pull away. She tries to stop me but I break free. I'm staring up at her, breathing hard.

She's reaching, tentative, unsure.

For stupid reasons I want to cry, so I take her hand to stop her getting closer. I look down so she can't see my face, and see that she bites her nails. I find this is a relief, which is just wavy.

She's touching my face, lifting my chin.

"What's wrong?" she asks.

"Nothing," I say. "Can we go somewhere?"

"Not tonight," she says. "Meet me tomorrow at the library—it's by the bus stop. At eleven? And don't forget my bag."

"Which library?"

"In Fraserburgh—where I live, mind," she says, and bends down to kiss me.

She might as well plug me into the mains, swear down, my toes are curling and my privates have turned into a halogen hob. Luckily she stops before my knickers catch fire.

"I'm away," she says, and turns to go.

"Laters," I whisper, but she's gone.

I catch my breath and then I go looking for Nightingale.

One of the things I've learned from the foxes is how to walk softly and keep quiet. It's basic tradecraft they say—discreet is good but unnoticeable is better. Nightingale's got this spell that sort of thickens the shadows around you, and when I've learned that one I'm going to be a ninja.

Still, the fake moonlight casts such black shadows that it's almost as good as that spell for sneaking, and I skirt the crowds by walking the gaps between the caravans, cars and vans. The bonsai unicorn pauses nomming its nosebag long enough to watch me go past.

I judge that I'm far enough away from Ione and her creepy uncle, and step out into the crowd. I'm used to getting looks when I'm outside London, and this crowd of donnies is no exception. Only it feels different. Varvara says the demi-monde doesn't look at people the same way.

"You're not some little black girl to them," she said once. "You're something else."

I like being something else, but I'm careful not to let it go to my head.

I am walking between two lines of stalls and booths, and the fake moonlight is making everything strange and sparkly. I pass a booth selling tartan cloth, another china bowls in white and blue. Another smells sticky and sweet, with jars full of things I don't recognize.

There are posses of gyaldems my age showing a lot of leg and milky muffin top, who hustle past pretending not to stare. Got matching gangs of wannabe roadmen who do stare but are too prang to come close. There are olds, some in their best suits and some in baggy jeans, walking arm in arm, checking out the stalls or standing around drinking beer.

I pass a stall selling translucent face masks, each lit from behind by a candle, that seems familiar. Next is a booth selling musical instruments, with acoustic guitars and fiddles lining the shelves while bagpipes hang from the ceiling like tartan spiders.

There's one selling old leather-bound books in a language I don't understand.

"Gaelic," says the stallholder when I ask. "Breton, Irish, Pictish."

I'm thinking of buying a present for Postmartin, but someone behind me is trying to attract my attention.

"Psst," says a voice. "London."

I look around and see, stuck between two larger stalls, a blue and gold booth I recognize. Shaped like a Punch and Judy booth, but with a pointed canopy and a sign reading *Artemis Vance: Purveyor of Genuine Charms, Cantrips, Fairy Lures and Spells*. Framed in the booth's proscenium arch is a familiar white face with candyfloss hair and a long hooked nose.

"Over here," he hisses at me, and ducks out of sight.

I cross over, and the front of the booth opens like a pair of curtains and Artemis Vance sticks his head out. He looks quickly left and right and beckons me inside. The fabric walls of the booth form a narrow corridor which opens up into a clear space at the back of the stalls. There's the rear end of an antique van, back doors open to reveal piles of storage boxes on the left, and a single blow-up mattress dressed with a patchwork quilt on the right. An awning is attached to poles extending from the roof and stretches all the way back to the booth behind me. Sheltering beneath is a folding table and a pair of green canvas camp chairs. On the pink laminated tabletop is a bottle and two mismatched glasses.

Vance sits in one chair and gestures at the other. I sit down and he lifts the bottle—which is made of smoky green glass and unlabeled—and offers me some.

"What is it?" I ask.

"A cordial," he says. "Nonalcoholic, a restorative of my own devising which I am sure you will find both flavourful and efficacious."

I hesitate.

"A melange of the finest herbs, spices and other natural things," he says.

I give him a look.

"Also obligation-free."

"You sure?" I ask.

"I am not so foolish as to pit myself against the prodigious might of the Nightingale," he says. "And that would only be if I were fortunate—the glorious Beverley would no doubt stake me out to wait for high tide, and the ire of the Parliament of Foxes is feared throughout the land."

"So you're not worried about Peter?"

"In such circumstances, one could only hope for the harsh but fair ministrations of the Starling," he says. "Which brings us to—"

"What about my charm?"

"Charm?"

"The one you sold me ages ago at the Summer Court," I say. "For a whole fiver."

"Has it not brought satisfaction?"

I take it out to show him—the stone is as dull as ever.

"It never does nothing."

"And that, my little sorceress," says Vance, pouring cordial into the glasses, "is entirely to the good. For should that charm ever start to glow, it would signal the swift approach of a dire consequence. In which case, your only recourse would be to take to your heels and run, as they say, like fuck."

He pushes a glass toward me and picks up his own. I wait for him to take a sip before I try mine. It tastes like summer sunshine, exactly like the feel of waking up with the sun on your skin. I look at the glass and then at Vance, who smiles so widely I think his face might unzip.

"Can I have a bottle?" I ask.

The smile gets even wider because he's thinking obligations, but I'm thinking chemical analysis. Also "synesthesia," which is not a word I've got to use in conversation very often.

He fetches a bottle from the van and hands it over.

"Don't give it to any fairies, foxes or falloys," he said. "It can make them obstreperous."

I put the bottle between my thighs so I won't forget it.

"Now," says Vance. "Glad as I am to render this small service, my true purpose in engaging your attention was to pass on a message to the Nightingale."

"He's here now," I say. "We could go see him."

Vance starts and waves his hand.

"Alas not," he says. "It would be presumptuous for someone such as I to approach one such as him directly. Not to mention imprudent, inopportune and dangerous."

"You're his snitch," I say.

"I beg your pardon?" He's acting all outraged, but that's the point—it's acting. These fae types think they're so subtle, but they make the girls on *Made in Chelsea* look like Machiavelli.

And I know who Machiavelli is—right? Just so we is clear on that point.

"You totally are," I say, and he slumps.

Real time ting—no stamina either.

"I prefer to see myself as an informal conduit for the transmission of necessary information," he says. "The world is not like a wheel. It turns on many axes at once. And the interests and obligations of oneself and others intersect in subtle and complex ways. A wise man looks to maintain separation, if only to avoid unwittingly entering into alliances one might regret later."

"You want to grass someone up," I say. "But you don't want anyone to know you did it."

"Including the Nightingale," he says. "You see my problem. If I tell you, will you keep my secret?"

"Dunno," I say. "What's in it for me?"

"I can do you a nice line in love charms," he says. "Guaranteed to bring the person of your dreams into the waking world."

"No thanks," I say. "I've got that covered."

"Alas, my little troublemaker. Nobody in this sad world ever has that covered," he says. "Still, you are a practical girl, so I will give you information about your furtive furry friends."

"What about them?" I ask.

Vance raises a long finger and wags it slowly from side to side.

"Nice try," he says. "Do we have a deal?"

"Better be solid," I say.

"Believe me, you would need a metaphorical diamond to pierce the surface of this intelligence," he says.

"What do you want me to tell Thomas?" I say, because sometimes these games go on far too long.

"There have been people abroad in the land, in Ireland and Germany, too, asking questions," he said. "Who is the Nightingale? Where is he from? Who gets inside the Folly, and what is it Nightingale is hiding there?"

I know what is hiding in the basement of the Folly, although Peter would lose his shit if he knew I knew. Vance def doesn't know, and I make my face a mask to make sure nothing is given away.

"People is curious?" I say. "So what?"

"These are foreigners," he says. "Some of them smell of power, others are a bit too curious and a little bit too well read—if you know what I mean."

"What kind of foreigners?" I ask.

"I have yet to meet any of these curious folk or ascertain their origin from other sources," says Vance. "But from what I've gleaned, they certainly wouldn't be counted among the admirers of the Nightingale." Vance makes an airy gesture. "Who are, of course, legion."

That's all he's got, but I promise to pass it on to Nightingale.

"What about payment?" I ask.

Then Vance is telling me things that I'm going to have to deep before I pass on to the foxes. They may not like what I have to tell them—they may not like that I know.

9

Westhill

I WOKE UP to find Indigo slumped bonelessly on the end of the mattress.

"Where's Abigail?" I asked.

"How should I know," said Indigo without looking up.

"Good," said the lump in the bed next to me. "You can help me today."

Indigo sighed and would have slumped further, had she not already been as slumped as far as it's possible for a fox to slump.

Given all the vulpine drama, I was a bit surprised to find Abigail monopolizing Brian's bathroom. She was singing, which I know from experience means somebody has settled in for a long session, so I went down and had breakfast. Brian and Abdul had a laptop open in front of their bowls of omega-enriched porridge, and were entering data between mouthfuls.

"Mapping analysis," said Abdul when I looked over his shoulder. "We're looking for a focal point."

Police analysts call this geographical profiling, and use it to produce exciting-looking maps and PowerPoint presentations. It was developed to locate serial offenders, by plotting any incidents and then seeing whether there was an anchor point around which all their crimes revolve. Abdul and Brian were doing the same, only with reported sightings of our black panther.

Which reminded me. I had to pick up Abigail's pictures.

Nightingale joined us for breakfast, dressed in his serious outdoor best—half of which dated back to the Second World War.

He was carrying one of the double-barreled shotguns that usually live in an ornate gun case in the Folly's upstairs study. Following their "deployment" in Herefordshire a few years back, I'd made a point of ensuring that Nightingale was licensed to carry them.

Given that he was capable of taking out vintage armored vehicles with a fireball, I did wonder what the gun was for.

"Baton rounds," he said. "In case I need to distract it."

"Do you think you're going to find it today?"

"I received some intelligence last night," he said, and told me about the magic horse, the Moon Fair at Aikey Brae, and the mysterious gent who might be a fae, or the *genius loci* of Glen Lanar.

"Or somebody else entirely," he said. "He remarked that the cat was far from being the only anomalous creature let loose in the countryside. He hadn't heard of your gull, but I think we can assume that they're related."

"Anything about people from the sea?" I asked.

"No," said Nightingale. "But then, he was a creature of the hills and glens—he may not know the sea."

"Did he say where the sightings had taken place?" asked Brian.

"As a matter of fact, he did," said Nightingale. "Is that helpful?"

Brian and Abdul launched into an explanation of geographical profiling, and I went upstairs to see if I couldn't wrangle Abigail out of the bathroom. I was just about to do the copper's slap on the door when it opened, and out she popped in a cloud of fragrant steam.

"Finished," she said.

She was dressed like normal, only something seemed different. I was already inside the bathroom when I realized that she was wearing lipstick and eye liner. There was also a waft of what I recognized as Beverley's Chanel Sycomore perfume. I've seen Abigail dolled up before, just not at nine o'clock in the morning.

Once I'd showered, I did what I always do when I want to know what Abigail's up to—I asked a fox.

"It's like Paris didn't happen at all," said Indigo, and made a huffing sound.

I didn't even know Abigail had been to Paris, although I had a vague memory of a school trip that happened years ago. Why would Indigo have been on a school trip?

"What happened in Paris?" I asked, and Indigo became suddenly very interested in the flight of a bird over the garden.

"Did I say Paris?" she said. "I meant Wales."

"What happened in Wales?"

"Nothing," she said. "Just a trip."

"Just a trip?"

"Like what happened in Norfolk."

"What happened in Norfolk?"

Indigo sighed and slumped down into the patch of sunlight she'd been moping in when I'd found her.

"Obviously nothing of importance," she said.

Beverley was equally unhelpful.

"Don't worry, I've got my eye on it," she said. The twins had taken the opportunity of my absence to climb into bed with their mother.

"Got your eye on what?"

"Aren't you supposed to be policing today?"

I knew that tone, so I kissed them all good-bye and headed for the Asbo. No doubt I'd find out what it was all about when something exploded or burned down or triggered a major civil disturbance.

Alice MacDuffie, our temporarily misplaced geologist, lived in a two-bedroom semi down a cul-de-sac in Westhill, a semi-detached town to the west of Aberdeen. The town was laid out in a series of whorls and dead ends, just like an American suburb, only with everything scrunched closer together to save on utility costs. The houses were similarly scrunched together and narrow, as if they'd all recently been on a crash diet. Most of the front gardens had given up their lawns to low-maintenance gravel or additional parking space, the attached garages being too small to accommodate anything larger than a Mini.

Me and Blinschell arrived in separate cars within a couple of minutes of each other. He had a front door key and a copy of the MISPER inquiry on his tablet.

These days all MISPERs are rated as high risk, especially where the media is concerned, but of course some missing people are a higher priority than others. Children and vulnerable adults get the full monty—media appeals, massive search teams, press conferences, families tearing up on the news. Adults in their mid-thirties who go unexpectedly absent at the start of the summer holidays, taking their car and their passport with them, create less concern. The only reason Alice MacDuffie got any attention at all was because she missed a series of crucial meetings at the university and with the oil exploration company she was consulting for. Potentially lucrative meetings, according to the file. Added to that, there'd been no social media activity or transactions on her bank account, and no calls to or from her phone, for three weeks before she was reported missing.

Still . . . maybe she was getting away from it all? People do that all the time. And resources, in case you didn't know, are stretched to breaking point as it is.

But the report of the large and ferocious gull was bugging me, and since Robert Smith refused to change his tune, it's not like we had any other leads.

Before he could use the key, Blinschell hesitated and squatted down to examine the lock.

"This has been forced," he said, and nudged the front door open with his elbow. It swung inward. I squatted down beside him and had a look—it was a standard Yale lock, but the latch bolt had been shorn right off level with the faceplate. I checked the corresponding striker plate on the frame—the rest of the bolt was still in the socket. It was a very neat cut, and there was no sign of damage to striker- or faceplate or any other part of the lock.

"What the fuck does that?" asked Blinschell.

I pulled a glove on to my right hand and touched the cut section of the bolt.

I heard animals—screaming, yodeling, shrieking, yelling—a sensation of wet heat, and the smell of decay like leaf mold.

"Magic," I said.

"Really, magic?"

"Really. Magic."

"Can you tell how long ago?" asked Blinschell, displaying the fine pragmatic qualities that makes some police a joy to work with.

"Not that recent," I said and, when he gave me a long-suffering look, "Yesterday or later. I think. It's not an exact science."

So we checked the house was clear first. For all that he wore his stab vest, Blinschell didn't routinely carry his extendable baton and was surprised I did. Nightingale's tailor has added a deep inside pocket to my jackets and weighted them so they don't hang crooked.

"I'm pretty sure that isn't legal this side of the border," he said when he saw it.

"I have special authorization," I said, and clacked it out.

There was a short porch with coat hooks and fitted storage. The inside door was open and I stepped into it, singing the song of the slightly paranoid copper.

"Hello, this is the police—we're coming in. Is anyone here?"

Unless they're pharmaceutically impaired or pissed, most criminals aren't stupid enough to pick a fight with the police, so it's best to identify yourself.

There are always exceptions, though, so I like to have my baton handy and an *impello palma* spell lined up just in case.

The inner door opened directly into the living room—comfy blue three-piece suite, bookshelves, big flat-screen TV, Blu-ray player. It was obvious from the papers and books strewn across the floor that somebody had already searched the flat.

"It was definitely not like this during the initial inquiries," said Blinschell.

There was an open-sided staircase up to the first floor and a door through to the kitchen. Blinschell watched the stairs while I checked the kitchen. The furnishings were older than in the living room, except for a brand-new fridge-freezer. Through the back windows I could see the whole garden. Paved patio, steps up to an untidy lawn and neglected flower beds.

Upstairs the bathroom still had a hideous avocado bath-shower, toilet and sink. The grouting was flaking in places and some of the tiles had fallen off. The front bedroom had been converted into an office, with brand-new stripped pine desk, swivel chair, fitted bookcases and books and papers strewn across the floor.

Whoever had done the search had been in a hurry and an amateur. Police or other professionals work methodically and disturb things as little as possible. That way, not only do you know what you have and haven't searched, but you don't have to bend down to check things you've already looked at.

The back bedroom was an actual bedroom, with new-smelling

carpet and a queen-size bed with the covers pulled off and the mattress turned over. The mattress also smelled brand-new.

Once we were sure that nobody was going to jump out and stab Blinschell, he went back outside to call it in while I did a sweep for more *vestigia*. Not a sausage. Blinschell came back in and said that DCI Mason was sending over some uniform to secure the scene and do a bit of house to house.

"This can't have been quiet," he said. "Somebody must have heard something."

We divided up the work—he'd check the back garden and I'd have another look at the study.

For all its rushed chaos, there was a definite pattern to the search. The desk had been thoroughly ransacked, every bit of loose printed material spread on the floor. There was a pile of magazines thrown to one side—discarded? I had a look—they were trade magazines with titles like *Geophysics*, *Geophysical Prospecting* and *Petroleum Geoscience*. Super serious stuff. There were two Billy bookshelves from which the box files had been pulled off, opened and their contents scattered. But a neat row of fiction paperbacks had been left untouched. Obviously the hypothetical searcher hadn't been interested in Carole Matthews's *The Cake Shop in the Garden*.

Even with my gloves on, I didn't want to disturb too much before the fingerprint team could have a go. I was about to check the bedroom when Blinschell called me out to the garden.

There was a waterlogged patch in the middle of the lawn, which was a neat trick given it hadn't rained for a while, and it stank of ammonia. Planted on the edges were two paw prints like what might be left by a cat, only they were almost ten centimeters long.

"What made that?" asked Blinschell.

"Possibly a large wading bird?" I said, as a joke.

"Looks more like a cat," said Blinschell, who obviously wasn't as well-read as me.

"That would explain the smell," I said.

"An affa big cat," he said.

"We need to get a cast of this," I said, and took a geolocated photo so I could send it to Dr. Walid to add to his geographical profile and pass on to Nightingale and Abigail.

"So what the fuck is it?"

"You're right. It's a very big cat," I said, and explained that it was why me and Nightingale and the rest had schlepped up to Scotland in the first place. Blinschell gave me a hard look.

"This isn't a coincidence, is it?" he said. "You being up here and all this weird shit happening."

"No," I said. "Weird shit was happening, so we came up here. Just in time."

"Lucky for us," said Blinschell, but strangely he didn't sound like he meant it.

DCI Mason seemed equally unimpressed when he turned up just ahead of the forensic team.

"You're not telling me a great big cat broke into the house," he said.

Unless you're talking murder, kidnap or other major crimes, DCIs almost never visit crime scenes. That's what sergeants and constables are for. DCIs are responsible for making sure that their junior officers are capable of hoovering up any relevant clues and bright enough to filter the information they pass on. If their juniors can't do the job, then turning up to contaminate the crime scene and bark orders is not really going to help push the investigation along.

Of course, for certain DCIs, particularly those who originate in small towns outside Manchester, barking orders is an intrinsic component of their job satisfaction. When I saw that DCI Mason was waiting for us on the driveway, I did wonder if he was one of those. Although, to be fair, rather than barking he went for the kind of soft-spoken, sharp-edged sarcasm that is the glory of Scottish conversation.

"No, sir," I said. "We believe that it was more of a surveillance asset."

We held another one of those impromptu police briefings outside the house while the forensic team zipped up their Tyvek noddy suits.

"A surveillance asset?" said DCI Mason. "A big black cat?"

"Possibly a melanistic leopard," I said before I could stop myself.

DCI Mason looked—a bit theatrically, I thought—at the scattering of neighbors who'd left the comfort of their semis to stand on their driveways to watch the excitement. I couldn't blame them. From what I'd seen of Westhill, it was hardly a thrill a minute.

"And nobody noticed?" said DCI Mason.

"It was dark, sir," said Blinschell.

"Who broke in through the front, then?" asked DCI Mason. "Roger Rabbit?"

Only if it was funny, I thought but did not say.

"Person or persons unknown," I said.

DCI Mason gave me a look that suggested he couldn't even be bothered to use sarcasm any more.

"Any idea what they were looking for?" he asked.

"Judging by what they concentrated on in the search," I said, "something to do with her work."

"Good," said DCI Mason. "Then at least we know where to go next."

The University of Aberdeen, just for a change, was mostly built out of granite, as if someone wanted to replicate an Oxford college, right down to the ivy-covered walls, only this time make it really sturdy. Granite has a reputation for being a bastard to work, but you have to hand it to those Victorians—they never let practicality get in their way.

It also wasn't short of turrets, crenellations and conical roofs. I'd looked it up on my tablet the night before and found that this was an actual architectural style called Baronial, the Scottish equivalent of the Gothic revival that gave us the Palace of Westminster and the St. Pancras Station Hotel. Into this gray extravaganza, later generations had thrown some of the squared-off blocks that were too nondescript to even be called Brutalist.

It was in one of these blocks lurked the university's geology department.

The world-renowned school is considered to be one of the leading centers for petroleum geology, and don't you bloody forget it—according to the head of school who showed us around. His name was Kristian Jørgensen, who, despite having an "o" with a slash in his name, sounded like he'd arrived in Aberdeen via an expensive British private school.

"We were hoping you had good news," he said. "Or any news at all."

He led us through tan-colored corridors lined with display cases and framed geological maps.

Alice MacDuffie's office was of a type familiar to me from institutional buildings across the UK. Narrow, with a window at one end, the room had probably been earmarked, in the architect's mind, as cleaning storage—if they'd given it any thought at all. Dr. Walid had an office just like it at the UCH in London, and I'd worked out of one in Leominster during Operation Manticore. The walls were the same tan as the corridor, with a table fitted lengthwise against the wall to serve as a desk, a double line of bracket shelves above, a pair of steel tubular chairs upholstered in the same royal blue as the rest of the building. There were a pair of flat-screens but no computer, and everything else had been pulled off the shelves and dumped on the floor.

"Shit," said Jørgensen. "It wasn't like that last time I looked."

Blinschell took Jørgensen back down the corridor to take a preliminary statement, but only after he'd called the SOCO team back at Alice MacDuffie's house and told them to add her office to their action list.

While he did that, I slipped off my size elevens, pulled on gloves and booties and started a preliminary search. Everything seemed to be on the floor, so I squatted down and picked up the first thing that caught my eye. This turned out to be a laser-printed copy of an academic magazine article—"Reconstruction of linear dunes from ancient aeolian successions using subsurface data: Permian Auk Formation, Central North Sea, UK." According to the header field, this had been from the March edition of *Marine and Petroleum Geology*. There was a scatter of glossy magazines among the loose hard copy, the same serious journals with "geo" in the title, and moody backlit pictures of fractionating towers or false color maps of the sea floor on the covers.

I wondered if us working wizards would ever get a trade journal. Historically there hadn't even been a *Transactions of the Society of the Wise*, let alone a monthly magazine called *Modern Wizard*, or even *Practical Thaumatology*.

A glossy brochure still in a sealed plastic wrap caught my eye. It was for a business called FPXPLORE, and featured an aerial picture of an oil rig at sea with huge gray waves crashing around it. Had to be fake—nobody would be flying a helicopter in that weather. Under the company name was the slogan—*Future-Proofing Scottish Energy Production.*

FPXPLORE had had a mention in Alice MacDuffie's MISPER file. Since she wasn't regarded then as high risk, the people at FPXPLORE had only been asked the routine questions—when had they last seen her, had she exhibited any unusual behavior or stolen any money? If Police Scotland had asked FPXPLORE what work it was exactly Alice MacDuffie been doing for them, it hadn't been in the file.

But surely her university boss, Mr. Jørgensen, must have known.

"Enhanced oil recovery," said Jørgensen.

We were in a large classroom down the corridor, with the same tan walls and blue upholstery as everywhere else. Jørgensen sat across from me and Blinschell, who was nursing a coffee as if it was a Scotch.

"What's that when it's at home?" I asked.

"Basically it's a number of techniques aimed at improving output from exhausted fields," he said. EOR, as it was known in the trade, was the big new hotness in the North Sea oil industry. Given that oil rigs were expensive to run and almost as expensive to decommission, it would be better, from the point of view of the oil companies, if they could make their current fields last a squidge longer.

"And better for the Exchequer and the wider Scottish economy," said Jørgensen.

North Sea oil production had peaked in 1999 and was currently running at about a third of that level. Offshore extraction cost more per barrel than pumping it out of a desert, so the lower the oil price, the less incentive to spend more money to exploit difficult fields. Oil prices had hit a record low three years previously but were bouncing back, so now there was money available for experimental EOR.

"And this was what Alice was working on with FPXPLORE?" asked Blinschell.

"Yes," said Jørgensen.

"Doing what exactly?" I asked.

He started to explain, but we had to ask him to back up and explain in words we might understand.

"It's not really that complicated," said Jørgensen.

Basically, the two main approaches to enhanced oil recovery were a) drill more holes in the seabed, or b) pump stuff down your existing holes to force more oil out. The first was like sticking a second straw into your milkshake to mop up the bits you missed. That is, if you thought your second straw cost half a million to insert.

"Better to increase the pressure in the reservoir using your existing wells," said Jørgensen.

And that involved pumping stuff in.

I asked what kind of stuff.

"Carbon dioxide, sea water, anything to increase the pressure. Or if you want to release more oil from locked-up areas, you can use hydraulic fracturing with a variety of mixtures. That creates cracks in the rocks so the oil or gas can escape."

"That's fracking, right?" asked Blinschell.

"Precisely."

"Doesn't that cause earthquakes?" he asked.

"Nothing serious," said Jørgensen. "And out at sea they barely register."

I wondered if Beverley's giant squid was so blasé about earthquakes—assuming there was a giant squid. Could Alice have masterminded something that made her serious be-tentacled enemies?

"And Alice was working on which one of these techniques?" I asked.

"You could say all of them at the same time," said Jørgensen. "What she posited was a system by which you varied your injector material by type and quantity from minute to minute, to maximize the return flow. It was an elegant conception but very difficult to implement."

"How so?"

"The original subsea well heads were set up for continuous flow," said Jørgensen, "with maybe a maintenance dive every two to three years. Alice's proposal requires the ability to change the inputs in near real time."

Rebuilding the well heads wasn't an option because of cost and time. So the alternative would be to have people continuously in place to remake connections, turn valves and attach tanks.

Which meant divers working as deep as three hundred meters, where you had to breathe some weird gas mixture and spend weeks in a pressurized chamber so you didn't have to decompress between work shifts.

"Deep-sea divers are expensive," said Jørgensen. "To have a team working continuously in shifts is *really* expensive, especially since at the experimental stage you're going to have to constantly shift things around until you find something that works."

Jørgensen shrugged.

"I would have said the cost was prohibitive. I think Alice assumed that the theory behind the approach would have been refined before it could be implemented."

"But?" I asked.

"FPXPLORE approached her directly," said Jørgensen. "They must have heard about her ideas from somewhere."

"Had she published?" I asked.

"No," said Jørgensen. "But oil exploration is a small world and geophysicists like to gossip as much as the next physical scientist. We also hate to keep our good ideas to ourselves. Alice probably told someone, who told someone." He didn't sound as sure as he thought he did. "I suppose."

"Did she say how the work was going?" I said. According to the original case file, Alice had struck her friends and colleagues as "mildly stressed," with the additional caveat of "aren't we all?"

Jørgensen hesitated and then spoke slowly. Choosing his words carefully.

"Initially she seemed pleased, but you have to understand, a project like this doesn't happen overnight. They had to find a suitable platform, with a suitable well, organize a diving team, satisfy the HSE and the NSTA."

"HSE I know—Health and Safety Executive," I said. "But who are the NSTA?"

"The North Sea Transition Authority," said Jørgensen. "They have to sign off on any changes to the well head. And all of that doesn't happen overnight. I would have said a year minimum of prep before you'd get any results."

Another unvoiced "but"—this time I didn't supply it.

"Something was worrying her," he said finally. "But because it was too early to get results from the field, I assumed it was personal."

The original MISPER file had looked into "personal" and found no boyfriends, girlfriends or favorite sheep. She'd certainly never cohabited, and nobody at the university had seen any signs of a relationship beyond a loose network of friends. Many of them confined to social media.

"How upset?" asked Blinschell.

"Not upset... Maybe that's too strong a word," said Jørgensen. "Preoccupied, perhaps—I thought it was personal. Are you saying it wasn't personal?"

Pissed-off lovers might wreck your bedroom, but they don't search your office. Well, not very often.

"We're reassessing the case in the light of recent events," I said. "Do you know what kind of deal Alice had with FPXPLORE?"

"I imagine a pretty standard one," said Jørgensen. "A monthly retainer that doubles her salary, share options, and a big bonus if it all goes well."

"Despite all that," said Blinschell, "could she have been worried financially?"

"Isn't everyone?" said Jørgensen and started to chuckle, but thought better of it in the light of me and Blinschell giving him the old police stone face.

"Oh, she'll have had a watertight contract," said Jørgensen. "You don't grow up in Aberdeen without learning how to deal with oil companies."

"Tricky?" I asked.

"These people have overthrown governments that get in their way," said Jørgensen. "They don't need to be tricky. They have a shedload of money and an office full of lawyers. Besides, what to you or me seems like a great deal of money is probably less than ten minutes' operating overhead—even for a medium-sized outfit like FPXPLORE."

Even in what we in the Met call Falcon cases, if the motive for the crime isn't sex, then it's usually money or power. Since in the oil industry those two seemed to be the same thing.

Back out in the car park, Blinschell stopped to show me his phone.

"You're going to love this," he said.

On the screen was an image of the tourist map they'd found in Aquaman's pocket. Blinschell zoomed in to show the circle someone had scrawled around a location in the west of the city.

"Rubislaw Hill," said Blinschell. "Guess where FPXPLORE is headquartered?"

10

What Abigail and Ione Did at the Museum

I KNEW THE library ting. Everyone does. Anyone who has had to share a bedroom with a sibling, or grow up reading in a family who think *Love Island* is overly intellectual, or just needed somewhere quiet or that has an unsupervised link to the internet. Your parents can never question the library or ask why you never answered your phone. That's why you get teenagers in every library everywhere, big or small. They're even outside the British Library in King's Cross, where the Muslim kids from Somers Town come to court. You see them on the benches behind the front wall, sitting two per bench each at opposite ends—talking but never touching. So I knew about the library ting when I ditched the bus outside Fraserburgh Library, which looked like it had been built for the Addams Family's Scottish cousins.

It didn't look out of place, being right next to an equally Goth church and on a long straight road lined with granite houses with pointy roofs and sharp bay windows. Above the entrance, PUBLIC LIBRARY was carved in stone. Inside, a long corridor with three, count them, three automatic doors led to the library proper, which was basically one big room with a skylight, a work island, shelves and an open area with lilac-colored sofas. I nod at a random librarian, who smiles back, and spot Ione lounging on one of the sofas. She's looking drip in a black sleeveless T-shirt, mum jeans and white creps. That weird silver shawl is still wrapped around her waist. It's got to be something arcane, but what?

She's reading a book and hasn't seen me.

It's weird, innit, but I almost turn around and walk away. My heart is going like a beatboxer and there's a freaky feeling in my stomach, and I'm thinking you shouldn't be this into someone after one snog and a bit of a grope. It's not healthy.

But it's not going away—so no point trying to pretend it is.

I pattern myself and cross the stretch of boring carpet between us. It must be a good book, because she doesn't look up until I sit down beside her. Then she looks pleased, but she doesn't kiss me or anything. Not that I thought she would in a library, right? Because that would be improper. But just a peck maybe? Her free hand is kind of fluttering like she wants to touch me, but it might be something else.

I watched a ton of YouTube videos on how to know if a girl is into you, but most of it involved being an American and none of it had melanistic leopards or creepy uncles.

"I brought your bag," I say, and hand it over.

I've been thinking of excuses if she asks me whether I went through it. Like "I was just checking it was OK," or "It got a bit wet so I had to dry it out." And I had decided to blame the foxes, which is realistic because they're always up in other people's business . . .

But all Ione says is "thanks" and, taking it from me, tucks in neatly behind the sofa.

"What you reading?" I ask, because I can't think of anything else.

She shows me the cover. It's called *The Indispensable Beauregard* and has an old-fashioned picture of the New York skyline.

"What's it about?" I ask.

Ione frowns and leans closer so she can whisper. Her hand rests lightly on my arm.

"I don't know," she says. "I only picked it up because I was waiting for you."

I touch her hand and she doesn't pull away, so I'm feeling pretty chill, especially when she takes my hand and stands up. She grabs her bag and leads me out the side to an old-fashioned wooden staircase.

"What happened to my spear?" she asks.

"Sorry, I sent it to the lab in London," I say. "It had blood on it."

"London?"

"Was it expensive?"

"Nah," she says. "But it will be a bugger to make a new one."

At the top we walk through a room with reference books, tables, chairs, a microfiche reader and a printer. In the corner it opens up into a round room that is part of a tower that climbs the side of the library. There's six windows with a view of gray rooftops under a blue sky, and pastel-colored cushions to sit on underneath. We sit down side by side, heads close together, holding hands down by the wall where it won't be obvious.

I take a deep breath because now is the moment of truth.

"You're fae, aren't you?" I ask, and wait for her to snatch her hand away.

She doesn't. Instead, she smiles and tilts her head.

"But you're not?" she says.

"I'm a wizard," I say, because it sounds cooler than apprentice.

"Truly?"

"On my life."

"You're the Nightingale's apprentice?"

"So you've heard of him?"

"I've heard stories about him, but I wasn't expecting him to turn up at the Stone Fair."

"What kind of stories?"

"War stories, mostly," she says. "The aul mannies talk about him when they're drunk and maudlin—but who listens to them these days. You any good?"

"In what way?"

"At magic, of course," she says. And, before I can say something safe, "Because I already know you can kiss."

Whatever I was going to say, I've forgotten it now.

"Got you," she says.

"I've told you me," I say. "What about you?"

"I don't know what it's like in London," she says. "But up here there's folk that go back a long way. Mine are from the Orkney Islands originally, but things got a bit uncomfortable and they shifted to the Broch and Banff and as far down as Aberdeen."

"Uncomfortable how?"

"In the stories we all lived on an island called Eyinhellig, but it sort of sank into the sea," she says. "Bit like Atlantis, and also a myth. I think it was the witch hunts."

It being easier to hide your business on the mainland than on an island where everyone knew everyone else. Especially when your business included moneylending.

"Nobody likes people they owe money to," says Ione. "So they make up stories."

"So your lot are bankers," I say, and she laughs.

"That branch went to Edinburgh ages ago," she says. "We're the families that stayed by the sea. If you leave the sea forever, you lose that part of yourself."

"What part of yourself?" I ask.

The red lips curl up into a smile and she squeezes my hand.

"I might show you when I know you better," she says.

I wonder when that will be, but I ain't so hazy that I don't spot when I'm being blocked. But talk is like boxing, they block you one way so you come at them from another. In case you're wondering, Nightingale is teaching me magic boxing, so I've got some technique.

"What's your beef with the big cat?" I ask.

"What's yours?"

"We want to know what it is," I say. "You're trying to kill it."

"I already know what it is," says Ione. "That's why I'm trying to kill it."

"So what is it, then?"

"It's a monster," she says.

"It's a melanistic leopard," I say, hoping stupidly that she'll notice how clever I am.

"It's a melanistic monster leopard," she says. "Wait—it looked like a panther to me."

"Same diff," I say. "Just because it's a monster, that's no reason to kill it."

"It doesn't belong here," she says. "It was summoned here to cause mischief, and it needs to be dealt with before it kills someone."

OK, because Ms. Melanistic Panther was def flicking in and out of our world like Peter's unicorns. Only they had been intrusions from what we were definitely calling an *allokosmos* because you can't say parallel dimension—the donnies get the wrong idea.

"Summoned?"

"Yeah."

"Who by?"

"I don't know," she says with a fierce grin. "Or I'd go after them instead."

"You're sure it's not fairies?" I ask.

"Fairies?"

"From wherever it's coming from, sort of pushing it—not summoning it."

She takes my other hand and leans in. It's not funny how much I want to kiss her.

"What do you know?" she asks.

I like that's she's bare sharp. "There's people I know back at base been looking into things," I say—meaning Nathan, who's totally cracked, by the way. "They found a reference to a big cat going back to the nineteenth century."

"What kind of reference?"

"Only that it's a cat, but the source document is up here at some place called the Discovery Center in Mintlaw."

"Been there," says Ione. "With my school. Years ago."

"Want to come have a look?" I say, squeezing her hand.

"It's not like a proper museum," says Ione. "They're not just going to let you rifle through their archives."

"They'll let me," I say. "I know the magic words."

"Which are?"

"You'll find out when we get there."

Ione has a dented 49cc Vespa parked outside the library and a spare lid for me. It's pink, sparkly, and has a dolphin sticker on the side.

"My sister's," says Ione.

So I get to climb on the seat behind Ione and put my arms around her waist all the way down the long straight road from Fraserburgh.

"How is the old book thief?" says Will. "I thought he retired years ago."

The magic words are Harold Postmartin, keeper of the Folly Archives, Oxford scholar, and notorious, he claims, the length and breadth of academia. He's called ahead all the way from Greece to let Will know we're coming.

"Nah," I say. "Still stealing books."

Will is white, plump, black-haired, and wears glasses with tortoiseshell frames to go with their big brown eyes. They're wearing a pronoun badge—they/them—on the collar of their sports jacket.

"You're not his dastardly confederates, are you?" they ask.

"No," I say. "Just students."

The Aberdeenshire Museums Discovery Center is a low concrete warehouse set among other low concrete warehouses on old railway land. I knew it was old railway land because I'd traced the path me and Nightingale had ridden the horse on, and it ran right past. That, and the street they were built on is called Station Road.

Inside, it was all breeze blocks and metal-framed storage racks.

"Eight hundred square meters of environmentally controlled storage space," Will says proudly. Not that we get to see it—they've already laid out the papers in the open-plan staff office.

"It looks like a school office," whispers Ione. "Only messier."

Will is hovering nervously, but I learned my document handling from uber-archivists so they've got nothing to worry about. I know about having clean hands, handling at the edges and not licking your fingers between pages.

And the document we're looking at needs careful handling. It's a nineteenth-century pamphlet, and printed on cheap paper that was flaking on the edges and cracking at the folds.

It's a religious tract, according to Will, fulminating against the evils of modern society and is, they say, what people used to shout at strangers before the internet.

"Although they used to shout directly at strangers as well," they say.

The author signs himself as the Reverend Wilbur Wallace, who Will thinks may have ministered to a parish near Peterhead in the mid-nineteenth century. He has a definite beef with George Ferguson, laird of the Pitfour Estate which once owned most of the local postcode.

There had been two lairds called George Ferguson, the three before them all being called James, but Will had identified which when cataloging the document. The giveaway is the line . . . *proves once more that bastardy breeds bad character . . .* Which meant it had to be George Ferguson, illegitimate son of George

Ferguson, former Governor of Tobago and major slave owner. Owning slaves was not a problem for the reverend. What he objected to was the establishment of a house tenanted by *the most unchristian Blacks as ever set foot in Scotland.*

We asked Will, but they said that since there were no other records of the house or its tenants, the exact nature of occupancy was unknown. An American historian interested in the matter had asked the same questions a year ago and had promised to get in touch if he discovered anything more. I got the historian's name and contact details—James Albright, in Oxford, MS—which turned out to be in America.

George the bastard had gone so far to build them a pagan temple deep in the woods where . . . *the inhabitants were said to have summoned up a devil in the shape of a black cat which did lie with the women of the house and in exchange granted them the power to curse their neighbors so that all the country around was afeart. When challenged, the Admiral claimed that it was but an observatory from which he could watch his horses* . . .

Ione asks Will if the Reverend Wallace is talking about the observatory in Drinnie's Wood. Will looks suddenly shifty.

"In a manner of speaking," they say. "There were two so-called observatories, the one that's standing now and the first one that was burned down."

Postmartin says that a lack of linguistic precision is the bête noire of the academic mind. And I had to agree—once I'd looked up what bête noire actually meant. Librarians always got to use the right words—even when they're trying to keep something from you.

"Who burned it down?" I ask, and Will slumps—they knows they're busted.

"If I show you something," they say, "you've got to promise me you won't tell Postmartin we've got it."

I cross my heart, and off they trot to fetch whatever it is.

Ione swivels in her chair and rolls over until our knees are touching.

"That was impressive," she says, and takes my hand.

I'm trying to play it cool and pretend like my heart isn't banging away at my ribs.

"Nah," I say. "They were dying to tell me. Archivists are bare proud—they love to show off their stuff."

And what Will has to show off is a copy of a letter that they say is too fragile to handle. Me and Ione separate as they come in, trying not to look too obvious. The copy, Will explains, is of a letter from the Reverend Wallace's even more extra Presbyterian sister who is . . . *proud of your valiant actions against the darkness . . .*

Said actions being burning down George Ferguson's heathen "temple" with some of the heathens still inside. She'd been particularly thrilled by that.

Me and Ione were less thrilled to learn that Will didn't know where the burned building was.

"The open grounds are pretty well surveyed," they say. "So my guess is that the remains are in Drinnie's Wood, to the west of the observatory." Awaiting a proper LIDAR survey, that being the hype thing in archeology these days.

"Is it all right if we have a look?" I ask.

"You're welcome to try," says Will. "But I don't rate your chances."

"That's because," I say to Ione as we walk back to her Vespa, "they don't have my resources."

I call Bev, who picks up on the seventh ring.

"Beverley's twin-drowning service," she says. In the background I can hear happy squeals and splashing.

I say hi and ask whether Indigo is with her. Bev calls Indigo over, who's aiming at vex but ain't fooling nobody.

"I thought you were with your new friend," she says.

"I am," I say. "But now I need your help."

"I'd love to, but I'm babysitting."

"Yeah," I say. "But this is mission-critical."

Indigo goes quiet, and in the background I can hear Bev telling Taiwo to "put the vole down." Indigo is trying to punish me, but none of the talking foxes can resist a bit of spycraft. Especially Indigo.

"Mission-critical?" she says.

"Vital," I say.

"Fine," she says, trying to sound casual. "What do you need?"

"You still in touch with the locals?"

The Pitfour Estate was once called the Blenheim of the North, which meant it was huge, grand and, according to Will, paid for by exploiting the rural poor. It had been expanded and "improved" by lairds one to four before being bankrupted and shrunk by laird number five. One of his many expenses was the building of a folly called "the Observatory" from which Georgie boy claimed he used to watch his horses exercising.

"Unlikely," Will said. "Given how far it was from the stables and training fields."

Also it was in the middle of a wood, one that me and Nightingale had checked the edges of during our first sweep. It was less than three kilometers northeast of Brian's house, and just over three from the Aikey Brae stone circle. Five minutes' drive from the Discovery Center with Ione's Vespa, buzzing up the narrow lanes and then bouncing along an unsurfaced logging road among dark stands of conifers.

We skid suddenly to a halt.

"Missed the turning," says Ione.

We back up twenty meters and turn on to what is def a footpath going deeper into the forest. Then another turn on to a gravel path, stones clattering in the mudguards. The path is dead straight through an avenue of trees. At the end is an octagonal tower, fifteen meters high, with a crenelated roof. Standing at the base watching us approach are two white men in sensible walking gear and a fox. It's Brian, Dr. Walid and Indigo.

Before I can dismount, Indigo throws herself onto the scooter seat and squirms between me and Ione.

"Look, Abigail," she says. "It's an observation post."

"Good afternoon, Abigail," says Abdul. "Is this the famous Ione?"

Ione is not happy that I've been telling people her name, and Indigo isn't happy about us getting off the Vespa just when she was getting comfortable. But I finesse Ione by doing proper introductions in a chipper voice that I copied off a senior civil servant I know, and Indigo by letting her climb up on my shoulders. She smells of pine needles, sugar and jam. The last two means that somebody's been feeding her jam doughnuts, which explains the zoomies.

I ask Brian and Abdul what they're doing at the observatory.

"The focal point for our geographical profile is thirty meters over there," says Abdul, pointing west into the forest. "This is the only nearby structure." He gives me his best narrow-eyed doctor look. "And what brings you two here?"

I tell him about the Reverend Wilbur Wallace, and his complaints against the fifth Laird and his coven of wicked blacks and the Devil summoned as a black cat. Indigo stiffens and hisses.

"That explains a great deal," she says.

"West of the observatory, you say?" says Brian, and pulls a map from his shoulder bag. It's a reprint of the 1870 Ordnance Survey map of the woods at six inches to the mile. It shows the observatory, but nothing to the west but a rectangle enclosing the symbols for deciduous trees mixed in with the conifers.

"There's nothing marked," says Abdul.

"Indigo," I say, "you're up."

Indigo launches herself from my shoulder and races for the treeline.

It's almost midday but there's a haze across the sun, making the light hot and diffuse. The boundary of the cleared rectangle around the observatory has a dense stand of Christmas trees—the better to deter casual hikers. I push my way through spiky branches until I reach the older trees beyond. Indigo is waiting for me, so I crouch down and ask where Sax William and Reid King are.

"Close by," says Indigo. "Perimeter."

Ione joins me, I stand up, she takes my hand, Indigo snorts.

"Bloody hell," says Brian, pushing through the Christmas trees. "Right in the face."

Beverley says that the only virtue of commercial conifer forests is that they're easy to walk through. Otherwise, she says, they have all the biodiversity of a banana plant. That hadn't stopped the ferns springing up wherever daylight penetrated the canopy.

The air is still and smells of resin.

"Is everyone ready?" asks Indigo.

Abdul joins us and we set off after the fox.

Sweat prickles my back and forehead.

There's a gap between the trees that's too small to be called a clearing but big enough to let the daylight in. It's covered in cut bracken, twigs and soil.

"Here," says Indigo, and points her nose at a spot where the foxes have dug away the covering. We crouch down for a look. There's a granite block embedded in the ground. Even before I touch it I get flashes of pain, white light and dirty water. Strong enough to show on my face, because Abdul asks what's wrong.

"Bare strong *vestigia*," I say.

"Natural? Human?" asks Abdul.

"Dunno," I say, and look at Ione, who is resting her fingertips on the rock and frowning. "You?" I ask.

"Nothing I recognize," she says.

"We need to clear this," I say. "But careful in case it's booby-trapped."

The bracken has been cut long enough for the stalks to turn brown and the fronds to shrivel up. Underneath is a rotten layer going slimy, and under that a stone floor. It's deeper, at least six centimeters lower than the modern ground level. I've done a bit of archeology on "youth trips," and this looks like it's been excavated before and covered over again. The floor is made of brown ceramic tiles, most of them intact, others cracked.

"Victorian," says Brian. "My house had a floor like this, but I had to take it up."

It's obvious once we've cleared it that it's only a section of the original floor. The granite block wall runs for two meters before making a right-angle turn and running another two meters until it's covered by the modern ground surface. At the edges of the cleared area, the tiles have been broken up by tree roots.

"Is that a pattern?" asks Abdul pointing at part of the floor.

It's hard to tell against the brown tiles, but it does look like a pattern has been painted onto the floor. Tracing it out, there's no doubt that it's an enclosed pentagram—a classic summoning circle.

"Yes, it is," says Abdul when I point this out. "I've never seen one of these in the wild, so to speak. Only in books, or when Peter is doing experiments."

I cautiously touch the closest edge of the pattern and snatch my hand back. The *vestigia* is bare loud, snarling and screaming with the taste of dirty water and mud. But I don't think the pattern had been drawn in mud.

"Indigo," I say. "Give it a sniff."

Indigo is suddenly still and stares at me, eyes big.

"Just a little sniff," I say.

Reluctantly, Indigo creeps forward and cautiously gives the line a smell. Then she sort of wriggles backward until she's beside me again.

"Blood," she says. "Old blood."

11

Rubislaw Hill

BEFORE WE PURSUED the professional life of Alice MacDuffie, we stopped for a late lunch at a nearby café that Blinschell knew. There we had a traditional Aberdonian copper's meal of great big floppy baps filled with—whatever you fancied, as long as the fat content exceeded 10mg per 100mg, at the very least. Preferably, according to Blinschell, you want your arteries to panic on the first bite.

I had bacon and egg and tried not to get yolk or ketchup down the front of my suit.

"Oil companies don't disappear people," said Blinschell, once he'd safely finished his steak pie butty and was drinking an Irn-Bru in blatant contravention of the Flagrant Stereotype (Scotland) Act (2006). "They don't need to."

"Either she ran," I said. "Or somebody snatched her."

"Or she's dead and buried somewhere," he said. "Or all of the above."

"Or that," I said, and had a sip of my tea. "Her car was found down by the beach. Suicide?"

"If our amphibious friend came out of the water," said Blinschell, "who's to say she didn't go and visit wherever he came from?"

"Or wasn't an amphibian herself," I said.

"You'd think someone would have noticed the gills."

"Like who?"

"The people she worked with? Boyfriend, girlfriend, gym partner?"

"It might be worth re-interviewing people on her contact list."

"It's a hell of a question, though, isn't it?" said Blinschell. "'Did you ever notice your girlfriend was part fish?'"

"Maybe they'll know at FPXPLORE," I said. "Maybe that's the real reason why they hired her."

We decided to start with the man listed as Managing Director— Derek Patterson.

Blinschell directed me up a road lined with Victorian villas, all set back from the pavement with garden walls and gravel drives. All of it built with granite blocks and half of them decorated with turrets and crenellations.

We turned right up a steep hill that leveled out to run past a chequerboard of car parks and modernist glass cubes separated by pedestrian-unfriendly grass verges and box hedges. We passed a sign for Chevron on the left—obviously this was where the big boys of the oil industry hung out. I'd checked the route on my phone before we'd set off and spotted what looked like a lake to the south, but the road on that side was lined with square-cut hedges interspersed with some serious palisade security fencing. The fence was topped with triple points, and while it wasn't tall enough to be intrusive it was definitely there to deter casual trespassing. I wondered what was on the other side.

"The quarry," said Blinschell when I asked him. "That's where the stone that built the city came from."

When it started, he explained, it was out in the countryside, and for two hundred years they cut and dug six million tons of granite out. While they did that, the posh suburb of Rubislaw Hill grew up around it—made from the very same stone. Blinschell had been taught this at school by a teacher whose dad had worked at the quarry all his life.

"They used it in the Houses of Parliament and Waterloo Bridge," said Blinschell as we turned right and pulled into the car park signed as FPXPLORE EMPLOYEES ONLY.

"Then when they closed it down it filled up with water," he said.

"And they just left it?"

"No," he said. "They stuck a fence round it to stop the wains from drowning each other." The pit itself was full of old rusting machinery and cables—not to mention slightly radioactive.

The much vaunted granite hadn't been used on the FPXPLORE HQ, which was another bland concrete low-rise whose architect had obviously been told to rein in their totalitarian tendencies and responded by sticking a row of picture windows across the front. It looked like my old school, but without the inspirational murals.

I found a slot right next to the company's main entrance that had a "Reserved for BANNERMAN" sign. I never park in an accessible space, but when I'm on the job everything else is fair game.

The foyer was cool and white and featured a lot of shiny high quality terrazzo. Beyond reception were the traditional ye olde security gates, designed to keep track of employee timekeeping or stop unwanted members of the public wandering in to interrupt the smooth daily existence of their corporate overlords—depending on your level of paranoia.

A tall blonde white woman sat behind a severely elegant beechwood desk marked RECEPTION and gave us an equally elegantly severe welcoming smile.

"Can I help you?" she asked as we approached. Her hair was pulled back into a French braid to emphasize high cheekbones and a triangular chin. She had icy blue eyes and her lips were a flushed red.

Blinschell showed his warrant card, introduced himself and asked to see Mr. Derek Patterson.

The receptionist tilted her head in polite inquiry. She was wearing an expensive black woven blazer, left unbuttoned to show off a sheer silver scale top. One that glistened like the skim of oil on water.

"I'm sorry," she said, and the harmonics in her voice were unmistakable. "But Mr. Patterson is not available at the moment."

For six years now, I've been glamoured by wizards, witches, revenants, jazz vampires, river deities big and small, ganja of all things, a haunted BMW, and that bloody plant in Kew Garden. As a result, I've built up an immunity to supernatural manipulation which has kept me, if not out of trouble, at least upright and still breathing.

Blinschell, who up till now has only had to worry about getting stabbed, started to turn away.

I did consider pretending to be under the influence, since I'm trying to keep a low profile with the local demimonde, but being police is all about going places you're not wanted.

"Stop it," I said, and the woman's eyes widened in surprise.

Blinschell reversed his turn and gave me a questioning glance.

"I'm sure he's available for a quick meeting with the police," I said.

The woman glared at me and opened her mouth. I could tell she was going to give it another go. The problem with the glamour, or so Bev tells me, is that it makes you lazy. When you expect people to jump at your every word, you tend not to develop vital social skills. I pointed out to Bev that she had perfectly good social skills.

"Lots of sisters," she'd explained. "So many sisters."

Obviously, the receptionist was an only child.

"No," I said. "Don't."

She closed her mouth with a snap and gave me an unkind look.

"Who are you?" she asked.

Blinschell snorted—amused.

"My name is Peter Grant," I said. "What's yours?"

She didn't want to tell me, so it came out quiet and reluctant.

"Calliste," she said.

"Callisto," I said, mispronouncing it on purpose. As a byproduct of being forced to learn ancient Greek and Latin, I recognized the name—sort of. Definitely a sea nymph, daughter of somebody. Turned into an island, I thought—I was going to have to look it up.

"No," she said crossly. "Calliste. And who are you?"

Abigail's new friend was named after a sea nymph, too. I wondered if there was a connection.

"I'm with the Metropolitan Police," I said. "I've come to see Derek Patterson. We only have a couple of questions relating to an ongoing inquiry."

Since it was obvious she wasn't getting rid of us, she defaulted to helpful receptionist mode and asked us to wait a moment while she picked up her phone to see whether Mr. Patterson was available.

"Please take a seat while you wait," she said.

We declined the seat, partly to maintain an air of dignified intimidation, but mostly because the seating on offer looked like it was designed by an architect and would therefore, like a Bauhaus chair, manage to be both stylish and uncomfortable.

"Where you from?" I asked, but Calliste held up a finger and tapped her handset in the unmistakable receptionist signal for "fuck off, I'm working."

"Fraserburgh?" I asked, and she frowned but continued to ignore me.

"I have two gentlemen from the police here to see you," she told the phone. "One of them is from London."

Interesting that she thought that that was important.

There was a response and she nodded.

"I'll bring them up, then," she said, and then turned back to us with a professional smile. "Mr. Patterson will see you now."

Derek Patterson was a fit middle-aged white guy who dressed like a Texan and talked like a drunk Glaswegian. The voice was down to a serious injury that made his face alarmingly lopsided, as if his jaw had been broken and reset crooked. Which turned out to be the case.

"I fell off a gantry in Borneo," he said. "I keep meaning to get it fixed, but who's got the time?"

That didn't explain the jeans, boots and the cowboy hat hanging from the hatstand beside his desk. Maybe the decade spent fracking in Texas and North Dakota accounted for that.

We knew all this because, after inviting us into his boringly Scottish office with its gray-green carpet and modern off-white zebra blinds, and ushering us to the black leather sofas by the window, he pretty much talked continuously for ten minutes while we waited for coffee.

"Nigeria, Kalimantan," he said. "Basically the wild fucking west."

Once we were settled with our coffees—good coffee, I noticed—we got down to business.

Patterson wanted to know if we'd discovered anything new about Alice MacDuffie.

"We're looking at a number of lines of inquiry," I said.

Patterson frowned.

"Like what, exactly?" he asked.

"That her disappearance could have been designed to disrupt your operations," I said, which just goes to show that in extremis you can come up with some quality bollocks.

"Is that a serious concern?" asked Patterson.

"That depends," I said. "How important was Alice MacDuffie to your ongoing plans?"

"That depends," said Patterson. "Have you any string on you? Certainly her theoretical work underpins everything we're doing, and we would expect her to monitor progress and refine her model to increase efficiency, but . . ." He paused to look suitably regretful. "We can manage without her. Although I suppose an outsider might not know that."

"Did she go offshore?" asked Blinschell.

Patterson hesitated—not for long, but enough to give him away.

"She didn't need to," he said—which was an unnecessary evasion.

When a witness slips like that, you have two choices—make a mental note to swing back to the topic later, or push straight away. You often don't know what the witness is trying to hide, but if they're trying to hide it, you want to know it.

Blinschell pushed—but gently.

"She wasn't curious to see her theories put into practice?" he said.

Again a hesitation.

"The data from the well head is collected remotely," said Patterson. He rubbed his jaw where it was bent out of shape—an unconscious gesture, maybe. "We're very safety-conscious these days. However routine we make transits out to the rigs, there's always an element of risk, and the best way to avoid accidents is to avoid unnecessary risk."

That was pure corporate-speak—if we hadn't been suspicious before, we were definitely suspicious now.

"Where is your rig?" I asked.

"Platform," said Patterson.

"What's the difference?"

"Rigs can be towed into new positions. Platforms are permanently situated."

"I see," I said. "And where is your platform?"

"We're currently trialing on Elgar Bravo," said Patterson. "It was due for decommissioning, so we got a good deal. The majors hate to decommission, since these days it costs more to shut them down than it did to construct and install them in the first place."

"Is it working?" I asked.

"That would be telling," said Patterson. "Let's just say that we expect the trial to continue for some time."

When dealing with corporations, publicists and other professional liars, you need to know when to break off an interview. Unless you were looking to intimidate them, you want them to think they've outsmarted you while you collect more evidence to throw in their smug little faces.

Before we wrapped up, I asked Patterson how he'd come to hear of Alice MacDuffie's research in the first place.

"It was brought to us by an information broker," he said, because there were people who made a living spotting promising bits of tech and then finding investors or companies that might be interested. The broker had also helped organize outside investors to help finance the project.

"This sort of thing isn't cheap," said Patterson. "The platform alone costs three hundred kay a day." He gave us a cool, lopsided smile. "That's just the platform, you understand. Not the actual work at the well head."

I asked after the name of the broker—in case he might have some insight.

"Sherman Brown of Buffalo Ventures," said Patterson. "They're based in Houston, but I can e-mail you their contact details."

I pulled a Columbo as he was showing us out of his office.

"You didn't notice anything odd about Alice, did you?" I asked.

Again, Patterson hesitated.

"No," he said. "Odd in what way?"

"Did she like to go swimming?" I asked.

Patterson relaxed.

"We really didn't socialize," he said.

"Did she like to go swimming?" said Blinschell as we headed out of the foyer, in what I think he thought was a London accent.

"It was worth a try," I said. "Do you think anyone from Buffalo Ventures is here in Aberdeen?"

"Did that name sound made up to you?" asked Blinschell.

"Shouldn't be hard to check," I said, and turned in the doorway to give Calliste a cheery wave through the window. She scowled back and her annoyance chased me into the car park. Once we'd reached the Asbo, we took a moment to write up our notes. I made a point of adding Bannerman, the guy whose parking space I'd nicked, and noting all the other names with reserved spaces. I clocked a mustard-colored Citroën C3, the VT with the dinky 1.1 liter engine, parked away from the main building.

A good candidate for our Calliste's motor, I thought, and made a note of its index.

We stopped at the car and looked back at FPXPLORE.

"They're dirty," said Blinschell.

I thought of the circle on Aquaman's map. He'd been on his way here, but why?

"Yes, they are," I said. "But is it the right kind of dirty?"

There's nothing like a completely inconclusive interview to generate paperwork, but before we headed back to DHQ we stopped to drop off Abigail's latest roll of film and pick up the first batch as prints and on a USB pen.

"Is this going to be more cats?" asked the unfortunately named Donnie as he took the film. "Because that was a big cat. They're fake, right?"

"Totally fake," I said. "Couldn't be more faker."

I don't think he believed me.

Blinschell didn't think so, either, after I let him flick through them on the short drive back to the police car park.

"These are going to be all over the internet . . ." He made a show of checking his watch. "About five minutes ago."

"Might generate some feedback," I said.

"Is everyone in the Met such an optimist?" said Blinschell.

"Oh, it's all sunshine and roses down south," I said.

He showed me a dramatic close-up of the panther that, judging by the tilt and the motion blur, Abigail had taken by accident.

"Do you think this is what was outside Alice MacDuffie's house?"

I said I thought so, and he asked whether it flicked in and out like the toothy gull we'd tried to grab.

"What's next?" he asked. "Dragons?"

"Unlikely," I said, which proved later to be unwarranted confidence on my part.

"Unlikely," he said. "But not impossible?"

"Definitely not a dragon," I said, and decided it was not the right time to tell him about the wyvern and why NPAS was never ever going to let me up in a helicopter again.

We parked on the raised car park at the back of DHQ and waved at the uniformed vapers lurking around the back door. We were halfway up the first set of stairs when we heard an eldritch screech from above, and Blinschell pulled me off the landing and down a corridor.

Somebody in a tearing hurry ran down the stairs, followed by slower, more labored footsteps. A woman. I recognized the voice. The same woman Blinschell had avoided on my first day.

"Stand still, you sodding fudgemonkey."

Then stamping down the steps.

"Sodding thieving cockwomble." This time, a grumble that faded into the distance.

Blinschell waited for at least a minute before opening the fire door and looking out.

"Coast is clear," he said, and up we went to our narrow little office.

Where there was a note instructing me to visit DCI Mason as soon as I got in. Blinschell showed me where Mason's office was and wished me luck before I went in.

Office design has been converging for years now, so that software developers, local council departments and international charities all have the same IT set-up, the same task chairs and the same shelving. The desks vary from repurposed trestle tables to grandiose expanses of piano-finish hardwood, but everything else is the same. So DCI Mason's office could have belonged to the MD of a pet wrangling firm in a romantic comedy from the 2000s.

Apart from all the pictures of dead people on the wall.

He waved me into a visitor chair and gave me the eye. In return, I gave him the look of attentive interest that has been the shield and comfort of the lowly ranker since the dawn of time.

"Do you know what our homicide detection rate is?" he asked.

"No, sir."

"Since we were established five years ago . . . one . . . hundred . . . percent." He said it slowly, with gaps between the numbers.

I was so tempted to say "good for you, sir," but I'm thirty and a father now and have learned to think before I speak. Most of the time.

"Yes, sir," I said. "I wish ours was."

"I'm sure you do," said Mason. "In fact, I made a few calls and do you know what I found?" He didn't wait for me to answer. "I found that your lot, the Special Assessment Unit, better known as 'The Folly,' doesn't actually have a detection rate."

I winced, knowing what was coming next.

"In fact," said Mason, lowering his voice and leaning in, "you're famous for having a negative detection rate." It was a bit of classic interview room intimidation and, given my sudden urge to confess, Mason must have been wickedly effective in his sergeant days. Not that I had any idea what I was supposed to confess to.

"In fact . . ." he said, and then another pause for effect. "The SAU is quite famous for reducing successful outcomes for any unit unlucky enough to encounter them." He straightened up and gave me what, on any other man, would have been a winning smile. "But that's not going to happen here, is it? Because we're going to find whoever it was slaughtered the poor wee selkie and hand them over to the Fiscal all tied up in a nice neat bow."

Another, longer, pause.

"Is that clear?"

"Crystal," I said.

"Good," said Mason, and sat back down behind his desk. "Now—awa' wi' ye!"

Away with me I went, and outside I found Blinschell loitering in the corridor.

"What was that about?"

"We were talking comparative outcome statistics," I said. "And the need to focus on our core competencies in order to promote optimum outcomes."

"That bad, huh?"

"I know a DCI a bit like him in London," I said. "They must never meet."

The general rule with paperwork is—the longer you leave it, the harder it gets. So as soon as we were safely back in our office, Blinschell hit his terminal and the PNC while I updated my day book and called the Folly. DS Danni Wickford, who was Falcon liaison while I was on my hols, picked up.

"Chaos central," she said.

In the background I could hear Toby barking.

"Wagwan?" I said—suddenly homesick.

"How's Scotland?"

"Very sunny."

"I see you've already found some trouble."

"Holidays," I said. "Overrated. How's it going without us?"

"Possible poltergeist," she said. "Attacked a bunch of scrotes in Sutton, and still no progress on the Battersea cat mutilator."

"You're coping, then?"

"You know me."

"I want you to tell Nathan to look out for pictures of a black panther in Aberdeenshire—see if he can find any patterns of interest."

"Where did the pictures come from?"

I told her about Abigail, the Leica, and the slightly too helpful Donnie at Jessops.

"You can bring in another analyst if you need one," I said.

"Is that an official authorisation?"

"I'll e-mail it over tomorrow morning."

For historical reasons the Folly isn't chronically underfunded, like the rest of the Met, but even our budget has its limits. This is the sort of thing you have to start worrying about as you go up the ranks. As Uncle Ben says—with great power comes greater bureaucratical accountability.

"I need you to check the library," I said, and got a groan in response. Normally I'd ask Professor Harold Postmartin, our semi-official archivist, to do that, but he was away on the island of Lesbos, researching rumors of a society of British sorceresses that had been based there in the 1900s.

"Chirpsing Hatbox, more like," Abigail had said when I told her. Elsie "Hatbox" Winstanley being a special collections librarian at the British Library. "She says she's going to stop him taxing any rare manuscripts he takes a fancy to, but I bet you they're sharing a hotel room."

I'd said that, providing it didn't constitute a breach of the peace, I didn't want to know about Harold and Elsie's love life, to which Abigail had said I might want to take an interest at some point.

"What's that supposed to mean?" I asked, but Abigail refused to say.

"Don't forget to check the card files first," I said to Danni. "Might save you some time."

Despite Robert Smith's determination to be sent up the steps for murder, spurious gay panic defense or not, there still had to be a full investigation. One that had been assigned an operational name BARLEYCORN, and because we were in Scotland—where my legal status was uncertain—I was summoned to a nearby conference room to give a proper witness statement to the same deputy procurator fiscal I'd met at Aquaman's postmortem. There I spun a straightforward narrative of CCTV, to Footdee pub, he ran, we chased, we interviewed, he confessed, we utterly failed to believe him.

"Why's that?" asked the deputy procurator fiscal.

"We believe he was acting as part of a group who specifically targeted the victim," I said.

"Because he was gay?" he asked, which I admit was the next logical question.

"You were at the PM," I said. "We think he came out of the sea for an unknown reason and was killed, possibly unintentionally, in an attempt to prevent him reaching his objective."

"What objective?"

"Possibly FPXPLORE at Rubislaw Hill," I said. "Certainly a nearby location."

"And I suppose you don't know why Robert Smith and his accomplices wanted to stop him?"

I admitted it was so, and the DPF nodded.

"Investigations are ongoing," I said, which got me a snort.

That chore took us to the end of useful work, and Blinschell asked if I wanted to come down to the pub.

"You can meet the rest of the numpties," he said.

"Love to, mate," I said. "But I've got a shift with my other job."

Beverley was waiting with the twins and my parents at chez rock star. Dad was playing at a place called Drummonds that night, but it was Bev's turn to enjoy the music. She likes jazz more than me, which has endeared her no end to my mum, who ranks love of jazz somewhere between faith and hope on the virtue scale. Bev had arrived that afternoon, found a paddling pool in the garden shed and got Zach to blow it up. Daniel had found the garden hose and the whole band had ended up "cavorting" around the lawn while one or other of the twins tried to soak them.

"They're a disgrace to the jazz fraternity," said my dad, but only after he got accidentally splashed himself.

It did mean that after we swapped keys the twins fell asleep as soon as we'd secured them in the VW, and I drove back up to Mintlaw in blissful silence. It was early evening when I arrived back to find Abigail sitting on the patio, reading her Kindle.

"Where is everyone?" I asked.

"Brian and Abdul have gone to Dundee to look up mates from uni," said Abigail as she helped me decant the twins into their bed. "Nightingale is guarding the summoning circle in case somebody tries to summon something."

Because Abigail was sure that's what it was. And Abigail has spent more time in the Folly's library than I have, probably more than anyone else in fifty years. She filled me in while I made sure my own creatures from the pit were sound asleep, and set up the folding table and chairs in the tent's vestibule so we could drink beer and still keep an eye on them.

"What was the name of the American researcher?" I asked.

"You think that was sus?" she said.

I said everything was sus, and she opened her notebook and I took the details down in mine. I gave her her first notebook six years ago in the hope of keeping her out of trouble. Not that it worked, but at least now we have contemporaneous records.

I handed over the photos and divvied up the beers.

"You're sure it was a blood sacrifice?" I said as I fished out the Tennent's from the childproof cool box.

"Indigo gave it a sniff," said Abigail. "Def blood."

"Animal or . . . ?" I left it hanging.

There's four ways of getting power out of a human being. You bring it out of yourself when you cast a spell. Somebody can give you their power as part of a ritual—although they don't always know that's what they're doing. A revenant spirit like Mr. Punch can get in your head and suck you dry from the inside out, or . . .

Or you can kill someone and soak up the magic that's released on death. You can use animals, but the amount of power you get from a death seems proportional to the complexity of their central nervous system. So a mouse is like a triple A battery, a dog or a cat is like the battery pack for a laptop, and sacrificing a human being is like plugging straight into the mains.

At least, that's the theory.

This is why you don't get many ghosts in graveyards, but they're all over battlefields, hospitals and slaughterhouses.

"Indigo says animal," said Abigail. "Abdul sent samples to a lab."

"Where is Indigo?"

"Off sulking," said Abigail. "She's vexed with me because of Ione."

On that subject, I said I thought she'd be out with her new friend. Abigail pulled a face and said that Ione had family business to attend to.

"We're meeting up tomorrow," she said, and handed me a picture. She'd caught the panther looking straight at her.

"Scary stuff," I said.

"Check the eyes," she said. "They're slotted. Big cats don't have slotted eyes."

Just like gulls don't have teeth—at least, not birds on planet Earth.

"Does your friend have a sister?" I ask.

Abigail didn't look up from her photographs.

"She's twelve," she said. "Why do you want to know?"

So I told her about Calliste, the receptionist with the compelling voice, and the mustard Citroën C3 that was registered in her name at an address in Newburgh, a village twenty kilometers up the coast sitting right on the tidal estuary of the Ythan river.

"Ythan," said Abigail. "That's a *Star Trek* name, innit?"

"Anyway, if there's a chance . . ." I said. I wanted to ask her about Calliste, but let it trail off because Abigail was giving me the legendary side-eye that has terrified teachers, social workers and unsuspecting members of the public since she turned nine. I'm immune, but I still know when not to push it.

"That'll be on a need-to-know basis," she said.

"Like I needed to know about the local foxes?"

"Yeah," she said. "Just like that."

12

Acronym City

I WOKE UP that morning being twinhandled off my nice warm air mattress while the girls took it in turn to tug at my arm and yell "shout" in my right ear. "Shout" meant my phone was playing *The Sweeney* ringtone, which I used to differentiate job-related calls from everything else.

Who'd taught them to say "shout" was a mystery I had yet to solve.

Beyond the tent door it was a gray morning, and my phone said it was 05:21 and that Bridget Don was calling.

"Shout, shout," yelled the twins. "Trousers on, you're nicked."

My own river goddess told the twins to be quiet, ushered them into the warm spot I'd just vacated, and got them settled without apparently opening her eyes. I unzipped the insect screen at the front of the tent and stepped outside before answering. There'd been rain over night; the sky was still gray with rain clouds but the air was fresh—I took a deep breath.

"Peter Grant," I said.

"This is Elric," he said. I noticed that it obviously didn't occur to him that anyone would forget who he was. "You need to come over right away."

"What's the problem?"

"You need to see something."

"What kind of something?"

"You want to see it," he said, and gave me an address and then more directions on top of that.

The Brig o' Balgownie was built across the Don in the fourteenth century out of sandstone and, unsurprisingly, granite, with a single Gothic span and a steep climb up the valley either side. It must have been a bugger to get horse-drawn carts up those slopes in the rain, never mind the armies that had regularly marched up and down the east coast of Aberdeenshire.

Now it was well known as a scenic view down to the mouth of the Don—I knew this because of the Wikipedia article my phone read to me on the drive down.

It *was* a bugger to get to, I can tell you. Involving a detour through yet another dispersed suburb of gray Scottish semis, then switchbacking down past a line of granite Victorian cottages with overflowing gardens before my way was blocked by a set of bollards. There I parked and, following Elric's directions, walked along the granite approach. Just short of where the bridge proper bent to the left, there was a section where the parapet was completely overshadowed by a lime tree. Hidden by that was a wrought-iron gate. As I touched it I thought I heard the clash of swords, the shouting of men and the creaking of wagon wheels. When I stepped through into the warm shade of the tree the quality of the air changed, became richer, older—untainted by particulates or petrol fumes.

If they spend any time in one place, *genii locorum*, such as my beloved, can subtly alter the nature of their surroundings—or at least our perception of them. When I asked Bev about this, apropos our shared gaff in SW20, she said I was probably immune to her influence. That particular influence, anyway.

A short flight of granite steps led to a landing that projected from the side of the bridge and a wrought-iron spiral staircase leading down into the shadow of the tree. It was beautiful work—Victorian, at a guess—with decorated balusters and delicate fascias like metal lace.

As I descended, I saw Elric waiting for me at the bottom.

"What is this place?" I asked.

"One of the river houses," he said, and pointed at the sandstone and granite causeway which supported the bridge approach. Between two squat buttresses a doorway stood in the recess. It was built in classic Jacobean style, with a shallow four-centered arch and a solid wood plank door with matching period iron latch and keyhole. The wood was stained dark by centuries of whatever passed for Ronseal in the late Renaissance. Above, about where the first floor would be, were a pair of narrow unglazed windows that probably had more to do with field of fire than interior lighting.

"Bridget used to let the trolls bed doon here, but they got too unruly so she sent them away."

Elric led me away down to where a small gravel bar projected out beyond the mature trees lining the riverbank. There I saw Bridget crouched down by a large pink lump that I took for some kind of industrial pollution, until I got closer and saw that it was an animal—a walrus. A very big, very toothy, very dead walrus.

The carcass was slumped belly down on the gravel bar, its tail in the water, its comically small head propped up on its tusks in the grass, as if it had been biting the bank. Its eyes had been ripped out, leaving bloody sockets and streaks of red down its wrinkled pink cheeks.

As I got closer, I felt Bridget's anger like the weight of a glacier grinding rocks into dust—vast, slow and inevitable. When I crouched down beside her I saw she was trembling.

"What is this?" I asked.

"An outrage," she said softly.

"I need you to step back so I can work," I said. "You're drowning everything out."

Bridget turned her head and gave me a confused look.

"Your anger," I said. "It's too loud."

She nodded and slowly stood up, then turned on her heel and walked away. Elric took her place.

I've dealt with dead animals before. Sheep, mostly; a very unlucky horse in Basingstoke. But there was something infinitely depressing about the sheer mass of blubber and dead meat slumped in front of me.

"I didn't know they came this far south," I said.

"His name was Willy," said Elric. "He's been visiting us since 1694."

"I didn't know they lived that long."

"Willy was special," said Elric. "Understand?"

He reached out and gently touched the ruined head.

"This is a provocation," he said. "He did not die here. He was killed and dragged and dumped on our Bridget's doorstep."

"To what end?" I asked.

"The world has been getting strange of late," he said. "There are new people, people like you, stirring things up."

I put my hand on the walrus's wrinkled pink cheek. The skin was cold and smooth.

Now Bridget was clear I could feel the faint flickering of a *vestigium* clinging to the body, but nothing definite. Then I thought to grasp its tusk. There was rage and blood and a rank smell, like rotting food.

The rage and blood were familiar—I'd felt something like that in the skies over London. When a wyvern decided to roost at the top of Center Point. That had been of faery, a creature of fire and air and rock and roll. This was like that, only darker. With the stink of bloodlust about it.

The gull, the panther . . . now this.

I got down on my front and examined the great blubbery belly. There were deep lacerations near where it met the gravel, and visible indentations in its flanks. I checked the other side and I found similar but not identical marks. When I stood up and stepped away, Bridget shouted, "Who was it? Who did this?"

Something big enough to lift a full grown walrus, something that definitely wasn't native to Scotland, or probably the world. Something out of mythology and fairyland.

"I don't know," I said, although it was all beginning to form a pattern.

"You'd better find out quickly," said Elric.

"Really?" I said. "I thought I was supposed to be staying out of this? Remember?"

"Yeah, but you didn't, did you?"

"I did my job," I said. "The one I'm supposed to do. You guys are going to have to decide whether you're part of society or not."

"The fuck," said Elric with genuine astonishment.

"I'm here to keep the peace." I thought it prudent to leave the Queen out of this. "If you want my help, you've got to swear that you're not going to take vengeance."

"You don't know what you're asking," said Elric.

"The fuck I don't," I said. "Do you want me to get the Nightingale down here?"

"Go on." Elric stuck his face in mine, puffing up his shoulders like we were having a beef outside the Hippodrome at Leicester Square.

"Oh, for fuck's sake," shouted Bridget from up the bank. "Stop waving your dick and do as he says."

Elric looked at his sister and then, turning back to me, nodded. "Fine," he said.

Given DCI Mason's attitude, I didn't think it was a good idea to dump a thousand kilos of dead aquatic mammal on Police Scotland's local forensic team. Not when I had an alternative, anyway. I called Abdul.

"I've got a specimen you're going to want to see," I said. "But if you take it away you're going to need a boat." I looked at the sad bulk of poor Willy. "One with a hoist."

I told Elric what we were doing, and he warned me that they wanted Willy the Walrus back after any post-mortem.

"He deserves a proper send-off," he said, and I promised to pass it on.

By the time Abdul arrived it was pushing nine, so I headed for DHQ, where Blinschell had been hard at work since eight. Once I was out of earshot of the custody suite and the canteen, the place was eerily quiet. Only uniform on shifts and poor sods with active cases like me and Blinschell came in on a Saturday—everybody else stayed at home.

I told him about Willy the Walrus and he rolled his eyes.

"That wouldn't be a gull, then?" he asked.

I said it would have to be a bloody big one.

"It wasn't a small walrus," I said. "I'm thinking more kind of mythological."

"You mean like a roc?"

I was impressed by Blinschell's grasp of obscure mythical beasts, but not so much that I was going to explain the taxonomical differences between dragons and wyverns.

"More sort of dragonish."

"You're kidding me," he said. "Where are they all coming from?"

"We think they're being summoned from another realm of existence," I said.

"I'm sorry I spoke," said Blinschell. "Last night people were asking me what I was working on, and I didn't know what to tell them. Selkies—fine, whatever. Panthers—well, panthers are a real thing. Gulls—sure, plenty of gulls... Dragons? You said a dragon was unlikely."

"Possibly a wyvern," I said.

"What's the difference?" asked Blinschell, and I was tempted to say *about two hundred hit points* but decided against it.

"For our purposes, not much really."

"How do you cope with this stuff?" he said. "Seriously—how do you cope with it?"

"It's like the rest of the job," I said. "You get on with the work in front of you."

"I don't think my stab vest is rated for dragons," said Blinschell.

"My advice is, don't try to arrest one until you have backup," I said.

Possibly to avoid thinking about the operational difficulties re: restraining a dragon. I mean, would it count as a dangerous wild animal under the Animals (Scotland) Act 1987? If it did, would we be required to take due care with regards to its welfare?

To avoid such thoughts, we took my advice and concentrated on some real policing—nailing down Alice MacDuffie's movements prior to becoming a missing persons statistic.

In these days of health and safety gone mad, nobody went offshore—at least, nobody covered by corporate insurance—without having at least their BOSIET—Basic Offshore Safety Induction and Emergency Training—certificate approved by OPITO, the Offshore Petroleum Industry Training Organization. BOSIET certifies that the bearer can escape down an emergency chute, use the compressed air emergency breathing system, CAEBS, and escape from a drowning helicopter, HUET.

"They put you in a mock-up fuselage and drop you in a swimming pool," said Blinschell. "Upside down."

This sounded like a personal experience, so I asked Blinschell whether he had a BOSIET certificate. He said he had because like many young Aberdonians, he'd felt the lure of the sea and, more importantly, the hefty wage packet.

"But you didn't stick at it?"

"I don't have that sense of adventure," he said. "I joined the police for an easy life."

Then, before his certificate could expire, he was instructed to get a FOET—Further Offshore Emergency Training—which extended the certificate for another four years.

"They wanted to have someone qualified to go offshore in case they needed someone arrested out there," he said.

"Has that ever happened?"

Blinschell rapped his knuckles on the tabletop.

"Not yet," he said.

All OPITO-approved safety training certificates were registered with the Vantage system and were searchable online, so while I'd been contemplating a dead walrus Blinschell had done just that.

Alice MacDuffie had done her BOSIET course and registered two months previously.

"Which only proves she could have gone out to the platform if she wanted to," said Blinschell. "If she did it, then it means there are divers working her well head."

Workers who might have had direct contact with our MISPER.

"If they're so safety-conscious," I said, "somebody must be keeping track."

"If you can be bothered, the harbor keeps records of who's going in and out and you can always check with the NSTA," said Blinschell. "If you've got the energy."

"Or?" I asked, because I know a story when I hear one.

"You can go down the Crown and Anchor and ask the landlady," he said.

Because the legendary landlady of the Crown and Anchor, which sat on Regent Quay by the docks, made a point of knowing who was coming in and going out, what they drank and whether they were trouble. She knew the difference between her divers and her roustabouts.

"She said there hadn't been any scientists or divers in from Elgar Bravo," said Blinschell. But that wasn't too unusual, because she mostly only saw the guys working off boats. "If they're flying into Dyce or Dundee, they drink in different pubs."

"So what does that prove?"

"Divers either work off support ships or off rigs and platforms," he said. "If they're not going off the ships, then they must be based on the rig—narrows the field."

"Not by much," I said.

"Yeah," he said. "But I've got a mate at the airport."

Of course he did.

His mate had checked the last flight back from Elgar Bravo and passed over the passenger manifest. Blinschell had rung each passenger in turn until he found one, an electrician called Alex Muir, who was sober enough to answer the phone, conveniently located, and admitting to having seen Alice on the platform.

"What are the chances that Derek Patterson didn't know?" I asked.

"More impossible than your dragons," said Blinschell. "Shall we go back and ask him?"

"Can we talk to your witness first?"

Blinschell checked his watch.

"We'd better hurry," he said, "if we're going to catch him sober."

Alex Muir was still sober, but it was a close thing.

"It's bloody ice cream for the next two weeks," he said, "so I'm stocking up."

He was a small, wiry, bald white man of the type you don't want to fight unless you've got a mate with a taser standing by. He had surprisingly long pianist's fingers, which he was currently using to hold a pint glass steady while pouring in a can of Hazy Jane.

Alex was drinking in what, had we been in London, I would have called a *shebeen*. An illegal drinking club, which was the roughnecks' response to the contraction in the Aberdeen oil industry.

"Pubs are too expensive," he said.

The unnamed establishment was located in a basement reached down some stairs in an alley off a sunken road not that far from Union Street. The bar was taking the Aldi approach to product presentation—there were stacks of beer multipacks and crates of spirits behind the bar. A very bored young black woman in jeans and a leather jacket was handing out cans and plastic pint glasses to order.

I'd caught her eye when we came in and she gave me a look that said, quite eloquently, *Oh fuck, not the police.* I'd given her what I hoped was a reassuring nod but, to be honest, I've had mixed results with that.

The basement had a series of shadowy alcoves outfitted with plastic garden furniture and lit by old fluorescent tubes. Despite it being half past breakfast, there were a dozen patrons sitting around in small groups and looking to get hammered as fast as possible. Alex Muir had been sitting alone, and raised his hand when Blinschell called his name.

"Who the fuck are you?" he'd asked, and we spent at least ten minutes identifying ourselves and convincing Alex that he'd spoken to us on the phone.

"Why the fuck did I want to do that?" he asked.

"Because I'll buy you a six-pack," I said.

I asked the woman behind the bar for a six-pack and she reeled off a list of beers that sounded made-up, so I asked for the strongest she had available and that's why we ended up with Hazy Jane. She overcharged me, too, but I let it pass—working down here all day was punishment enough for her.

Once Alex had wrapped his laughing gear around half a pint, we started asking questions. Like, was he sure the woman he'd seen on Elgar Bravo was Alice MacDuffie? He said he was because they'd chatted in the rec room.

"They weren't running a full crew," he said. "On account of them not drilling, so the string wasn't moving. So there weren't that many people to talk to."

"How did she seem?" asked Blinschell.

"Entirely fuckable," said Alex. "But not by me."

I asked what her mood was, and Alex said that she seemed excited.

"Happy in her work," he said. "That's what these university types are like. It's all a grand adventure, not a grind like it is for the rest of us."

"Who was she fucking, then?" asked Blinschell.

"Don't know for sure," said Alex, and cracked another can. "They were a tight crew on that rig. Kept their secrets."

"Like what secrets?" I asked.

"They were trying out some hush-hush experimental bollocks

that they weren't supposed to talk about," said Alex. "So we didn't talk about it. I'm an electrician—I just fix the wiring. Even so, I had to sign an NDA and I didn't even know what they were doing."

"Did you see Alice again?" I asked.

"We saw each other all the bloody time," said Alex. "It's not that big a place, a platform."

"How about on other rotations?" asked Blinschell.

"I only did the one rotation," said Alex. "Temporary replacement. It was a good gig, though, easy shifts. Not much work going on." He finished his pint glass and started refilling it again. There was something disturbingly mechanical about the way he drank, as if he was under a compulsion.

"Has anyone else talked to you about Alice recently?" I asked.

"Why would anyone be interested in Alice?" said Alex.

"Well, somebody was, weren't they?" said Blinschell. "You said she was banging someone on the rig." Deliberately misstating a witness being an oldie but a goodie in a copper's conversational arsenal.

Alex gave Blinschell a blank look before turning to me, as if he expected me to explain.

"Was she close to anyone on the platform?" I said.

"No, nothing, nobody," said Alex. "People are careful about that sort of thing. No questions, no gossip, no fraternizing with the natives." His tone was weirdly dull, as if he were reciting an instruction.

His mood and robotic attitude was making me suspicious that somebody had put the fluence on him. Or he could be drinking himself senseless because he hated working offshore. But if he hated offshore, why did he do it? And if he'd been glamoured to shut up about Alice, why was he willing to talk about her in the first place?

"The money," said Blinschell, after we'd left Alex to the remains of his six-pack. "He's making £40,000 a year—minimum."

That explained the work. But what about the—possible—glamour?

"When did you first call him?" I asked, and Blinschell checked his notebook.

"8:50," he said.

"Where was he, do you think, when you rang?"

"In bed, or at least asleep. I woke him up."

I thought through the timings. Imagine Calliste comes into work bright and early, boss calls her in and says, Calliste, be a dear and pop down and put the fluence on this electrical engineer for us.

Sure thing, boss, says Calliste, and hops into her underpowered Citroën and drives over, since they know his address from their files. A bit of glamour later and Alex Muir has a memory like Swiss cheese.

Impossible to prove, and a good example of why Falcon cases are a bugger and nobody wants to work with us. Still, somewhere there would be an official record that Alice MacDuffie visited Elgar Bravo. Once we had proof, we could re-interview the lying fake Texan in the hope of shaking something loose. Blinschell grabbed a pool car and headed for the airport to find the records, while I headed back to our office to check my emails.

Strictly speaking, there's a procedure for contacting members of foreign law enforcement agencies. A whole sodding international bureaucracy, in fact, involving such bunches of letters as NCA, EUROPOL and INTERPOL—which American movies seem to think is a cross between the FBI and Team America. They might even do good work, but when you need something in a hurry, your hard-working copper opens their little black book and calls their low friends in high places.

Or, given it was still morning in America, emails them. In the clear, you note—because you don't want the NSA or GCHQ thinking you've got something to hide. No doubt there's a cubicle somewhere with a bored analyst who keeps track of us between sharing goat videos and spying on antiwar activists. I'd sent the message first thing from my phone while waiting for Abdul and Brian, and thrown in some walrus pics for good measure. Fuck knows what the NSA made of those. Probably made a nice change from goats.

There was an e-mail from Nathan the analyst, who probably hadn't gone to bed at all. He informed me that he'd done an extensive check of available public sources and that James Albright, alleged American academic and Aberdeenshire history aficionado, was not and had never been on the staff at the

University of Mississippi. But there were several at other universities in the US and two in the UK. It was quite a common name, which might explain why a J. Albright appeared, once, on a list of consultants working for FPXPLORE.

Abigail was right. It was definitely sus. But it could also be a coincidence.

But that wasn't the way to bet.

You don't action a senior officer, but you can ask them nicely to go interview William Sinclair, who's been foolish enough to let Abigail into the Discovery Center. Only if they have a moment to spare in their busy panther-chasing schedule, though. I sent that as a text to Nightingale, and was shocked to get an immediate thumbs-up emoji followed by—*already taken care of.*

I was about to call Blinschell for an update when a slim white man in a good suit appeared in the doorway.

"Sergeant Peter Grant?" he asked in what even I could spot was a posh Edinburgh accent, although no doubt Blinschell would have pinpointed its origin within a five-kilometer radius. "My name is Andrew Rae, I'm with the Economic Development Directorate. Is it all right if I come in and have a word?"

I knew trouble when I saw it. I could tell from the clothes, the confidence, and the fact that he was wandering around at will inside the perimeter of a police station, that this was a senior civil servant.

And senior civil servants make you come to them; they don't pop into your office for a word unless what they are about to say is off the record. And nothing good gets said to coppers off the record.

I acknowledged that I was the aforementioned Peter Grant and offered him the spare office chair.

He had a triangular face that narrowed down to a pointy chin, blue eyes, and curly brown hair of the kind my mum used to dream of. He sat down with exaggerated pleasure and gave me a sunny smile.

"Thank you," he said. "The trip up from Edinburgh is a trek. It's a scandal that there isn't a high-speed link from Waverley."

And you came all this way to discuss peripheral region transport priorities, I thought, but kept my mouth shut. According to the king of the goblins—although don't call him that—you should never show your hand first.

And I should never have introduced *him* to the Ferengi Rules of Acquisition. But that's another story.

"How can I help you, Mr. Rae?" I asked.

"As I understand it, you're up from London," he said, and there was a definite edge when he said it, although I'm not sure he knew he was doing it. "From something called the Special Assessment Unit?"

"We've been asked to advise on a case," I said.

"You're basically the English version of *The X-Files*," he said.

"We don't do UFOs," I said. "Or alien conspiracies."

"Are there alien conspiracies?"

"Not that we know of."

"I suppose that's a relief."

"I've always thought so."

Andrew Rae glanced around the office as if looking for inspiration before refocusing on me.

"I understand you're investigating FPXPLORE Limited," he said.

"Only in connection with a missing person case," I said.

"That seems a mite parochial, considering," he said. "Does the SAU often investigate MISPERS?"

"More often than you'd think," I said. Especially when the fae were involved. But I felt that Andrew Rae didn't need to be burdened with that kind of detail. "We cover a wide range of cases."

"So I've heard," said Rae, and now his smile was thin-lipped and lacking in sunniness.

I gave him the look of bland inquiry that has been my refuge since my first day at infants, when I ate my first crayon. I think it was orange. Mr. Rae wanted me to know that he'd done his homework and knew who I was. The question was, what else did he know? And what was his interest?

"Do you have an interest in FPXPLORE?" I asked, because otherwise we might have fenced all day.

He was smooth, I'll give him that—he didn't hesitate.

"They're a component in our wider energy strategy going forward."

"Who's 'us' in this instance?"

"The Scottish Government."

"How big a component?"

"At this stage, in the field of resource renewal, quite important."

"Resource renewal," I said. And because this sort of thing is close to the heart of a certain river goddess I know, I added, "Not renewable resources?"

That stung, I could tell—for all that he kept his bland mask in place.

"We're planning a managed transition," he said. "Ideally we'd prefer to switch straight over to renewables. God knows the need for a properly organized transition was obvious decades ago, but for some reason the Westminster government failed to do so."

"Shocking," I said. "But to put your mind at rest, as of this moment FPXPLORE is only involved in the investigation because the missing person consulted for them. If you leave me your contact details, I'll have my governor call you with any updates."

"You still haven't said what your interest in this missing person was," he said.

Bugger, I thought. And it was such high-quality bollocks, too.

"Their case was connected to a murder case that we were asked to consult on."

"This would be the unidentified victim found on Beach Boulevard?"

"That's right."

"Was he killed with magic?" asked Rae. "Bitten by a werewolf? Attacked by a redcap?"

"He was found severely beaten and suffering from several stab wounds," I said. "The actual cause of death is still unclear." And before Rae could follow up, "What's a redcap?"

"Vicious little goblin thugs," he said. "They use their victims' blood to dye their caps."

"I'll add them to my list of things to avoid."

"Very wise," said Rae, and stood. I followed him up. He handed me his card, nicely judged to be good quality but not too ostentatiously posh. I clocked that it said Economic Development Directorate and gave his e-mail and mobile, and made a show of slipping it in my back pocket.

Rae smiled and held out a hand—we shook.

"I'm up here for a couple of days on other business," he said. "If you think I can be of assistance, don't hesitate to call."

I said I wouldn't hesitate to do so, and he left.

I closed the door, sat back at my terminal and sent his details to Nathan for a background check. I was about to call Nightingale when Blinschell rang me.

"Here's the thing," he said. "I've been through the personal manifest of every flight to and from Elgar Bravo in the last three months, and I've got her flying offshore but no record of her coming back."

13

Bayview Court

"COULD SHE HAVE come back by boat?" I asked.
"We'll have to check," he said, and swigged from his bottle of Highland Spring.

Unlike the Met, which has largely abolished canteens as a cost-saving measure, Police Scotland still likes to feed its officers. Blinschell had an anemic curry and rice, while I played to its strengths by having a macaroni cheese the consistency of hot asphalt. If asphalt was cheesy and delicious.

"We're going to have to re-interview her work colleagues as well," I said.

I'd double-checked the files, and nobody had reported seeing Alice MacDuffie between her departure to Elgar Bravo and the finding of her car parked on the Esplanade.

"We'll have to ask Mason for more bodies," said Blinschell.

"Do you think he'll authorize that?"

Blinschell forked in some curry while he thought about it.

"I think he'll have to escalate the MacDuffie case to a suspected abduction or murder," he said.

"He's going to love that," I said. Not least because that would make him SIO. And there isn't a major crimes unit anywhere that doesn't already think it has enough work to do, thank you very much.

I was right—DCI Mason didn't like it.

But he did it anyway.

"Is there anything you can contribute to this investigation?"

he asked before we could safely leg it out of his office. "Apart from doubling my caseload?"

"We do have a Falcon line of inquiry that may be relevant," I said.

"I'm afraid to ask, but I suppose I'd better," said Mason. "What's this line of inquiry?"

"Somebody has been summoning eldritch creatures from another world," I said, because sometimes no amount of management-speak bollocks is going to help. "We need to catch him."

"Eldritch creatures?"

"Yes, sir."

"From another world?"

"Yes, sir."

"This would be the seagull and the big cat I've heard so much about?"

"Yes, sir." I felt it better not to mention the possible dragon.

Mason carefully lowered himself into his office chair. For a moment he looked longingly down at his desk, then up at the ceiling, and then at me.

"In that case, you'd better get on with it," he said.

Only it wasn't that simple—first Blinschell had to brief a couple of keen young DCs who were going to complete the re-interviews. Following my advice, he kept the weird bollocks to a minimum, although, judging from their questions, rumors had been flowing.

"Is it true that she was a selkie?" one of them asked.

To which our only reasonable answer was, "Not as far as we know."

"*Could* she have been a selkie?" asked Blinschell after the briefing.

"Who knows?" I said. "Is anyone looking into her family background?"

"Mason has an analyst on it," said Blinschell.

"We'll have to follow up if they find anything strange," I said.

"Stranger than a dragon?"

"More likely a wyvern," I said. "And that hasn't been confirmed."

But five minutes later it was, when Abdul called me to report his preliminary findings of the sad corpse of Willy the Walrus.

"Judging from the marks left on the body," he said, "whatever snatched him up had claws of similar size and structure to the Center Point wyvern."

"How similar?"

"At a guess, same species," said Abdul. "If you see it, make sure you get some photographs."

Correlation is not causation, but our wyvern confirmation may have been why Blinschell decided to arm himself with a taser.

"You authorized for that?" I asked as I strapped on the holster.

"Most definitely," he said.

"Don't use it without checking with me first," I said.

"I make no promises."

"And don't shoot me in the back," I said, and asked whether they had a spare stab vest I could borrow. They didn't have one in an undercover sleeve, so I borrowed a uniform version in black with a blue and white chequerboard pattern and "POLICE" on the front and back.

Stab vests are a pain, but when faced with uncertainty I find the weight comforting.

There's never just the one way to conduct a major investigation. For a start, you could look at a crime scene and ask yourself, what's the common denominator? Did the perpetrator take their time or prepare in advance, or did they just like to stab and run? Did they know the area well enough to be confident they wouldn't be disturbed?

Or you can rely on physical forensic evidence and good old Locard's exchange principle. These days you can gather a ridiculous amount of information from a crime scene providing you — or, more likely, your governor — is willing to shell out the readies. Some of it might even be useful.

Or you can track someone's mobile phone data, the so-called snail trail it leaves behind as it pings every cell tower. You can even analyze the communications data from a cell tower near the scene and try and cross-check individual phones with known villains or those unlucky enough to end up as nominals on HOLMES, or any unknown phone that turned up at multiple scenes.

Or, even better—all of the above.

With the full, if grudging, resources of NE Division's MIT picking up most of the slack, it was up to me and Blinschell to do the deductive reasoning. We decided this would be easier on the Esplanade, where the sea air would clear our heads and the lack of senior supervision would free up our mental processes. We ended up on the south end, where Alice MacDuffie's car had been found abandoned.

It had been fingerprinted as part of the initial investigation, but only her prints had been found. Likewise, the driver's seat was adjusted to match someone of Alice's listed height and estimated weight. Mason was probably dreading having to call in forensics to do a DNA examination. As we drove down Beach Boulevard, past the initial crime scene, I was beginning to get that familiar sense of dislocation you feel when a case starts spiraling out of your ability to grasp it all at once. Supposedly, that was what information management systems like HOLMES were for. But in truth you generally solve most cases by trudging through the evidence until something turns up. Starting with, if Alice hadn't returned from Elgar Bravo, who had driven her car to the Esplanade?

By the time we'd reached the spot, the clouds had cleared and sunlight sparkled off the sea, the wind turbines, and the dayglo orange service vessels cruising in and out of the harbor.

"That's Aberdeen," said Blinschell when I commented on it. "If you don't like the weather, wait twenty minutes and get something else."

It certainly explained why any sunseekers on the beach had their fleeces handy and swam in wetsuits.

I looked at the sea. Aquaman, aka the selkie, aka the poor sod whose murder had started the whole ball rolling, had walked naked out of the sea. If Alice MacDuffie was an amphibian like him, then could she have swum back from Elgar Bravo, picked up her car, driven it down to the beach and swum back out? It seemed unlikely.

"Or she had another amphibious friend," said Blinschell, "who borrowed her car, drove down and swam away."

"Or more likely," I said, "someone drove it down here to throw . . ." I was going to suggest that it was to throw us off the scent. But of course we weren't even on the scent at that stage—nobody was. I said this to Blinschell, who nodded.

"Yeah," he said. "But maybe, being proper neds, they didn't know that?"

A gull squawked somewhere above, and we both looked up in case it was a dragon.

"This is not proper police work," I said, once I was happy it was just a gull.

"You do not get to say that," said Blinschell.

"Let's assume the gull that attacked Aquaman at the bus shelter served as a sort of alarm system," I said.

"Is that possible?"

"Fuck knows," I said. "But it's not impossible. Let's say it alerts its handler, who is probably the one summoning it." I paused, because that was a stretch. But overthink these things and you can drown yourself in loose threads. "Then they alert some accomplices, who come from over there."

I pointed south, to where Footdee lurked hard up against the futuristic spike of the harbor control tower.

Where, according to Robert Smith's gay friend Stud, reside families that have a long-time connection with the sea.

"Our boy Aquaman looked like he was on a mission," I said. Grabbing clothes like John Connor as he went. "He was desperate to get somewhere inland, and I think the gulls and the boys from Footdee were there to stop him. The question is, where was he going and why didn't they want him to get there?"

While I was chatting, Blinschell's phone bleeped and he checked his emails. When he finished, he looked up and gave me a proper copper's grin.

"We might be able to ask your mysterious American about that," he said.

Because one of our earlier actions—getting MIT to check suspicious traffic around the Pitfour summoning circle—had paid off.

The thing about amateur criminals, especially well-off ones from good schools, is that they're used to getting away with shit. Grow up skirting the law and you'd know that you don't use your own car to do crimes. Otherwise, thick plods like me, Blinschell and whatever poor sod it was who trawled through the ANPR data from cameras on the A952 and the A950, which bracket Mintlaw and the ruined observatory, wouldn't be able to match their plate against the DVLA records, and find that one particular 2017 Range Rover Evoque with the 2.0 liter petrol engine and the driveline gearbox and match it to two nominals held on HOLMES.

One, that the car was registered to FPXPLORE of Rubislaw Hill. And two, its registered keeper was one James Albright—our phantom American academic. The DVLA even had a current address.

"Oh, I do love it when they're stupid," said Blinschell. "Makes our job so much easier."

"It probably never occurred to him that we'd spot the crime," I said.

"And I love it when they think *we're* stupid," he said, and grinned again.

"Where is this Bayview Court, then?"

Blinschell turned and pointed along the Esplanade, to where a clump of tower blocks stood about a kilometer away.

"First one in the row facing the sea," he said.

"Dragons and gulls," I said. "If you were summoning creatures of the wind and sky, you might want to be high up."

Bayview Court was nineteen stories of 1970s utilitarian council housing that had been reclad in the recent past and was, even as we approached, having a little work done around the main entrance.

We cruised the car park in front of the block and found the black Range Rover Evoque with the correct index among the battered Fords, Hondas and second-hand Kia Sportages. As per our instructions, an elderly Peugeot in Police Scotland livery was parked discreetly in the corner, where it could keep an eye on the Range Rover. I parked right in front of it so it couldn't leave without ramming somebody's car—hopefully mine. Blinschell waved the uniforms over and, after I'd had a quick shufti in the back of the Range Rover—nothing obvious on the seats or in the boot—we proceeded to the block.

The main entrance had the access-controlled concierge door that was pretty standard for council flats nationwide. Blinschell called the supplier's control room in somewhere called Tillydrone and got the override—but not before having to recite his Police Scotland identification number first.

No amount of cladding was going to improve the sunless space that was the foyer, where we left the uniforms watching the emergency stairs and the second lift, and took the first up to the eighteenth floor. The lift smelled weirdly of lemon floor cleaner and peppermint. We stepped out into a lobby that showed the same flecked terrazzo flooring as in the Divisional Police HQ and the mortuary—obviously a municipal favorite. The tower was an old-fashioned design built around a central structural core housing the lifts and emergency stairs, so only two of the flats' doors were visible. Fortunately, Blinschell had arrested people in one of the nearby sister blocks just the other month, so he knew the layout.

"They built all the towers on the same plan," he said, and pointed at the door we had listed as James Albright's address.

I've stepped on a few traps in my time, and it tends to make you a bit cautious. You've got to watch the paranoia, though. Otherwise you get a bit flaky, and your therapist gets that little crease between her eyes that spells trouble. But given that I was approaching the lair of a possible practitioner, I took a moment to check the door for *vestigia* before I so much as knocked.

The door was heavy, fire-resistant, and had a three-point lock. I touched the metal of the keyhole as the place most likely to retain *vestigia*, and got such a shock of sweaty heat and decay stink that it made me snatch my hand back.

I stepped away from the door and hustled Blinschell back up the corridor.

"Take the battery out of your phone," I said.

"Does this mean you're going to do some weird shite?"

"Oh yeah," I said, and handed him the small flat-head screwdriver I keep just for such occasions. iPhones are a hassle, but with Galaxies you just pop the back off and pry the battery out. I kept my eye on the door while Blinschell scrabbled and cursed behind me. Then he grunted and said he'd got it.

Back on the Peckwater Estate when I was young, you could open the front door with a well-aimed kick at the right spot. You knew which flats the drug dealers lived in by the reinforced doors or the external security bars—all the better to slow up the filth when they came knocking. These days, local authorities have decided to make their tenants less vulnerable to random burglaries, building fires and police raids, by installing reinforced hardwood doors with square bolt three-point locks.

Also, up in Scotland you're not supposed to kick in doors without a warrant. But I didn't like the *vestigia* on the door, so we were going to go for a flexible hybrid approach. There's a standard spell called *clausurafrange* that pops the barrel of a Yale lock right out, but with three locking points, me and Nightingale have had to invent something a bit more sophisticated. It took a lot of trial and error, but we ended up with a spell that shears all three bolts at the same time, and could be cast—and this was the important bit—from three meters away.

It was from that safe distance that I lined up the *formae* and let the spell go.

I heard the satisfying *snick*, *snick*, *snick* of the bolts shearing through.

Then I felt a burst of hot damp heat, like getting a face full of steam. I staggered back a meter before the fact that it wasn't a physical sensation registered with my brain. Behind me, Blinschell swore.

Somewhere below us somebody screamed, while somewhere else below us a baby started crying. I held up a hand to stop Blinschell asking what the fuck just happened, because I wanted to listen. No alarms went off, the front doors of the other flats on the floor didn't fly open, nobody ran screaming or charged out with a baseball bat. I exhaled.

"What was that?" asked Blinschell in the calm voice of a man who has decided that freaking out, however much he'd like to, would be counterproductive at this particular moment.

"Demon trap," I said. "Like a sort of landmine, only magical."

Blinschell considered this for a long moment.

"Do you think it's safe to go in now?" he asked.

"Let's find out," I said.

"You first."

I pulled the extendable baton and flicked it out to full length. Then I advanced cautiously toward the doorway. Blinschell, I noticed, kept a nice prudent two meters behind me.

The smell of burned plastic got stronger as I reached the open door. Beyond was the too-narrow corridor that planners have inflicted on the proletariat since the 1950s. There was a white door opposite where the corridor turned a corner. The off-white paint of the walls was unburnt, the wood-effect flooring was untouched, the light fitting was intact but the bulb was dark. Just inside the threshold was a welcome mat with *Fàilte* printed on it—heat had turned a fist-sized circle in the center the color of burned toast. Motioning Blinschell to stay back, I used the tip of my extendable baton and flipped the mat over.

Underneath was a breadboard-sized sheet of white plastic with a hole burned at its center. It was a demon trap of the modern plastic type I associated with American practitioners. They used to be metal and easier to detect. I touched it lightly with my finger and felt the now familiar sensation of dank heat, but faint—an echo, not a threat.

To be on the safe side, I stepped over it. Then I used *impello* to knock open the door ahead, but nothing else happened. I told Blinschell to stay in the corridor while I checked the rest of the first room. It was obviously a furnished rental. The walls were neutral whites and tans, the carpet was hard-wearing and khaki, the furniture generic flatpack. The bed was unmade, the wardrobe empty, but there was an open sausage bag on the floor with clothes spilling out.

I did a quick sweep of the rest of the flat. A second, smaller, bedroom was bare and unoccupied. Opposite was a bathroom with shaving gear carelessly scattered on the sink counter next to an electric toothbrush in its charger.

The kitchen and living room were surprisingly large for a council flat, with astonishing views out across the sea.

I shouted to Blinschell that it was clear and he helped me do a search. Either James Albright was a neat freak or he didn't spend much time in the flat. The remote control for the stingy 20-inch flat-screen TV sat on the smoked-glass coffee table next to an old cup ring, but there were no books or magazines in the room. Although there were a pair of fluffy purple slippers placed neatly by the door.

"Either he didn't eat much," said Blinschell from the kitchen, "or he does a lot of takeaway . . . Shit!"

I looked into the kitchen and found Blinschell with his palm placed on the dome of an old-fashioned kettle, the kind that you heat on a hob and whistles when it's done.

"Still warm," he said.

I tested it myself—lukewarm, but definitely used in the last half-hour or so.

Blinschell started wrestling his battery back into his phone, but I stopped him and used my Airwave. The protective cover had done its job, but it took me a minute to find the right settings for our uniforms downstairs. They reported that nobody had come in or out in the last ten minutes. Blinschell told them to stay alert.

"Maybe he's on the roof," he said. "What do you think?"

I looked out of the kitchen window at the long sweep of the Esplanade far below, and blue sea stretching out to the white windmills.

"I'm thinking that the roof would be a really good place to put a summoning circle," I said.

The emergency stairs smelled of bleach and distant urine. They terminated on our floor, but there was a metal ladder with a safety cage bolted to the wall leading up to an obvious access hatch. I'd assumed that, if he'd been in the building, he'd have felt the demon trap go off and should, by now, have come down to investigate.

Unless he was waiting at the top—ready with an ambush—and with that in mind, I went up as quietly as I could. When I reached the top I brushed my fingers against the cool metal of the hatch but there were no warning *vestigia*. Noting where the hinges were, I gave it an experimental push and felt it lift. It should have been securely locked, which was definitely sus, so I raised it a bit and peered through the crack, but all I could see was the cement facing of the lift equipment tower. I lifted the hatch all the way open and laid it down carefully, so as not to make a noise.

The tower was basically two square towers rammed together so that they merged at the central core. There was no sign of anyone standing on the section with the hatch, but most of the other section—the top of that square tower—was hidden behind the lift equipment tower. I pulled myself up on to the roof, definitely not swearing as a Velcro strap on my stab vest caught on the lip, and motioned to Blinschell to come up. Once he was up, we flattened ourselves against the equipment tower and I risked a quick look around the corner.

He was there—a tall white man in a checkered shirt, dad jeans and black and white trainers. His hair was brown, streaked with gray and long enough to be tied back in a ponytail. He was turned away from me so I couldn't see his face, and he had his arms flung up in a dramatic gesture. Around him was what I assumed was a summoning circle painted in reddish-brown splashes. If there were occult symbols, they'd been too badly painted to make out.

There was a shimmer in the air—as if a heat haze was rising from the rim of the circle. That would be for protection from the things he'd summoned. It also dampened sound, although not enough to mask the fact that he was chanting. I didn't recognize the language. I ducked back out of sight.

"Fuck me," I whispered. "It's bloody Saruman."

This got me a blank look from Blinschell.

"Sorry," I said. "I want you to stand behind me and to the left. Get the taser out and if I shout 'now,' shoot the fucker. Do not shoot me by mistake. Understood?"

"I'll do my best," he said.

We're the police and we're not supposed to smack unsuspecting people from behind without authorisation from a senior officer. So I stepped out boldly and approached to within about a meter of the summoning circle. As I got closer, I smelled dirty water and something like rotting bananas. Any real smell should have been blown away by the brisk breeze coming in from the sea. So should the clammy warmth that clung to my skin like a damp flannel.

"Excuse me, sir," I shouted. "Do you have permission to be conducting a magical ritual on these premises?"

My Saruman wannabe kept on chanting. Maybe he couldn't hear me. I eyed the shimmering heat haze rising from the circle and did a dynamic risk assessment—there was no way I was getting near that.

"Sir," I shouted in my loudest and best authoritative cop voice. "Cease any magical activity and step away from the conjuration circle." And then, because he didn't even turn round, I broke the circle with a nifty little *impello* variant I'd invented to get persistent stains out of carpets. I wanted to call it Vim, but Nightingale objected—presumably for copyright reasons.

A ten-centimeter length of the red-brown "paint" rolled itself into a sphere the size of a billiard ball—along with any loose grit, fecal matter and all the other detritus you'd expect to find on the roof of a tower block.

With no drama whatsoever, the haze dissipated as soon as the circle was broken. Saruman the Checkered faltered, and then stopped chanting. He spun to face me and I saw, to my complete lack of surprise, that he wore his facial hair in a neatly trimmed goatee.

"Mr. James Albright?" I asked, and he didn't answer but the little jerk of his head gave him away. "Please immediately cease your conjuration and step out from the circle."

He actually goggled—which I've never seen in real life—before regaining control of his face. You could almost see him selecting *weary contempt* from the menu of middle-class responses to police.

"You don't know what you've done," he said. His accent was American, but the best I could do beyond that was vaguely Southern.

"Please step out of the conjuration circle, sir," I said.

I felt him start a spell. He was clumsy, and his *signare* was all swamp water and elephant feet. I threw a blinder at his face but the fucker had outsmarted me—the spell was a distraction. Instead, he ran for the parapet as if to throw himself off.

I know a couple of ways of breaking your fall from a height, but you'd have to be crazy or desperate—or, more likely, crazy desperate—to want to do it on purpose. Maybe he had a spell I didn't know about that would slow his fall. But we didn't give him a chance to show off.

"Now," I shouted, and Blinschell tasered him.

14

What Abigail Learned About the Queen

"DR. WALID SAYS it's animal blood," I say. I'm standing with Ione and Nightingale back at the summoning circle. Ione picked me up on her moped first thing and we drove out together. Indigo didn't come home last night, so I presume she's off doing classified fox things with Sax William and Reid King.

Nightingale asks whether they know what kind of animal, but I say that takes longer. Establishing an animal's genotype is still tricky, even with faster machines and bigger databases.

"Where was the first place you encountered the leopard?" Nightingale asks Ione. He's playing it casual, not even looking at her. Instead he's scanning the trees as if checking for clues.

I'm standing close enough to Ione to feel her stiffen, and she hesitates.

Nightingale waits—he's good at waiting. He once told me that the most important thing he's learned in his long life is how to wait. Mind you, he can wait in lots of different ways—this is the way that says, *I'm so old and patient, I can do this all day.*

"I'd have to check my phone to be sure," says Ione, pointing. "But I think over there—a couple of miles."

"By accident?" he asks, and his tone is vexing me because he's being suspicious of Ione and I don't like that. But a part of me that isn't thinking with my hormones is also wondering—*Yeah, what were you doing jamming in the woods just so you could meet Ms. Melanistic Leopard?* She looks at me and maybe she sees some of that on my face, because she sighs.

"I heard rumors that somebody had brought in a stranger to do some work," she says.

"A stranger?"

"Aye," she says. "But 'stranger' is a wide word among the families. It could mean from anywhere. Plenty of strangers bide up the road in Ellon."

"What kind of work?" asks Nightingale.

Ione's obviously decided that we're on the same side, because she admits that her uncle Atlas is involved in some way—although she doesn't know how or how deeply. She thinks all the old families are involved, from somewhere called Fittie to the Broch—which I remember is the other name for Fraserburgh.

"With my family there's always a scheme," she says with a bit of pride. "We're famous for it. But I didn't like the smell of this one. Fiddling quotas, poaching and moonshining is one thing. But breaking older laws than that . . . old alliances."

"Alliances with whom?" asks Nightingale.

"I've never met them," she says. "Part of the old laws is we don't mix. But there's supposed to be people living in the sea."

"People that can breathe under water?" I say, thinking about Aquaman, the fish man who had gills and an extra layer of subcutaneous fat.

"I've never met them, or even seen one," she says.

"And yet there was an alliance?" says Nightingale.

"More of a ceasefire," says Ione. "If you listen to the old stories."

Nightingale looks at me and raises an eyebrow. He wants *me* to listen to those old stories. Then he says he's going to do a sweep of the perimeter and strides off, leaving me alone and with no excuses not to ask a difficult question.

"Quick," I say. "Before he comes back. Do you know a woman called Calliste, lives in Newbury?"

Ione frowns and actually looks both ways before leaning down so she can whisper.

"Do you mean Newburgh?" she asks.

"Yeah," I whisper back. "Is that important?"

"What about her?"

Nightingale is far enough away that I could probably talk normally, but I like having Ione's lips this close to mine. She smells of the sea and the wind among the grass, and I can hear the crash of waves against the stones. I'm trying not to get distracted but, oh my days, it's bare hard. I concentrate and tell her about Calliste, who works for FPXPLORE, who are definitely involved in something—even if we don't know what.

"We?" she says, straightening up. "You keep saying 'we' like you're police, too. Like him." She jerks her chin in the direction Nightingale has taken. "Is that so? Are you undercover?"

"Nah," I say, because I reckon a bit of swagger is called for. "Like I said, I'm a wizard."

And because she gives me a proper *Yeah, right* look, I conjure a werelight right in front of her face. Which I probably shouldn't have done, but it's worth it to see Ione standing with her mouth hanging open. Then she smiles.

To be honest, I'm expecting her to tell me her secret in return, but sometimes life doesn't work like on TV and she says nothing. Just takes my other hand. I puff out the werelight with a little flourish that two out of three of my teachers say is an unnecessary affectation. Well, one of them says affectation—the other says it's showing off.

"I thought you were full of secrets," she says. "Still doesn't say why this is any of your business."

"It's wrong, innit?" I say. "It's a problem, and who else are you going to call?"

"So it's not because you want to help me?"

"Why not both?"

She lets go of my hand, which is disappointing, but I'm bare stoic about disappointment. Or maybe dense—we're still waiting on the phone vote for that. I make myself not fold my arms.

She gives me a long look, which I give back, and her lips twitch and a little thrill goes through me because we're there. I know it.

"We could always ask her grunny," she says.

"Will she know what's going on?"

"Definitely, she knows aathing about aabody."

"Then why haven't you asked her about our panther?"

"There was no way I was going to visit Aunty Clio on my own," says Ione. "She's frichtsome."

"But you're willing to ask her now?"

"Ah," she says and takes my hand again. "I'm with a mighty and cunning wizard—am I not?"

Cunning, yes, I think. Mighty is off playing big game hunter somewhere to our west.

I text Nightingale—*Following lead, Newberg.*

I ride down to Newburgh on the back of the pink scooter, with my arms wrapped around Ione and the landscape rolling up and down around us. We cross a causeway across a flat expanse of glittering water, and Ione starts a humming so deep that I feel it through my arms. Like I'm hugging a subwoofer and the tune is Janelle Monáe singing "Make Me Feel," vibrating up the bones in my arm, shoulders and neck until it rings the small bones in my ears.

Ahead there is a cluster of white houses with purple roofs by the water, and we pass a warning sign with a silhouette of a duck in a red triangle, then a housing estate with that new car smell. We scoot past the new houses and after them, old new houses, and then old stone bungalows before turning left out onto an isthmus with more houses, a graveyard and something that looks like a small factory, until we reach the end of the road. There, surrounded on three sides by water, sits an old stone two-story cottage with a sign above the door that just reads *THE SEA*.

We pull up outside and I follow Ione to a front door windbleached to gray-blue. She knocks, we wait, and a wind is blowing up the estuary making me cold enough that I'm thinking that Ione wouldn't mind me grabbing her round the waist again—for the warmth, of course.

The door is opened by a teen boy, maybe sixteen or seventeen, with curly black hair, a sharp nose and a sulky mouth. He's wearing a black T-shirt with a picture of a werewolf baying at the moon on the front. He doesn't seem hyped to see us, especially when Ione calls him Ponty.

"Don't call me that," says Ponty. "You know I don't answer to that."

"You prefer Pontus," says Ione, and then to me, "God of the sea, father of all life in the water."

"What—even the whales?" I ask.

"Duncan," he says. "You can call me Duncan."

"OK, Duncan," says Ione. "Is your grunny in?"

"'Course," says definitely Duncan. "Where else would she be?"

He leads us into a house full of stuff, every centimeter of the walls covered in photographs and muddy paintings of moors and sad-looking cows. Ione kicks off her trainers, so I follow suit. The hallway has thick purple carpet which clutches at my toes.

Duncan scampers ahead of us.

"Gran," he calls. "Ione is here with a wee stranger."

We are sitting in a room full of memories. Windows look out across the estuary to the lumpy green moors beyond; there's a door back to the hallway and every other wall is covered in framed photographs. They start a meter up and stop half a meter short of the ceiling, and come in any kind of frame and size. Some are bare ancient, showing men in caps and jumpers standing by boats, some are clearly modern prints of young women in little black dresses or bridesmaid outfits. One frame, close by the old lady's chair, is a digital display on which an endless number of toddlers and pink and white babies appear. I keep my eye on it and I swear it doesn't repeat itself once.

The Old Lady is sitting in her armchair like everybody's favorite nan, if you thought your nan was tall and thin and terrifying. I'm sitting on the sofa opposite, next to Ione, and trying not to grab her hand for comfort. Ione introduced me as "my friend Abigail from London" and I don't know what the Old Lady thinks that means. Friend or "friend" or "whatever."

Ione introduced the Old Lady as Aunty Clio, but she's staying the Old Lady to me—complete with caps. Peter's going to be bare vexed with me when he knows I'm having tea with a power like this.

And the tea is being served by a thin clumsy white girl with long purple hair, which don't go with her cherry-red lips or the blue T-shirt with a picture of Tom Hiddleston on the front and printed with the words *I am burdened with glorious purpose*. We're getting delicate blue and white cups and saucers and, real talk, there's no way I'm drinking nothing until I get some assurances first.

The girl with purple hair is introduced as Polly, short for Polynoe, which I'm guessing is another Greek nymph. Which is a puzzle . . . Calliste, Ione, Clio, Pontus, Polynoe? Why Greek? Why not Celtic or Nordic?

"She's an affa bright lassie," says the Old Lady. "We're hoping to send her off to Norway."

Ione asks about a bunch of other people—sons, daughters and grandchildren. Some of them with nymph names, too, but the rest all named out of the big book of Scottish baby names. My tea is getting cold when Ione asks after Calliste.

"Working in Aberdeen," says the Old Lady. "Working for some exploration company."

"Offshore, then?" asks Ione.

"In an office, thank God. Your uncle Atlas fixed it for her and she's making good money, too. Na like her poor da," she says. "The rigs were the death of him." She stops suddenly, and there is pain on her face. She sees me looking and turns away. "My glaikit dother wint toot searching for him and nivver came back."

"When has Uncle Atlas been cozy with the oil industry?" asks Ione.

"He isn't," says the Old Lady. "But he thinks he has an in with those indy eejits at the Executive. Independence, fah! Fools."

I'm surprised. Online, anyone even vaguely Scottish, even if they're from Texas, is dead keen on independence. I thought it would be the same in Scotland, so I've been careful not to bring the subject up—not even with the foxes. Definitely not with Ione, for obvious reasons. People can get funny about these things.

"So you're not in favor, then?" I ask, and Ione sighs.

Oh, shit, I think, now I've done it.

"Independence," says the Old Lady. "Those fools in Edinburgh think they can talk themselves into independence. They have no idea who they're dealing with." She flings up her arm and points to a point on the wall behind her. "Not while she's in charge."

I look where she's pointing, and there's a framed black-and-white photograph of a young white woman in an army forage cap. It looks like a professional studio shot and the woman is posed, staring out at the camera, doing her best to look dignified but she looks distracted to me—like she's thinking about something else. She seems familiar, and I'm wondering whether she's like some old-time film star.

STONE AND SKY   191

"Who's that?" I ask, and the Old Lady chuckles.

"Don't you know your own sovereign?" she asks.

"That's the Queen?" I say, and this gets another laugh. It's good to know I'm so funny. But I do recognize her now—the Queen from all the way back, from Nightingale's war. Yeah, we did this in school and even Miss Redmayne was OK with Princess Elizabeth doing her bit.

I say OK and that I see it now, and the Old Lady turns and stares me in the eyes. They're bright blue, the pupils big, and behind them the long slow sad song of sea, of ships and men lost, of wives waiting, of dreams foundering on the rocks.

"But you don't see it," she says. "That's not her true face."

I'm going to say that, well, yeah, it's definitely a PR glamour pic, and in any case HRH is like ninety or something now. But the look in the Old Lady's face stops me.

"She's had many faces and goes by many names," she said. "Matilda, Mary, Elizabeth, Anne, Victoria. But they are all Gloriana, queen of the unspoken court and one of the true rulers of the world."

She pauses, like she's waiting for me to say something, but I'm thinking about that time in Wales that I ain't ready to talk about. I don't think the fae I met back then think Queen Liz rules them. Still, one thing's for certain. The fae lie like a bunch of boys in a Relationship and Sex Education class. So who knows?

"You know something of the mysteries," says the Old Lady, obviously having got bored waiting for me to answer. "I can smell it on you, and see it from your rudeness." She glances down at the tea I haven't touched. "You have a master—yes?"

"I have teachers," I say, because obviously I'm not a dog or a Jedi.

This surprises the Old Lady, who cocks her head to one side and stares at me hard. I think she thinks I'm lying, so I stare back to show that I'm not. She gives me a small smile and nods.

"Faerie-touched, too," she says. "But not by her, thank God. Still, we all do her bidding in the end."

I think she's talking about the Queen, who my mum thinks walks on water.

"Someone is summoning monsters," I say. "They need to be stopped."

"If only for the sake of the monsters, aye?" says the Old Lady. She waves an airy hand at the door. "Ask Pontus—he'll know."

Definitely-Duncan-not-Pontus's room is reassuringly normal. If it wasn't for the view of the sea from the single dormer window, we could be in the lair of any teenaged boy from Hackney to Chester. That includes the random underwear, festering plates, mugs and that smell. Even Paul had that smell, although it was mixed in with disinfectant and orange blossom air freshener.

He's got a ninja PC, though. But instead of FPS mayhem, he's playing a strange puzzle game set on a sailing ship that plays out in a series of static monochrome pictures. It looks like something Molly might like, but before I can ask what it's called, Ione accuses Duncan of letting his nan on the internet.

"You knows she gets ideas," she says.

I sit down on the bed, because it's covered in a tartan blanket and so should be safe—germ-wise. Ione sits next to me; the bed sags a bit under our weight.

"Oh, you got her going about the Queen, didn't you?" he says.

"You've let her on to the chat rooms, haven't you?"

"Don't be stupid," says Duncan. "She still thinks I cycle over to Tesco's with a shopping list."

"So what's with the Queen?"

"Ah, they all believe that," says Duncan. "A' the al wifies. That's fit they tak aboot fan they come for tea. I bet your ma thinks it's true."

"That the Queen is an immortal fae who secretly rules the world?" asks Ione.

"You'd think Charlie would use some of that magic to grow his hair back," I say, which gets a grin from Duncan. He swivels away from his PC and faces us straight.

"It might even be true," he says. "Who knows for sure?"

"Does Uncle Atlas believe it?" asks Ione, and Duncan goes bare quiet. "Does he?"

"Uncle Atlas does what he does and believes whatever suits him best," says Duncan, which sounds like a quote to me.

"Do you know what he's done this time?" asks Ione.

"Not him," says Duncan. "FPXPLORE. They brought in a cunning man to summon up beasts and the like."

"What kind of beasts?" asks Ione.

"Your wee pussycat, for one. I don't know about anything else for sure." He nods at his PC. "There's sites where people talk about these things, but you can't believe everything you read. They talk about birds and dragons. Like the one in London."

"It was a wyvern," I say.

"That's not what they say," says Duncan, nodding at the PC again. Like people on the internet are the last word on anything.

"How do you know?" asks Ione.

"I was there," I say. "Def a wyvern—two legs, not four."

So I had to tell them about how I was at the Winter Wonderland in Hyde Park when a wyvern snatched some woman's dog right off a ride. Which served her right, really, 'cause she shouldn't have been carrying her dog on that ride anyway.

"It was on YouTube," I say.

"I saw that," says Duncan. "I thought it looked well fake."

"I know the people that caught it," I say. "But that's not the point, is it? Do you know who the Isaacs are?"

"No," says Duncan.

"They're the magic Feds," I say. "The ones that caught that wyvern. They're already up here because of the panther, and it won't be long before they're knocking on your nan's door asking questions."

Duncan, teenaged boy, sticks his chest out and says he'd like to see them try.

"No, ye widna," says Ione quietly. "Trust me, Duncan, ya dinna want your grunny mixed up in this."

"But Aunty Callie?" says Duncan.

"Calliste can look after herself," says Ione. "If Abi and I handle this, the Isaacs will be none the wiser."

"Why are they called the Isaacs?" asks Duncan.

"Help us and I'll give you the whole story," I say.

"Fit maks ye think I ken onything av a'?"

"Oh, please," says Ione. "You're famous as the nosiest loon in the families."

"OK," he says. "But you keep Aunty Callie and Grunny oot a this."

"As far as we can," I say, because while I've been known to lie when I have to, Nightingale says I shouldn't make a habit of it. In the long run, he says, it's always easier to tell the truth. And he should know about the long run—right?

Anyway, honesty is the best policy with Duncan, because he says that he reckons the person we're looking for has a caravan off Rattray Point. When Ione asks how he knows this, he grins.

"Because they rented it off my mate Stuart's da, and he said the man had filled it up with candles and sheep skulls and the like," says Duncan.

"That's it?" asks Ione.

"And me and Stu cycled over to have a look and he was out on the beach drawing pentagrams in the sand," says Duncan. "And when we went to have a wee look in the caravan, this monster gull swooped down and tried to take my head off."

That was enough for Dunc and Stu—they were off as fast as they could pedal.

The gull was enough for me, too, so we make our goodbyes to Duncan, but as we step outside, a black Toyota SUV pulls up in front of the house.

"Shit," says Ione. "It's my uncle. Stay quiet and look pretty."

"Pretty I can do," I say. "But I'm not famous for quiet."

Ione shushes me as a man unfolds himself from the backseat. I recognize the punchbag face and the pork-pie hat. The sense of solidity is less in the daylight, but enough remains to make me think that maybe shutting up is not a bad idea.

"Ione," he says. "Visiting your grunny?"

"Aye."

Uncle Atlas looks at me and it's like the Old Lady, except with the weight of the sea behind it and the wide sky and shoals of silver fish racing through the water. I make myself look stunned, because powers like this like to know they're having an effect.

"Fa's this?" he asks.

"This is Abigail, up from London for the summer," says Ione. "This is my Uncle Atlas."

"Pleased to meet you," I say.

"Likewise," he says, and then to Ione, "How's she deein?"

"She's fine," says Ione. "You know. Still ga'n on aboot the Queen."

Uncle Atlas's lips twitch and he looks from Ione to me.

"It's good to have a hobby," he says. "Far are ye awa tae noo?"

"Peterhead," says Ione. "I'm going to introduce Abigail to the Dolphin."

Uncle Atlas nods.

"The superior fish supper," he says. "Bon appétit."

Then he turns and heads for the house. Duncan has the door open before he even reaches it.

When I climb onto the moped behind Ione I can feel her trembling.

"That was close," she whispers.

"What now?"

Ione takes a deep breath, lets it out slowly, the trembling stops.

"Fish supper," she says.

So we stop at a place called the Dolphin in Peterhead for fish supper, which is really fish and chips—and which I have to pay for, by the way. I decide that Peter's def going to reimburse me for expenses.

But, swear down, it is the best fish and chips I've ever had.

"They get it fresh off the boat," says Ione.

Then we scoot northward until the landscape is flatter than a pancake and the roads are straight and narrow. Then there's this box-shaped white building on a mound, and stuck between it and these high dunes is a car park. I'm remembering that Bev and Peter came here with the twins and didn't notice nothing, so maybe definitely-Duncan is shitting us. But then I see the caravan.

The car park is deserted but for a couple of battered hatchbacks, both with roof racks.

"Windsurfers," says Ione.

We leave the scooter on the road and head for the caravan. It's silver and white and modern and expensive-looking, with a rounded nose. It looks unscuffed and brand-new and has the word *Buccaneer* in embossed letters beside the door. We walk around it, peering in through the tinted windows. The bedroom end is properly neat and tidy, with the bed made up and an absence of clothes hanging on door handles, et cetera. The living room bit at the other end is almost as neat, but covered in books and stacks of papers. It looks like the study at the Folly when I've been looking stuff up.

No sign of candles or sheep's skulls, though.

We circle back around to the door and I rest my hand on the handle. There's a tingle, faint, a whisper of insects and smell of stale water. It's enough—I snatch my hand back.

I draw Ione away and she asks what's wrong.

"The door might be booby-trapped," I say.

I'm thinking about calling Peter, but I'm not sure I want to get Ione mixed up with the Feds unless I have to. I call Nightingale, because while technically he's a Fed he's not always on duty, like Peter. His phone goes straight to voicemail—which ain't unusual if he's working, doing magic, or has forgotten to turn it back on.

We check the windows again but they're all closed and locked. Then Ione points through the front window at the living room skylight.

"Does that look unlatched to you?" she says.

It does, and Ione boosts me up onto the roof. Now, I'm small and I've been skinny since I can remember. But she just puts her hands around my waist and up I go. High enough to scramble onto the roof and check the skylights. There are three, but only the front one is unlocked. Looking down, I can see the books and the empty coffee mug. Also a notepad with scribbles.

I try the skylight and it comes up a bit, but stops. It's got a restrictor. I'm feeling around to see if I can unlatch it from the outside when I hear Ione swear. She's running back toward where we left the moped.

Which isn't there.

Ione stops and looks left and right, and then back at me.

"Some fucker's stolen my bike," she shouts. "See if you can spot them."

I jump up, which is a mistake; the roof is smooth and the caravan rocks a bit. I check my balance and look around. Up here I can just see over the dunes to the sea and the lighthouse, and I think I see a reflected flash from a high window. Behind me is the square white building with its walled enclosure, but no sign of any wasteman on a stolen moped. I look back toward Ione, who is still swearing, and spot a flash of pink among the dune grass a hundred meters away.

I point and shout and Ione runs off to look.

Sunlight flashes off the top of the lighthouse; it's very quiet and I get this booky feeling. I do a full 360, but all I can see are the shadows of the clouds racing across the fields.

I realize what's wrong.

There's no gulls.

They've been crowding us all up the coast, and now they're nowhere to be seen.

Ione has reached the moped and is swearing again, her voice small and snatched away by the wind.

I hear a noise. I try to turn, but something hard smashes into my back and thighs. I go flying off the caravan roof. I get that slow-motion sick feeling when you see the inevitable rushing up to meet you.

Only the ground is going in the wrong direction.

I can hear Ione screaming far away.

Things start to make sense and I wish they didn't.

There's a sound like sails flapping slowly in the wind. When I grab the band around my chest, it's rough like bark but hot like skin. I don't want to look, but I do—there's the neck outstretched like a goose in flight, the head, the jaws, the teeth. The smell like the inside of an overheated handbag.

It's a fucking wyvern.

I'm more dead than a bag full of VHS tapes.

I can't help notice that it's laboring a bit, trying to climb.

Last time we met a wyvern, we all agreed that the bloody things shouldn't be able to fly. Their bones might be hollow and their metabolism amazing, but physics hates them and biology only gets you so far.

We reckon magic keeps them airborne, but fuck knows where it's coming from.

I look down—mistake.

The sea is way too far away, we're higher than the lighthouse. I grab the claw that's holding me. *Don't let go.* I may have screamed that last bit.

OK, I think. If it was going to eat me straight away, I'd be in bits by now. Maybe it's taking me somewhere, hopefully not to a nest full of bitey things. But down, even with bitey things, would be better than high up. Once I'm down I've got resources—magic, fists, guts . . . Let's not think about guts. I'm feisty, that's me. Ask my teachers. You just put me down, sunshine—gal den fuck you up. See if I don't.

I'm just getting some confidence back when the fucking thing disappears. Pops out of existence the same way the melanistic leopard did—although this close, I feel the air rushing in to fill the vacuum.

Then I'm falling.

15

How Abigail Came to Fall So Hard

I'VE GOT A friend called Simon who literally doesn't know the meaning of fear. I'm using the word "literally" literally here 'cause he's never afraid—at least not for himself. He worries about other people, obviously.

Right now he's in Pakistan climbing Nanga Parbat, which ironically means he's at a higher altitude than I am, but unlike me, he probably got a plan for getting down again safely.

Not that he's going to be worried about that.

When I asked why this particular mountain, he said because it was beautiful, and when I asked why he wanted to climb it, he said because it was beautiful—and difficult.

Anyway, a brain like that only thinks in possibilities of survival, don't it? But not being stupid exactly, Simon knows it's best to be prepared. So he makes a list—what to do in every emergency situation. Like . . . meet a bull, back slowly away; meet a vampire, make a sign of the Cross; meet a werewolf, shoot it with a silver bullet—which is just rude, actually. Werewolves are good fun when you get to know them. He's right about the bull, but if you meet a vampire you better be running, because unless you've got a flamethrower you're dead meat.

On that list was things to do if you fall out of an airplane without a parachute. The following advice is . . . reduce terminal velocity as far as you can and aim for a slope, the steeper the better. Trees and bushes will help, and deep snow even more.

"There was this guy," Simon said. "Jumped out of a bomber

without a parachute at five thousand meters, hit small trees, then snow on a slope, and walked away with a sprained ankle."

And then I had to explain how all that reduced the rate of deacceleration. As they say, it's not the falling, it's the sudden stop that kills you. The longer you take stopping, the more chance you will finish up still breathing.

So my big problem right now is that I'm falling into the wide flat sea, def no slopes or trees or snow, and past a certain velocity, water might as well be concrete.

The average terminal velocity of a human body is about 190 kph, which you reach in about twelve seconds. So there's the good news. I'm too low. I'm not even going to reach terminal velocity before I hit the water. Yay for me.

Part of me that's not doing the math is screaming.

Actually, it's most of me.

But enough of me lives in the same cool happy place as Simon's brain. And it's thinking of a spell that might just save my life. It's got a Latin name, but people have been calling it *feather fall* since forever. Peter says it's a terrible name because you def don't fall like a feather, but you *can* stop yourself going splat.

If you're lucky and you get the timing right.

It thickens the air beneath you so that you slow before you hit the ground. It needs a surface to work on, so you can't float down. And without a physical boundary, the cushion effect dissipates bare quickly.

Nature doesn't just abhor a vacuum, she also likes to keep things nice and even.

Peter says he used it to soft-land a helicopter once, but I'm skeptical.

However, it's one of the four safety spells that Peter insists every apprentice has to learn. And I was the guinea pig selected to refine the spell. We did it up the Thames at Kingston Bridge, and Beverley was on hand to be lifeguard. Took me thirty jumps to get it right, another thirty to get it consistent. We used a laser rangefinder to log the results.

The screaming part of my brain is screaming that that was less than a ten-meter drop. And I couldn't have been going more than 26 kph then. And there's no way I'm going to get the timing right.

And a treacherous part of me, that lives in the hole where my brother once was, is saying that maybe I should just not, you know, try, at all...

Obviously it works, since I'm chatting about it, but not quite in the way I was expecting.

The waves rush up to meet me and I get the timing wrong.

Too late, the useless part of my brain screams.

The air is catching at my arms, legs and face, but too late. Here comes blue death.

Only suddenly there's a hole in the water below me, and into it I drop. I get my arms over my face before I hit the bottom, which is just as well because I'm still falling fast enough for it to hurt.

My ears pop as the sea crashes back into the hole, and the screaming part of my brain starts up again because now it thinks we're going to drown. But I did swimming classes in primary and got a Level 3 Water Safety certificate for not drowning in my pajamas. The trick is not to panic, get disorientated and swim downward. You're supposed to relax and let yourself float upward while shedding your shoes and any other heavy items of clothing.

At first I don't get a chance to panic. I'm freezing. The cold is squeezing me and I have to clamp down to stop myself breathing out. Doing magic is about control, and I reckon that saves me because I keep my breath in, and suddenly my face is out of the water. Then I sort of panic trying to keep my face up while kicking off my trainers. I swallow water, spit, breathe, sink, thrash, break surface—it's not going well. My right trainer is refusing to come off and I can feel my jeans dragging at my legs.

Kick, surface, breathe. I lose the trainer and, bonus, the sock with it. I unbutton my jeans. My fingers are numb and freezing and a wave swamps me. I'm supposed to get my legs up and float on my back. But my legs are too heavy, and when I try and lean back I get a face full of water. I'm sinking backward. I can see the blue sky through the rippling surface and it's not fair. I survived a fall from a killing height, but now I'm going to drown because I can't get my fucking jeans off.

I'm sculling with my arms but the surface is just as far away. Some wasteman giant has their arm around my chest and is squeezing it. My body is betraying me like it's desperate to give me a quick taste of Paul's final years before I go wherever he did.

And that tiny evil voice whispers—*You could of looked harder for a cure, this is what you deserve.*

Then I hear someone calling my name and the flickering sky is eclipsed by a face. Arms enfold me, the water rushes past, and I am in the sunlight, breathing air, and the face and the arms are Ione's.

"Are you OK?" she asks, but I can only nod and breathe and think how beautiful her face is.

My brain starts to work again and I realize she's floating on her back, holding me half out of the water. We are well past the lighthouse, the beach is out of sight and the dunes a green smear across the horizon. Ione is topless, which is sensible, because she has swum to rescue me. But such a long way? I put my arms around her and she pulls me close. I feel something that is not legs pressing against mine. I'm thinking she's wearing a long skirt, which is seriously weird. But not as weird as when I reach down to touch her thigh and feel scales.

Now, I don't handle fresh fish much, so I don't know if what I'm touching is fish scales. But it definitely ain't human skin. I feel it undulate between my legs and we zoom back toward the beach like she's got an outboard motor attached to her backside. I give it a feel, just to make sure, and it feels like metal scales, only soft and warm. And underneath is the most muscle.

"Stop that," says Ione. "That tickles."

"Fuck me, you're a mermaid," I say, and she laughs.

"What gave it away?" she says.

She's swimming on her back to keep my head above water. I'm twisting my head to look at the sky, because I'm thinking maybe the big motherfucking wyvern is planning a comeback. I can't see it, but I didn't see it coming the last time either.

"How fast can you swim?" I ask.

"How long can you hold your breath?"

"About a minute."

"Then hold on."

I wrap my legs around her hips and my arms around her neck. She puts her arms around my waist and holds me tight.

"Deep breath," she says.

I take a breath and then she rolls over and we're under water. Freezing water is rushing past my head and pulling at my T-shirt; the muscles in Ione's tail pulse and shift beneath my thighs. Just like the horse, only I didn't want to kiss the horse as badly as I want to kiss Ione now.

Is this what it's like for Bev and Peter?

I feel her tail surging between my legs and we fly out of the water, breaching like a dolphin. Sunlight, spray, a breath, and Ione twisting so that she takes most of the blow when we hit the surface.

We breach again, and this time I'm ready and take a deeper breath. I'm squinting so I can see when we're under water. And so I see the beach shelving beneath us before Ione makes a half breach that sends us sliding up to the water's edge.

We are lying in the surf, kissing and getting wet sand ground into our crevices. Ione lets me kiss from her bare neck down to her navel. She's kept her tail on, and I kiss down to where the scales meet the skin. There's a seam, a raised ridge of silver that hugs her hips and dips down at the front. As if she's wearing one of the fake mermaid swimsuits . . . only when I run fingers down the front, there's no dip between her legs—it's all solid muscle.

I run my tongue along the seam, probing to see if there's a gap, and she gasps, the muscles in her stomach twitching. I'm wondering whether she's sensitive in the same place when she isn't wearing her tail. I let my tongue trace down her scales.

"What does that feel like?" I ask.

"You really don't care, do you?" she says, her voice far away.

"I don't lips every mermaid I meet," I say, and kiss my way back up. Belly button, left nipple, right nipple, neck—lips.

"How does it work?" I ask.

She puts her hand on the seam where her tail meets her hip and hesitates.

"I don't normally do this in front of other people," she says.

I say nothing 'cause I'm bare prang I'll say the wrong thing.

She grabs the seam with her hand and pulls her tail open to reveal her bare legs. It happens so fast it makes my eyes water. Now there are legs where there was a fish's tail, and the scaly skin has become a shimmering silver shawl. Ione lifts her hips so she can pull the shawl out from under her bum and, swear down, there's no way there's enough of it to cover her legs all the way down to the bottom.

She rolls it up like it's a beach towel.

"What is that?" I ask.

"It's my secret," she says. "Passed down to me by my grunny."

I run my hand down her thigh to see if her skin feels different, but a wave breaks over my head and reminds me that the water is cold.

"Can we go somewhere?" I ask.

"Are you usually this pushy?"

"No," I say, and stop myself from saying something lame. "But can we go somewhere?"

Another wave hits us, and we stand up and walk hand in hand up the beach.

"Like where?" she asks, and my heart turns over.

"My tent?"

We walk on to where Ione says she left her bag tucked into a hollow in the dunes. Her clothes are piled messily on top, and she has to shake out the sand that's drifted into them. I ask if her phone is still working and when she says it is, I borrow it to bell Peter.

When you practice magic you learn to memorize people's digits.

I tell him about the caravan and the wyvern, but leave out the whole bit about being dropped from altitude. I'm going to tell Simon when he gets home from Pakistan, but Peter and Nightingale . . . never going to know, bruv. Ignorance is bliss and all that. Peter's going to organize a Fed mobile to come and secure the area, so I tell Ione that we might want to shift unless we want to be secured with it.

"Can't," she says, and takes me to where the pink moped waits. It's got some dents and a flat front tire.

I borrow her phone again and call Bev. I tell her to bring a trailer for the moped, then we wait. It's warm; the sun is out but we have to shelter in the dunes from the wind. I start to shiver. Ione puts her arms around me.

Beverley arrives before the Feds, so that's one less thing to worry about.

"Hello," says Beverley, looking Ione up and down. "You must be Ione."

"Yes, ma'am," she says, and then, to me, "Should I curtsy?"

She's taking the piss, I think. At least I hope so.

"There's no need for formality," says Beverley. "You can call me Bev."

She's borrowed a motorbike trailer from a garage near Brian's house and we'll drop Ione's moped off for repairs on our way back.

"What happened?" asks Bev, examining the dents.

I think the wyvern picked it up and then dropped it, but I tell Bev that we didn't see. Which is true. And Bev's a scientist—you don't want to be giving her false information.

I climb into the back of the Asbo with Ione and we hold hands, out of sight.

Beverley calls Peter and tells him that she's got me.

She turns in her seat to look at us, clocks we're holding hands. She looks at Ione and narrows her eyes.

"Did you save her?" she asks.

"Yes," says Ione.

"Did you show her?" asks Bev.

"Yes, she did," I say, because Ione is blushing.

"How did you know?" asks Ione.

"I can smell the sea," says Bev. "And I know the songs, although you were just a rumor until now."

"Shouldn't we be getting back?" I say. "I want some dry clothes."

Bev nods, starts the car, and as we drive off starts singing the opening lines to "Summer Nights," which I only know because my mum had a thing for John Travolta when she was seven and used to sing it in the bath.

"Bev," I plead, but we drive back to Mintlaw with Beverley playing embarrassing older sister the whole fucking way.

Indigo ambushes me, leaping into my arms as soon as I'm out of the Asbo.

"You're alive," she says, and sticks her snout into the hollow of my neck. "Why are you wet?"

"I went for a swim," I say.

Indigo squirms, being hyper even for Indigo.

"I was worried," she says, and, swear down, she sounds a bit guilty.

Ione has her hand over her mouth to hide her smile.

"I need to change," I say, and lurch toward my tent.

I'm wondering how to ditch Indigo when Beverley calls her name.

"I have a reward for you," she says.

Indigo immediately twists in my arms.

"What kind of a reward?" she asks.

"That's a secret," says Bev.

Indigo leaps down and scampers over.

"What kind of secret?" she asks.

"The top secret kind," says Bev, and winks at me.

I grab Ione and drag her to my tent.

"That fox is in love with you, you know," says Ione.

I'm so excited I fumble the zip on the tent door. I crawl inside feeling clumsy and stupid.

"She's not going to steal one of my trainers, is she? Only . . ." Ione stops and looks at me, probably because I'm shaking.

"Hey," she says and takes my hand. "It's OK, you're safe."

But am I? I don't feel safe, I feel like a stupid blonde teenager who's walking down the steps to the basement even though the lights aren't working. I feel small and pathetic and useless.

"I don't want to be . . ." I say, but I can't finish.

Ione zips the tent closed and leans closer so she can whisper.

"What are you afraid of?" she asks.

"I don't know," I say.

"Shall I tell you what I'm afraid of?"

I nod.

"I'm afraid," she says, "that if I spend any more time with you I'll never want anyone else. And when you go back to London, I'll be left sitting on a rock singing sad songs at the sailors."

I giggle stupidly, like a schoolgirl in an anime.

"Sad songs?" I say.

"I could sing you a song that would break your heart," she says, and gently pulls me closer.

"Sing me a song," I say.

So she does, singing very softly so that it's just for me. I don't understand the words, but they sound Swedish or Danish. And the tune is so sad and full of longing that I feel tears running down my face, and I hate to cry but it's like a dam that's reached its limit. I'm still shaking. I want her to stop, but I can't make sentences, words or even sounds.

She stops singing. There are tears on her cheeks.

I kiss her and she kisses me back. Then she helps me out of my wet clothes.

It's still light when I wake up, but I can feel the world turning away from the sun. Which is fine, because I'm warm and happy and sleeping with a mermaid. She sang me a song, and now I'm sharing an unzipped sleeping bag with a woman who swims through the sea like a dolphin. Which reminds me . . . were the fins at the end of her tail horizontal like a whale's, or vertical like a fish's? Ione rolls over to face me, and watching her legs moving under the sleeping bag reminds me that I have questions.

"Where does the extra mass come from?" I ask.

Ione pulls back her head to look at me.

"What?"

"Your tail, right," I say, and she stiffens.

"What about it?" she asks.

"I love your tail, but when I was touching it—it felt like solid muscle."

"That's 'cause I stay in shape," she says, and slips her arm around to stroke my back. But I refuse to be distracted because this is going to bug me until I get some answers.

"The thing is . . ." I say. "The thing is, I reckon your tail has got to have a volume of at least 0.09 cubic meters."

"You just worked that out in your head?"

"I assumed it was a truncated cone with a starting diameter of thirty centimeters, a length of about seventy, and an ending diameter of about ten. I didn't count . . . What's the fin at the end called?"

"Depends. Some call them flukes, some say fins. But it's not something we talk about."

"I can stop if you like," I say, because all my days I've been warned to respect other people's boundaries. Which would be easier if other people knew where their boundaries were.

Ione shakes her head.

"No, I want to know where this is going," she says.

"Your cross-section is actually probably an oval, but that makes it harder to calculate, and it doesn't matter because given that the average density of the human body is 945 kilograms per cubic meter. Your tail masses about eighty kilograms, which I'm guessing is a third more than your legs."

Ione scrunches up her face and then relaxes.

"I'll take your word for it," she says.

"So where does that extra mass in the tail come from?"

"No idea."

"No?"

"Like I said. We don't talk about it," she says. "It's just what we are." She smiles, and her hand cups my bum and she pulls me closer so that I can feel her legs as she slips one between mine.

"Which do you prefer? Legs or tail?"

"Both," I say, and then we're kissing again. But then I have an idea.

"Water," I say.

"What?" says Ione.

"You wrap your magic shawl around your hips, yes?"

"Yes."

"And you get a tail—yes?"

"Yes."

"Can you do it out of the water?"

"Put on the shawl?"

"Yes?"

"Yes," she says. "But the magic only works in the sea."

"You've never tried it in the bath?" I ask. "Or a swimming pool?"

"No and no," she says, and I think she might be getting vexed so I back off.

"Just wondered."

She gives me a long look.

"What are you thinking?"

"Water," I say. "I think the extra mass comes from water."

"I'm in bed with you, all naked and alluring and full of the mystery of the sea, and this is what you're thinking about?"

"It is mysterious," I say.

Water is great, water is heavy, water is dense, and if you know the right *formae* you can shape it and make it dance. And theoretically cut through solid metal, although so far I've only managed a breeze block.

We kiss again, but then Ione's stomach gurgles so loudly it sets mine off. We get dressed, step out into the long evening in search of food, and find Bev and Peter having a row.

16

Dyce

WE'D DONE THE whole Scottish caution and everything, so there was no doubt that James Albright knew he had a right to a solicitor and a right to remain silent, only he didn't ask for a brief and he didn't seem to have the capacity to stay silent. Me and Blinschell had been watching from the observation room while we had a quick coffee. We'd left a uniform in there with him with strict instructions not to open their mouth. Not that a lack of response slowed Mr. Albright down at all.

"You can feel it, right?" he said, gesturing around the interview room. "All the emotions that have seeped into the walls. Places like this are my bread and butter. I didn't know the meaning of history until I found myself in Scotland."

He pronounced Scotland like it was two separate words—Scot Land.

We decided I'd have first crack.

"And here come the English," he said when I entered. "Right on cue."

"Punctuality is the politeness of princes," I said.

James Albright waved vaguely at a seat.

"Have a seat, Your Majesty," he said. "Have you contacted the American embassy yet?"

"That's in train," I said, which wasn't quite a lie. "And we called the FBI."

"Whyever would you want to do that?" he said.

"They like to keep track of their magicians," I said, just to see his reaction.

He snorted and shook his head.

"The FBI," he said. "I wouldn't put my faith in them—especially now the great orange one is in charge."

"You're not a supporter of President Trump?"

Albright actually shut up for a moment, first eyeing the digital interview recorder behind me and then the CCTV camera mounted on the wall.

"He has his moments," he said carefully. "And he will make America great again. Although maybe not in quite the way he imagines."

Something for our American liaison to look into, I decided, and moved on.

Blinschell entered the room and identified himself for the recording. Albright eyed him up with the same cool disdain as he had me.

"So, what brought you to beautiful Aberdeenshire?" asked Blinschell, playing cheerful local cop, because he reckoned that in his experience Americans were suckers for a Scottish accent.

"I came for the hunting and fishing," he said.

"Oh yeah?" I said. "What were you hunting?"

"You mean what was I hunting with?" he said.

He so wanted us to know what he was, so we could be impressed.

"OK—so what were you hunting with?" asked Blinschell—keeping it casual.

"Hunting was probably an exaggeration," said Albright. "It's more akin to hawking. You guys are familiar with hawking, right?"

"That's where you wear a funny hat and get a bird to jizz on your head," said Blinschell, which stunned both Albright and me into temporary silence.

"No," said Albright in a tone that suggested that the avian shagging hat thing had wound him up a bit. "When you train raptors to hunt on command."

Angry can be good. But, for an interview, annoyed and impatient is better. I was going to ask him if he meant that he was like Chris Pratt in *Jurassic World*, but he started talking before I could open my mouth. Which is a pity. I don't often get to demonstrate my erudition within a policing framework.

"I summoned forth eldritch creatures to do my bidding," he said, and smirked.

We took a moment to pretend we were impressed because we wanted to encourage him. Then, to wind him up further, I deliberately didn't ask about the summoning creatures thing.

"You said hunting," I said. "What were you hunting?"

Albright scowled at me for not being a cooperative audience.

"Fish mostly," he said. "Rabbits, foxes, vermin."

"Did you think to apply for permission before summoning these creatures?" I asked.

"I wasn't aware that was necessary," said Albright. "Is there a website I should have checked—an app?"

Not yet, I thought, and made a note in my daybook.

"So these elderly creatures—" said Blinschell.

"Eldritch."

"Sorry . . . eldritch creatures," said Blinschell. "Are you saying they're magical?"

We were hoping he hadn't twigged that we were the magical police despite me getting cocky on the roof earlier. I've been warned about that, but if you can't have the occasional laugh, what's the point of doing the job?

"Isn't that why I'm here?"

"No," I said. "We're detaining you for behavior likely to cause a breach of the peace—to wit, dancing around on the roof of a tower block. Plus we're looking at vandalism charges, but we want to talk to the council first."

"The council?"

"It's their tower block," said Blinschell.

"Do you truly have no conception of the nature of my business," asked Albright.

"Summoning eldritch creatures," I said, and me and Blinschell exchanged smirks.

"With magic," said Blinschell, and waved his fingers like a stage magician.

And with that, Albright popped—just as we hoped he would.

"Yes," he said, leaning forward over the table. "With magic."

"Magic isn't real, Mr. Albright," I said.

Albright sat back and, with a tight smile, held up his hand and conjured a ball of electricity. It was a hollow sphere, formed of crackling blue lines like cartoon lightning and the size of a honeydew melon.

I felt the *formae*; it was a third-order spell at least, and unfamiliar. With it came the smell of ozone, old water and the sense of things gliding under the surface.

"Magic is real," he said, and then hesitated. Something must have given me away because he gave me a hard look and snuffed the spell out. "I see how it is." He folded his arms across his chest. "Very clever."

There was the smell of burning plastic, and I looked over to see that the digital interview recorder was on fire.

"Oh, fuck shit piss bugger," said Blinschell.

We suspended the interview while Blinschell booked us into a second room and informed the custody sergeant that, weirdly, the digital recorder had caught fire—*Jist een o' those things, I suppose*. While he did that, I checked that the interview room's camera hadn't been sanded by Albright's magical display. And then I called the States.

There were the usual clicks and whirrs, and then the call went through.

"Reynolds," said Kimberley. "Is that you, Peter?"

There was a definite in-car ambience.

"It's me," I said. "Sorry, I thought you'd be at your desk."

"I'm in California following up a bank robbery."

"Don't tell me they let you out of the Basement?" The Basement being the FBI's very own department for weird bollocks. If one special agent plus clerical staff plus an analyst on timeshare with the Aviation Support Group counted as a department.

"This is a very special series of bank robberies," she said. "The vaults were emptied without the doors being opened."

"Nice," I said, and asked for details when she was done. "Did you get my e-mail?"

"We looked into James Albright," she said. "I'll e-mail you the details once I'm at a secure terminal. But our preliminary findings are that he's not a professor, although he is accredited with the Light of the World Bible College in San Diego."

I said that Albright hadn't struck me as particularly religious, and Kimberley said her analyst was ninety percent certain that while it had started as a training center for evangelical missionaries, it wasn't teaching theology any more.

"Or at least not proper theology," she said.

I asked what she thought they *were* teaching.

"You might ask your guest," she said.

I promised I would and let her get back to her road trip.

It was getting on by then, and the custody sergeant insisted that the prisoner was fed, although what he made of the microwaved penne pasta Bolognese was anyone's guess. Me and Blinschell pulled rank on one of the DCs and sent them to the canteen for big floury baps full of square sausage, ketchup and grease. Once we were suitably fortified, we sat down with James Albright for the interview part two—electric boogaloo.

"Mr. Albright," I said, once we'd done all the introducing ourselves to the recorder business. "Have you ever summoned a extradimensional gull in or around the Aberdeen Esplanade?"

"What if I have?" asked Albright. The penne Bolognese must have agreed with him because he was definitely more relaxed this time around. "Is that even a felony?"

Which was a good question. Technically, since he was in control of a dangerous non-native animal, he was responsible for and thus liable for any damage they might cause.

"You forget this is Scot Land," I said. "The rules are different here."

"Why do you want to know?" he said, and I thought, Oh, you want to tell me. Practitioners tend to be vain. Even Nightingale likes to do a little flourish when he's casting something fancy.

"I'm not familiar with the technique," I said.

"You mean summoning?" he said, and because he was American, added, "Isn't this the home of the Newtonian Revolution? Isn't that what they call it? I thought you fellas knew everything."

The way he said "fellas" annoyed me, so I thought I'd get straight to the point.

"I've summoned ghosts and *genii locorum*," I said, although the last involved me phoning her up and asking a favor. "Not animals, especially not ones that aren't native to the local ecosystem."

"That's Louisiana for you. They do things differently there."

"Like what?"

"Like summoning kin," he said.

"Kin?"

"That's what my master called them," said Albright. "He liked to pretend he was a Cajun, but I reckon he was from Denver or some such place."

"Really?" I said. "What was his name?"

Albright shook his head.

"No," he said. "I think not."

This is how an interview works. Even the non-answers tell you something. Louisiana, Denver, a master. All points of information that could be sent across the Atlantic, to where Special Agent Kimberley Reynolds was no doubt too busy catching bank robbers to read any of it. But I was sure she would be riveted once she had some free time.

My American geography is a bit vague, but even I was pretty certain that San Diego was in California and a fair whack from Louisiana. So the question was whether Albright had learned his summoning skills from the Light of the World Bible College, or had picked them up in the Deep South first. Kimberley had already identified half a dozen distinct magical societies operating in the continental United States. Not counting all the native American traditions she suspected were being forcibly contained on the reservations.

We'd done *stupid cop* and *oblivious cop*. But when it's time to drill down into the details, nothing beats *relentlessly pedantic cop*. The ultimate weapon in the interviewer's arsenal.

"When you call these summoned creatures 'kin,' what do you mean?" I asked.

"Kin," said Albright. "As in kinfolk, as in people you are related to. Although in this case, the relationship is more metaphysical than genetic. As I was taught, there are correspondences across the veils that lie between worlds." He made a strange fluttering gesture with his hand and then pointed at me. "You can play the dumb flatfoot if you like. But I know you've seen across the veil—I can see it in your eyes. So why don't we just cut the bullshit? What is it you want?"

And because Albright was focused on me, Blinschell asked the next question.

"So what is it you do for FPXPLORE?"

Albright hesitated—he obviously hadn't expected us to make the connection, despite the Range Rover, which tells you all you need to know about amateur criminals.

"Flexplore?" he said, to buy time and choose an answer. "Who are they?" he asked, choosing poorly.

"The company who lease your Range Rover," said Blinschell.

"You mean eff-pee-explore?" he said. "I'm sorry, sometimes I have difficulty with your Scotch accent."

There's a trap you can fall into when interviewing a suspect. You can let your biases cause you to underestimate them. This man was playing the stupid American tourist partly for fun, partly to bait us into making mistakes. But mostly so we wouldn't see how clever he really was.

"Scottish," said Blinschell, but mildly—a friendly correction.

"Noted," he said.

"That's fifty thousand pounds' worth of vehicle," I said. "What services are you providing for FPXPLORE in return?"

"Supernatural security," said Albright. "They were worried that there might be metaphysical incursions on their offshore operations."

"And what were the nature of these incursions?" I asked.

"I'm afraid that that information is covered by commercial confidentiality," he said. "I signed a contract."

Me and Blinschell went a couple of tedious rounds testing that, including that this was Scotland, where the duty to inform the police about potential criminal activity superseded any duty toward his client. He said in that case, he'd take local legal advice before answering.

"Surely you can tell us whether such incursions took place?" I asked.

"None that I was aware of," said Albright. "But it always pays to take precautions."

"These precautions involve summoning eldritch seagulls?" I asked.

"Gulls," said Albright. "The general term for the family is gull."

"Does that include summoning *gulls*?" I asked.

He said it did. They made excellent sentry birds because of

their ability to hover stationary relative to the ground. Their main drawback being that they weren't very bright.

We asked whether they'd been effective against these unspecified "incursions." He said that they hadn't been tested.

"As I believe I already said," he said, "there were no incursions that I was aware of."

"So FPXPLORE weren't exactly getting their money's worth, were they?" said Blinschell.

"These oil companies have cash to burn," said Albright. "They're probably paying me out of their lunch money."

"Just to clarify," I said—which, by the way, if you're ever the wrong side of an interview is a cue for you to shut up and call a solicitor. "In fulfilling your contract with FPXPLORE, did you ever summon anything other than the eldritch gulls?"

"No," said Albright.

I pulled out one of Abigail's photographs from a folder and showed it to Albright. He did his best, but he couldn't hide the flinch.

"Did you summon this melanistic leopard?" I asked.

"No comment," he said.

That was the rest of the interview done. It was no comment to the claw marks in the sides of poor dead Willy the Walrus, but not to the caravan, which he said was part of his remuneration package from FPXPLORE.

"Why Rattray Head?" asked Blinschell.

"Because it's so silent," he said. "Aren't you supposed to provide me with an attorney?"

DCI Mason, as senior investigating officer, wrangled the custody review officer into granting us a twenty-four-hour extension to detain Albright. The US consulate in Edinburgh worked office hours, so we waited until they'd gone home to leave a message with their answering service. We also told them that the charges were not serious, which was unfortunately true, and provided them with Albright's passport number.

"Here's hoping it's a fake passport," said Blinschell, because that would not only piss off the Americans, but also give us access to a ton of draconian immigration laws to keep him banged up pretty much indefinitely.

I did think that the level of response from the consulate would also tell us something about Albright's importance to the US government. That I seriously thought this was a sign that I'd been hanging around with the NCA too much.

Nightingale turned up at the custody suite around seven. He apologized for keeping me waiting, but said that he'd had to help log stuff from James Albright's caravan into evidence.

"I needed to ensure the caravan was safe before the forensic team went in," he said.

I asked whether he'd found anything interesting, and he said he was quite impressed with the haul.

"A large number of books," said Nightingale. "Many of them legitimate works on the craft." Some had been antiques with library stamps from the universities of Philadelphia and Virginia while, much more interestingly, a couple were brand-new. "Printed, according to one of the evidence boys, on demand," he said, and then had to have POD explained to him.

Given the short work magic would make of a Kindle, tablet or phone, you wouldn't want to rely on PDFs for your arcane textbooks.

There had also been a great number of mundane books on the history and folklore of northeast Scotland. Nightingale thought this might be significant.

"It occurs to me," he said, "that he may be using local folklore to locate suitable targets for summoning."

"Like what?" I said. "Weak points between us and other *allokosmoi*."

"Possibly. It would explain his interest in George the bastard's first observatory."

"I haven't run into any local legends about angry seagulls."

"Gulls are ubiquitous on the coasts," said Nightingale. "Panthers are rare this far north. Perhaps he was working the probabilities. Specialized intelligence for the leopard, a general understanding of bird habitats for the other."

"And the wyvern?"

"If we had leverage and time we might be able to ask Mr. Albright for clarification, but alas . . ." Nightingale shrugged.

We didn't have either. The extension deadline meant that unless we could develop an actual case—i.e. one that conformed to

Scottish legal practice—twenty-four hours was all we were going to get.

"There were a couple of things that struck me as out of place," said Nightingale, and he called up some pictures on his phone. They were of maps of some kind, lots of white space and thin lines labeled with incomprehensible strings of letters and numbers. One of the forensic techs had identified them as geological charts of the seabed. There was no need to ask of where, because Nightingale had taken a close-up of a symbol in the middle of nowhere. It was a hollow square with a purple teardrop attached at the top right-hand corner. Beside it was printed—ELGAR BRAVO.

One does not simply fly off to an oil rig. There are safety protocols there that never sleep.

Ultimately it's about insurance. The insurance companies aren't going to be liable for anyone flying out to a rig without their BOSIET certificate. And the oil companies certainly don't want to find themselves legally liable if they negligently let untrained personnel wander around one of the most dangerous workplaces on earth. That's doubly true of the logistics companies that fly the workers out across the perilous North Sea.

But in extremis an officer of the Crown can overrule all these objections, even in Scotland, because should said officer get himself killed or injured in the line of duty, then that will be between him and the Crown.

Well, in my case, the Met. But when push comes to riot shield, that's pretty much the same thing.

"I'll have to go out with you," said Blinschell, and he did not seem happy.

"You don't have to," I said.

"I'm the one with the up-to-date BOSIET certificate and the unambiguous powers of arrest," said Blinschell.

"I thought we were going to be in international waters."

"Don't argue," said Blinschell. "We can't let you go alone, and I'm the only one qualified to go with you."

I was suddenly struck by the memory of all the poor sods that have said that to me at one time or another. Sahra Guleed outside Number One Hyde Park, before we went in to tackle the

Faceless Man—*"If it's all the same to you, sir, I think I'm going to have to see this through*—inshallah." Dominic Croft saying, "*My patch, my village, probably my folklore*," as we waited for a ton of enraged horned equine to turn up and skewer us.

"*If you're going to shoot, then shoot.*"—Miriam Stephanopoulos facing down an armed and desperate Lesley May.

And all the other dumb flatfoots that ran in when they should have run away. Even poor old Phil Purdy, who was a waste of space as a copper except that once, when it cost him his career and his health.

I thought about saying something, but instead I asked whether he could get us on a flight the next morning.

"I'll see what I can do," he said.

I drove back to Mintlaw on autopilot, rehearsing my arguments for the upcoming discussion I was about to have with the light of my life.

Generally, me and Bev try to avoid having rows. Apart from anything else, we have a responsibility to large stretches of southwest London not to do anything that will bring on major flooding. Also, the twins don't like it and get surprisingly kinetic if we get too loud.

Beverley wanted to know why I was putting myself in danger—again. I tried pointing out that this was hardly a portal into a parasitical *allokosmos*, or even the lair of a megalomaniacal techbro.

"This isn't dangerous," I said. "I'm flying out to an oil platform to ask some difficult questions. They're going to be more worried about me turning up than the other way round."

Beverley sighed.

"Is there something else I should be worried about?" I asked.

Beverley shrugged.

"Is this about the giant squid?" I asked, because according to Beverley, a pair of bottlenose whales she'd guided out of the estuary in the spring had confirmed rumors that there was a giant squid living in the North Sea.

Or, more precisely, the bottlenose whales might have confirmed those rumors.

"They're not dogs or cats," she'd said. "They didn't co-evolve alongside *Homo sapiens* so there's an absolute conceptual barrier to communication. I'm saying stuff to them, they're saying stuff to me. But how much of it means what we think it does, beyond 'danger stinky river stay away,' I don't know."

"You called your mum's river stinky?"

"I didn't have the necessary vocabulary for 'navigation hazard.'"

"Are they sentient?"

"Well, they can be really stupid sometimes," Beverley said. "But that doesn't prove anything either way."

"So, is there a giant squid?" I asked.

I thought we were far enough from the tent. But, no, on the word "squid" the twins started shouting random words.

"Banana, hazelnut, squid, squid, squid."

We both marched over to the tent and grabbed a twin each, and that was the end of the row. Or, more precisely, that was the end of the row for the moment.

Aberdeen Airport is the busiest heliport in Europe. They've got loading hung-over oil workers safely on to their helicopters down to a fine art. First, though, you climb into a yellow passenger immersion suit which is supposed to be waterproof, flameproof, NASA-approved and idiot-proof. There were a surprisingly large number of toggles and hooks that Blinschell had to talk me through.

We'd hitched a ride on a Sikorsky S-92 that was flying half-empty to a platform further out and was willing to do a drop off at Elgar Bravo. I've done a couple of flights with NPAS, but this was more like climbing aboard a small plane with forward-facing seats in a two-one configuration. We weren't allowed to carry our carryalls in the cabin, so I spent the first couple of minutes worrying that they'd end up on the wrong platform, or maybe even in Stavanger.

They were about to close the door when Beverley entered the helicopter, clocked me, sat down beside me and strapped herself in. Unlike the rest of us, she hadn't bothered with a survival suit, her one concession being an outsized high-visibility bathing cap to protect her dreads.

"Where are the twins?" I asked.

Bev nodded at Blinschell.

"His boss put me on to one of his sergeants to babysit," said Beverley. "He says she's very reliable, got her own kids."

Before I could say anything else, she held up her hand.

"If we go into the water," she said, "you do nothing, go limp, hold your breath and let me handle everything. Understand?"

I would have kissed her, but it would have been inappropriate.

"Understood," I said, and she shook her head.

"Sometimes I think I can't let you out of my sight."

"The accident rate is less than 0.4 per 100,000 flight hours," I said. "And the weather outlook is clear."

"I, for one, feel safer already," said Blinschell.

17

Elgar Bravo

ONCE WE WERE past the coast and the lazily turning wind turbines, there was nothing to see but the sea. Despite the blue skies, the surface was as humped and jagged as a mountain range and topped by white foam. Blinschell sat with his eyes closed, trying to look calm. Beverley practically climbed into my lap to get a better look out of the window. Which is why she saw the platform first.

"There it is," she shouted, and pointed.

It looked ridiculously tiny—like a movie miniature that was waiting for its close-up, or an unrealistically scaled tidal wave.

And it stayed looking small even as we came into land and dropped the last couple of meters on to the helipad. There we sat for a minute with the rotors still turning until the side door opened and a man in a reflective waistcoat over a fire engine red boiler suit climbed inside. He was a big white man in late middle age, with a sad round face and thinning red hair in wisps. He pulled his ear protectors down around his neck and scowled at us.

As a general rule, the police like to arrive as unexpectedly as possible. That way your target doesn't have a chance to tidy up the living room, stack the dishwasher or stuff anything incriminating into the Aga. Alas, you can't be completely spontaneous when your target is offshore—the best we could manage was to not tell them we were coming until we were in the air.

Still, whatever we were looking for, I doubted it would fit in an Aga.

"Which of you is from the police?" he shouted over the noise of the rotors.

The three of us put our hands up, and if Beverley's unconventional attire surprised him, it didn't show. He beckoned us off and we followed him down into the folding steps and onto the pad.

Unless you're an old hand, you crouch when you step out from a helicopter. Even if you know, intellectually, that the blades are at least a meter above your head, the prospect of sudden decapitation causes you to hunch your shoulders. There were a couple more white men in orange boiler suits with built-in high-viz flashes waiting for us. One of them by our luggage—two nylon carryalls and a blue backpack with a picture of a cheerful cartoon fox on it—and another man by the stairs.

Under the stern mimed guidance of the redhead, we picked up our bags and headed off the helipad. We were led down a steep flight of stairs with metal handrails wrapped in red and white tape. I could smell salt spray in the air, and away from the rotor wash there was a sharp breeze. We descended through a labyrinth of scaffolding until we were through a hatch and into a narrow, brightly lit cream-colored corridor lined with noticeboards and cautionary posters. The hatch closed behind us and our red-headed guide turned to glare at us.

"What the fucking hell is going on?" he said.

Since he was the representative of a proudly independent-minded nation, I let Blinschell do the talking.

"I'm Detective Sergeant Martin Blinschell from the Aberdeen Major Investigation Team," he said, thrusting out a hand which the man reluctantly shook. "This is Detective Sergeant Peter Grant from the Metropolitan Police Special Assessment Unit." I shook the guy's hand as well—he had a firm grip and calluses. "And Beverley Brook, who is acting as a technical consultant."

Beverley smiled, but didn't offer her hand.

The man introduced himself as Rory Carroll, the OIM—aka the offshore installation manager. The top boss. He had the kind of non-specific American accent associated with Canadian actors who have trained themselves out of politeness.

He frowned at Beverley.

"What happened to your safety gear?" he asked.

"I'm wearing it," she said. "It's the latest thing."

"Which brings me back to my original question," said Carroll. "What the fuck's going on?"

"Not in the corridor," said Blinschell.

Carroll led us through a blue and white room with plastic seats and a Perspex-enclosed reception desk, then through a set of fireproof doors with *Administration* on the lintel, down another corridor, and into a small office with a desk, chairs and filing cabinets. On the walls was an empty corkboard and a 2016 wall planner. The desktop was equally bare, but for an old-fashioned corded phone. This was obviously not Carroll's office.

Carroll perched himself on the edge of the desk.

"Where's your specialist?" he asked as me and Blinschell sat down.

Beverley had peeled off before we entered. She'd assured me that her natural glamour was pretty ineffective this far from home, but it's not good policy to have her attend an interview—however informal. People can spontaneously do and say things to please her, regardless of whether it's true or not. This is dangerous—and not just as a temptation, either.

"We're here about Alice MacDuffie," said Blinschell.

There was no disguising the shock on Carroll's face, but he quickly got it under control.

"What about her?" he asked.

"She's missing," I said, and again there was that too-long pause while Carroll sorted through his options. He wanted to deny any knowledge, but he wasn't sure whether that would come across as suspiciously callous.

"I heard something about that," he said.

"Only there's no record of her coming onshore," I said.

Carroll nodded, glanced at the obsolete year planner as if for inspiration.

"As far as I know, she flew back to Dyce," he said.

Usually in an interview the junior-most officer takes the notes. But since me and Blinschell were both sergeants, we'd tossed a coin for it. He lost, so it was his job to make an inarticulate grunt to draw Carroll's attention and then make a long scribble in his notebook.

"Did you see her board the helicopter?" I asked.

"This is a busy platform," said Carroll. "I don't have time to wave everybody good-bye. But trust me, the chopper manifest is sacred *and* it gets sent to Dyce as soon as it leaves."

"Yeah, and chain of custody is sacred, too. But "accidents" happen.

"So you don't know for sure that she left the platform?" said Blinschell.

"Look, even assuming she didn't get on the chopper, there's no way she could have stayed hidden," said Carroll.

"Are you sure?"

"Anything's possible. But to stay hidden she'd have to be actively hiding," said Carroll. "Why would she do that?"

"So you think she went overboard?"

"What?"

"If she's not on the platform and she didn't fly back to Aberdeen," I said, "where else could she be?"

"I think she got on the fucking helicopter," said Carroll.

"I see," I said, and exchanged deliberately meaningful looks with Blinschell.

Carroll opened his mouth to speak, but then thought better of it.

"We're going to have to interview your crew," I said.

"We'll need a roster of everyone on board," said Blinschell. "And somewhere to talk to them."

"This will be a serious disruption," said Carroll. "Are you sure you want to do this?"

"A woman is missing," said Blinschell. "We're here to determine whether there's been a crime or not. If it turns out it was an accident . . ."

Carroll didn't take the bait; Blinschell had said he wouldn't. An accidental death would be worse than a murder—it would be his responsibility, for a start. And, worse than that, the company might be found liable.

Carroll slumped and nodded.

"How about here for the interviews?" he said. "I'll get Phyllis to provide a list."

"Meanwhile, our technical adviser will take a look around the platform," I said.

"Fine," said Carroll. "Whatever."

Phyllis turned out to be Carroll's administrative assistant. A windblown white woman in her late thirties, dressed in an Aran jumper, black cargo pants and boots, she kept her glasses on a lanyard around her neck and her hair wrapped in a red scarf. What with the nose stud and a big pair of gold hoop earrings, she looked like a librarian who'd run off to join the pirates. She even had a bit of a West Country accent. Her lair was down a couple more narrow corridors in an office adjacent to the central control room. Carroll had his own office here, too. We passed several other empty offices on our way there. When I pointed this out to Carroll, he said that they were partly de-manned as the platform wasn't currently operating at full capacity.

Once we'd handed Blinschell over to Phyllis, who didn't look happy about it, Carroll knocked on the door of another nearby office and introduced me to Ryan Griffiths, the platform's production manager. A skinny white Scouser whose accent had that tinge of fake Texan drawl I was beginning to associate with people in the oil industry.

"This one needs a tour," said Carroll. There was definite emphasis on the word "tour"—as in, make sure they don't see nothing that might upset them.

"No problem," said Griffiths. "What do you want to see first?"

"First I need to find my technical adviser."

Who was playing pool in the recreation room with a pair of bulky young white men who were losing badly, but with good grace. The room itself looked like a students' living room, only extended and with better furniture. It certainly had the same smell, but with overtones of diesel, old water and rotten eggs. Like the rest of the platform, it was obviously built for many more people than were currently using it.

We let Beverley finish her frame. Fortunately she never plays for money—because, she says, that would be unethical.

Your modern production platform comes in two bits. The bit where the oil comes up the pipe, is processed and pumped away, and the bit with the accommodation block, the helicopter landing pad and the control room. Theoretically, all the dangerous stuff happens on the satellite platform, so that if it happens to, you know, catch fire, you get a head start for the lifeboats.

Elgar Bravo was not a modern platform, so the accommodation block sat like an enormous stack of Portakabins to one side of the drilling platform, with the helipad perched on top. While Blinschell went off to start interviewing the crew, me and Beverley were issued with yellow hard hats and ear protectors and led down the stairways to where the thirty thousand barrels of oil was processed.

"That's on a good day," Ryan shouted. "Since we're a production platform we don't drill on a regular basis. That's why it's so quiet up here."

Yeah, I thought, you hardly need the ear protectors at all.

I caught the difference when we went down into the well bay, which was full of pipes and wheels and dials, all of which rumbled and shook. He showed us the well head valve assemblies, where the sort of hand wheel I associate with submarine hatches stuck out at random intervals from a dense tangle of pipes. Growing out of the big pipes and valves were thin green pipes, that branched out to flower into mechanical gauges with white faces and analog displays. I've ridden a traction engine that was cleaner and less complicated.

Griffiths called it the "Christmas tree," and said it controlled the flow coming up the production string, which is what oil people call the pipe you suck oil up, and into the well bay, by means of turning the hand wheels to open and close the valves.

I let Beverley, who did industrial chemistry as part of her degree, ask all the questions. Like why still turn the wheels by hand, why not remotely controlled servomotors?

"We do for some valves, but these..." He waved a hand at the whole thrumming tangle. "These are easy to access. When you turn a handle manually, you know it's turned and you can watch the effect on a gauge that's directly connected to the valve. Fewer points of failure."

Assuming that the people turning the handles don't fuck up, I thought. As police, I have a low opinion of people's general levels of competence. And that includes many of my fellow officers.

We were shown the test separator and the control room for the test separator. We let Ryan chatter on about the normal procedure for testing the quality of the oil, before asking him about the diving deck.

"Why do you want to see that?" he asked.

"Isn't that what this new process is all about?" I said, pointing at where a brand-new monitor had been slapped down next to a bulky 1990s terminal whose display looked even older—all cursors and asterisks, as if it was running on MS-DOS. The display on the new monitor was all high-resolution lines, gradient shading and drop-shadowed dialogue buttons. I didn't need to be told which one belonged to Elgar Bravo's super high-tech experimental oilfield recovery system.

A young white man with long blond hair and a headset was monitoring the screens. Insufficiently hidden under a ring folder was the spine of a paperback book. Obviously he wasn't expecting any excitement this shift.

"Sure, OK," said Griffiths. "I'll have to get the OK from Garrett first."

While we waited to hear back from "Garrett," Griffiths continued his heavy machinery tour, including showing us what was essentially a jet engine turbine that amped up the pressure of the excess gas from the separator, so it could be pumped back down the well to maintain the pressure within the "payzone" to force oil back up the pipe.

It was surprisingly quiet.

"That's because it's not running," said Griffiths. "Controlling the mixture of gas, mud and other inputs—that's at the heart of the new process." He sounded proud of the process. I could sympathize; it's nice to set something up that actually works. "We only fire up the compressor when the controller determines a need for it."

As if on cue, the turbine suddenly kicked in, a high-pitched whine that rapidly descended into a roar that vibrated in my chest. Griffiths grinned at me and we retreated from the noise.

Beverley asked what pressure the turbine produced.

"About 147 bar," shouted Griffiths.

"That's almost 15 million pascals," Beverley shouted in my ear.

"Thanks," I said. "I was wondering." I don't think she heard me.

We descended further down into what Griffiths called the module deck, and down further still by ladder into the dive control center. This was a long narrow room with control stations in front of angled windows that overlooked a platform, the dive skid, crammed with winches, and what looked like a late Soviet space capsule.

A man in a survival suit was outside with a clipboard, checking gear. He waved when he saw us through the window and climbed up a short flight of stairs and in through a door at the end of the room. There was a strong waft of sea salt and diesel before he closed it behind him. He was a short, middle-aged white guy and the survival suit made him look squat. He had a square face, blue eyes and brown hair shorn to a pelt.

"Hello," he said. "Who's this, then?"

He had a Black Country accent that made him sound like a stoned Brummie, but his eyes were intelligent and wary. He was pretending to be surprised to see us, but he'd been primed ahead of our visit.

Still, he made a good show of it when we were introduced. Especially when shaking hands with Beverley. But then Beverley is a constant surprise, even to me.

His name was Garrett Partridge, the dive manager.

"Yes, I know," he said. "Every single variation."

"Including the pear tree?" asked Beverley.

"And the bloody pear tree," he said.

Griffiths left us with Partridge, who took us out onto the dive skid, where diverse divers would have gone into the water to carry out repairs.

"If we had any divers," said Partridge.

We were about as far down as you get on the platform without swimming, and the sea looked gray and cold and very close. In fact, I was sure the waves were getting bigger. But I decided to wait until I could get Beverley alone to get a weather report.

"I thought you were the dive manager," said Beverley.

Partridge nodded at the winches trapped in their yellow metal cages, the crane and the Soviet-era space capsule hanging from its crane.

"Somebody has to manage all this," he said. "Just in case."

I was about to ask, Just in case of what? But Beverley got in first.

"I understood that this exciting new process required continuous adjustments at the well head," she said. "So you must have divers down there . . . right?"

"That's the beauty of it, isn't it?" he said. "They live down there. You ever seen a film called *The Abyss*?"

Beverley laughed and nodded at me.

"He's got the DVD box set," she said.

"You remember the underwater drilling rig?" said Partridge. "Basically that, only it doesn't do the drilling." He sighed. "Ultra-long-term saturation diving. Wave of the future."

Spray bounced off one of the vast metal-jacketed pillars that held up the platform and beaded Beverley's hair. Partridge suggested we go back to the control room, where he had a flask of tea and some cups.

"Have you seen it yourself?" asked Bev as we settled into the operator chairs.

"No, it was built in Norway and has its own support ship," said Partridge as he divvied up the tea. Beyond the diving skid, the strip of visible sky between the sea and the bottom of the platform had gone from blue to a misty white.

Partridge was explaining to Beverley about how the support ship had lowered the module down to the well head, and then transferred the umbilical to the Elgar Bravo before sailing away. He pointed out the well head umbilical, which was a thick orange and white striped cable running up the production string before vanishing into the platform above.

"Do you talk to them?" I asked.

"That's all handled by the operation center upstairs," said Partridge.

"Have you ever visited?" asked Beverley.

"The well head?" he said. "No chance. Long-term saturation—strictly for the young and stupid."

"When was the last time you made any kind of dive?" asked Beverley.

"Not for years," said Partridge.

Although five years ago, he'd spent more time under than he did onshore.

"The money's so good and the work was always there."

Two hundred grand or more and, unlike others, Partridge tried not to waste his on booze, fast cars and ex-wives. But then the oil price collapsed, and with it production, new drilling and the demand for divers. Partridge had been stranded on shore for three years before he'd got this gig and found he didn't really miss it.

"This suits me perfectly," he said, and drank his tea.

"Be honest now," said Beverley. "You don't think there's anyone down there."

Partridge kept his eyes on his tea.

"What makes you say that?" he asked.

"You're the dive manager," said Beverley. "You're responsible for diving operations on this platform and under it. There's no way you'd go without a link down to the well head if there were people working there."

Partridge shrugged.

"I just do what the management tells me," he said.

"Have you ever talked to them?" I asked.

He shook his head.

"Comms is text only," he said, and jerked a thumb upward.

"So who do you think's down there? Giant squid?" I asked, which got me the side-eye from Bev. "Aliens?"

"Robots," he said. "It's got to be robots."

Because robots didn't need to decompress or take time off or die in messy and media-unfriendly ways. Or worse, join the National Union of Rail, Maritime and Transport Workers. Eliminating human workers of all kinds, let alone divers, had always been a long time aim of the oil companies.

"Their holy grail," he said. "And this is a low-profile experimental project. The perfect place to test the robots. Make sure they work, and then quietly lay off the divers before anyone notices what you're doing."

He lapsed into silence and we finished our tea.

Against my will, Beverley dragged me back out onto the diving skid while telling Partridge that it was all right. He could stay nice and dry, she just wanted to show me the diving bell. Which turned out to be the Roscosmos-surplus capsule hanging from the crane by its own umbilical cable—this one striped green and yellow. Spray was regularly washing across the skid, and every so often a wave rose high enough to kiss the metal grating beneath our feet. We moved into a sheltered spot beside the bell, which was—I checked—securely fastened to a bright yellow frame that looked much cleaner and newer than the bell itself did. There were definite dings and rust spots on some of the tanks that bulged off its base.

"Could it be robots?" asked Beverley.

I thought about it. You've got to be careful about making assumptions in the Job. Or as a wizard. Just because I was neck-deep in weird bollocks didn't mean everything I encountered was going to be supernatural. Robots would make sense, and yet...

"They'd have telemetry," I said. "You'd have cameras and the ability to override any robotics and operate the machinery remotely."

"That would be up in the control room," said Beverley, "Where Mr. Carroll hasn't shown us."

"We'll make that our next stop, then," I said.

Beverley looked thoughtful. This close, I could see the droplets of spray evaporating off her face—the ones on mine were running down my neck.

"And if it isn't robots?" she said.

"We've met mermaids and we've met . . . whatever we're calling Aquaman."

"Selkies," said Beverley.

"So it's either mermaids or selkies."

"Or something else," said Beverley, "that can work that far down."

"Or something else," I said. "Could you work down there?"

Beverley squinted at the diving bell.

"This far from my ends?" she said. "Maybe I could do a bounce dive if I was breathing helium. I'd have to be quick, or I'd saturate and have to spend time in a decompression tank." She grinned at me. "Do you want me to go have a look?"

"Fuck, no," I said, which only made her grin wider.

"You're right," she said. "Probably not a good idea."

"I'm going with the selkies," I said. "I don't think they can survive long out of the water—I think they're *of* the sea. The mermaids seem more like people with magic. I bet they stay close to the surface."

"Let's call Abigail," said Beverley, "and ask her to ask Ione what her diving envelope is."

"First, let's rule out robots," I said.

Thankfully there was a side staircase up from the module deck to the accommodation block, sparing us the clanking, roaring confusion of the well head deck. We clumped up the steps being buffeted by the wind, which had definitely picked up. Although as we got higher, at least I wasn't getting spray in the face. Halfway up, Partridge handed us over to Rory Carroll. Between the wind, the machinery noise and the ear protectors, conversation was limited.

"I hope you weren't planning to fly back today," he shouted. "It's too windy for a landing."

We were halfway up the side of the accommodation block when Carroll stopped and cocked his head to one side—obviously getting a message via his headset. Judging from the scowl, it wasn't good news.

"Tell them to wave off," he shouted into his walkie-talkie.

Whatever the reply was, it was obviously more important than us, because he took off, clattering up the stairs. Me and Beverley followed him up five flights until we arrived, panting, at the top. Carroll was an orange blur heading toward the helipad that stuck up on a metal framework at the far end of the roof.

I ran after him. What can I say? It's a bad policing habit.

As I followed him up the stairs to the helipad, a gust of wind nearly knocked me off my feet. So I stopped short of the actual pad and peered over the top. Carroll was having a shouted conversation with a group of grim-faced men in yellow survival suits. They all stood crouched, braced against the wind. On Carroll's command, the men scattered and started lowering the capture nets into position around the pad. Carroll scuttled back toward me and shouted angrily for me to get off the ramp.

"What's going on?" I asked.

"Some moron is trying for a landing." He pointed to the reception door. "Get inside."

I collected Bev at the bottom of the stairs and we got inside. So, as a result, we didn't see the crash.

We definitely heard it, though.

The rising whine of engines, then a collision that made the whole accommodation block shudder. Beverley dragged me down another corridor, away from the helipad. The engines screamed behind us and there was a *thwack thwack thwack* which I guessed was rotor blades smashing into things.

The engine sound died and we found ourselves in the reception area.

We stayed where we were . . . listening.

There was shouting up ahead, but it didn't sound panicked and nobody was screaming, which was a hopeful sign.

A bunch of guys in orange suits, carrying green medical bags and various bits of unidentified engineering kit, banged into reception through one door and thundered out through another. It was strangely, reassuringly familiar. Like watching the TSG gearing up for a major disorder.

Blinschell followed the herd in, spotted us and walked over.

"You guys all right?" he asked.

We said we were and asked if he knew what had happened.

"An incoming chopper crashed," he said. "They told it to stand off but it came in anyway."

"Did you see it?"

"Watched it on the monitor."

"And?"

"Could have been worse," said Blinschell. "Nearly made it, but I think a rotor hit something and it dropped three feet."

"Casualties?" I asked, and started heading for the exit.

Beverley grabbed my arm.

"Wait," she hissed. "They know what they're doing out there—you don't."

There were shouts from outside and heavy boots clanging on the metal deck, then the door at the far end of the access corridor opened and big men in survival suits and life jackets started filing into the reception area. I recognized one of them.

"You know what they say," said Derek Patterson when he saw me. "Any landing you can walk away from . . ."

"What the hell are you doing here?" asked Blinschell.

"It's my platform," said Patterson. "And you should have informed FPXPLORE before coming out."

"And what are you doing out here?" asked a slim man who'd come in behind Patterson. It was Andrew Rae, suspicious special adviser at the Scottish Executive's Economic Development Directorate. From a certain point of view, this was good news. They wouldn't have come out, let alone risked that landing, if we hadn't been close to discovering something we shouldn't.

From another point of view, Andrew Rae's presence suggested political connections. And that never turns out well for good honest coppers.

And then it got worse, as a large man rocking a ponytail and an American accent shouldered his way over to us.

"Detective Grant," said James Albright. "Isn't this bracing?"

18

What Abigail Did When She Woke Up the Next Morning

I WAKE UP with the warmth of Ione's back against mine and I want to stay there forever, only I have to wee. So I get up. Since I'm going into the house, I reckon I might as well have a shower and a coffee, and if I'm all clean and sweet-smelling when Ione wakes up, so much the better.

Indigo squeezes out from the flysheet of Peter's tent and bounces over to wait for me on the patio table. She's pretending like she's not really waiting, so I pretend not to notice her as I walk past. So she jumps down and trots after me.

"Ask me where I've been," says Indigo.

"Where have you been?" I ask.

"Scampering," she says, "in the woods."

"Where's everyone else?"

"Nightingale is on deployment in Aberdeen," says Indigo. "Peter and the Bev are flying out to an oil platform, whatever that is. Everybody else is asleep. Miss Fishy is back in your tent." Indigo's ears twitch. "She's waking up now."

I ask who's looking after the twins and am pleased to find it's not me.

"They were taken away by a very nice golfing lady," says Indigo.

"How do you know she was a golfer?" I ask. "And for that matter, how do you know she was nice?"

"Very nice."

"How did you know she was very nice?"

I've spent enough time jammin' with the foxes to know smug when I hear it.

"Had a golf bag in the back of her vehicle," says Indigo. "Plus she smelled of happy kits, plus overheard conversation—her mate is a police sergeant."

I'm not sure that proves anything, but it isn't really my problem.

"Do your Scottish friends have any human-rated transport available?" I ask.

"Roger that," says Indigo, which surprises me.

"Really?" I say. "The foxes up here have wheels?"

"Operational necessity in low-density rural environments," says Indigo.

"I want you to pop back and ask Ione, nicely, to join me at the house," I say. "Then after breakfast, bring the transport here."

"Mission?" Indigo asks eagerly.

"We're going to find out just what that dragon was guarding."

But first breakfast, which starts simple but gets complicated when Peter's mum turns up and takes over the cooking.

"Is that the enticing aroma of a proper fry-up?" asks Brian, coming downstairs.

Scrambled eggs, bacon, mushrooms, toast, and basmati rice. Plus microwaved knuckle and pepper soup for those that didn't mind having their taste buds burned out. Brian, who'd pitted himself against Aunty Rose's cooking a couple of nights earlier, chooses not to risk it.

I have some to show off in front of Ione, who tries it herself and then has to stuff a white bap into her mouth to soak up the spice.

"Now that's hot," she says with her mouth full.

Abdul, when he arrives, sticks to coffee and toast. He wants to know about the selkies, but Aunty Rose wants to know why Ione thought it was a good idea to go magical leopard hunting.

"Well, I wasn't going to tell the police, was I?" says Ione. "And I couldn't let it run around unchecked. What if it ate a child?"

"I like this one's heart," says Aunty Rose to me, and turns to Ione, who's actually preening. "But chasing a devil? You need to be more careful."

Fox transport turns out to be a blue Vauxhall Corsa that looks surprisingly good, given it's fifteen years old and owned by a consortium of talking foxes. Although that isn't as surprising as the fact that it's driven by Ione's cousin Duncan.

"You crafty wee bugger," says Ione when he turns up. "I knew you hadn't biked all the way to Rattray. You don't even have a license."

Duncan says that, *au contraire*, he has a provisional license and that he never drives anywhere without a responsible adult in the passenger seat. Even though the responsible adult was often a fox.

I ask Sax William, the fox responsible, whether he has a license.

"No," he says. "But I aced the theory test online."

"Move over, Duncan," I say. "I'm driving."

Nightingale insisted that I learned to drive, although not in the Jag. Also Peter insisted that I get professional lessons, on account of Nightingale's relaxed attitude to the Highway Code, speed limits and the laws of physics.

Which is why I'm driving three foxes, two people and an inflatable dinghy to Rattray Head. Where we sneak past the Feds guarding Albright's caravan by pretending we're a bunch of kids going to the beach—which I suppose we are.

I set the foxes to keep an eye on the Feds while Duncan guards our stuff on the beach. I make him turn his back while I pull on my wetsuit, but I let Ione watch because I'm generous that way. Besides, I get to watch her strip off and wade into the surf in nothing but a yellow and red tankini. I climb into the dinghy, she wraps her shawl around her waist, flips her tail at me in a flirty way, and off we go.

I'm riding a sea chariot drawn by a beautiful mermaid.

And to think Ms. Redmayne used to complain about me daydreaming.

Rattray Head Lighthouse is built in two parts. The lower section is made of gray stone blocks and, according to the internet, used to house the foghorn and the engine room. The top section looks like a proper lighthouse—a slender white tower with a light at the top. At low tide you can pick your way across the causeway from the beach, but now the tide is coming in so we can start halfway up. We tie the dinghy to the metal ladder and climb up to the entrance.

The metal is old and slick and smells of electricity and barking seals. I go up first and wait for Ione in the shadowed recess of the entrance. Our way is blocked by a thick metal door with a surprisingly modern lock, and I wish I'd thought to bring Zach with us.

I think the Northern Lighthouse Board is going to be pissed with me as I burn the lock out. While we wait for it to cool, Ione kisses me on the neck.

"That was surprisingly sexy," she says.

"I got more of that," I say, and I'm blushing.

Inside it's dark and the sound of the sea is far away. The walls are lined with cream tiles, like old Tube stations, and there's a narrow metal staircase that spirals upward.

I call hello up the stairs, because you wouldn't want any sudden surprises on something this steep. We go up a flight and run into another thick iron door. This one is barred on our side, like it's there to keep somebody locked in. The brackets holding the iron bar are crudely welded and unpainted.

"This was done recent, weren't it?" I say.

"Looks like it," says Ione, and together we lift the bar off and leave it propped up against the wall.

We step through and emerge into the hollow top half of the lighthouse. Now the curve of the stairs is visible all the way up to what I assume is the floor of the living quarters.

I call hello again, and a woman answers from the top.

"Don't come any further," she calls. "I have a toaster and I'm not afraid to use it."

"Are you Alice MacDuffie?" I call.

"It's a big old-fashioned one, too," she shouts back. "You wouldn't want it landing on your head, I can tell you." There's a pause, then, "Who wants to know?"

"We're here to rescue you."

There's a slapping sound and a woman comes far enough down the spiral stairs that I can see she really is holding a toaster. A big old-fashioned one. She's right. You wouldn't want that landing on your head.

She stops three meters above us and asks how we got in.

"Through the door down there," I say.

"How did you get past them?"

"Get past who?"

"You didn't see anyone . . ." She hesitates. "In the water?"

I tell her no. Ione backs me up.

"How can they not be there?" she says, but to herself. "They said they'd be watching. I could have broken a window or made a rope out of sheets. It's two hundred meters. You can swim that in your sleep. And you can walk across at low tide."

"Do you not want to come away?" asks Ione.

"Wait there," says Alice, and slaps back up the stairs.

We can hear muttering and cupboards opening and closing, and then she slaps back down the stairs. When she comes around the final twist in the spiral stairs, I see that she's barefoot and wearing a pair of blue nylon pajama bottoms and a shabby yellow waterproof jacket. Both are way too big for her. She has pink cheeks and auburn hair tied back in a ragged ponytail.

"Did you see me flashing?" she asks. "I used one of the stainless steel spoons to try and signal."

I say I saw it, and then ask her who trapped her in the lighthouse, and she gets all shook and says she won't tell us until she's safely out.

"You've got a boat, right?" she says. "Because you don't want to be getting in the water."

"What's wrong with the water?" asks Ione.

"You don't want to know."

I said not only did we want to know, but that was the whole point of us being out here.

"There's creatures living in the sea," she says.

We step into the shadowed alcove at the top of the ladder.

"Like what?" I ask. "Seals? Dolphins?"

She hesitates and I decide to push a bit.

"Selkies," I say, and looking over her shoulder at Ione, add, "Mermaids?"

"What do you know?" asks Alice.

I wait before telling her, because I've done enough falling in the last couple of days and would like to concentrate on climbing down the ladder. Alice follows me down quick enough, although she's not happy about the dinghy.

"You couldn't manage anything bigger?" she says.

If I'd deeped it properly, I'd have at least brought like a paddle or something. Instead, Ione has to push from the back, going slowly as if she were swimming with legs, while I sit in the front and try to distract Alice from looking behind us.

Luckily, I think Alice is so pleased to be out of the lighthouse that she keeps her eyes fixed on the beach.

"You'd think they'd have a radio, wouldn't you?" she says. "For emergencies. I thought I might cut the power and force the lighthouse people to come out, but I didn't dare mess with all that high-voltage cable. And what if I cut the light and a ship ran on to the rocks—not that that would happen these days, with GPS. But still . . . Who did you say you were?"

"Who stuck you in the lighthouse?" I ask.

"Selkies," she says. "You don't seem surprised. Why's that?"

"Really selkies?" I ask, 'cause even though I have no intention of becoming a Fed I've picked up some good habits. Like not leading witnesses. And some bad habits, too—like not answering questions unless I have to.

"Amphibious people who live in the sea and bark like seals," she says, giving me a hard look. "You know them, don't you?"

"Not socially," I say. "But enough to believe you. But what we don't know is how you got off the oil rig."

"Platform," she says. "Not a rig. There's a difference. And you haven't said who you are."

"I work with the Special Assessment Unit," I say. "We deal with weird shit like this."

Then we have to go through the list, which is why I didn't want to bring it up. No, not MI6 or MI5 or the Home Office or the Fortean Society. When she brings up the police, all I say is that they know who we are.

Since I'm facing backward to keep Alice distracted, I can't see the shore, but I can hear the surf. I need to get a move on.

"How did you get from the platform to the lighthouse?"

"Some bastard pushed me overboard," she says.

She was on the diving skid, which is at the bottom of the platform, otherwise she probably would have died from the fall. It was the middle of the night and she wasn't wearing a survival suit or life jacket.

"What were you doing there in the middle of the night?" I ask.

"I was trying to find out who was doing the work down at the well head," she says.

"Did you find out?"

"Not until I was in the water."

Survival time in the North Sea without survival kit, even in summer, is about an hour. If the shock doesn't kill you in the first ninety seconds. I shudder, and she sees.

"Yeah," she says. "You know what I'm talking about."

And that was if a wave didn't dash you against a support pylon and kill you that way. Nobody—except the fucker who'd pushed her in—knew she was even out of her room. It was pitch dark and she was definitely going to die.

"Only that's when I met the selkies," she says.

In the dark she really did think they were seals at first, what with the barking and the feel of smooth skin under her flailing hands. Then she realized they had hands and arms and human-shaped heads, and stopped struggling.

"It's not like I had a lot of options," she says. "If they wanted to drown me, all they had to do was let go."

Instead, they started swimming with her in the middle like the sausage in a roll.

"For how long?" I ask, thinking how like Ione rescuing me this is.

"Hours," she says. "The sun came up and I couldn't see anything. I was that exhausted that I fell asleep, drifting in and out. And then I woke up and that . . ." She waves at the lighthouse. "That was in front of us. They carried me up the ladder, dumped me in a bed, and off they trotted."

"How long have you been in there?"

"Two weeks, I think," she says. "Maybe a couple of days more."

The external doors were locked, the windows were sealed, but she knew that the Lighthouse Board would be round.

"Eventually."

And every two or three days the silent selkies delivered fresh fish.

"And they were patrolling around the base, too," she says. "They made sure I knew that."

Then ten days ago, an older selkie arrived, as naked and

dripping as the rest, but he carried a waterproof bag from which he pulled an old tourist map of Aberdeen and a laminated visitor pass for FPXPLORE. It didn't take much in the way of pointing and grunting to make it clear he wanted to know where the HQ was.

"So I drew a circle around it on the map and he got very interested in the quarry," says Alice, who could tell he wanted to ask more questions. But they were stymied by the language barrier. In the end they resorted to drawing pictures on the inside covers of some tatty old paperbacks that Alice had found in the kitchen. The man had drawn big stick figures and next to them small stick figures — children, Alice guessed. Then he'd drawn a box around the children and an arrow leading away from the grown-ups. Then he savagely drew lines curving down where their mouths should be.

"Then he pointed at the quarry in the map," says Alice, "Then he stared at me, as if he could make me understand just by staring. I've never seen anyone so angry and sad at the same time. And then he stuffed the map back in his bag and left."

"What do you think happened?" I ask.

"I think someone has stolen their children," she says.

"But why?"

"I don't know," she says, and the dinghy grinds up against the beach.

Ione slips off her silver shawl and joins us on the beach.

"Aren't you cold?" asks Alice.

"Well," says Ione, dragging out the word. "I'm from the Broch, see. So, no."

We drag the dinghy to the top of the dunes and I point out the Feds jamming around the caravan.

"You should go down and introduce yourself — they've been looking for you."

"Shouldn't you come with me?"

I wave Ione ahead and spot a streak of fiery red among the dune grass as Sax William runs for the car.

"Nah," I say. "I don't want to deal with the police."

"What do I tell them?"

"Tell them everything," I say. "Actually, better ask to talk to

Inspector Nightingale. He's the boss man and my teacher, so he'll believe you about the selkies and ting."

Alice starts down the dune toward the Feds.

"Inspector Nightingale," I call after her, then I catch up with Ione and help her carry the dinghy the last twenty meters to the car.

Once the dinghy is safely on the roof rack, the foxes are in the back and I sort out the squabble between Duncan and Ione as to who gets to ride shotgun—Ione, obviously—we're out of there as fast as a Vauxhall Corsa can go on a rough track.

I ask Sax William if they have any assets in Aberdeen.

"We have a team on standby," he says, and I tell him to put them on surveillance at the FPXPLORE HQ at Rubislaw Hill. When we reach Brian's house in Mintlaw, the foxes bounce off to make arrangements. There's no sign of Brian, Abdul, Aunty Rose, Uncle Richard or the twins, so we raid the fridge for drinks and sit down outside so I can have the talk.

"Your family's up to no good," I say, and Ione nods glumly.

"I told you," she says.

"But you don't know what?"

She shakes her head.

"But it's got something to with FPXPLORE?" I ask. "Because your cousin works there." I tell her about the elder selkie and the little kids who were in a box in a flooded quarry right in front of FPXPLORE's main offices.

"So what do we do next?" she asks.

"Have you got anything against fresh water?"

19

What Abigail Did To the School

THE TALKING FOXES think they're spies. I don't know why, and I'm fairly cert that they don't know why either. But if someone taught them to be spies then their teachers left some major gaps in their vocabulary. This is why Sax William's briefing on Rubislaw Quarry contained such fox-speak as "an affa big diggy-thing, I mean affa, affa big, mony winters afore Violet and a hale lot o' stone dens."

But I'm used to this now, so I manage a running translation while we drive into Aberdeen. Occasionally Ione looks things up on Wikipedia.

The quarry was opened in 1740 when Rubislaw Hill was countryside, and over the next two hundred years they dug out six million metric tons of granite. This figure impressed the foxes, who I knew all dream of extensive split-level, hunt-proof dens, with hot and cold running mice and all modern amenities. I reckon they're ten years from doing a deal with the Quiet People, after which no oligarch's super-basement will ever be safe again.

"Do you want this briefing or not?" asks Sax William.

"Sorry," I say. "I was distracted by the road conditions."

Sax William snorts and continues to explain that all the stone was used to build the sparkly gray glory that is Aberdeen. The foxes say that the stone smells different from brick, and that a Aberdonian fox always knows when they're home. Then 25 years after Violet—1971, says Ione—they turned off all the really big diggy machines and walked away. Fox legend is that the first intelligence assets to come this far north used the quarry as an initial base, but had to move out when it filled up with rainwater. Now it was surrounded on three sides by dense suburb and on the fourth by oil company HQs.

"It's a hundred and forty meters deep," says Ione, not waiting for Indigo to translate six-and-a-half fox scurries. "That's below sea level."

"It's also around the same depth as that oil rig," I say.

Sax William has marked the best access point to the quarry on Queen's Road, and we park opposite and cross over on foot. There's no official entrance, so we climb over a low wall of granite blocks and up an earth slope beneath some trees. There's a crumbly flight of stone steps that leads to a ragged chain link fence. It says DANGER KEEP OUT, but I don't think whoever put it up was serious, because some of the concrete uprights that hold up the fence look like they're going to fall down and there's no razor wire along the top. Indigo and the foxes don't even slow down, they wriggle under the wire and sit waiting for us with smug expressions.

There's a gate and a padlock, but before I can burn it Sax William coughs and indicates where the wire has been neatly sliced open just to the right of the gate. We push the wire aside and carefully step through. We continue up a bank and stop when we can see the quarry.

Swear down, it's not as impressive as I imagined. It looks like a big version of the ponds up Hampstead Heath. But when I say this, Ione shakes her head and says it's depth that counts.

"The deeper it goes," she says, "the easier it is to hide things."

Ione has said this before when I asked about the Loch Ness Monster. Which she claims is simply for tourists.

"Loch Lochy," she said, which sounded like a made-up name to me. "That's where Lizzie lives."

When I asked who Lizzie was, Ione said that if I was good she'd introduce me.

I looked up Loch Lochy and it's much bigger than Rubislaw Quarry, although not as deep.

About a hundred meters across the quarry from where we're standing is a steep slope covered in trees and bushes. The blue glass façade of the Chevron HQ peeps over the top of the trees, and further to the right are is the blocky white upper stories of ConocoPhillips. FPXPLORE is just visible as a gray concrete parapet at the far end. That end has a sheer sand-colored cliff, but I think I can see two vertical grooves cut into the granite. I take a pic with my phone, but the camera is not good enough to make out what it is.

I settle Indigo's headset on her head and tell her to ask the fox team watching FPXPLORE to check it out.

Ione takes my hand and we pick our way down the muddy bank to where a short pier has been constructed out of modular PVC blocks—the foxes spread out along the shore. Although Indigo stays with me. She wants to ride in my backpack with the rest of the comms gear, but she's bare heavy, so I make her walk when we're not in public.

It's sheltered down by the water and the sun makes it warm. Ione strips off down to her tankini and hands me her clothes. Then she walks to the end of the pier, lies down and sticks her head under the water.

She pulls her head out and looks at me.

"Anything?" I ask.

"It's not as cold as the sea. It's fresh water. There's fish, so it can't be that toxic," she says, and swivels around to wrap her shawl around her waist.

The transformation is too blurry to see properly; the silver scales smear out over Ione's legs and then suddenly she's got a tail. She slips into the water, I see a ripple of silver and she's gone. I clutch her clothes tightly to my chest.

Sax William and a couple of the local foxes join me and Indigo on the pier.

Ione hasn't been in the water for more than five minutes when she suddenly breaches the surface and flies toward me in a cloud of spray. The foxes scatter, and for a cracked moment I open my arms as if I was going to catch her until my brains catch up and I jump back out of the way. She lands hard, swearing, her tail thrashing around exactly like a distressed fish until she gets her shawl off and rolls over on her back. Still swearing.

I ask if she's all right and she swears some more, but rolls over and I help her to her feet.

"Ow," she says, and takes my hand. "We need to get off the water."

She leads me up the pier. She's limping, but I wait until we stop halfway up the bank before asking if she's hurt.

"There's something doon there," she says. "Either big eels with teeth or some kind of octopus thing with tentacles. I *did* not stick around to find out which."

"Was it a natural thing or another summoned creature?"

"It wisna fae aroon here," she says. "That's for certain."

I ask if she found anything else but she shakes her head.

"I was deterred by the things with teeth," she says.

"But that's their mistake, innit?" I say. "'Cause if there was nothing to hide, they wouldn't have put something down there to guard it."

"So what now?" asks Ione, never taking her eyes off the water.

"We see what the foxes have found," I say. "And we call Thomas."

We slip back out through the hole in the fence and cross the road back to the Vauxhall. We seem to have acquired a dozen extra foxes, who fill the backseat in a pile of red fur. It's a good thing that we left Duncan in Mintlaw and picked up snacks on the way. I drive us up Rubislaw Hill and call Nightingale while Ione distributes grapes and raspberries to the foxes in the back. Abdul has been lecturing us about feeding the foxes too much processed food—that's why it's fruit. Although Indigo complains.

"Cheese puffs," she says sadly.

Nightingale answers the phone just as we pass the glass walls and neat hedges of the Chevron campus.

"We've lost contact with James Albright," he says. "Keep a look out, but for God's sake don't engage. Where are you?"

I brief him as to Ione's encounter with a possible sea monster in the quarry, and he agrees with me that its presence indicates that FPXPLORE are hiding something down there.

"Have you deployed the foxes?" he asks.

I tell him that I have initial teams out, with more in the car.

"Tuck yourself out of sight. See what the foxes find, but stay put until I get there."

"Roger that," I say.

"And, Abigail?"

"Yes, boss."
"Be careful."

Nightingale has brought Zach with him.

"Just in case," he says—meaning locked doors and security systems.

After Nightingale's call I drove into the FPXPLORE visitors' car park and tucked our reasonably priced car next to an SUV so that it was hidden from the office proper. Checking no one was looking, we let the foxes escape out the windows. Except Indigo, who squirmed into my backpack. The fox team leaders and Sax William have their own headsets connected via encrypted short-range radio sets.

Ione wants to know where all this specially adapted gear comes from.

"Remember the vet?" I say, and she nods. "Same thing, only spy gear."

By this time, Nightingale and Zach turn up in his totally inconspicuous vintage Jag with the bad news that, not only had the time run out on James Albright's detention, but he'd given Nightingale the slip when he tried to follow.

"He had a car waiting," says Nightingale. "And I wasn't quick enough. DCI Mason has a notification alert for the car, but I suspect he may either be out of the city by now . . ."

"Or here," I say.

"Quite," says Nightingale. "The presence of one of his monsters in the quarry makes that a distinct possibility."

"Monsters?" says Zach, raising his hand.

"Big ones," says Indigo. "With lots of teeth."

"Don't go in the water," I say.

"The trouble is, we don't know how persistent his summonings are," says Nightingale.

There was very little in the Folly's records about summonings and ting. Not only because the Folly didn't hold with demonology or spirit summoning, but they also thought such activities was immoral, dangerous and, above all, the preserve of heathen foreigners.

"What have your foxes uncovered?" asks Nightingale.

What they've uncovered is a small door inside a bigger door

inside an underground car park. At just about the same location where I'd spotted the vertical grooves in the granite cliff.

Defo not a coincidence.

The small door, according to Sax William, is metal, has an electronic entry pad and smells of fish. The big door is made of older metal—the foxes can smell the difference—and is freshly oiled.

"There used to be tunnels through the rock," says Sax William. "The men used them to get their smaller diggy things up and down the hole. When it was a hole, and not full of water. That's what Control says, anyway."

Nightingale looks straight at me.

"Suggestions?" he says.

This is the thing about Nightingale. He's the only elder I know who looks right at you—like he's seeing the real person you are. And he never asks a question unless he's actually interested in the answer. This can get bare uncomfortable sometimes.

"We put a fox perimeter around the grounds," I say. "Then you go in the front door and flash your ID and demand to see the management. Meanwhile, me, Ione, and Zach go down and get this door open and see what's on the other side."

"And if there's resistance?" asks Nightingale.

"If there's serious resistance," I say, "we fall back and wait for you to reinforce."

"Make sure you do," he says. And just like that, we're going with my plan.

Before he leaves, Nightingale nods at Indigo, who is poking up out of my backpack wearing her headset. There's this bare strange smile on his face, but swear down, his eyes are misting up. Which is just weird if you know Nightingale.

"Radio operator?" he says to Indigo.

"Yes, sir."

"*Omne vetus novatur*," he says to himself. *Everything old is made new.* And then, to Indigo, "Carry on."

"Yes, sir," says Indigo and then, when he was out of earshot, "I wish he was a fox."

"Seriously?"

"I'd drag him into my den and never let him out."

"That was an overshare," I say. And she's never fancied a

human being before. Not even my friend Simon, who's so peng he has a teen fan club on Snapchat. "What's that about?"

Indigo sighs.

"It's that time of the year," she says.

"I thought that was in January?"

"That's civvies," says Indigo, meaning normal foxes. "With us it's a bit more random."

"You've never said," I say.

"It's never come up before," says Indigo.

"Are we doing this or not?" asks Ione.

Opposite the front of the FPXPLORE offices, on the other side of the car park and the access road, is a line of trees and bushes. Sax William leads us behind the shrubbery, where there is a narrow path between them and the fence around the quarry. It's a much more modern fence compared to the one we'd slipped through down the hill. This is made of solid green metal palisade slats with pointy tops to deter curious kids and urban explorers. The path is fox-sized, and me and Ione have to crouch to get under the overhead branches.

The space is warm and green and something bites me on the neck.

"This takes me back," says Zach behind me, and Indigo shushes him.

We pass behind a wooden fence that smells of old rubbish and, after waiting for Sax William to give the all-clear, we step out onto an access ramp that curves down and around into the lower floor of a two-story car park. Sax William breaks into a scurry down the ramp, and we jog after him until we are inside the car park entrance and hidden from view. Obviously everyone at FPX-PLORE takes global warming very seriously. There's no cars parked down here at all—they must all cycle to work.

We wait while Sax William and a bunch of local foxes check the end.

"Clear," says Indigo, and we creep down the left-hand side of the car park until we reach the door within a door.

They haven't tried to disguise it—there's a KEEP CLEAR box painted in front of it. The yellow paint is much fresher than the white lines marking the parking spaces. The big door is two and a half meters tall and four meters across—and old. When I put my palm against it, I can feel the grind of metal teeth against rock. The small door is on the left-hand leaf, is much newer—a retrofit, the plastic casing on the security number pad clean and blue.

"You're up," I say to Zach.

Zach steps up and bends over to peer at the pad.

I ask Indigo for a status update on Nightingale.

"Sierra Five," she says into her headset. "Sitrep, please."

She listens for a moment.

"He's stopped arguing with the receptionist and is penetrating deeper into the facility," she says.

Ione touches my arm and nods at Zach, who appears to be smelling the keypad.

"What's he doing?" she asks.

"Watch," I say—I've seen this trick before.

Zach stands up, puts his left hand over his eyes, and stabs in a six-digit code with his right. There's a *klunk* inside the door and it opens when Zach pulls on the handle.

"Ta-da," says Zach, and stands aside. "Ladies first."

Actually, foxes first. But me and Ione are close behind. Zach gives us a good two-meter leeway before following.

The secret tunnel has roughly the same dimensions as the big door, a square cross-section two and a half meters tall and four wide. The walls were smooth—cast concrete at a guess—with horizontal scratches along the sides. Modern LED strip lighting has been fixed at intervals just below the ceiling level on both sides.

We haven't gone three meters in when Sax William and the advance fox scouts come running back—much faster than they went down.

"Bandits," says Indigo. "Dead ahead, three, human-sized."

I ask what human-sized means.

"They're the size of humans," she says—which serves me right for asking.

The scout foxes are regrouping a nice safe distance behind us. Foxes don't fight unless they have to—and definitely not "human-sized things." Asymmetrical warfare has a very specific meaning when you're the size of a two-year-old child.

Three human-sized mandem walk toward us.

"It's my uncle," says Ione as the man approaches.

He's still wearing the Two-Tone revival suit, still as squat and dense as a cast-iron postbox. He has his magic silver shawl loosely knotted around his neck and wears expensive-looking shoes. He's flanked by a pair of low-rent white wastemen in jeans, donkey jackets and work boots. One of them has a skinhead, the other has stupid spiky dyed blond hair.

They don't have the silver shawls, so I'm thinking they're just local muscle.

"Indigo," I say softly. "Falcon fight. Shut down comms."

"Roger," she says, and my earpiece goes dead. I don't take my eyes off Ione's uncle Atlas while the weight shifts on my back as Indigo jumps out. As we've practiced, she's going to retreat to what the foxes call a tactical scamper, so that whatever happens will get reported back to Nightingale.

The big men standing either side of Atlas shift uneasily. I've met killers and these are not them—Atlas is the real danger.

"Abi," hisses Ione, "what are you doing?"

"She's being foolish, Ione," says Atlas. "You should talk some sense into her."

This is the wrong thing to say, because I feel Ione get all tense, and I'm hoping that she's not going to do anything stupid because I've got plans.

Nightingale says ideally, in a fight, you want your opponent to be in one of three states. Overawed, over-confident or utterly confused. Uncle Atlas didn't strike me as easily intimidated or stupid, so I was aiming for bafflement. Nightingale says this is Peter's specialty, and since he's gone PvP with some total nightmares, I'm going to make this my approach.

I risk a quick glance around—Zach is nowhere to be seen.

"Dinna be sae feel," says Uncle Atlas, and now there is power in his words. There's rain and wind in that voice, the smash of waves against rocks and bits of pottery. It's like the dig I went on in Norfolk when the sea was eating the cliffs—a sense of an inevitable doom.

Ione steps back, grabs my arm and I pretend to go with her. Atlas starts to relax, so I cast a treaclefoot spell that glues his and his wastemen's feet to the floor of the tunnel. You couldn't do this to a practitioner without them spotting it, but I'm counting on Uncle Atlas being something else. He's still doing his voice of the patriarchy thing. He's saying that if we walk away now, everything will be forgiven.

I smack the two henchmen with an *impello palma* that hits at chest level, and they both go over backward. With their boots glued to the floor, they bend over backward at the knee and smack their backs into the cement. They keep yelling, so I know they're not dead, and before Uncle Atlas can react I smack him in the chest as well.

The LED strips near us flicker and go out.

He rocks backward, but he doesn't fall—which is a shock.

He straightens up and glances down at his henchmen, who still haven't patterned enough to get out of their boots. He shakes his head wearily and carefully pulls his feet out of one shoe and then the other. He looks down at what I reckon are expensive silk socks and sighs. Then he takes a deep breath and turns to face me.

"Ye'll hae tae dee better than that," he says, and charges.

Ione shrieks and stumbles backward, and I have to shake her off to stand my ground. Normally I'd follow up *impello* with a couple of freezing water bombs to the face, but Atlas is a merman, isn't he? Cold water's not going to faze him. I try a blinder to soften him up, but he runs through it with his eyes narrowed into squints. I lay down a sheen of ice in front of his feet and plan to try for another knock-down. But when his silk socks hit the ice it cracks and breaks. He doesn't even slow down. More of the overhead lights flicker out.

In the half-darkness it's like he's getting bigger and heavier as he runs. It's like staring down a Class 66 freight locomotive that isn't planning to stop just because some squishy young woman has decided to stand in front of it. I can see the breath streaming from his nostrils like smoke, his eyes burning like headlamps—his arms and legs pumping pistons.

He's going to hit me with the same inevitable impact as my brother's death.

It's going to happen.

Then Ione grabs me and spins me out of the way. There's an impact and she screams. Her hands let go of me and she flies off to land on her side. Atlas the locomotive lumbers to a halt, turns and looks at where Ione lies, and then back at me.

"See fit ye've deen noo," he says. "Ye gleckit wee shite."

I try and get my mind clear enough to do magic, but the sight of his face, the set of his shoulders—the bare fucking total weight of him—has scrambled my brains. He stalks toward me, leaning forward like a cartoon prizefighter.

My brain still ain't working. I've always managed to deep my way out of shit, but nothing useful is coming out of my head.

Then somebody even smaller than me, and covered in red and white fur, jumps on Uncle Atlas's back and bites him on the neck. Kilo for kilo, a red fox bites as hard as a dog, and Indigo is a talking fox so those jaw muscles get a fuckton of exercise.

Atlas's eyes bulge in surprise. His mouth opens, then clamps down in pain. He straightens up and reaches back for Indigo, but it's too late. I have remembered the wisdom of my mum, who grew up small like me and has never backed down from a fight in her whole life.

"The thing about big men," she said to me once, "is their bollocks are at a convenient height."

So while he's reaching for Indigo I jump forward, grab his squishy bits, give a sharp twist to the left, and then pull as hard as I can. He nearly brains me with his head as he doubles over, but I let go and step to the side. Indigo does a neat little jump onto my shoulder, which does nearly knock me over.

Uncle Atlas is lying curled around his pain.

I'm not sure what to do when he gets up again. I'm considering kicking him in the head a lot when, luckily for him, Nightingale arrives. He has me unstick the henchmen so we can make them all lie down together and wait for Police Scotland to turn up.

Only I can't, 'cause Uncle Atlas was trying to block us from something, and I'm not sure we want to wait to find out what that is. I scoop up Indigo and she climbs back into my pack.

"You step on this lot," I say to Nightingale. "We'll scout ahead."

"Abigail," says Nightingale, sounding half vexed, half amused.

"I'll be careful," I say and, skirting around the fallen goons, head down the tunnel.

The walls of the tunnel go from cast concrete to brick, but at least the lights are working here. I don't need Peter's architectural geekiness to know that this is an older section. Maybe a century older, I'm thinking. It starts to slope downward and curve to the left. Indigo reports that she's losing comms and we start being careful and moving slower. The slope and the curve end in a large flat square of concrete. This is definitely modern. I can tell because of the yellow hydraulic hoist hanging from the ceiling. It hangs over a squared-off hole big enough to drop a car through, and is surrounded by safety railings wrapped in yellow and black hazard tape.

I test the railing first—see? Careful—and then look down. There's a shaft descending at least ten meters before vanishing into the gloom.

"This is a bit James Bond, innit?" I say.

"Nah," says Ione. "This is the oil industry."

There's a breeze coming from two slits in the wall ahead. They're three meters high, and when I peer through the one on the right I see they're a meter deep with a view over the quarry at the other end. These must be the vertical features I could see from the pier.

On the other side of the floor is another hole, a meter and a bit square with a railing and a metal gate. Opposite the gate, gray metal tracks run down the wall from head height into another shaft. There are lights at the bottom of this one, allowing us to see that it descends a long fucking way. There's a big rubberized control hanging from a bracket by the gate. It has two large buttons marked with an up and a down arrow.

I look at Ione, who cocks her head and then grins. We both make a grab for the control, but she beats me. She waves it triumphantly and then presses the *up* button. There's a clanking and whirring from down the bottom of the shaft and then the lights start up toward us.

I tell Indigo to run back and tell Nightingale that we're going to have a quick look in the basement.

"Is this wise?" she asks.

"I think it might be mission-critical," I say.

Indigo harrumphs and scampers off.

It takes ages for the lift—or, more accurately, the hoist—to reach our level. It has a blue mesh cage with GEDA on the side. It rocks as me and Ione clamber in. There's a duplicate set of controls inside, and I beat Ione to them and press the *down* button.

Unlike a proper lift, this has its motor as part of the cab at the back, so it engages directly with the track down the wall of the shaft. Although it's not so noisy we couldn't talk, we don't. But we do hold hands.

Every three or four more meters we pass gaps where unlit tunnels lead off into the darkness. Then there is light rising up to meet us. We descend into a concrete-lined corridor brightly lit with LED strips. The hoist clanks to a halt and we get out.

The air is still, and there's no mistaking a sense of depth—although that might be my brain playing tricks. Still holding hands, we follow the corridor around a sharp right-hand bend. There's a metal pressure door on our left. Ione rests the palm of her hand on it for a second.

"There's air on the other side," she says.

"How can you tell?" I ask.

She shrugs.

"Just can," she says.

We pass another pressure door—also with air on the other side, according to Ione.

At the end of a corridor is another pressure door—this one's ajar. We sidle up and have a listen. Inside, we can hear someone moving about and grumbling under their breath.

Ione grabs the edge of the pressure door and I mouth counting down from three. On "go," she yanks the door open and I jump through.

"Stay where you are," I yell. "And put your hands on your head."

The small white woman in front of me gives a little shriek and drops her mug of tea.

We're in a gallery five meters long and about two deep. In the wall opposite the pressure door is a long window made up with panes of glass separated by grids as thick as my arm. Positioned in front of the window is a big fake wooden desk cluttered with a laptop, stacks of papers and an in-and-out tray piled with bits of colored felt.

The mug hits the cement floor and breaks. Tea splashes.

The woman looks down and swears under her breath. Then she looks up and glares at me. She doesn't look older than thirty but she's dressed older, in straight jeans and a flowery blouse, with brown hair hanging loose to her shoulders and big round glasses.

And a glittering silver shawl folded and wrapped around her waist.

"Look what you did," she says.

"Phoebe?" says Ione. "What are you doing here?"

Phoebe turns her attention to Ione.

"Ye're nae supposed to be doon here," she says. "Uncle Atlas is gan tae be raging."

Not as raging as he already is, I think, and while Ione and Phoebe have their family reunion I cross to the window and look out. The water beyond is dark, and the glass is cold and at least six centimeters thick. I press my cheek against it and look upward—I can see a pale oval that might be sunlight playing on the surface of the quarry. I think there might be a diamond mesh between here and the surface.

Something flicks past the corner of my eye and I jump back.

There's definitely movement out in the dark.

"I thought you were teaching in Inverness," says Ione.

Phoebe is crouching down and picking up pieces of her mug and plonking them angrily into a metal waste paper bin.

"I got fired, didn't I?" she says.

"How come?" asks Ione.

"You know what it's like," she says, swirling the bits around the bin as if she's looking for treasure. "Dealing with strangers." She straightens and gives me a suspicious look. "Who's this?"

"Never mind that," says Ione. "What are you doing here?"

"Would you believe, teaching?"

"Teaching who?" asks Ione, and for a mad moment I think it might be the thing with teeth that Ione met under the water.

"Them," says Phoebe, and points out the window.

There's a row of faces on the other side of the glass—pale ovals caught in the light, dark eyes and hair. On their necks and upper chests I can see the slits of their gills rhythmically pulsing.

Not really selkies, says a mad part of my brain. Seals don't breathe underwater.

They don't look much like seals, or friendly, or grown-up. The eldest are a pair of teens, floating opposite me and scowling.

I give them a wave and one of the little ones waves back—the teenagers don't.

"What are you supposed to be teaching them?" I say.

"The three R's," she says, and has enough conscience to sound guilty.

There's an old-fashioned desk microphone on the window ledge. I lean in and speak.

"Hello," I say, but get no reaction.

Ione slaps Phoebe's arm.

"Ow," she says.

"Turn it on, Phoebe," says Ione.

"All right, all right," she says, and walks over to the desk, clears some papers and flicks a switch.

"Hi," I say, and wave.

The younger kids open their mouths and the room is filled with chirping sounds that run from high-frequency squeaks to proper bass.

"They don't speak English," says Phoebe.

"Can you understand me? If you can, thumbs up. If you can't—thumbs down."

One of the older teenagers turns to the younger selkies and opens their mouth. There's a blast of bass that shuts the young ones up. They turn to me and give me a thumbs up.

"I've got good news," I say. "School's out for summer."

20

The Diving Skid

EVERYWHERE YOU GO on an oil platform there's a constant background hum. You mostly tune it out, but every so often it breaks back in to remind you that you are inside an enormous machine. One in which you are definitely an afterthought, a necessary inconvenience that was dropped in after all that expensive plant had been installed. Add to that the storm—although Rory Carroll, the offshore installation manager, made a point of doing the whole "Call this a storm? This is just a light blow" routine. You could hear it faintly blowing all around the sides of the accommodation block and moaning through the main derrick. Occasionally the recreation room would shake. Which all the workers would studiously ignore.

The offshore oil industry was not what you'd call testosterone deficient, even by the standards of the police.

Carroll was off interviewing the helicopter pilots, with Blinschell looking over his shoulder. I should have been with him asking questions like "Who the fuck told you to land in this wind?" except I had to stay to keep an eye on James Albright, evil wizard, Derek Patterson, evil company head, and Andrew Rae—something slippery and political.

It doesn't take much to distract men like Albright—all Beverley had to do was challenge him to a game of pool and then fail to lose. He'd have stayed playing all night if necessary.

Since we were stuck here, I reckoned this was a good opportunity to ask Derek Patterson some questions. As MD and chief organ-grinder of FPXPLORE, he was the most likely to know the answers. Since I couldn't separate him from Andrew Rae, special adviser and political fixer to the Economic Development Directorate, I thought I might as well find out what the role of the Scottish Executive was. Nothing official, was my guess, since they hadn't brought anyone from the NSTA—the North Sea Transition Authority—the people who are supposed to oversee everything offshore.

We were eating ice cream because apparently that's what you do offshore instead of necking Scotch.

"Gets priority maintenance, too," said Patterson. "Otherwise the workers stage a riot."

"Who's down there?" I asked, and Patterson and Rae exchanged looks. "And don't say robots."

"Foreign workers," said Patterson. "Highly skilled foreign workers."

"Uniquely skilled," said Rae.

"So what's their unique skill?" As if I didn't know.

"They can breathe under water," said Patterson. "More importantly, they can work at depth."

"We call them *ee-sow*," he said and spelt it out. ESAO—externally sourced amphibious operatives.

I winced. I work for the Met so I've heard some terrible acronyms, but this was worse than CHIS.

Patterson gave me a rueful smile.

"Selkies," he said.

"They fill that ecological niche, at least," said Rae. "Although they don't shed their skins and marry unsuspecting fishermen."

"Does the government know?" I asked.

"Which one?" asked Rae. "Westminster or Holyrood?"

"Either."

"Well," said Rae. "You know, don't you? So that covers Westminster."

I felt a little chill, and got a horrible suspicion that I'd just become the man who knew too much. I kept my eyes fixed on Rae—was he a killer?

Not face to face, I thought. Most murders, like most assaults, are committed on the spur of the moment. The prisons are stuffed with people, mostly men, with poor impulse control and a belly full of anger. These are usually caught easy because nothing was planned—no clever schemes to hide their fingerprints, forensic awareness or complicated motives. *He fucking pissed me off, I hit him, he died. She had it coming, but I didn't mean to kill her. I swore if he hit me one more time . . .*

Most of the other murders are for stupid reasons. Jealousy, gang affiliation, football, religion or politics. I was us, he was them—what else was I supposed to do?

But a tiny number of murders are truly cold. People get done in because they're in the way, or to make a point or . . . to keep a secret.

No, Rae wasn't a killer. Neither was Patterson, for all his oilman's bravado.

I didn't look over to where Albright was losing to Beverley.

You utter cunts, I thought. Leopards and seagulls and wyverns. And legally, it doesn't even look like a murder. Doesn't even feel like murder, does it? It's something that happens in the realm of legend and stories. And even when it gets messy and your local muscle goes too far—that was an accident, wasn't it? You can get on with your pragmatic economically vital work. It's just business.

Nothing personal.

Allow me to differ, I thought, and smiled.

"So not the Scottish Executive," I said.

"They don't need to know," said Rae. "It'll be a nice surprise after independence."

"So there'll be employment records," I said. "PAYE, National Insurance, contracts?"

"We're working on that," said Rae. "These things take time. I'm sure you have more experience of this than I do."

Because Aquaman risked his life coming ashore because he was worried that he was ineligible for a state pension—right?

Out of the corner of my eye I spotted Ryan Griffiths, the production manager, standing in the doorway and staring in our direction. I looked back at Patterson and caught the moment when he noticed Griffiths, and the involuntary nod he gave when he caught his eye.

He'd have been better to just openly wave—if you're any good as police, you notice surreptitious more than the obvious.

Especially if you're in a pub, which this was, sort of. Anyway, Griffiths left. Then, a couple of minutes later when Patterson got up and said he had to drain the snake, I let him get out the door before I followed him.

I brushed Beverley's back with my hand as I passed the pool table to let her know what I was up to. She glanced over at Andrew Rae and smiled to let me know she knew she had to watch him as well.

Patterson didn't seem to be worried about being followed, so it was easy to keep up as he headed down a narrow corridor festooned with noticeboards and the ever-present safety posters. One with an HM Government crest—*Health and Safety Law: What You Need to Know*, and another complicated one with a red border and lots of illustrations entitled *Life-Saving Signals*, which I rather wished I'd had time to look at. Life-saving signals are something I've definitely needed in the last six years.

I walked past a couple of offices with their doors open. One of them belonged to Phyllis, the pirate personnel manager, who was too intent on her computer to notice me. There was a door at the end of the corridor marked *Control*. I reckoned Patterson had had a three-minute start, and decided to give him a couple more minutes to do something nefarious before bursting in.

That was the plan, anyway.

It lasted right up to the point where the door slammed open and a young man ran out the door. I didn't get much of a look at him and I don't think he saw me at all, just hurtled down the corridor.

I heard Phyllis yell, "What the fuck is it now?"

I slipped into the control room, and then really wished I hadn't.

It was a big room with the same mishmash of technological eras as the rest of the platform. A wall of steel-blue cabinets with analog dials and illuminated push-buttons, a row of workstations with built-in flat-screen monitors and festooned with even more push-buttons, old-fashioned telephone handsets and lots of stuff I didn't recognize. Further back were desks with better, more modern terminals on them. Swivel chairs. Slanted windows looking out into misty darkness, with hazard lights and girders gleaming through the rain.

And a man with a gun.

Patterson, with a compact semiautomatic pistol and shitty trigger discipline. His grip was solid, though, and it was aimed at Griffiths, who stood with his hands up—shaking with rage.

"Do you know what you've fucking done?" he shouted.

"Of course I know what I've fucking done," said Patterson. "I fucking did it."

I was about to do something clever, honest, but Patterson spotted me and shifted his aim to cover me.

"Oh, for fuck's sake," he said in a tone of weary annoyance that I've become strangely familiar with. He gestured for me to join Griffiths.

Now, these days I've acquired a particular set of skills that can come in handy during an armed confrontation. The problem being that all of them involve magic and—I don't know if I've mentioned this—magic has a tendency to render microprocessors down to their original constituents. Since I was standing in a room full of delicate instrumentality which in turn was controlling what Griffiths himself had described this morning as *a barely controlled geyser of inflammable hydrocarbons*, I decided to restrain myself.

I put my hands where he could see them and sidled over to stand beside Griffiths. Usually I wouldn't make things that easy for an armed suspect, but I wanted to draw his attention away from the door. Somebody was bound to come rushing in. Although hopefully not Phyllis.

"What has he fucking done?" I asked.

"There's a device," said Griffiths. "Attached to the well head. It's designed to seal off the well in event of a subsurface blowout."

"Seems sensible," I said.

"We modified it a bit," said Patterson.

"He's allowed an uncontrollable flow of hydrocarbons up the riser," said Griffiths, and I judged from the way he said it that this was not a good thing. "When the device fails, the control rig blows up in the faces of the divers."

"They'll be long gone," said Patterson. "If they're sensible."

"And we get a blowback all the way up the string," said Griffiths through gritted teeth.

"There's two sets of preventers between them and us," said Patterson. "There's a good chance they'll hold."

Griffiths was making spluttering noises.

"How long have we got until the blowout happens?" I asked.

"Oh, the device is on a delay," said Patterson. "I'm not a monster."

No, but you're probably going to have to shoot me, I thought. Or better, throw me overboard. You probably think you can pay off Griffiths, but you won't want to take that risk with me.

Or Blinschell. Or Beverley.

Patterson told Griffiths to order an emergency evacuation and kept the gun on him as he hit a button. An emergency klaxon started to sound and an orange spinner light came on, just to add that extra bit of visual excitement. Griffiths picked up an old-fashioned PA microphone and gave Patterson a dirty look.

"Don't even think about it," said Patterson.

"This is not a drill," he said. "This is an emergency evacuation, get to your muster stations. Boat captains to drop as soon as you have your complement. Repeat, this is not a drill."

He repeated the alert a couple of times while I eyed Patterson, looking for an opportunity. If he was going to shoot me, I was just going to have to take my chances with the geyser of hydrocarbons.

I heard Phyllis shouting outside. Somebody answered and Rory Carroll barreled in, saw the gun and demanded to know what the hell was going on.

"They raided the holding area," said Patterson. "Where's the other police?" Under stress he gave the last word the full *Taggart* treatment.

"I sent him off to a muster station with the others," said Carroll, and then looked over at me and Griffiths. "What about these two?"

"Rory," said Griffiths, "what are you talking about?"

"Don't worry, Ryan," said Carroll. "Everything is going to be fine, we'll take care of everything."

"You two stand over there," said Patterson, and pointed over to where an exterior door led out onto an exposed gangway.

Overboard it is, then. So much for company loyalty.

Patterson had Griffith open the door and wind drove water into my face. I couldn't tell if was rain or spray. Before we could be ordered, I pushed Griffiths ahead of me out onto the gangway.

"Run," I shouted, and gave him a shove.

Patterson yelled and, to my disappointment, shot at me.

It was probably a combination of surprise, inexperience and a face full of sea spray that caused him to miss. But not by much. Occasionally I wake up with the sound of that bullet going past my ear.

I didn't give him a second chance.

Nightingale can daintily snatch a weapon out of an assailant's hands and throw it into a convenient rose bush. I ain't reached that level of control yet, so I cast an *impello scindere* variant directly on the gun, so that it stuck to the wall above the lintel. Patterson was too startled to let go, so he was jerked upward and his wrist hit the top edge of the door with a nasty snap.

He screamed, and then I ran right over him, knocking him down and accidentally on purpose stepping on his face as I charged back into the control room, yelling at Carroll to lie down on the floor and put his hands on his head.

Amazingly, he did it straight away.

I dragged Patterson in through the door and closed it. That way, the gun was outside, although I knew from experiments that it would stay stuck for at least half an hour. I made him roll over, despite his whingeing about his wrist. Back in London I might have had a couple of Plasticuffs stuffed into my back pocket, but I was supposed to have been on holiday.

We'd gone to Greece the year before and I hadn't had to do any policing whatsoever. Let's do that again, I thought. Or Italy—they like kids in Italy. Everyone always says so.

I was still catching my breath and planning our next holiday when Blinschell and Beverley sauntered into the control room. I told them about the "device," the kick, the potential blowout, and the chance that the whole platform might explode.

"Probably won't," said Patterson, slightly muffled from being face down on the floor.

Blinschell went to fetch his bag and the cuffs he'd packed just in case.

There was a tentative knock on the outside door and Griffiths let himself in. He glanced nervously at Patterson and Carroll before moving purposefully toward the control consoles and pressing buttons.

"I need to contact the standby ship," he said. "Tell them to move downwind for a possible lifeboat recovery."

I told him to knock himself out.

"Is there any way of contacting the divers?" I asked. "We need to warn them."

"Stop bothering him," said Patterson. "The man is busy. You can't contact the 'divers.' I cut the umbilical."

Carroll hissed at him to shut the fuck up.

"Don't tell him shit," he said. "First the chopper and then a gun? What were you thinking?"

Which reminded me to caution the pair of them, although the "anything you do say" bit got a chuckle out of Patterson. He was still laughing when Blinschell came back with the cuffs.

I heard Carroll tell Beverley that there was no way to warn the divers about the device—which we were assuming was probably a bomb. Well, obviously, if they knew about it they might have disarmed it themselves. Then she strode over to Carroll, reached down, grabbed him by the front of his jumper and pulled him to his feet—one-handed. She shoved her face in his and softly said...

"You do not have to worry about the police, or NSTA, or even The Hague, because what you have done is break a much older set of agreements. Do you think you can just fuck with the people of the deeps and not face the consequences? You live in the Kingdom by the Sea, and the sea will follow you into your dreams. And in the end you will beg to drown, so it will be over. Do you understand me?"

Carroll nodded.

"How do I disarm the device?" she asked.

When me and Bev do row, it's usually about the little things. Her inability to ever put anything back after she's cooked. The random hours of the Job. And, now, her insistence on doing something really fucking stupidly heroic.

"You don't even know if you can disarm it," I said.

"Patterson told me how," she said. "It's not booby-trapped or nothing."

We were heading down the internal stairs to the diving control. The production modules were still loud, but there was something missing. We were already down the next flight when I realized that it was the roar of the compression turbine.

Given that Beverley's information came from Carroll and Patterson, I was dubious about its reliability. They wanted the well head to be obliterated.

"Even if I can't disarm it," she said, "I can at least warn the selkies to get clear."

I wasn't the only one with doubts. We'd warned Partridge, the dive manager, that we were on our way down so he could prep for the dive. But when Beverley presented herself to get suited up, he almost refused.

"Are you qualified for this?" he asked.

"Way more qualified than you are," said Beverley, and I felt her put some *oomph* into the words and I didn't even think of stopping her. Which shows how desperate we were.

"I doubt that," said Partridge, who didn't seem affected at all. Not a good sign.

"Let me rephrase," said Beverley. "Lives are at stake. I'm going to put the suit on and dive, whatever you say. So what do you say?"

He could have stood on regulations and said no, but he didn't. Plus the fact that Bev seemed to know how to put on a warm suit and how to climb into the worryingly scuffed diving bell seemed to reassure him.

The sea spray was practically horizontal across the diving skid and, despite the spare high-viz jacket I'd borrowed from the control room, I was getting cold. Still, I stayed to help with the umbilical winch while Partridge swung the bell out over the sea and lowered away. Once it was in the water, we retreated to the control room so that he could keep an eye on the pressure system as Beverley descended. I watched the green and yellow umbilical that followed her down—it seemed a very slender thread.

A bounce dive, she'd called it. If you go down fast enough and you don't wait around on the bottom, you can come straight back up before your body is saturated with helium. You still had to come up in stages, but Bev had said she'd be able to judge how long to take.

"I have an instinct for it," she said. "I've done this before."

"When?"

"Off Southend," she'd said. But that was practically in her mama's lap. We were all the way in Scotland now, and swimming out to Rattray Lighthouse had knackered her.

At least we had comms, even if her voice was squeaky from the helium.

"It stinks in here," she said. "When was the last time you cleaned it?"

"They always smell like that," said Partridge. The chat seemed to calm him down and he and Beverley exchanged instrument readings, which seemed to calm him further.

Beverley called off the depths.

Twenty meters, forty meters, sixty meters...

Everyone but us and Partridge were holding at their muster stations. Blinschell had bundled Carroll and Paterson into a lifeboat, on the basis that it was both a small confined space they couldn't get out of *and* satisfied his duty of care. He hadn't seen James Albright, which was worrying me. But hopefully he was sensible enough to have attached himself to one of the lifeboat groups.

Eighty meters, a hundred meters...

Estimated descent time was eight to ten minutes.

Albright wouldn't be stupid enough to stick around... would he? I kept an eye on the door back to the platform's interior.

"I'd forgotten how weird this feels," said squeaky Beverley.

One hundred and twenty meters...

Something hit the window in front of me—hard enough to crack the glass. There was a confusion of blood and feathers. It took me a crucial moment to link the impact to Albright, to decide it was an obvious diversion, and turn my head to look at the door.

Albright was stepping in, quietly. I think he'd expected me to be distracted for longer.

I jumped and got in his way.

There was a smash behind, Partridge swore, and I felt a blast of cold wet air. I didn't risk looking behind me, but it was enough of a distraction that Albright thought he had a chance to kill me.

I don't have a name for the spell he used, although judging from the opening *forma* it was a bit like the *impello* variant that

I use to cut restraints and slice through deadbolts. At the moment of attack all I was thinking was, *spell, attack, dodge.*

I jumped back and something as sharp as a stiletto and glittering like a disco ball swished past my face. It was attached to the palm of his left hand, so as it went by I grabbed his wrist and kicked out. I was hoping to trip him flat on his face, but instead he stumbled, flailed with his free hand, and we twirled round like a crap pair of celebrities on *Strictly Come Dancing*. The glittery stiletto slammed into the wall and sunk all the way until Albright's palm slapped into the surface.

He started another spell, but I didn't wait, and slammed myself into his back. Normally when you smack someone's face into a wall, it breaks their concentration. But this fucker was made of sterner stuff. He finished the spell and I was thrown right across the cabin and against a control panel.

If he'd been trained like me, by the school of street policing and the university of pragmatic Nightingales, he'd have followed up with a physical attack. Instead, he started running up another spell. I never found out what, because I hit him in the face with a freezing water bomb. And while he was dealing with that, I went in for a tackle. I tried to get him face down on the floor when a big white bird came screaming in through the broken window and tried to bite my face off.

Suddenly the control room was full of screaming mutant gulls, and Albright wised up enough to slam his elbow into my chest. I tried to roll with it, but it hurt. He went out of the door, and what with the control room being full of avian psychopaths, I decided to follow.

I left Partridge crouched down under a console with his arms protecting his head.

A wave—and I mean a wave—of spray struck from the side as I got out onto the skid, and I could hear the gulls coming up behind me. Albright spun around to face me while I made a sharp right turn, my trainers skidding across the slick metal floor. The stream of gulls tried to follow me but, as I'd hoped, they couldn't make the same sharp turn and instead flew straight into Albright's face. He staggered back, but dodged just enough to avoid giving me another opening.

I decided to try de-escalation. It's been known to work before. And, besides, it bought time for Beverley to finish her business and get back up to me.

"What is this in aid of, James?" I asked. Although what with the wind, the spray and the waves smacking the metal support pylons, I had to shout. I like to think it was a friendly, de-escalatory kind of shout. "This operation is bust. What's in it for you?"

"There are secrets I don't want coming out," he shouted back. "And there's such a thing as professional pride."

"Professional," I shouted. "Yeah, I see that. The seagulls I get, the wyvern, OK—you needed to watch the coast. But what was with the panther? And what did you have against poor Willy?"

"Who the hell is Willy?"

"The walrus," I said, and risked a quick glance to see that Partridge was back up and manning the console. Behind me, the umbilical winch stopped turning. Maybe Bev was at the bottom.

She had ten minutes at depth and then she had to come up.

"It had a name?" said Albright. The wind was slacking off and we definitely weren't getting sprayed quite so often either. "The gulls are morons. But the wyvern has a mind of its own. It got away from me and scooped up the walrus before I could regain control."

I definitely wasn't going to tell the Dee and the Don that their ancient friend had been a bit of accidental collateral. I liked Aberdeen too much to want to inflict serious flooding on it.

Magic is about control. Outrage gets you fuck all. And raw anger usually just causes you to trip over your *formae*. All us practitioners know this, which is why we spend time trying to wind each other up. That Albright was trying it on was a given. What I should have considered was that he had other things to throw at me than spells.

If his eyes hadn't flicked to a point over my shoulder, I would have been seriously dead in the next couple of seconds. As it was, I only just dived out of the way in time as several tons of scaly mythological creature landed where I'd been standing.

Wyverns have two legs. That's how you can tell them apart from dragons. On the ground they walk like a *T. rex*. Only not computer-generated. And they smell of fire, anger and the Sunday roast. The platform's supporting cross-struts forced it to crouch awkwardly, its claws scrabbling on the metal deck, and use its wings to hold itself up.

I popped a snapdragon in front of its face. As a spell, it's designed to distract and deter wildlife with a flash and a bang. It doesn't do any damage, which was good. I didn't have anything against the monkey. It was the bloody organ-grinder I planned to mess up.

Said organ-grinder was staring up in concentration at his wyvern. He'd said it was hard to control, so while they both were distracted I ran at him. He had enough awareness to raise his hand, but I already had my shield up and angled, so that whatever he threw at me would deflect left and up. He definitely threw something. I got another whiff of old water, and over that a smell like a sweet pine forest. A spray of hundreds of things glittering and sharp bounced off my shield. It must have clipped the wyvern because I heard it bellow with rage, and hit the platform crossbeams with a sound like shotgun pellets hitting corrugated iron.

I'm not sure why what happened next happened.

My plan had been to get behind Albright, so that he was between me and the wyvern, put him in a highly unauthorized chokehold and render him unconscious. Hopefully, at that point the wyvern vanishes into a puff of metaphysical uncertainty.

The first part went well. I got behind him, but he wasn't as distracted as I thought he'd be. He spun around and got a shield up—it was green and semi-opaque, and I didn't recognize the *formae*. I jumped back and got mine up again even as he started conjuring something pretty complicated.

I never got to find out what it did, though, because the wyvern lunged forward, twisted its head sideways and seized Albright around the waist. There was no blood, and Albright seemed too startled to scream. Looking back, I don't think it bit down. But I can't be sure, because the fucking thing swung around and its tail smacked me clear across the skid. If it hadn't been for the safety rails slamming me across the chest, I'd have gone swimming. I bounced off and rolled over in time to see the wyvern, Albright in its mouth, launch itself off the skid and flap away in a way I was pretty certain was against the laws of physics.

I picked myself up and limped back toward diving control. Through the broken windows I saw Partridge poking at the console.

"Hey," I called. "How's the dive going?"

When he looked up his expression told me everything.

The diving bell's umbilical was gone.

Something—the wyvern, one of the spells that got flung around—had cut the cable and taken a chunk out of the crane.

We'd lost the diving bell.

I stood staring for quite a long time.

Somebody has to do something, I thought. And that somebody is you.

I ran back to the diving control.

"What can we do?" I asked.

Partridge wouldn't meet my eyes.

"There isn't anything we can do," he said.

There'd been another warm suit in the locker. I'd seen it when Beverley suited up.

"There's another suit," I said. "I'll go down."

Partridge shook his head and sort of laughed in an unfunny way.

I had trouble staying normal.

"I shouldn't have let her go down," he said. "I'm certainly not letting you."

"I'll take responsibility," I said, managing to keep my voice calm.

"Not the point," said Partridge. "Even if you could operate the suit, which you can't, you won't make it down fifty meters. And if you found her, what were you planning to do?"

"Can I take down emergency oxygen?"

"Do you know how to cross-rig the gas supply? Of course you fucking don't. In any case, you can't go down without a bell. And that was the bell she went down in."

There was a pain in my chest, and I wondered if I'd bruised myself in the fight and not noticed.

"You have to have a backup," I said.

"That was the backup."

The adrenaline was wearing off and I was feeling suddenly dizzy. I found myself, bizarrely, sitting on the floor of the control room.

"Who do we call?" I said.

"I don't know," he said. "We can call the NSTA. They can ask the navy to help."

"Can you do that from here?"

Partridge tapped one of the screens. It was black. All the screens were off.

"Everything is fucked down here, I'll have to go to the control room."

"Go and do that," I said. I knew I should get up and go with him, but I couldn't make myself stand up. It might have been the fumes, but I felt sick and my chest was tight. The bruise on my breastbone throbbed. Rubbing it didn't help.

"She still has the reserves in the bell," said Partridge. "A rescue might be possible. There's bound to be a dive gearing up somewhere in the North Sea."

"Then stop talking and go and get them."

He hesitated.

"Are you going to be all right down here?"

"Fucking go!" I shouted. Jesus, why were people so dense?

For some reason, a memory of the way the twins smelled when they'd been rolling around in the garden with the foxes came to mind. What would I say to the twins, what would I say to Mama Thames? Oh shit, never mind her mother. Her sisters would kill me. My mum would kill me. I couldn't stay in London. I'd have to pack up and go somewhere far away—Auckland, maybe. Nightingale would have to train a new assistant.

This, I decided, was not helping.

But the terrible thing was that there was no helping. There was just sitting and waiting.

I think Blinschell might have come down and talked to me.

The klaxon and the emergency lights stopped.

I should be up and dealing with shit, I thought.

"What are you doing on the floor?" asked Beverley.

I didn't stay on the floor, obviously. Once I was up, I grabbed her to make sure she was real. The warm suit was wet, and so was her hair. She kissed me and she smelled of salt water and vulcanized seals.

After the kiss I started to say something, but nothing came out.

"Yes?" she said.

"I was worried," I said.

"Good," she said. "You should have been."

I kept my eye on her as she changed out of the warm suit and she told me about the "device."

"It's not like the movies, Peter," she said. "Like I said, it wasn't booby-trapped or anything. Once the selkies pointed out where it was, all I had to do was yank the cables out. Last I saw of it, the selkies were swimming away with it."

I wondered what they planned to do with a couple of kilos of plastic explosive.

Beverley explained how, with the selkies' help, she'd decoupled the bell from the remains of the untethered umbilical.

"Then they gave me a shove, and after that it was just a matter of lowering the pressure immediately above the bell to pull it up."

We were at least 600 kilometers from the Thames Valley, the source of her power.

"You lowered the pressure?"

"It wasn't easy," she said. "Plus I had to come up slowly to avoid the bends."

"I was worried," I said.

"You said."

"Really worried."

"You were right to be worried," she said. "I nearly died. And given that it's me that we're talking about, that's something."

"But you didn't," I said.

"Well spotted," she said. And then gave me a funny sideways look. "Are you all right?"

"No," I said. "I don't think I am."

My face was unaccountably wet. Beverley put out a hand and wiped my cheek dry. She sighed and put her arms around me.

"So did you meet the giant squid?" I asked.

"Nah," she said. "I think he was taking the day off."

21

The High Road

I WANTED TO prosecute everyone we could get our hands on under the Human Trafficking and Exploitation (Scotland) Act 2015, and then go after everybody else under the maritime provisions of the Modern Slavery Act 2015, but we lacked that one crucial element needed for a successful prosecution—evidence. What with the victims having swum away into the sunrise.

"They wouldn't have survived for any time on land," said Abdul, who'd managed a brief health check on the selkie kids before they were ferried up to Rattray Head.

The North Sea Transition Authority did come after FPXPLORE for safety violations, not least when Blinschell handed over the statements he'd taken from the helicopter pilots with regards to the crash. The company went into voluntary liquidation and Elgar Bravo was to be decommissioned—again.

Apart from Calliste's and Phoebe's employment record—Phoebe was listed as personnel officer—there was never any paper trail between FPXPLORE and Ione's uncle Atlas. I was pretty sure Atlas had headed the group that waylaid poor Aquaman on that desolate stretch of Beach Boulevard, but Robert Tarry Smith never cracked. He was remanded in custody awaiting a trial date, and the old families of the Broch and Fittie and Peterhead demonstrated that, compared to them, the Mafia were a bunch of mouthy slags.

James Albright was dead. At least, I hoped he was, because I didn't fancy his quality of life if the selkies got hold of him.

People don't like it when you hold their kids hostage—it makes them excitable. I created an official briefing document and sent it off to Kimberley at Quantico.

Abigail pointed out that at least the oil rig hadn't exploded.

"Oil platform," I said.

"Whatever," she said.

Because of the wrecked helicopter on the landing pad, we had to wait for the weather to clear enough for the support vessel to arrive. It then had to stand off because the Royal Navy arrived first in the form of a Type 23 frigate, and saw their role of rendering assistance as a chance to practice their boarding procedures and "jolly good fun."

"Who talks like that?" asked Blinschell, once the happy navy lieutenant was out of earshot.

"You wouldn't guess he was from Sunderland, would you?" said the Marine sergeant leading the boarding party.

Given our questionable jurisdiction, me and Beverley got off straight away while Blinschell stayed as Police Scotland liaison until the cavalry, in the form of some very seasick colleagues, could arrive.

Apart from anything else, we had to pick up the twins from DCI Mason's "reliable" skipper. Actually, from her wife, who, dealing with her own two preschoolers, had shown remarkable forbearance by not locking the twins in a cupboard. They had a nice granite semi on a posh leafy road in the west of the city.

"Thanks, Susan," called Beverley as she came down the front path with a twin under each arm. I was lugging the vast kitbag that had to accompany the twins whenever they stayed somewhere overnight.

"Fudgemonkey," said Taiwo as we belted her into her seat.

"I didn't teach her that," said Beverley.

"Cockwomble," said Kehinde.

After five days, evenly split between wrangling the twins and answering difficult questions posed by senior members of Police Scotland, I received a call from Andrew Rae. The *special* adviser appeared to have slithered out from under the whole incident without even ruffling his hair. He said he wanted to meet and give "his side of the story."

We met down on Pocra Quay, at the place where Robert Smith went to dive into the water.

"I'm from there," he said, pointing across the harbor to where ranks of gray terraces climbed a low hill. "From Torry. But you wouldn't know what that meant."

Actually, I thought I did. Both socioeconomically and in terms of the demimonde. There are families, the boy with the stud had said, with their own connection to the sea. Old families. Andrew Rae wasn't wearing a silver shawl, but maybe his branch had given that up.

Still, I played ignorant. People tell you all sorts of shit if you keep your mouth shut. Andrew was no different.

"I'm not some extremist," he said. "I don't hate the English. I don't even mildly dislike them. My objective is for Scotland to join the roster of independent nations, not because I think we're oppressed but because it is right, natural and just that we govern our own affairs."

"And the whole slavery thing?"

Andrew had the good grace to look away.

"There's no point being independent if we're broke," he said. "Westminster had the best of North Sea oil and pissed it away on tax cuts and nuclear weapons. If we can resuscitate even a fraction of the oilfields, then we can take advantage of what were supposed to be *our* natural resources to the benefit of *our* nation."

"That's not what I asked."

"It's for their own good in the long run," he said. "They live in Scottish territorial waters. Who's more likely to protect their interests in the long term—us or the bloody Tories? Look at the way they shit all over northern England. They're not going to care about a bunch of aquatic mutants." He paused, as if something had just occurred to him. "Except maybe recruit them into the navy."

Who knows, I thought, maybe they'd think it was jolly good fun.

"What do you want?" I asked.

"I wanted to warn you," he said. "I know you think your branch of the British Establishment is having a bit of a resurgence, but I wouldn't get too comfortable. You've attracted attention now, and there are actors out there who smell power and influence. And they're not the types to share power."

"Well, there can only be one Lord of the Rings," I said. And just for once, someone got the reference.

"The unblinking eye has nothing on these people," he said.

"You should meet my sister-in-law," I said.

"I think I have," he said, and I felt a chill. "You have a reputation as a networker. I thought it was an exaggeration, but now I've seen it in action . . . You should remember that not everything can be solved through stakeholder engagement. And not everybody's going to want to be your friend."

Dad did a last gig at the Lemon Tree. While he was on stage I went with Blinschell to the nearby Wetherspoons, where I was properly introduced to the rest of the MIT inquiry team and made myself popular by buying a round. Not even Scottish coppers drink as much as they used to in the good old days, so me and Blinschell were remarkably uninebriated when we returned to the Lemon Tree and found two junior river gods propping up the bar with my beloved designated driver.

I introduced Elric and Dee to Blinschell.

"Is he our community liaison now?" asked Elric.

I thought of Andrew Rae's snide remarks about networking.

"He's got my phone number," I said. "Everything else is up to Police Scotland."

Dad and the Irregulars crushed it, of course. And my mum was happy. I watched her in the garden at Mintlaw later, chatting to Beverley, and thought about how close I'd come to losing one of them.

I glanced over to where Abigail's tent was watched over by a pair of foxes.

Nightingale brought over a bottle of BrewDog Punk and joined me propping up the patio wall.

"I was rather hoping for more of a holiday," he said.

"We're spread too thinly," I said.

"You can't solve every problem, Peter," he said. "You can only do what you can."

I thought about that lost period of time I spent waiting for Beverley.

"How do you cope?" I asked.

"With what?"

"With losing people?"

"I rather think I'm the wrong person to ask," he said. "I didn't cope. Or, rather, I merely carried on until enough time had passed for things to settle."

"That's not very helpful," I said.

"As I said, perhaps I'm not the right person to ask."

Somebody nearby was sniggering—I think it might have been a fox.

22

What Abigail Did At The End

IT'S OUR LAST day before I head back to London, and me and Ione have gone swimming. Or actually, Ione is swimming while I cling on with both arms and legs. I'm not going to lie, it's well hot feeling the pulse of tail muscles as we power through the water. We go under, we breach into the sunlight, and I take a deep breath as we fly through the air. Then, splash, down we go again. We're way out beyond sight of the shore, and if she drops me now I'm going to drown.

We're not only out there for fun and chirpsing. And sure enough we come out of the water and find two guys breaching either side of us. Ione comes to a graceful stop and holds me up while her tail sculls to keep us afloat.

The two guys look like old-fashioned wrestlers, lots of smooth fat over muscle. They glide over toward us, showing us their hands. I show my hands and, swear down, they both high-five me. Then behind them a dozen, smaller, heads bob to the surface. I recognize the kids from the prison school.

They wave and I wave back.

The water boils in front of them and a bare massive shadow rises from the deep. I see no detail, just get a sense of size and power. Beside me, Ione is shaking with fear. I squeeze her hard.

In front of us two figures rise from the water on the back of the shadow. A man and a woman, the same wrestlers' physiques, black eyes and straw-colored hair. I feel smooth, slippery skin beneath my bare feet, and suddenly I'm standing as well. Ione coils her tail to stay upright beside me.

The North Sea is never still, and the waves rise and fall around me but whatever—whoever—I'm standing on is so big I might as well be standing on a reef. I have a quick look around, but there's no sign of any tentacles. Although I suppose that just means they could be lurking underneath.

The adults open their arms wide and step toward us as if they want a hug. I've never been good at hugging strangers, but I manage not to flinch as the man embraces me and does that French kiss-on-both-cheeks thing. His chest is like a slab of concrete in a wetsuit. All that high-protein fish and healthy exercise, I'm thinking.

The children and the young men are barking their approval as the adults let go of us. Then the vast thing beneath us is sinking, taking the adults, the young men and the children with it.

Ione puts her arms around me from behind before I can sink with them. I feel her wet hair against my cheek as she kisses my neck.

"What was that about?" I ask.

"Alliances," says Ione. "Or maybe they just wanted a hug."

"Are you going to be all right?" I ask, hoping she'll say, *No, I'm going to have to move to London. Do you know anywhere I can stay?* Only she doesn't.

"I'll be fine," she says. "I'm starting uni in September, so I'll be in halls in Aberdeen. Away from my family, thank God."

"What about Uncle Atlas?"

"He's in disgrace. And anyway, he's scared of you."

That really shouldn't please me as much as it does.

For our last night we planned to go and sleep on the beach, but it started to rain, so we sleep in the tent instead. In the morning, we carelessly deflate the pop tent and stuff it into its bag. Nightingale gives us disapproving looks for treating our kit this way, so I promise to unpack it and leave it to air when I get back. I'm trying not to think about not being with Ione, and also how strange it is that I'm thinking like that. We sneak in some lips while Peter and Bev negotiate the twins into their seats. But too soon we have to let go, and I'm watching Ione in the rearview mirror of the Jag.

Nightingale is letting me drive it for the first time, but only as far as Aberdeen.

Abdul is heading off in another direction, to visit his parents in Oban, so the backseat of the Jag is rammed with sample cases, a pile of old books tied up in string, and a stuffed creature mounted on a board. It looks like a catfish, only it has legs. Nightingale says it's a souvenir from the Highlands. "From an adventure I had with Abdul before he became so serious."

"Before *he* became serious?" I say.

"He used to be a bit of daredevil in his youth," Nightingale says.

I'm riding in the back of Peter's Ford Focus with Indigo. Bev is driving us while Peter chauffeurs his parents and the twins in the camper van. Indigo has been quiet since we left Aberdeen, which is bare sus, 'cause normally she's either sleeping, spying or talking. Double sus because when I hit the M&S at the Stirling Services she doesn't even ask about potential sausage rolls. That's where we play musical drivers and we end up on our own with Bev. And once we're safely off, Indigo gives a big sigh.

This I recognize. We've been living in each other's pockets for almost five years, so I know this is Indigo's invitation to pay her some attention.

"OK," I say. "What's going on?"

Indigo sighs again and slumps down to rest her head on my thigh. I scritch the fur around her neck and she sighs for a third time. This is a worry.

"I'm going to assign you a replacement operative," she says.

I go into shock, 'cause my brain is thinking about the average lifespan of normal red foxes, which is about the same as a dog, and I'm not ready to live without Indigo. She's not gray or slow, like some of the senior foxes I've met, but we've never talked about it and Abdul says they always claim operational security when he asks about longevity.

"You're not sick, are you?" I ask.

Indigo makes that weird giggling sound that all foxes make when they laugh—talking foxes or not.

"Not exactly," she says. "But I will be incapacitated for a couple of months."

"So what are you going to be doing?"

"Exercise, eating, picking out a den," she says. "I've got my eye on a nice hole up at the allotments by the Hampstead footbridge."

"Yeah, but why?"

"Good hunting in the green, close to Gospel Oak, excellent transport links."

I'm being stupid, I know I'm missing something, but don't know what. It's bare vexing is what it is. I swear Indigo was planning to wind me up indefinitely, except Bev puts me out of my misery.

"Congratulations, Indigo," she says. "When are you due?"

"Three moons," says Indigo. "Give or take a night."

Part of my brain is going . . . *Interesting, the talking foxes have a longer gestation period than their mundane cousins.* While the other part is going, *What the fuck!* Which I suppose is ironic.

"How?" I manage.

"The normal way."

"Who?"

"Sax William," says Indigo.

"Oh," says Bev. "He was pretty."

"Yes, he is."

"When did you have time?" I ask, but I'm thinking that I was too busy with my own business to be keeping track of Indigo.

"A good operative knows when to take advantage of local conditions."

"You took advantage, then?" says Bev.

"We agreed on mutually optimal operational parameters."

"I'm a bad friend," I say.

"You had your own distractions," says Indigo.

"So is he coming down to London?" asks Bev—being practical.

"No," says Indigo. "We both have our assignments. His is up here. Mine is Abigail."

"So Sax William isn't going to see his kits?" I ask.

"It's Scotland, Abigail," says Bev. "Not the moon. Plenty of transport links. And aren't you planning to come back yourself?"

"You will never escape me," Ione had said as we lay together on our last night. "I'm a siren and we both live in the Kingdom by the Sea. Every evening I will sit on the rocks at Greyhope Bay and sing you home to me."

"Every evening?"

"Obviously I might have to work, or study, or go to the pub. But definitely Wednesdays and Sundays—minimum."

So, yeah, I'll be going back. And since I'm going, I might as well take a basket full of kits with me.

I look down to find Indigo staring up at me—inscrutable as ever.

"You sly fox," I say, and Indigo smiles.

Technical Notes

Rubislaw Quarry is as fantastic a place as I have described, although minus the supervillain underwater lair. That Hugh Black and Sandy Whyte bought a hole in the ground purely to preserve it from a fate worse than development is both admirable and totally mad. They should be supported by all right-thinking people. Likewise Footdee (Fitty) is as historically interesting as I have described it, but the pub the Cream of the Well is entirely fictional.

Some of the details of Rattray Head Lighthouse are wrong, for which I apologize.

The name of the island Ione claims as the original home of her people is actually spelt in Norn, the ancestral language of the Orkney Islands, as *Øjinhellig*. I apologize for the transliteration, but as well educated as Abigail is, I doubt she knows when and where to use an Ø in cold blood. I suppose we can be thankful that Peter hasn't got round to showing her *Monty Python and the Holy Grail* yet—although I suspect it is only a matter of time.

The Crown and Anchor Pub actually closed down in 2015, which makes this book officially set in an Alternative Universe—the magic, fae and talking foxes notwithstanding.

Aberdeen, Fraserburgh and the wider region is so full of fantastic detail that I had to leave too many wonderful things out—the lost Den Burn that runs under Union Street, the fabulous history of Kincaid Point Lighthouse, and some impressively internecine civic infighting during the Scottish Enlightenment could all have served as the basis of an entire novel on their own.

Acknowledgments

Writing a book set in a faraway city, seven and a half hours by train, is only possible with a great deal of local help. I'd like to thank Lee, Ranjit and Joe Barry for medical knowledge, tours of Aberdeen Royal Infirmary, Robert Gordon University, and introducing me to the delights of BrewDog. Likewise, Andrew Hurst let me roam the corridors of Aberdeen University. He also, along with Rob Wallace, helped with the geology and complexities of North Sea oil production although, of course, any technical mistakes are mine alone. Speaking of geology, Sandra Whyte and Hugh Black kindly took time to show me around the fenced-off bits of Rubislaw Quarry, which really, if there were any justice, should have a kraken living at the bottom. Localized fact-checking was provided by Kirsten Murray and Roderick MacBeath. Again, I reiterate, any mistakes are entirely mine.

I received more technical help from such widespread fields as the law, Andrew Coyle, Procurator Fiscal (is that not a cool title?), and Keith Nortrup. The intricacies of spoken Doric from Kirsten again and Fiona Bruce, ancient Greek from Sonya Taaffe, and Latin from Penny Goodman. Mark Yexley proved once more his worth advising me on police procedure and law and how it might pertain to things that go bump in the night. Finally, I'd like to thank Anne Hall for coordinating everything, and to Clive and Beth Hall for fact-checking the architecture and Abigail's romantic adventures.

Finally, I need to thank Andrew Cartmel for beta-reading the chapters, plus Stevie Finegan and John Berlyne for their constant support and encouragement.